TRANSGRESSIONS

TRANSGRESSIONS

James A. Jacobs

James A. Jacobs

TRANSGRESSIONS

Editorial Assistant: Susan Springer

Cover: David R. Johnson

Typesetter: Encore Design & Type, Martinez, California

Typestyle: Goudy

Library of Congress Control Number: 2010920269

ISBN 9780915685158

This book is dedicated to the memory of my mother, Mary Margaret Ida Francis King, and my father, David.

TRANSGRESSIONS

"I am poured out like water, and all my bones are out of joint: my heart is like wax; it is melted in the midst of my bowels.

My strength is dried up like a potsherd; and my tongue cleaveth to my jaws; and thou hast brought me into the dust of death."

Psalms of David, Psalm 22:14-15

"You live in a world of crooked and mean people. You must shine among them like stars lighting up the sky."

St. Paul's Epistle to the Philippians 2:15

PROLOGUE
Upstate New York/Iroquoia
Lafayette County
April 17, 1948

O n this momentous occasion, Mary scrutinized the reservation's terrain more purposefully. She drove slowly along the rain-slick dirt road—avoiding ruts and potholes, snaking the sedan over hills fringed with naked elms, pausing at particular homesteads and shaded glens where she and her brother had played as children. Finally, in the deepest part of the valley floor, she angled into a ravine, parked the car and, with her young son, hiked into a forested hollow to the place where she was born. After a reverent moment in front of her mother's house, she hurried her little one along a trail that would lead to the clearing.

It was spring, when the valley awakened from the despondency of winter to bathe and adorn itself. Everything looked so familiar to her and hiking playfully with her son made it feel as if she had never changed her life, as if her childhood and his had somehow converged, and she was a guide for her new playmate.

When they finally reached the clearing, she took off her shoes and put them in a paper bag, fastened her leggings, slipped into beaded moccasins, straightened her skirt, grasped the boy's hand, and hurried along the trail to join the last of the celebrants filing into the Council House. Just outside the door, a puppy strained at the end of a tethered leash. The puppy belonged to Jesse, her brother. It was the clan's gift to him to mark two occasions: the third anniversary of his military discharge and the clan mother's nomination of him to be Faithkeeper. The boy tugged at her hand. She glanced at clouds banked high in the windless sky and then let him go.

"Daniel, if those clouds part and the sun comes out, take him to shade…and don't forget his water dish."

She unhooked the puppy's leash from a stake in the ground and handed it over. Although she wanted Daniel to witness the ceremony, seeing Echo changed her mind, and she thought once again that her boy needed a puppy of his own. If only the scheme of their lives weren't so complicated by work, school, her husband's intricately-timed training schedules, and the constant strain of advancing his boxing career. As sweet as Daniel's life had become, she still believed he deserved a dog, especially like those celebrated in Iroquois stories, dogs who spoke to people, sacrificed their lives, and even reunited with their keepers in the afterlife.

Inside the Council House, the delicate throb of a water drum played over a murmur of conversation. She slipped inside just as the drum faded to complete silence, and the chief began a prayer of thanksgiving. *"It's the obligation of those of us who are gathered that we continue to be grateful, we who remain, we who can claim to be happy. And give it your thought: the first thing for us to do is to be thankful for each other and for the young man who will be installed today as maker-of-ceremonies."* Before she crossed to the women's side of the Council House, she glanced at Jesse—resplendent in his red ribbon shirt, sash, and feathered *gastoweh*—and at her husband Davey Mendoza, his father Jake, and Uncle Abe, who were seated by special invitation.

She had hoped to marry a man like her husband, someone who was ambitious and kind, and whose kin would accept her as one of their own. She just never dreamed he'd be Jewish. Unlike her family, who tried to steer her toward one of her own kind, the Mendozas accepted her immediately. She captured the hearts of Uncle Abe and Jake, who were widowers and appreciated her grace and beauty. Jake brought her into his business, a workingmen's clothing store, boasting he could double his profits just by her presence. And in fact, business did get better, which enabled him to focus on the principal family enterprise—advancing his son's boxing career.

Throughout their courtship, her family—orthodox practitioners of the Iroquois religion—regarded the intermingling of the two tribes as uniquely forbidden, as if they had nothing in common. But Mary pleaded with Uncle Abe to intervene, to meet with her family, because he was a scholar and a convincing preacher. She believed he was the only one who could persuade her parents how much she and Davey loved each other, how much his family treasured Mary, and—most intriguingly—how strikingly similar their two faiths were. All of these were important issues to convey and he did; he dissolved everyone's misgivings.

The final hurdle to acceptance was overcome by the way he shepherded Mary through the conversion ceremony. He persuaded the rabbi, whose perspective on rituals had softened after surviving Auschwitz, to perform Mary's ritual bath, her *mikvah*, at a reservation site sacred to her family, and to sanction her continued participation in Iroquois ceremonies.

And as if she no longer needed to justify her marriage to anyone, vindication stories soon cropped up on the reservation. Like the one Mrs. Tarbell told about her iron worker cousin who grew up Caughnawaga Mohawk and Jewish in Coney Island, or the one Ike Logan told about the recently-crowned Chicago Indian Princess whose mother was Apache and whose father had escaped a Russian *pogrom*.

Of course, it helped enormously that a tribe desiring their young men to be *hodeskeahgetduh* now had an undefeated professional boxer as a relative, a recently-crowned state light-heavyweight champion working his way up in the world rankings. And it was the way he did it, bucking the corrupt governing bodies, that made the biggest impression.

"Those who are sent to earth for this purpose have to go through hard times in order to develop strength and a good mind...."

Jesse was now being installed as Faithkeeper, and Mary hung on every word of the clan mother's narrative. As much transformation as she had experienced since their childhood, it couldn't compare to what had happened to Jesse.

"He was one of the most promising children of his generation: a good student, athlete, devoted son, brother, and friend...."

Everything changed with the war. At the outset, Jesse held back from enlisting until he learned that the Marines were specially training Indians and absorbing them into scout units. It made perfect sense to him, and when he found out some of the units incorporated dogs, he volunteered. He cut his hair, took a bus into the city, signed up, came back for a farewell party, then took the train south to training camp. But if he was a mature young man when he left, he returned a deeply-wounded ancient.

"...served with his war dog platoon on Guam and Okinawa; promoted to sergeant on the battlefield at Sugar Loaf Hill; awarded the Navy Cross, 2 Bronze Stars, and the Purple Heart."

After returning to the reservation, Jesse barely surfaced. He turned down good jobs, stayed away from hunts, gave up Red League lacrosse, ignored ceremonies. Whenever anyone inquired about these obvious lapses, he'd simply say he lost his *"good mind."*

It was only when Uncle Abe intervened and brought Jesse's company commander to the reservation that the family learned about how Okinawa had wounded him so deeply: the nine days on Sugar Loaf Hill defending high ground against continuous assaults. At the end, only he and Jesse remained from the original Echo Company—but severely wounded, surrounded, pressed into a ditch. Not one scout dog had survived. By dusk on that final day, Jesse was exhausted. His pockets seeped with blood. He sought a hiding place somewhere along a ridge, but he was lost.

"There's nothing else we can do," his captain whispered to him. "Hide us."

Jesse struggled to lift the captain onto his shoulder, but before he could take a step, an explosion flung them to the ground. When he came to—ears ringing, vision clouded—he tried to stand, but he'd lost all equilibrium. Desperate, drained of all but the last remnant of adrenaline that'd kept him going for so long, he dragged the captain into a cave behind a clump of trees. No sooner had he propped him inside than the enemy swarmed outside, bayoneting wounded marines and harvesting their weapons, ammo, and valuables.

The captain told Jesse's family how after the war he lived in his basement for a year, until a psychologist told him that his most grievous wound was the guilt of surviving. So the family finally understood Jesse's suffering and the terrible, secret burden that'd tormented him.

Uncle Abe and the captain took Jesse to a VA hospital, the beginning of his healing. When he came home, there was a ceremony at his clan mother's cabin conducted by members of the False Face Society, the final step in his transformation. It was a tradition that a man cured by False Faces became a member of the society. That was the beginning of his resurrected life. In time, he accepted a job at Brant University as groundskeeper at the chancellor's estate. This put him within walking distance of Jake's house and Uncle Abe's apartment, where he recovered his appetite and rediscovered sleep without nightmares.

After the installation ceremony, everyone followed Jesse outside. He stood so tall and square shouldered. The silver strands of his plaited hair gleamed. His face shined like polished wood.

Uncle Abe sidled over to Mary. "You can see God's light in him." Mary beamed with happiness. Davey stood next to her, staring in awe and appreciation, while Daniel lifted the puppy, struggling to keep him in his arms. In about an hour they'd all be back in the city at Jake's for the first night of the Passover *seder*, celebrating what Uncle Abe called the story of liberation, how the Jewish people were transformed from slaves into a free people. But on this night, Mary thought, we should celebrate the triumphs of both tribes. It seemed only fitting, given all that had happened.

CHAPTER 1
Lafayette County
Brant, N.Y.
December 10, 1952

*I*n order to begin my story, I have to take you back in time to a childhood
dream. Over the years, it's become not only a relentlessly-repetitive dream,
but also the epitome of my moral transgression. In the dream, it's autumn; I'm
wandering the leaf-strewn streets of my neighborhood, aimless and freighted with
a vague sense of unworthiness and a foreknowledge of leading a solitary life.
Uncertain whether to feel elation because I've escaped my legacy, or despair
due to its loss. I encounter Remson, 15, the oldest and most disturbed of the
three brothers who are displaced-person refugees living in a flat behind ours.
His goggle-thick glasses glare in the sun, and he strides with martial purpose:
lats flexed, bare and ropey arms cocked like a gun-fighter's.

Remson spots me and goes into his bravado stagger-walk, curling his fingers
into loose but ready fists. Fear pinches my chest. So little time to prepare for
his onslaught. My legs go rubbery. Only with the greatest effort can I try to
mentally focus on the basics: breathe deeply, relax, step away from Remson's
first move, counter. But a half-block away, surprisingly, and to my relief, his
arms go slack, and his body deflates. The fight has gone out of him. He's
recognized me: the great Davey Mendoza's boy. His ally, his fellow-Jew, his
12-year-old neighbor.

He approaches, and his expression is, as usual, enigmatic and unreadable.
I'm relieved, but worried nonetheless.

"Where are you going?" he demands, in a stolid European accent. "You better watch out for them polack-fascist Ram bastards. They're hiding somewhere around here. They beat my little brother Arthur and stole his bicycle."

Then a great idea suddenly dawns on him, and his expression changes; he grimaces a gap-toothed smile. "Hey, why don't you join me? The two of us...we could take revenge if we find them. Maybe even get Arthur's bicycle back."

Against my better judgment, I agree to accompany him, already dreading the next inevitability: another run-in with the Polish gang that raided our neighborhood. Sure enough, Remson spots three of them squatting surreptitiously in an alley a few blocks away, wearing their gang's black corduroy bomber jackets with large, yellow ram heads on the back, their slicked-back hair swept into ducktails, beginning to dismantle Arthur's bike into reusable parts.

Unself-consciously, and to my great dismay, Remson hails them.

"Hey!" My stomach roils and I can barely breathe. This is just what I don't want to happen, just what I dread most because, unlike Remson, I've never been able to muster his kind of unfettered commitment.

The fight starts this way: Remson strides directly to the bike, kicks it out of their hands, then turns and whales on the most startled Ram until he goes down. Then he traps the next closest one against some garbage cans and waves me into the fray. I trudge unwillingly toward the third Ram, a boy my age and, judging by his wide-eyed expression, a novice lacking guile. I'm relieved that he's inexperienced and transfixed by Remson's rage because he can't read me. Instead, he backs deeper into the alley—probably what I would've done had I been him—until he can go no further.

It's a long way to where he waits, trapped against a brick wall. But when I get close to him, he lashes out and lands a solid punch on my cheek which instantly goes numb. But, surprising him (and even myself), I laugh. It's reflexive. I'm grateful for his gift because now I can act out my lessons: move into him, cover up, deflect whatever blows he gives me, wait for the opening when it presents itself. After a weak, unconvincing flurry, my opponent pauses to reposition himself—a crucial mistake, according to my advisors—and I strike: a straight right against his jaw. I feel his teeth grind against my knuckles.

I don't really hit the Ram that hard, but already the fight has gone out of him, so I shove him into the brick wall where he slumps onto the pavement, thrusting one hand up for protection. His pathetic gesture gives me pause. But not Remson. He leaves his victim sprawled on the ground, runs over, pushes me aside, and kicks the young Ram in the head with the pointy toe of his shoe.

"What are you doing?" he yells. "Never let up when you got one down; finish with him." His glare admonishes me. Then he wheels to chase the other gang member out of the alley.

The boy on the ground lays still, whimpering, blood seeping out of his mouth. I peer closer and my mouth begins to water sympathetically. I kneel over him like a fool, inexplicably drooling, cowed by a fraudulent satisfaction that soon dissolves into guilt.

What I appear to have accomplished I know shouldn't be this easy. But, here, in the dream, I'll take the credit. It buys me time. Remson, once again puffed up the way he was when I first encountered him, marches back into the alley and grabs me by the shoulder.

"Leave him. Help me with the bike. We can go now. Get up, Daniel. Get up."

The dream ends with my bedroom bathed in light and Grandfather standing over me, nudging my shoulder.

"Get up, Danny. You need to eat breakfast if we're gonna stay on schedule," he whispers hoarsely. I moan in belated embarrassment because a puddle of drool has spilled onto my pillow, and I move quickly to wipe my jaw clean with a pajama sleeve. At the same time, I have to flutter my eyelids to pull them loose from their crusty mooring.

The dream was so vivid that this other level—consciousness—confuses me. Especially so this morning when, dazed and inert, I squint at my first sight, a snow squall raging outside the bedroom window. My grandfather, Jake Mendoza, stands beside me, smiling a tight, knowing smile, an unlit Cuban cigar clenched at the side of his mouth.

The sight of him prompts a sliver of awareness: today begins my Christmas vacation from school, and today is my father's final sparring session before his first-ever title fight, one week away, in St. Louis, against Joey Maxim.

"Di...did I oversleep?" My speech is slurred, as if waking to the winter storm had numbed my jaw.

Grandfather chuckled. "Just a little, Daniel. But so did we all."

He sighed. "The heavy snowfall created such a tranquility last night. Morning just crept up on all of us." He stared out the window.

"Your father and Uncle Jack have already left for the Armory. They took your mother to open the store. You've been up before dawn nearly every morning this past month, so I didn't see any harm in letting you sleep late today." He patted my feet. "But you better get up now; this is going to be a very busy day!" Grandfather, still grinning with anticipation, ambled from the bedroom.

I pushed away the heavy layer of bed covers, astounded that, overnight, a storm had blanketed and transformed every exposed and familiar landmark of drab, aging Burt Street and my lower East Side neighborhood, once predominantly Jewish, but now becoming an increasingly Negro enclave. Grandfather and my parents shared ownership of our big, boxy, tarpaper-shingled house. But, after Davey wins the title fight, the plan is for us to move to a new home just now being built, farther east from the city center, following the lead of Uncle Jack.

I slid out of bed, stepped to the frosty window and wiped a clear view. Below in the backyard, drifting snow obscured the crude dirt boxing ring where my father first learned his craft and where I was being tutored.

Looking down, I experienced the beginning of a fainting spell, or vertigo, and I lapsed into the tail-end of my dream, triggering a state of armpit-dripping anxiety until Grandfather returned with a pile of freshly-laundered long underwear, wool socks, my favorite flannel shirt, flannel-lined dungarees and matching jacket, wool gloves, and a blue wool watch cap.

His eyes crinkled. "By the time you wash and dress," he promised, "I'll have your breakfast ready." His voice broke with nervous enthusiasm.

For breakfast, Grandfather allowed me half a glass of hot coffee with milk and sugar. Coffee-milk, we called it. Next, he sliced a big hard roll in half, slathered the flat sides with butter and browned them in a skillet. Then he flipped them onto a plate and spread generous portions of his home-made strawberry jam.

"Your father ate two poached eggs, one-half a hard roll, some yogurt and jam, a couple of bananas. Because of the snow, he couldn't run, so Uncle Jack drove him to the Armory."

"Davey'll warm-up inside: skip rope, do some calisthenics, work the bags, then spar with Joey DeYoung about mid-morning."

Grandfather stood at the kitchen sink, contemplating the dregs of coffee at the bottom of his cup. "The first thing we'll do today is go over to Meltzer's and pick up lunch; I've already phoned in the order." He emptied his cup, flushed it with hot water and set it upright on the counter.

While I ate breakfast, Grandfather lowered the gas heat in the living room and shut off the glowing gas heaters in the bedrooms. I finished eating, washed my dishes, and went back upstairs for my jacket, gloves, and cap. From my bedroom window, I watched him walk outside to brush snow from his truck. He jerked hard on his door handle to break an icy seal then slid into the front seat to start the engine. In a few minutes, melting moons formed on the windshield, freeing the wipers, and he tapped a signal on the horn.

I scrambled downstairs, let myself out the side door and locked it and jogged through a plume of billowing exhaust fumes to the passenger door. At any other time of year, driving straight up the big Adams Street hill would've been the quickest way to Meltzer's. But today, Grandfather headed north along gently sloping side streets. He parked curbside at the deli, leaving the engine running while he trudged in for the food: a dozen rolled beef sandwiches on pumpernickel, dill pickles, buckets of potato salad and cole slaw, a gallon of barley soup and a case of cream soda.

From this hilltop vista, I scanned the open panorama of downtown: Burt Street and north to Central High School, past the War Memorial Auditorium where, last September, Davey had K.O.'d the ex-champ, Freddie Mills, sealing my dad's long-shot bid to finally challenge the Commission for the big fight against Maxim. Just beyond stood the Boy's Club, and past that, adjacent to the Armory, Grandfather's workingmen's clothing store. Every step in Davey's arduous, seemingly hopeless preparation for a title fight had been taken within this 12-block circumference.

Winning fights had actually been the easiest part of Davey's quest. The hardest had been skirting and fending off mob influence, right up to this fight, our family's greatest anxiety yet proudest accomplishment. Meltzer, wearing a buttoned-up cardigan sweater over a knee-length apron, helped Grandfather carry the crated order to the truck. Grunting laboriously in the chill air, his breath feathered behind him.

After they loaded the crate onto the truck bed, Grandfather reclaimed his seat. Meltzer leaned into my window and grazed the side of my chin with a fake punch. "We're really proud of your dad," he said, beaming with admiration, "and of your grandfather and your Uncle Jack for wangling this title shot." He shifted his gaze toward Grandfather. "You never let that *dago* take him over." Meltzer spoke this as a straight, declarative sentence, but a rising intonation toward the end made it appear that he just might be asking a question. Grandfather's brow furrowed and he gunned his engine; its guttural roar over-powered Meltzer's final words.

"We gotta go now, Mort!" Grandfather yelled. "This is a big day for Danny, and we don't want to be late!"

The deli owner shivered but waved with benevolent enthusiasm as we pulled away from the curb, made a u-turn, and headed towards downtown and the Armory.

"What did Mr. Meltzer mean about 'the *dago* taking over?'" I said, shouting to be heard over the truck's laboring engine. I felt a vague sense of unease by the sudden fading of Grandfather's enthusiasm. "Is DiNardi still trying to worm in?"

Grandfather waved off my question. He shook his head inconclusively. "We'll talk about it later," he said grimly, pretending to search the snow-covered road for hidden, potential hazards.

When we arrived at the red-brick Armory—where hundreds of amateur and pro bouts since the turn of the century had been staged and where, for the past ten years, my father trained—Grandfather parked in back. I followed him into the locker room entrance where two men who served as Davey's seconds sat alertly near the door. Grandfather ordered them to fetch the food and move the truck to behind his store across the street. Then we kicked off our overshoes and made our way to the arena proper where Davey—ruggedly handsome and tall, lean yet broad-shouldered, his curly black hair dripping sweat—dug strong-armed combinations into a heavy bag. Each powerful blow dented and re-shaped its contour. With slight turns of his torso, he bashed the bag in contrary directions, finishing with a combination which sent it way off center against the limit of the clanking chains that anchored it overhead. Then, pivoting smoothly and measuring perfectly the bag's return, he planted and checked its momentum with one final, shuddering hook.

Uncle Jack, the head trainer, stepped in and embraced the bag, grunting in contrapuntal rhythm to Davey's finishing blows. He looked comical in a baggy gray sweat suit topped by an extra-large Army surplus Eisenhower jacket, white towel encircling his neck. When Grandfather and I approached, my uncle placed the towel over Davey's steaming head and helped him into a wide-sleeved terry robe—not his formal white silk robe with the Lion of Judah embroidered on the back—knotting the belt with a rough, jerking motion. Davey opened his arms and embraced me. "Danny, you sit ringside with your grandfather," he ordered, as Uncle Jack handed me a stopwatch. "Keep time for us."

I sought out a small table just beneath the ring apron and took my seat. Behind me, scattered among a dozen rows of wood benches, a cluster of spectators sat expectantly. I recognized most of them: cousins and close friends of the family who were regular guests at Burt Street pinochle games, including the Brant University boxing coach, Ray Sammons, and his son, Slugger, one of my friends from the Boy's Club. Sportswriters from both the *Morning News* and *Times-Herald*, and a few others from out of town, rested spiral-ringed notebooks on their knees, waiting for the action to begin.

Side-by-side and waving at me were two uncles: Abe—a great-uncle, actually, my grandfather's brother—and my mother's brother, Jesse.

Before sparring began, I noticed three men standing opposite the ring, draped in unbuttoned, double-breasted, ankle-length overcoats. Their rakish fedoras hooded coarse, baleful expressions. Grandfather leaned close.

"Those three characters are Joey DeYoung's sidekicks from the North Side. They don't look too happy, do they?"

Grandfather may have chuckled with nonchalance, but I reckoned the men's greater significance—their association with Raymond DiNardi, "Rotten Raymond," the man Meltzer had referred to earlier, a boxing promoter and manager and local protege of a man of greater authority who Grandfather referred to only as "the overlord of the boxing world."

Although the men projected studied, inert expressions, their eyes smoldered with hatred, and I dropped my gaze to the stopwatch in my hand. But Grandfather continued to study them, through squinting eyes framed by mottled, variegated scars.

"Yup, they're *paisans* of Joey's."

I flinched as Grandfather pulled the lever on a polished, brass prizefight bell. Its high-pitched CLAAANG! echoed throughout the Armory. When Davey entered the ring, he began a pre-fight dance, springing side-to-side, which impelled his robe to swing open. His white satin shorts, with the blue Star of David, seemed too large for his narrow hips and slim legs.

Perspiring in a hooded robe of his own, Joey DeYoung emerged from a dimly-lit area cluttered with medicine balls, dumbells, and other training paraphernalia. He climbed the steps to the ring where Uncle Jack separated the ropes for the veteran fighter to duck through. He wheeled and snapped punches and shuffled in tight circles, clearing his nose against the side of one glove and jerking his head side-to-side.

Davey waved cordially to the small crowd of onlookers. After nearly 90 amateur and Golden Gloves bouts, culminating with a national middleweight title, and a 10-year professional record of 72 wins—43 by knockout—only two defeats, and one draw with the current champion, Maxim, this was to be his final tune-up. And who better to go against than this friend of the family, Joey DeYoung, a cunning, roughhouse middleweight contender who had spent most of his career trained by Grandfather.

Uncle Jack, who would referee three regulation rounds, routed both fighters to their corners where seconds helped them out of their robes. He checked Joey's gloves then walked to the center of the ring. Davey smiled confidently, eyes closed, as a second wiped vaseline across his broad, slightly-protruding brow and burnished cheeks, the only noticeable effects after hundreds of rounds. As the fighters donned headgear, Grandfather briefed me, once again.

"Joey's tall for a middleweight; but he's a banger, one of the roughest. Today he's above his weight, so he's a good match for Davey. Except he can't quite put it all together like Maxim, especially since his idol, LaMotta, took him out. And he hasn't trained with me since he's gone back to 'Rotten Raymond.'

"Since then," Grandfather continued, "he's fallen into some bad, old habits. Still, Joey's cute; he can be dangerous."

I had known Joey DeYoung for several years and liked him. Most recently, at a top-ranked welterweight fight at the War Memorial, Joey and my father had embraced in the ring as they were introduced to the crowd.

It'd been a night to remember. Davey and I had just entered the auditorium when Dick Tobin—a Runyonesque ring announcer with a flattened nose, wearing a perfectly-tailored tuxedo—spotted us. He asked Davey to be part of the pre-fight introductions.

"Sure, but only if my son can come to the ring with me," Davey said, grinning, sophisticated in a double-breasted blue suit, his lotioned hair combed back from a widow's peak in undulating waves. Together, bathed in bright light, Davey and I climbed the stairs and ducked through the ropes.

Joey had preceeded us, dressed casually in slacks, sport coat and open-necked shirt. The lights amplified his permanently swollen brows and cheeks, cauliflower ears and splayed nose which he'd gained during the first, inglorious years of his pro career—before he trained with our family—because he'd absorbed as much punishment as he'd given.

To me, Joey's distorted facial features seemed like a mythic mask, sculpted over several suffering years of disdaining caution in favor of relentless attacks, patterning himself after LaMotta, his hero.

I'd watched him train, watched him grimace as he hit the heavy bag, watched his face contort into profoundly amplified menace. However, on most days when he trained at the Armory, when he walked by the bench where I sat and paused briefly to chat and shake my hand—beaming with genuine affection, his eyes barely visible behind puffy, hooded slits—Joey's battered face became suffused with an apologetic, endearing tenderness, like that of a tragic circus clown.

My father's face, which remained smooth, even regal, projected an even more frightening menace because his twinkling amiability could disappear and be replaced by a volcanic anger so quick and complete that no man mistook his intention.

Even that evening, during a minor traffic dispute that occurred while Davey tried to find a parking space outside the Auditorium, the other driver—offended and believing he was wronged—shrank from confrontation and backed off once he discerned Davey's look of profound fury. He realized that the cocked fist jerking in and out of Davey's side window telegraphed an intent to seriously harm.

That night, before we were all introduced in the ring, Joey's clown face wrinkled with laughter when Tobin kidded with the milling crowd in his best, practiced delivery—million-dollar vocabulary coming out of a smothered tough guy nasal rasp—something about license plate numbers and illegally-parked cars: "…we have been alerted by constabulary officials that they will remove your vehicles from the premises." Tobin was a funny man, but he always seemed incongruous, like a comedian at a strip-tease club.

In fact, this light-hearted tone was a constant in pre-fight ceremonies at the Auditorium. Davey, Joey, the fighters, and other dignitaries—current and former rivals—gabbed with an incestuous gaiety that always seemed to me to be misplaced, almost irreverent. I marveled at their nonchalance before a zealous crowd and the two warriors nervously flicking their arms of excess energy who would soon fling themselves at one another, committed to inflicting serious harm, if not annihilation.

Finally, the announcer gave a signal and the ringside bell rang several times, reverberating over the buzz of the crowd, loud and insistent; then he cupped the overhead mike with a more appropriate levity and exclaimed:

"Ladeez and gentlemen…I would like to introduce to you a well-known contender for the world's light heavyweight title…a hometown favorite and a descendant of one of the pioneers of the sport…ranked fourth by the International Boxing Commission…Daaayveee MenDOHza!"

The crowd burst into cheers as Davey gracefully circled the ring and waved. When he returned to the celebrity corner to embrace Joey and whisper in his ear, the announcer piped up again, studying a hand-held card.

"Aannd, ladeez and gentlemen, before I introduce to you another popular contender, a rising young middleweight from another illustrious family in the city, I'd like you to give a big round of applause to a real up-and-comer…the youngest member of the pugilistic Mendoza family—named after the patriarch—weighing approximately 135 and one-half pounds, winner of the Boy's Club summer camp boxing championship in his age group—he's only 12, ladeez and gentlemen—DANyel Mendoza!"

With that, the crowd again exploded into cheers, and Davey took my arm and lifted it high, as if I were a celebrity, the heir-apparent. Then Joey raised my other arm and, together, they escorted me around the ring to shake hands with the fighters and everybody else.

It was a fraudulent moment, but I basked in it nevertheless, and beyond. Throughout the prelims and main event, my ears continued to burn with the adulation of the crowd, a remarkable multitude of voices suffused with euphonious passion, a roaring wind that ratcheted in pitch and velocity and decibel-level and swirled in vicariously-shifting gusts. Fans cheered and coaxed the best efforts from their favorite fighters as loyalties shifted moment to moment based on surges, reversals, spectacularly-convincing blows or, better yet, combinations that lifted both fighter and fan onto yet another more sacred and communal level. However sham, it was still the highlight of my life.

Grandfather pulled the bell three more times. But before the fighters left their corners, loud shouts of derision resounded from across the ring. DiNardi's men were exhorting through cupped hands. One yelled: "C'mon Joey! Pound on this punk. Like a bull, *paisan*. Show him what fast hands are all about!"

Joey glanced obliquely at me, but it was not a look of acknowledgment.

Grandfather draped an arm around my shoulder. "Forget them guys, Danny. They're just here to needle your dad and me."

I met his gaze and nodded, marveling at the old man's practiced indifference.

"Joey's ranked, he's quick, and he's a helluva puncher," Grandfather continued. "Ambitious, too. He's won 29 of 31 fights just in the past two years.... But he don't use his head enough; he lets his temper rule.... He just keeps comin' through thick and thin."

Grandfather rang the bell once more and the fighters met at center ring, simultaneously flicking measured left jabs.

"This'll be more of a speed workout for your dad. He'll shift stances more.... Then we'll...."

Before Grandfather could finish, Joey lunged forward with a slashing combination. But Davey, especially alert, slipped it and countered with a stunning left hook.

Uncle Jack stepped between the two fighters, and Joey extended a glove apologetically. Now he circled more cautiously, right, then left, then right again, his feet scuffing rhythmically on the taut canvas—a special, prescient sound that sent chills up my spine.

"You want aggression from Joey," Grandfather conceded, as the two men sparred evenly, holding back the force of their blows, dancing in, then away, landing single punches, missing combinations. "It'd be my worst nightmare if Davey was a slow starter and got banged around because he hadn't trained properly. Sometimes he needs to be hit to know he's in the game."

At one point, Davey shifted to a southpaw stance, feinting a left. But when Joey, squaring his shoulders, rushed head-long towards him, Davey merely spun away and countered with a short, jolting hook, sending Joey back on his heels and into the ropes.

I knew well this aspect of my father's repertoire, the counter-punch mode: fake an attack against a rough-houser, maybe with a dropped shoulder or a tentative step forward, then draw back to slip and counter quickly and with power. It was why his face was relatively unmarked, why his ears remained flat and close to his head.

A searching, feinting pattern developed and caution ruled, except Davey began to work his jab, off-setting Joey's confrontational pace and rhythm. Because of his shorter reach, Joey tried to slip Davey's jabs by ducking inside and hooking to the body, but Davey backed smartly away. Frustrated, Joey unleashed haymakers, content even to land them against Davey's biceps and elbows. But his fury proved yet more futile as Davey slipped, dodged, and jabbed, and by the end of the round I sensed Joey growing more impatient, as if something more was at stake than just a paycheck and a friendly workout.

"See how Davey backs away and feints?" Grandfather said. "You negate the power of Joey's punches by backing away, by deception. He's got Joey reaching, off-balance, looping punches, just hanging out there. You lose taking a guy like him head-on."

At the beginning of the second round, after absorbing a series of flicking, harassing jabs, Joey again lunged recklessly, hooking Davey in the ribs. When Davey lowered his arm to block a second hook, Joey grabbed him, swung him around and hammered repeated rights to his head.

Uncle Jack stepped in to break the hold and Davey backed away, winging a weak hook that missed badly.

"That's not what I want to see!" Grandfather bellowed, referring not to Joey's holding tactic but to Davey's weak throw-away punch. "I want leverage, Davey. Step into your punches!"

To me, he whispered, "You want aggressiveness against Joey's type of boxer, a guy who's wild. But Davey's got to get low and rip those hooks."

Davey rebounded off the ropes with a series of jabs, but Joey made him miss with good head movement; he slipped and parried Davey's punches. Later in the round, he sprang inside from a flat-footed, wide stance, surprising Davey, hooking him to the ribs and shouldering him into a corner. Instinctively, Grandfather shouted a warning while DiNardi's men across the ring hooted with glee. Uncle Jack tried to separate the fighters but Joey raised both forearms and, like a blocking fullback, drove Davey against one of the ring stanchions.

Davey's eyes widened in alarm and Uncle Jack again tried to wedge between them. But Joey, cursing furiously, rammed Davey repeatedly into the corner.

Forced into an upright stance, trapped by Joey's leveraged thrusts, Davey could only raise his gloves and lean side to side to avoid blows and head butts.

Finally, amid shouted protests from Grandfather and partisan spectators, Uncle Jack elbowed between them and pushed with such force that both he and Joey collapsed onto the canvas.

Grandfather scrambled awkwardly onto the ring apron and piled on top of Uncle Jack to keep Joey pinned on his back. Aghast, I could only watch Davey grimace in pain as he test-shrugged his shoulders, catching his breath with his mouthpiece thrust out partway.

Rage transformed Grandfather. He spit out his cigar and shouted instructions while he and Uncle Jack shoved Joey into his corner.

"Fer Chrissakes!" he screamed in Joey's face. "This is a *sparring match*...! A week away from a title shot! What in the hell's gotten into you?"

Joey strained to get out of his corner and resume action, but Uncle Jack barked him back, swiping angrily at the fighter's raised, defiant arm.

From across the ring, DiNardi's men barged towards Joey's corner, startling spectators in the front row who shrank back to avoid being trampled. Uncle Jack traded glances with Grandfather who held a towel aloft, uncertain where to throw it.

Instead, he waved to the group of partisan fans standing a few rows back, their fists clenched. At this cue, they bounded towards DiNardi's men.

Disgusted, Grandfather threw the towel at Joey, then signaled to me with a hammering motion.

As I repeatedly struck the bell, Coach Sammons and three of our cousins—tough Jewish carpenters and contractors wearing workingmen's denim coveralls purchased from my grandfather's store—confronted Di Nardi's men, stalling them in their tracks.

Urging a standoff, Grandfather shouted everyone back to their seats and waved for me to keep hammering the bell, much as a judge might bang his gavel to regain order in an unruly courtroom.

"We still got a round to finish!" Grandfather shouted, veins bulging in his neck. "No brawling!"

He pulled scissors from a back pocket and cut deftly through Davey's tee shirt, unveiling red welts across Davey's back. Swiftly he smeared vaseline and called for a dry shirt, killing time, admonishing Uncle Jack to keep Joey in his corner.

My father glanced towards me. "Don't worry," he exclaimed. "We got a little temper here." His chest heaved. "Nothing to worry about, son; we're gonna keep going."

Uncle Jack waved the fighters forward; they touched gloves and withdrew a few paces. Grandfather backed out of the ring and returned to the bell table.

"Re-set your watch," he ordered, sucking in deep breaths and pounding the bell for the last round.

"Your dad's not worried about Joey's temper," he muttered, more to himself than to me, trying to regain his composure. "He just needs to find his place on the floor," he said cryptically, "and not fall behind himself."

The fighters resumed their prowl of feint and parry, only this time Davey shifted into the unconventional, highly-criticized stance invented by the patriarch in the 18th century that some were now calling the *peek-a-boo*: crouched, his feet closer and more parallel, gloves raised to each side of his jaw and poised to punch with equal effectiveness.

Joey continued to pursue and Davey backpedaled.

"Watch how Davey uses his gloves and forearms to protect himself from Joey's hooks; how he tucks in his elbows to deflect the upper-cuts. He knows Joey loves to unload…in times like these."

DiNardi's men sensed opportunity; they shouted encouragement as Davey's lateral movement grew wobbly, and he seemed barely able to slip Joey's lead lefts and rights.

At one point during this onslaught, Joey feinted with a cocked right and lunged with a left hook that Davey avoided only by turning clumsily away at the last split-second.

"Normally he'd duck lower in his stance from a hook like that, take it on his gloves, but his back's probably stiffening up on him," Grandfather said, his voice growing tremulous. His emotion transferred to me, and I bit the side of my cheek to prevent tears from welling.

Seeing his opponent off-balance and in pain, Joey came with a hard right that glanced off Davey's headgear, then dug hooks into the back of his ribs, driving him into the ropes. But before Joey could widen his stance to pump leveraged blows, Uncle Jack stepped deftly between, allowing Davey to carom listlessly off the ropes and backpeddle out of harm's way.

I rose from my chair to get a better look at the action and, at the same time, to keep an eye on DiNardi's men. They'd placed their overcoats and hats on chairs to stand and jeer.

Perceiving vulnerability, Joey attacked, winging crippling hooks that ricocheted off Davey's arms, while Davey back-shuffled, shrugging his stiffened, cramped shoulders.

"Shit! His mobility is gone," Grandfather mumbled, shaking his head. "He's gonna have to think deep to get the best of this round."

Stunned and unable to find my voice, I couldn't even cheer my father on while Joey stalked him around the ring, bulling ahead, over-running him, forcing him again into the ropes.

Grandfather winced. "He's either really hurting, or he's settin' something up."

Back against the ropes, Davey sank lower in his stance as Joey bombed wanton, arcing hooks, reaching again, off-balance. Suddenly, Davey swung a short, leveraged kidney punch, and Joey pitched to one side in mute, pale agony. Springing to the side, Davey raked an overhand right just below the brow of Joey's headgear that broke his nose. The impact swiveled Joey's head back over his shoulder, disgorging a plume of blood that spattered both fighters.

Grandfather punched his open hand—a sharp whack—and I raved incoherently, along with our partisan spectators, delirious with esteem. I'd never seen blood in a sparring match before.

"Might be the beginning of the end!" Grandfather yelled, jerking a sidelong glance at me.

My emotions of panic and glee crowded me. I could barely follow Davey's rapid turn-around. I struggled just to keep up with Uncle Jack, who chased the fighters, arms half-raised, more witness than referee.

"That kidney punch got him. Joey's blind with pain now," Grandfather told me. "Finish him!" he shouted.

A split-second later, Davey did exactly that: ramming a straight right through Joey's enfeebled guard that dented his cheek, following with a withering left hook that seemed to collapse Joey's ribs. Gasping for breath, Joey stumbled toward his corner, peering vaguely at his revived tormentor.

Davey followed him. He squared his feet and dropped his right shoulder as if to hook again. Joey winced helplessly and lowered his guard but, instead, Davey launched a three-punch combination: a right cross over Joey's lowered left hand that again swiveled Joey's head and caused him to bring up his hands protectively, an abrupt left uppercut through the opening of Joey's gloves to the point of his chin, and a right cross to finish him.

Joey swooned. His eyes went vacant, and he began a slow, crumbling slide, corkscrew fashion, to a sitting position, feet fixed where he last stood. Deeply unconscious, he tipped onto his side, bouncing off the bottom strand of rope before thudding to the canvas.

It took the clanging bell to remind me to stop the watch: a kayo with 42 seconds left in the third round. Way too far for sparring.

Our family's partisans sprang to their feet cheering as Uncle Jack embraced Davey, whirling him around, forgetting his bruised back.

DiNardi's men, on the other hand, gathered dejectedly behind Joey's corner and filed up the stairs into the ring. Trainers sponged twin lines of blood leaking from Joey's nose. It took an ammonia capsule to finally revive him. Then they raised him to his feet, leaning him into the waiting arms of his entourage.

Grandfather entered the ring with an ice pack. He tossed it to one of the men and peered inside their huddle. "After all I've done for you!" he shouted in disgust. "And you turn on us? You *schmuck*. You deserve what Davey gave you." He turned to a second. "Get him back to the showers. Pay him off and get him the hell out of here. We're through for the day."

Davey sat on his corner stool, towels draped over his head and shoulders, talking quietly to Uncle Jack. Alone now, prompted by a mixture of anxiety, relief and delayed exultation, I ran to my father's corner, calling repeatedly from below until he acknowledged, though barely able to turn his head. Our partisans swarmed next to me, including one of their wives, a tall, *zaftig* woman with peroxide hair stacked high on her head. I stared at her mouth, lustrous with a frosty-pink lipstick that veered beyond the outline of her lips. Her eyes were glazed with excitement.

Davey pulled Uncle Jack close. "I wanted to drop him, to send a message...," he whispered. Uncle Jack raised Davey's tee shirt and re-examined the bruises.

"This feud with DiNardi has gone too far," he retorted. "DiNardi wanted you out of the title fight. He sicced Joey on you today and sent those lugs here. Who knows what they're up to right now?"

Grandfather helped Davey off his stool. "Let's get you out of here and off your feet. I let you do too much," he said, berating himself. He cut through the tape and laces of Davey's blood-smeared gloves and jerked them off.

I leaned against the ring apron to get a better look at my father. His expression wavered between sardonic grin and grimace, as if he possessed some secret joke or knowledge. Uncle Jack helped him into his robe, gingerly, one arm at a time, while Grandfather smoothed back his hair and unfurled a dry towel over the top of his head, tucking the ends inside his robe.

When they parted the ropes for Davey to step through, I reached tentatively out to him. He pulled me close, and I buried my face in his robe.

"I'm okay, Danny," he said in a spent voice, trying to deflect my fear, reassuring me in a steady monotone, repeatedly, like a mantra, that he was fine, unimpaired. To prove it, he threw an unconvincing combination of shortened punches but, wincing in pain, he quit halfway. My stomach felt punched up into my throat. Not wanting to give any more away, Uncle Jack bulled a path through spectators, seconds and reporters bunched behind our corner. I trotted behind. In the dressing room, I positioned myself close to Uncle Jack as he took a pair of scissors and sliced deftly up the back of Davey's tee-shirt. When he pulled away the pieces, I could see raised, red contusions. My father met my stare. He cracked with feigned nonchalance: "Don't worry; it probably looks worse than it feels."

During his shower, I stood and peered through a mist of steam while he braced himself against a tiled wall, slack-jawed, his head thrust into a cascade of hot water until he sensed my presence and pushed himself erect. Later, Grandfather administered a slow, deliberate massage, working his oiled hands just clear of the damaged skin which he sponged repeatedly with hydrogen peroxide. Davey buried his face in the crook of an elbow. Even after the reporters left the locker room and I watched him begin to eat lunch, casually leaning on a table heaped with Meltzer's deli provisions, I still read discomfort in his eyes.

Grandfather, Uncle Jack, and some of the cousins slid chairs to the table, displacing their concerns by unwrapping the thick rolled beef sandwiches, scooping mounds of potato salad and cole slaw onto paper plates, and filling their coffee mugs with steaming barley soup. Tentatively, but then with unabashed enthusiasm, they recounted Joey's demise, re-casting what earlier had seemed like a perfidious assault into a standard sparring session which had got "only a little out of hand," as one cousin put it.

At the same time, however, as the conversation segued into a prolonged rehash of Joey's motives and strategy leading to the grudge-melee, a larger context was obliquely skirted: The scheming of Raymond DiNardi.

I knew they were intending to spare me. To them, I was only a boy in a man's world. But I'd already learned a lot. Like a fly on the wall, I'd accumulated acute observational skills, an ability I'd acquired and honed at annual family picnics, weddings, *Bar Mitzvahs*, and, most often, during pinochle games at the Burt Street house where stories about our family and fighting lore abounded.

My hovering devotion had been rewarded by the card-players: I was appointed their official waiter. And as I refilled drinks and snack baskets and served up sandwiches, I reconnoitered, insinuating myself inconspicuously, absorbing subtle nuances in their stories, boasts and jokes as they casually studied the cards cradled like miniature fans in their thick, workingmen's hands.

This was how I learned the most important aspects of family life. Detailed anecdotes that fit into a larger narrative of the family's history: the history of the 18th century patriarch I'd been named after, boxing's first prominent Jewish boxer and 16th champion of England; Grandfather's own immersion into boxing and subsequent emigration from England, and his quest to discover a new champion in Davey, his youngest son, after his own career faded.

It had been a primitive winnowing process conducted over a number of years in the backyard ring against cousins, playmates, neighbors and local toughs. And Uncle Jack's assignment when he finished college—even though he wanted to go to law school—was to be head trainer and business manager for what had become the family enterprise. All of it had been exalted to the status of legend.

I'd also learned about the man outside the family circle, DiNardi, acting on behalf of his benefactor, who tried to thwart my father's ascension. I'd learned about the quarrels that grew out of DiNardi's failed attempts to woo Davey, dissolve the family enterprise and add him to his own stable of boxers, which now included Joey. Once Davey came home from a post-fight celebration extremely agitated, a hand bruised and swollen. A quarrel between Davey's cohort and DiNardi's had come to blows, and in the process, DiNardi had been humiliated.

Around Brant, DeNardi was primarily known as a tavern owner, restaurateur and proprietor of a downtown nightclub featuring strip-tease shows—the Chez Ami. But these operations were really secondary to his main livelihood: managing local gambling and loan-sharking enterprises on behalf of his benefactor's multi-state syndicate, a syndicate that also influenced the International Boxing Commission and promoters and managers throughout the northeast.

Of course, Grandfather had another plan, an obsession, really, bordering on a crusade. Inherited, he believed, from his forebearer and nurtured over the years: to raise another Mendoza to be a world champion.

He was convinced that he had one in his son, who he began to teach to box since Davey could toddle and who now possessed the requisite skills, power, agility, style and temperament to inflict merciless, ruinous punishment. Now that Davey was a main event star, he could—despite the purse-killing impact of television—pack non-syndicate venues in cities like Baltimore and San Francisco, cities with sizable Jewish populations, deifying Jews who craved for one of their own to gain validation and glory in the ring.

Grandfather was convinced his son could capture the light-heavyweight title. And after Davey defeated Mills, Uncle Jack—after several weeks of negotiations—had somehow managed to get Davey signed. Some concessions had been made because, after all, the syndicate controlled the IBC and Madison Square Garden where all IBC title bouts were fought. But that wasn't important; the fight was going to happen (in no small part due to the clamorous demands by a coterie of sportswriters and New York columnists) and DiNardi and his benefactor were out of it.

My grandfather was already envisioning the ultimate possibility: that Davey would then gain a few more pounds, move up to the big-money division and challenge Rocky Marciano, a clumsy brawler with only a 67-inch reach, shortest of all heavyweight champions.

However, for the past four years, DiNardi had been harping on Uncle Jack and Grandfather to allow him to assume management of their fighter. At first, he paid them to tutor Joey in the finer points of ringmanship. Then, with this nascent association, he wanted to confer with them on a regular, amicable basis. Then he pressed a little harder, and Davey, no fool, got wise.

DiNardi grew frustrated, then angry as Davey refused to meet with him. On Davey's orders, Uncle Jack and Grandfather rejected all of DiNardi's offers, although their approach was to do this with disarming civility and humor, fearful that Davey's abrupt and heated rebuffs might trigger DiNardi's vindictive temper.

In the meantime, against family counsel, Davey took it upon himself to dismiss DiNardi with typical audacity, provoking him, needling him to a point where DiNardi had to be restrained, fuming and sputtering threats.

At one point, DiNardi altered his strategy, turning cordial again when he invited Davey and Uncle Jack to join him in a crowded booth at Poodle's, a late-night diner, after one of his boxing promotions at the Auditorium. He laid out his offer in flattering detail: join his stable, be guaranteed within six months a date with Bob Murphy ("He's diminished, Davey; not even in your class"), move up in rank, a title shot against then-champion Mills in London ("No waiting in the wings, no unnecessary bouts, no haggling with the IBC. And you can visit your *landsmen* in the old country! Big money guaranteed!"). A 40-60 split of purses (with Uncle Jack and Grandfather each getting 10 per cent of Davey's share) and all expenses covered. "By the first of next year, add some weight, take on a couple of *palookas* just to get the feel of it. Then the *moolonjon*—Ezzard Charles. He can definitely be taken, and you're our top contender...King David!"

But Davey laughed in DiNardi's face with such disdain that one of DiNardi's men felt compelled to reach across the table and grab Davey by the arm, signaling he'd gone too far. It was, of course, a mistake to provoke my father. Davey grabbed the man by his wrist and twisted it with both hands, torquing the man out of the booth and onto his knees. Everyone in the packed diner witnessed that humiliation.

Then, last July, there had been the post-fight victory party at the Yates Hotel, the night Davey TKO'd Tami Mauriello before a raucous, packed house at the Auditorium, which moved him up to number four ranking.

DiNardi showed up with Joey driving his Cadillac convertible, both of them drunk and recklessly boisterous. They sauntered into the hotel ballroom and took a table after surveying the buffet catered, of course, by Meltzer. DiNardi immediately alienated several adjacent partisans who bristled with disgust when he announced he didn't want any "Jew food." A band which Grandfather had hired to sustain the victory momentum smothered this affront with a loud rendition of "*Swing, Swing, Swing.*" But after a few more drinks and while Davey had gone to the bathroom, DiNardi pushed his way across the dance floor to where my mother sat with several friends and me, rejoicing, basking in the limelight.

DiNardi leaned heavily on our table, insisting she dance with him. Frightened, my mother shook her head no, but he grabbed her by the arm and pulled her from her chair. Standing nearby, talking to an assistant hotel manager, Grandfather heard the commotion and intervened, coaxing DiNardi to join him at the bar for a drink. But DiNardi simply shoved him aside.

That's when Davey re-entered the ballroom and glimpsed his father careening into the bar, crashing into a cluster of empty bottles and glasses. The band stopped playing. Everyone froze. Davey walked swiftly to DiNardi, separated him from Mary and grabbed him by the lapels of his sharkskin suit. He slapped him once, hard, across the face, so that DiNardi lost his balance and staggered ignominiously, hair drooping over his eyes.

But Davey held on and slapped him again, then again, until DiNardi fell to his knees, listing obliquely. Joey remained at his table, paralyzed by liquor, and it took Uncle Jack to step between his enraged brother and a bellowing DiNardi. He offered to drive DiNardi to the North Side tavern that served as his headquarters and watering hole, then take a taxi back to the hotel.

"This should've never happened, Davey," he complained before he left, pulling Davey aside. "It was bad enough at Poodle's. Now you've pushed him God knows how far."

"If he remembers any of it," Davey retorted, laughing.

Of course, throughout the next week the story of that confrontation circulated throughout the city. DiNardi remained sequestered at his tavern, seething. To sever the last strands of the relationship, DiNardi pulled Joey from the Armory gym. From then on, Joey trained at a storefront building near the Farmer's Market on the North Side. But recently, supposedly on his own, Joey arranged to spar with Davey. DiNardi was vacationing in Miami, he said. He'd begged Grandfather to "have the honor of such quality work," and Grandfather acquiesced. But it was obvious now that something else was at work, and he'd been authorized to subvert Davey's title shot.

"Daniel!" Grandfather called. Startled out of my reverie, I lurched from behind a gym locker where, after eating, I'd eavesdropped.

"Danny, get your coat and cap. We're going across the street to the store."

The family's entourage eased from their chairs and helped clear and crate leftovers, while Grandfather instructed Davey to stay put.

"Drink some hot tea. Jack will drive you back to Burt Street. When I close the store, Mary and I will bring the rest of the food home. You'll eat light tonight, have a good breakfast tomorrow and take the day off… stretch…rest your back…take ice and hotpacks. Another rubdown."

Grandfather escorted me through the Arena. We crossed the concrete floor, retrieved our overshoes and ambled to the exit door which he opened, pausing momentarily, looking askance at the darkening sky and furiously swirling snowflakes that attacked my face like bees. I kept blinking to avoid their sting. With a final tug on the front brim of his cap, he lowered his head and led me out, across the parking lot and to the curb, through an opening in a snow bank and across the street where we passed single file through a shoveled path to the front entrance of his store. The sidewalk in either direction was nearly empty of pedestrians. Grandfather pushed open the front door and herded me inside, accompanied by invading flurries which quickly dissolved from the warmth generated by three gas heaters, glowing bright orange, placed strategically among the aisles where tables and shelves were piled high with workingmen's apparel.

Beaming, my mother stepped away from a customer who was deliberating between wool and leather gloves and walked down a dimly-lit aisle to a point where she could better see me. I stood just inside the doorway, kicking one overshoe against the other to dislodge snow from the lower buckles.

"Well, dear, was it all you hoped it'd be?" she asked, modulating her enthusiasm in mid-sentence as I came into clearer focus.

Instead of brightening at the sight of her, my standard reaction, my expression sagged, then began to crimp. But I averted my eyes and dropped to one knee to unbuckle my boots, pausing halfway out of frustration to tear off the gloves that hindered my progress.

Mother shifted her glance to Grandfather standing behind me. I don't know what she saw in his eyes, but she knew what to do.

"Why don't you two go into the back office," she urged. "Get out of those jackets and I'll make you some hot chocolate."

Grandfather must've scowled. "Alright, Dad; for you, a snifter of warm blackberry brandy." She led the procession to the back office. I was second in line. She turned just enough to make eye contact with Grandfather, a questioning glance.

"Davey's okay," Grandfather attested. "Joey got a little carried away is all. Until Davey ended it. The kid's a little shook."

Mother nodded, her lips pursed. "After I make hot chocolate for Daniel and warm up some brandy for you, Dad, will you come help me stock some shelves?"

In his small, cluttered office, I sat at his work desk, warming my hands around a mug of hot chocolate and skimming absentmindedly through a current issue of *Ring* magazine, pausing only to review the lists of boxers ranked by weight class. I dwelt longest on the light-heavyweight division and my father's name at number four. As I studied the rankings in the glow of a hissing gas heater, I tried to ignore traces of conversation coming from the store proper: Grandfather's muffled account of the morning sparring session, and mother's reciprocal sighs and protestations.

Images reverberated of my father—bruised and cornered—staving off Joey's frenetic onslaught. I struggled to clarify the mixed feelings which seemed to always afflict me. While I was proud of my father and fascinated by the mythic, heroic nature of my family's enterprise, I worried about the title quest. Moreover, I worried whether I could ever share equally in it, given my secret disinclination to venture beyond the give-and-take of play boxing to that place beyond where men like Davey and Joey set out to annihilate others.

It's not that I didn't know that pain was momentary and bearable when one fought, that one focused on regaining rhythm, marshaled inner resources and regained control. I reviewed in my mind times my father would shadow box with me, poke me hard in the stomach and laugh, lovingly and playfully, and I learned not to moan or double over or fall if he knocked the wind out of me. I also trained at the Armory nearly every day after school, endlessly repeating drills supervised by one of the assistant trainers, or by Grandfather, or at least once a week by Davey himself. I also sparred countless rounds and had many fights already, by age 12, both competitively at the Boy's Club and on the playground after school. But at the playground, I'd fought only to defend myself against those who wanted to test me, and only to a point when I gained clear advantage and they finally recognized my determination and saw their own blood.

More-violent encounters that I'd witnessed always reminded me of my deepest misgivings. In the playground after school one day recently, I heard one angry boy screaming at my friend's older brother and the older brother just stared back. Then the angry boy called him "dirty nigger" and the older brother leaped at him, swinging one punch with all his might flush against the boy's throat. Reeling from the blow, the boy collapsed on the cinder lot, gasping desperately. No one offered to help him, and it was a long time before he could even get to his knees.

Even though I sympathized with the older brother's response to such a hateful slur, and even though I marveled at his efficiency, I felt ashamed that it was way beyond what I was capable of.

On the other hand, I was proud of my own ability and aspiration. I could box better than any boy my age, and I reveled in the acclaim that came my way at summer camp and at the Boy's Club and at home. But it was easy to fight in a supervised milieu. I never attacked anyone in anger. A true counter-puncher like Davey, I just agreed to take on all comers. I was grateful for the knowledge Davey and Grandfather imparted to me, and I adhered to the principle of self-defense. But I also knew that it was insufficient, and I worried: how could I ever ascend beyond minimal principle and become utterly ruthless?

Of course, I also understood the importance of being a tough Jew. Grandfather's brother, Uncle Abe, a sexton and scribe at the family synagogue who was a fixture at our house and regularly attended training sessions at the Armory and all of Davey's local fights, tutored me in the lore of fighting, from Biblical times to the five-year reign of the patriarch, to the present.

Uncle Abe was a kind but sickly man with pronounced curvature of the spine. He'd also been in and out of a tuberculosis sanitarium several times. But he'd sit for hours with me at the kitchen table, beside piles of *Ring* magazines, scholarly books, and a dog-eared copy of the *Talmud*, simultaneously nursing glasses of tea, teaching me my *Bar Mitzvah haftorah*, and teaching me the lore of Jewish boxers.

"At 5-7 and 160 pounds, your patriarch became a swift, graceful fighter—the first one to cultivate agility and speed, a counter-puncher and the first one who retreated rather than stand up in British bulldog style.

"Remember, there were no weight classes in the 1790s. And there could be only one champion; Daniel Mendoza fought them one and all. He could put them down or take them the distance. After he defeated the Irish champion, Squire Fitzgerald, he established a school in Ireland and taught his scientific style. He developed many fighters there."

Uncle Abe liked to compare Daniel Mendoza to "Chrysanthemum" Joe Choynski from San Francisco. "At 5-10, 165 pounds, he also had to fight the big boys and he also learned the value of science over brute force. He fought from 1888 to 1904. He was too big to be a middleweight and there was no light-heavyweight division. Never a heavyweight champion himself, he fought men who were much bigger—Corbett, Sullivan, Honey Fitz, Jeffries, Hart. Even Jack Johnson. Johnson said he hit harder than anyone he ever met."

Uncle Abe also took me through to the modern period of Jewish boxers: "Abe 'Little Hebrew' Attell, the featherweight champ for 12 years (1901-12)! He had over 300 fights in his lifetime. He was born right here in Brant, but his parents moved to San Francisco.

"Then there were the two bantamweight champs during the 1920s, Abe Goldstein and Charley Phil Rosenberg, both from the Jewish section of Harlem; featherweight champ Louis 'Kid' Kaplan (1925-27); the great three-time lightweight champ Benny Leonard, followed by Lou Tendler, Sammy Mandell, Al Singer, and Barney Ross, who held the lightweight, junior welter and welterweight titles and who fought with the Marines on Guadalcanal; junior welterweight champs in the 1920s Mushy Callahan and Jackie 'Kid' Berg; welterweights Harry Lewis and Matt Wells; middleweight champs Davey Rosenberg and Solly Kreiger; light heavyweights Battling Levinsky and Maxie (Slapsie) Rosenberg; and heavyweight champ Max Baer, who was only half Jewish."

I'd read all their stories, and more. All of those men loved to fight, through blood and gore, whatever it took to win. I, too, became obsessed with fighting. But it was more a reflection on anger and a fighter's sweet desire to inflict punishment and on the seemingly pre-ordained, ironic and nearly overwhelming anxiety about fighting that only I seemed to possess.

After conducting last year's Passover *seder*, Uncle Abe sat me by his side. He told me that Davey was one of the only Jews left in boxing. He also reminded me about World War II, how six million Jews were led to slaughter, like lambs. Of course, he conceded, there wasn't much they could do about it. But, Uncle Abe said, there was this popular sentiment among gentiles that Jews, hounded and oppressed for 2,000 years, were by nature passive and cowardly. Therefore, it was important, he said, to show the world that Jews were fighters, not lambs.

I also understood that the deep-rooted indignation about how Jews were perceived and treated helped motivate many Jewish boxers, including my father, whose animated, focused fury seemed to surface from a constantly-smoldering interior. Davey had honed a strong sense of aggrievement and responded to even hints of provocation; he would not suffer any slight, real or imagined.

I witnessed this again last October while waiting in line for matinee tickets outside of our neighborhood movie theater. A burly, scowling man attempted to bull his way to the head of the line. He bumped hard against my mother, causing her to cry out, but more from surprise than actual distress. Reflexively, Davey grabbed the man's shirt collar, jerked him backwards and off-balance, and angled a slashing, downward punch, unhinging the man's jaw, dropping him in a heap. Horrified, I and the other onlookers edged back as blood pooled from the man's mouth onto the sidewalk. My father's rage continued to boil over; he stood over the man, yelling obscenities, dark eyes glaring.

Mother grabbed him from behind, barely restraining him, trying to bring him back from that edge. And though she, too, was frightened by this vicious outburst, I could tell from the light in her eyes that deep down she was proud of the way he had punished this man, if only for his effrontery. But the explosive anger that erupted from my father both frightened and unnerved me. It made me aware that such unrestrained passion did not flow within me, and this was to be my secret burden to bear, my transgression.

My father's contentious temperament had manifested early, and I constantly heard about it in family stories like the courtship tale.

When my father was 16, he walked from Burt Street to the West End, an Irish neighborhood where my mother lived. She was the daughter of an Irish steelworker who'd been recruited from Pittsburgh to help start up a mill in Brant. But he stayed and married an Iroquois woman who worked as a secretary at the mill.

Only a few weeks after Davey had met Mary at a summer dance, he went to her house one afternoon and they decided, after some debate, to walk to the local ice cream parlor situated at a famous O'Connell Hill street corner where Irish toughs just waited to humiliate some unsuspecting intruder. Davey deliberately wore knickers that day to provoke those working class boys because, from their point of view, only rich sissies owned them to play golf. But his reputation had already been established city-wide and, as he and Mary passed under the O'Connell Hill traffic signal whose lights were symbolically inverted—green over red—the boys stood silent, provoked and resentful of this invasion of their territory, but dreading to brook an altercation over it.

The storytellers especially cherished that affront—a Jew, whose father had emigrated from England and whose patriarch had taught Irish boys to box after he'd retired, entering forbidden territory to date an Irish girl who bore the taint of Indian blood.

As I finished the hot chocolate, holding the cup high over my upturned mouth to shake loose the last dregs, Grandfather entered the office.

"There's no sense staying open on a day like today, Danny. Your mother and I are going to close up now. You can bring that magazine with you if you haven't finished it yet."

I marked the page beginning a photo essay on retired heavyweight champ Joe Louis, my favorite boxer besides my father. It was Louis, "The Brown Bomber," whose placid, indefatigable expression and hooded eyes conveyed to me an almost divine purpose.

I placed the magazine on top of two consecutive issues of *Life* magazine Grandfather had saved for me. They contained a two-part autobiography, *"My Story,"* in which Louis revealed his own troubled dealings with the boxing underworld.

I saw the film when he regained the title from Schmeling. I watched it while laying on the living room floor next to Davey where he stretched out every night after dinner to ease his aching back. I thrilled to the high-pitched, nasal voice of ring announcer Johnnie Addie working through the elaborate introductions, punctuated by the cheering crowd and a clanging bell and, later on, to the catch-in-your-throat enthusiasm of the ringside commentator's blow-by-blow analysis.

I was deep in that reverie when Grandfather approached and wrapped a new wool scarf around my neck. "Danny, help me carry these cartons of leftover food out the back door to the truck."

It had stopped snowing, but wind had swept deep drifts against the red brick walls bordering the parking lot.

"Boy this soup is gonna taste good again tonight," Grandfather said with renewed enthusiasm. He scanned the dense, gray clouds that blanketed the city. "Good thing we don't have to climb any hills to get back to Burt Street."

He opened the passenger door for me, then went around to the other side, got in, and started the engine.

I've had to imagine most of what subsequently happened after that moment, but this account is also based on what I learned years later, so bear with me. This is what is imprinted.

In the store, before she turned off the gas heaters, my mother walked back into Grandfather's office to fetch a box. She wanted to give her older brother, Jesse, who lived on the Iroquois reservation on the outskirts of town, a Midwinter gift of socks and long johns. But the sound of a door closing in the store proper gave her pause. She stopped and listened for movement. Nothing.

She left the office to check. A new chill had seeped into the store, but it was empty of customers. She shrugged and went to the front entrance door. It was securely closed, as before, so she locked it. But something pulled her glance to the carpet. A trace of crystalline snow appeared to be dissolving. She turned and scanned the store again. Empty.

A last-minute customer must have peered in while she'd been in the office and decided it wasn't worth it to wait. She turned off the gas heaters, flicked off the wall light switch and gazed one last time up the aisles at the shelves of stacked apparel.

From the parking lot outside, Grandfather yelled impatiently. "Mary, aren't you finished? The truck's warmed up. Let's go already."

Turning up the collar of her surplus Navy pea jacket so that it embraced her scarfed head, Mother pulled gloves from her pockets and hurried to the back door, holding the gift box under her arm in order to manage locking up. I held the truck door open for her to slide quickly in. She nudged me to the middle.

Grandfather gunned the engine once again. The motor and the

heater had sufficiently warmed to begin the drive home. But at that moment—and you don't know how much I've regretted it—I raised my hand in alarm. "Oh, darn," I complained, "I left my magazines in the office."

Mother suppressed her exasperation.

"Hold on for a second, Dad, will you?" she pleaded. "I'll be back in a jiffy."

Through pursed lips, Grandfather nodded a grudging ascent. Condensation glistened on his bushy mustache. He reached into the ashtray and withdrew a half-smoked cigar. He tried to pull matches from his jacket pocket, but I was sitting too close. He put the cigar back into the ashtray when mother, standing at the back door, turned and gestured helplessly.

"I can't find my keys!" she shouted.

Grunting again, Grandfather pushed open the driver's side door and slid out.

"Hold on, Danny; we'll be right back."

I watched Grandfather trudge back through deepening drifts of snow. As he unlocked and drew open the door, a wisp of smoke passed and surged into the swirling wind. Mother and Grandfather faced each other, mirroring disbelief. They glanced back at me in the truck, exchanging words I couldn't hear.

Feeling my stomach tighten with anxiety, I stared, incredulous, as first my mother, then Grandfather plunged into the darkened entrance. At just that moment, the gift box fell from my lap and, as I leaned to retrieve it, a shock wave from a nearby explosion rocked the truck, hurtling me headlong into the metal dashboard.

CHAPTER 2

Like embarking on a pilgrimage from a place of abandonment, I regained consciousness. The first part of the journey began with a revived sensation: hearing distant, muffled voices. This encouraged me to climb out, however feebly, from a vague nether-world I'd most recently inhabited.

Then, struggling upward through successive, daunting depths of insensibility, I realized that I was overhearing a story—one that I'd been told before but desperately needed to remember, or I wouldn't reach my shrine.

A suddenly-realized pain in my head felt strangely consoling, nearly euphoric, proof that I was, indeed, capable of heroic struggle.

Then, as if a support cable had snapped above me, I lapsed into a deep, plunging reversal. Perhaps it was decided that my circuitry had to be shut down after all. But my anxiety over this slide seemed to spark a resurgence and sensation returned, as if a radio program had been restored to normal frequency.

A narrator continued his story, and I resumed my climb. Then, another voice—whether inserting commentary, asking questions, or seeking clarification, I wasn't certain —drew me higher from the abyss.

The more I concentrated on making sense of the conversation, on hearing a story so clearly that I would have something to remember, the closer I came back to the surface of the real world.

At one point, I believed I heard a question being asked, one that I was expected to answer. In turn, I felt compelled to respond, but I couldn't figure out how, or summon the strength for a simple gesture, as if an unbreachable obstruction were deterring me from this last part of my journey.

But those murmuring voices persisted. With major effort, I finally turned my head toward the voices, and this first willed movement brought me close to revival. What I'd been hearing wasn't a story or a lengthy conversation, it was talk about me.

"He's moving…," a man's voice said. "Are you awake, Danny? Are you, son? Look at me, Danny…can you see me?"

It was my father's voice, breaking, close. And because it startled me, I blinked and opened my eyes. A face loomed into focus: puffy and creased with worry, eyes red-rimmed and carrying an unusually weary expression.

His elicitation seemed important, but I couldn't speak. I lay on my back in a cold, dimly-lit room, constrained by tightly-tucked bed covers, without a pillow to cushion my bandaged head.

"He's back! Thank God!" said another man emerging from behind my father. It was Uncle Jack, with the same forlorn look.

I was so astonished by their concern for me that I sought a reason for it.

That's when I remembered Grandfather and my mother entering the smoke-filled doorway. I felt a weakness, a sinking in my chest, and I realized that my shrine was unyielding grief.

When I came home, I learned that, after the explosion, a fire erupted, destroying the building that housed Grandfather's store. Four policemen had to restrain Davey when the fire precinct captain told him that all was lost, except me.

Davey's first reaction, I'm told, was to scoff, but when the captain persisted with his report, confirming the worst, Davey bellowed with rage and raced across the street where he could see for himself the black smoke and flames erupting out of the store's front window and doorway. He so disrupted the firemen's efforts that the commanding police sergeant ordered him restrained. Three policemen and Uncle Jack coaxed him back to the Armory, but he kept ranting that he wanted to go to the store, to see again for himself.

Cautiously, once enough water had been hosed into the building that it was at least safe enough to approach police lines, they relented, escorting him back across the street. This time, the devastation registered. The caved-in ruins of the store still smoldered and huge icicles draped the fire-blacked brick walls and hung down from charred rafters like stalactites.

By the time they re-entered the Armory gym, Davey's most fanatical expression of denial had relented, so the officers relaxed their vigilance. Uncle Jack eased next to his disconsolate brother, but Davey pulled free. He sprinted to the heavy bag and tackled it, ripping it from its swivel, and dove with it onto the floor. Astride it, he pounded blow after blow until he began to weaken, then sob, then slide off, sprawling onto his belly, hiding his face in the crook of an arm.

The next day, prompted by the mysterious nature of the fire and at Davey's insistence, the fire department's arson squad combed the wreckage. They found two charred bodies, Mary and Grandfather, but no precise evidence of foul play.

When this was reported to Davey by a police sergeant friendly to the family, Davey glared sardonically at the sergeant and at Uncle Jack. They both winced at the light of truth that burned in his eyes. He said he now understood how far DiNardi could go. His wounded mind raced and, in front of me, he blurted out a likely scenario to the sergeant.

"You said that a bartender across the street saw a man wearing a full-length overcoat leave by the front door, carrying a gym bag, at just about the same time Pa and Mary re-entered from out back?" he asked rhetorically, slipping on a surplus leather bomber jacket and rumpled newsboy cap. He faced the sergeant. "And then the bartender said he saw smoke seep from the door?"

Davey said that turning off the gas before locking up had been a constant practice with Mary.

"That man must've snuck in the front door just before closing. While Mary was locking up, he could've doused the place with fuel, turned on the gas and lit a match as he fled the store. The street wasn't deserted. You said so yourself."

He snatched the keys to Grandfather's truck from the kitchen counter.

"The guy probably left, confident that the place would go up, and he'd be safely down the street...."

"And no victims," the sergeant added, re-insinuating the accident theory. "He probably figured that your father was leaving for the day."

"But when Pa and Mary reentered the store...." Davey thrust open his outstretched hands and mimicked the sound of an explosion. "Don't soft-peddle this. It's arson and it's murder."

He believed his own explanation and despised himself for being

so blind to the possibility that DiNardi could instigate something
so destructive. He immediately asked that Uncle Jack drive him to
DiNardi's tavern.

"We'll stop at a gas station, fill up some gallon cans," he said matter-
of-factly. "And if any of his *shmucks* are there, I'll take care of them before
I torch the joint."

The sergeant's eyes fluttered in disbelief. "...Davey...." Uncle Jack
appeared speechless, afraid to expose my father's proposed revenge caper
as outside of the realm of rational possibilities.

But Davey shoved right past them, bounding out the door and down
the ice-crusted driveway. I could see that Uncle Jack hated to intimate
anything like what he said next, but the necessity of the situation demanded
he say something with deliberative finality.

"Don't act crazy!" he shouted out the doorway.

Furious, Davey turned, and Uncle Jack immediately corrected
himself.

"*This* is crazy!" He ran out to the truck. "Don't go off half-cocked like
this," he pleaded. "There's an investigation still going on." The sergeant
followed him and they peered inside the truck window.

"You've got to consider all the angles here," the sergeant reminded
him. "Your future, the safety of the rest of your family."

"Your son," Uncle Jack added.

"You're the manager and you're the investigator! You think about
it!" he shouted, choking on the last words.

"Maybe you don't care about yourself right now," the sergeant calmly
pleaded. "But DiNardi's a maniac. You retaliate the way you're planning,
he'll come right back at you, at your brother's family, at your son."

His protestations fell on deaf ears. Davey turned the key in the igni-
tion. The starter only whined, but Davey coaxed the choke and pumped
furiously on the gas pedal until the engine sputtered to life and burst into
a vengeful roar.

An hour or so later, three squad cars and a fire company converged
in front of DiNardi's tavern with its neon-red sign lit in cursive signature.
Officers jogged behind their vehicles to the sergeant's car where we sat
waiting. One of them reported seeing Grandfather's truck parked in a
small lot nearby.

Suddenly, a large metal ashcan exploded through the tavern's tinted
picture window, followed seconds later by a torrent of black smoke. Almost
immediately, the tavern door burst open and Davey staggered headlong
into the street, coughing and laughing like a madman, holding blackened

and misshapened hands aloft, as if in benediction. He careened into the arms of Uncle Jack who, along with the sergeant, didn't know whether to embrace or subdue him. "Jesus Christ," Davey rasped. "I nearly couldn't find my way out of there."

"Is anyone else in there, Davey?" the sergeant asked urgently. A fire engine u-turned and jerked to a halt a few feet from the curb. Firemen quickly unfurled a hose.

"Not really," Davey said, mockingly. He pulled away from Uncle Jack.

"Get some men in there, right away!" the sergeant ordered.

Firemen bashed in the remainder of DiNardi's picture window and a glass-plated front door. "If he found any of Raymond's boys in there, they'll be in no shape to make it out on their own."

The firemen, wearing sloping helmets and yellow slickers, plunged into the entrance. Within minutes, they emerged, dragging two dazed and soot-blackened men, their faces smeared with blood.

After wandering in semi-circles, reeling with the pain of his damaged hands, Davey finally acknowledged the pleas of Uncle Jack and crawled into the back seat of the sergeant's car where he sagged on my lap. Uncle Jack leaned in and tried to straighten him up.

"Your hands, Davey. Let me look at your hands."

Davey wrenched free and fell head-first again into my lap. "No!" he shouted. "Leave me alone! I don't care about them. I...don't...care!"

I could barely comprehend my father's total loss of composure. From what could later be pieced together, Davey swiped a tire iron from my grandfather's truck and wrecked the circular bar and booths, smashed bottles of liquor and assaulted the two men who, as it turned out, were among those jeering him at the Armory. According to the sergeant, only their heavy overcoats saved them from critical injury.

Davey was kept overnight at University Hospital where I'd been admitted a few days before. From the rampage, he'd fractured bones and dislocated knuckles in both hands and doctors cast them in plaster.

The following day, in City Court, he was charged with assault and attempted arson but, given the circumstances and the compelling need to prepare for a double funeral within 24 hours, he was released on bond into the custody of Uncle Jack. The judge also ordered that a police presence be maintained at the Burt Street house. Whether for our protection or to keep an eye on him, it wasn't exactly clear.

CHAPTER 3

B ecause my mother had converted in anticipation of my *Bar Mitzvah*, there would be a joint funeral and burial; she and Grandfather would be interred at a Jewish cemetery in side-by-side plots located near the top of a snowy knoll that overlooked the entire city and the valley to the south. The morning prior to the funeral, mourners congregated at Hertzberg's Funeral Home, a converted residence within walking distance of Burt Street. They milled about, spilling into hallways and vestibules in small, shifting pockets. Some joked and kidded the way I'd remembered it that night in the ring. Was it irreverence or a nervous response?

I sat away from the closed caskets, my forehead tightly bandaged, still throbbing from 20 stitches and a concussion. Most of the mourners wanted access to Davey, so he sat a short distance from me in an aisle seat, calm but severely downcast. Mourners mainly glanced at me in pity, or gave me the briefest attention. Although our family doctor considered my hearing, vision, and reflexes normal, I hadn't spoken since regaining consciousness. The doctor took my father aside and told him that I had temporarily lost my voice due to the trauma and the concussion. Well, it didn't make any difference to me; I had lost my voice, and I didn't even care if I found it.

The doctor suggested not putting any undue stress on me. Fortunately, the only one who purposely sought me out was the blonde who I'd seen at the Armory at the end of Davey's sparring match: Sarah, the wife of one of the contractors. She was especially solicitous, complimenting me on my resemblance to Davey ("another Mendoza in the making"), a possibility which I, of course, tacitly dismissed. Mainly she sat quietly beside me, wearing a black Persian lamb coat with a veiled fur hat. Her gaze held a certain knowing quality, at once serene yet consoling, and when emotions erupted nearby she held my hand.

The rabbi let Uncle Abe lead *Kaddish*, here and at the cemetery. At Uncle Abe's urging, the rabbi also allowed Jesse Isaacs, my mother's brother and an Iroquois Faithkeeper, to chant an invocation and a death song with its chorus of a short, matter-of-fact verse. Translated, it meant: nothing lives long except for the land and the mountains. I didn't understand how that was supposed to be relevant.

Uncle Abe and Jesse were of different generations; Abe was part of Grandfather's cohort, while Jesse was 35 and a recently-discharged Marine Corps war veteran. But they both believed they possessed commonalities that surpassed tribal identity. Abe was an ardent scholar of both *Talmud* and *Kabbalah*, devotions he inherited from a line of Spanish-Jewish scholars going back to the 13th century. Jesse was a scholar and devout practitioner of Iroquois religion.

A solitary person like Abe, Jesse—nominated to be his tribe's Faithkeeper—preferred to live in his late-mother's log cabin on the reservation. The two men saw quite a bit of each other. Abe lived near Brant University where Jesse maintained the grounds of the chancellor's estate. They often met for lunch. And Abe, who loved athletic competition, visited the reservation every weekend during the summer Red League lacrosse season. Most recently, he'd been invited to Mid-Winter ceremonies, which would be celebrated within a few weeks, to reciprocate for Jesse's being invited to observe High Holy Days.

Abe and Jesse had developed and cultivated a respectful inquiry into the other's religious practices, a natural outcome of the union of Davey and Mary and the fact that they had been the favored children in their respective families. But what really sparked the initial interest stemmed from Abe's and Jesse's shared scholarly curiosities when they discovered that their faiths shared a central symbol—a divine tree.

Then, the more they came to know one another, they uncovered more profoundly-overlapping, historical synchronicities: their people's apocalyptic tragedies and millenial hopes. Abe even joked about one: "We're still waiting for our savior to deliver his people; yours has already come and gone.... You're already redeemed!" Although a disinterested observer might've found that assertion hard to accept, given the contemporary Iroquois reality, Abe and Jesse were true believers who preached with identically-idealistic fervor about tribes poised at the onset of new greatness.

At the burial ceremony, mourners struggled against a biting wind. They filed past crusted snow banks to the grave sites where Davey, dazed with grief, and I, merely disbelieving, stared at the frozen ground and the two perfectly-rectangular repositories. Davey marveled at how they'd been dug so deep into frozen earth and with such precisely-squared corners.

The invocation, death chants and *Kaddish*—delivered in emotional, Old World vibratos by Jesse and Abe—were made even more tremulous by an obstinate wind which buffeted the canvas canopy covering the orators. Only a circle of tall pine trees helped corral and sustain their plaintive laments.

After the service, mourners gathered at our house, pausing at the porch before a white porcelain pitcher where we ritually washed death from our hands. Rented tables and chairs had been set up and all mirrors draped with cloth. I was shocked at the amount of food visitors had set on the dining room table for our meal of condolence: loaves of *challah*, trays piled high with corned beef, pastrami, turkey, beef brisket, noodle *kugel*, potato *knishes*, a green bean casserole topped with fried onions; another tray of bagels, lox, and cream cheese; and coffee cake, cheesecake, and *rugelach*. The top of a card table was crowded with a bottle of scotch whiskey, soda pop and ginger ale, a bucket of ice and two large urns of coffee. Uncle Jack's wife, Charlotte, and Sarah took charge of seating and serving the steady stream of callers, most of whom appeared ravenous.

Davey and Uncle Jack shared council—a *minyan*, actually, in order to say *Kaddish*—in a back room with me, Uncle Abe, Jesse and cousins and friends.

I resumed my fly-on-the-wall demeanor near a window where I looked out with the others upon the family boxing ring, squinting with pain from a headache that still throbbed with every pulse beat. Moments earlier, Ray Darcel, a trainer from New York City and a friend of Grandfather's, helped break the last vestige of Davey's vengeful spirit with a story about how he'd been badly beaten and driven out of Boston for promoting fights there. He said he never knew for certain who'd done it, but that if he'd found out and acted upon it he'd never again be able to go on the road with any of his fighters.

Uncle Abe also weighed in with a cryptic but resonant plea to desist, that it wasn't Davey's private affair, that revenge against DiNardi would just make the task of others who were weaker more difficult, and that the enemy would only become stronger.

"In time, he will be brought down," the old man predicted. "For now, exile is the best strategy; but it's only temporary."

It sounded as if decisions were being made that I hadn't yet been let in on.

Davey drew deeply from one of the last of Grandfather's Cuban cigars. He held it up to the window, smoky strands rising, wispy and delicate.

Uncle Jack broke the silence. "Maxim's people aren't postponing the fight, Davey. They've substituted Moore."

Davey remained silent, waving the cigar back and forth across his field of vision.

"The fight's tonight," Uncle Jack said. "We probably shouldn't begrudge the old-timer his shot; he's waited a hell of a lot longer than you have."

"Two hundred fights since 1936," Darcel added placatively. "Maxim's ready; he's recovered enough from the Robinson fight to handle Moore. But he would've been ripe for you, kid."

"We can't listen on radio, not while we're in mourning," Uncle Abe admonished.

Davey nodded absently.

Uncle Jack's gaze shifted from the ring to Jesse and Ray Darcel and back to the yard. "Pa made that ring when he first come over, in 1928. He started as a peddler, buying goods at the market and selling them in the countryside. Then he bought that land out in the valley near the reservation. Sold chickens and produce, too, during the summer. Shoes and workingmen's clothing he got wholesale and sold those to the farmers and Indians.

"He recruited all of us to help him start up his store," Uncle Jack added. "Had us boxing before dinner."

"When Mary stayed with me after our father died," Jesse offered, "he'd drive out to the reservation and take us both to the Armory or to the Auditorium for Davey's fights. He was crazy about her."

"At every family picnic, all the cousins from Brooklyn to Cleveland had to box... all of you had to box," Uncle Abe reminded. "He said if Davey could beat everybody that he would be the one to carry on."

Davey pulled hard until the ash of the cigar glowed deep red; he exhaled a long and steady stream of smoke against the window, trailing a glistening string of saliva which he wiped with the heel of his hand across his whiskered chin.

"His own boxing career was cut short by injury, but he knew he'd find another champion in the next generation," he said flatly.

Uncle Jack's son, my cousin Victor, seemed especially restless. He wandered evasively into the kitchen then reluctantly re-entered the room where we sat as Uncle Abe explained to us that we had to redouble our efforts to bring God's kingdom into being.

I was exhausted but acutely attentive to any altered sensibility, and I noticed a tremor in my cousin's passive, listless demeanor: a sudden contortion and near-grimace, and then his eyes rolled back. He teetered off-balance and, almost in slow-motion, crumpled to the floor, abruptly drawing all attention to him as he struggled through one of his epileptic seizures.

When he regained consciousness, he still seemed distant and unrevived. Much like me, I thought. Uncle Jack cradled him in his arms then summoned me into his embrace, so that Victor and I were evenly consoled, facing one another, mute yet tense with emotion. For a second, I felt as if Uncle Jack were a referee, turning his large, balding head first to Victor, then to me, improvising instructions.

"Danny will come live with us…after a while," he said to Victor. "He'll share your room and be like a brother to you." Then he faced me, his eyes red-rimmed and strained. "It might take only a couple of months…maybe in early summer."

By nightfall, the last of the mourners left and the council moved into the kitchen. Uncle Jack began the final discussion.

"Davey's won only a few big purses these last few years. I just moved into my new house. He and Pa were three months away from moving into theirs, on the same block, on huge lots with weeping willows." He shrugged. "But I agree with the judge. I think we have to leave Brant, and God knows how soon we'll be able to come back."

Avoiding further retribution was the council's greatest concern. Our police sergeant had recommended that we consider closing up our homes and leaving town, based on the destruction Davey had caused at DiNardi's.

Uncle Abe agreed, especially because he suspected that the police and district attorney were reluctant to become involved in the case.

"After all, DiNardi's a crook but he's still licensed to run a big night club, a tavern, two restaurants. And for all his arrests, including one for attempted murder, he's come out on top every single time. Not only that, but also there's never an eyewitness or evidence, only a theoretical motive."

So it was agreed that Davey and Uncle Jack and his family would move temporarily to a house owned by a second cousin in Crown Heights, Brooklyn. Uncle Jack would attempt to marshal the family's resources, including selling the Burt Street house. Jesse vowed that he would find Davey a job with an Iroquois steel-raising gang which worked out of the Brooklyn union hall on Atlantic Avenue in North Gowanus, just a short bus ride away. The job would provide a good income for him, and his part would be the least dangerous because it involved only helping to raise beams, girders and columns into position for the riveters, and he could work on the ground.

The loyal police sergeant told the council that DiNardi was still being sought for questioning about the fire, but he also said that they suspected he'd left Miami for Havana and might remain there "for at least the winter, considering the circumstances."

Uncle Abe and Jesse made a strong case that I live for a while on the reservation. Uncle Abe could visit, deliver money and other necessities, and keep up my religious instruction. It was the safest place, Jesse argued, given all the uncertainty. With the reservation's sovereign political status, not even the police could gain access without special permission, let alone unknown white men.

A cut-glass decanter was passed around, the last of Grandfather's home-made blackberry brandy which he'd laced with vodka and transformed into a strong liqueur. Uncle Jack, choking back emotion, offered a final toast: "To Pa, and to Mary." Except for Jesse, who abstained, they downed the liqueur in a few gulps, bracing themselves for a stealthy departure, while outside the sky darkened and a gust of wind raked across the yard.

"I'll drive you to the train station now," Uncle Jack announced.

Uncle Abe planned to accompany Davey to New York. Jack was anxious to not keep the police outside waiting too long for this special, extended favor. "Then I'll drop Danny off with Jesse."

Before we left, we walked outside and around the yard to stand once more in the ring, then returned to the house to sew broad, rough stitches on our torn, black mourning scarves.

Uncle Abe offered one last prayer: "As we mend this tear in our garments, let us strive to mend our torn hearts. Give us the strength and courage, o' God, to face our pain and our grief. May we find a means of comfort in your presence and in each other, and in *Olam Habah*, the world to come, where the wicked in this world will be annihilated and the suffering of the righteous will no longer be a factor when measured against an eternity of bliss."

Given what happened to us, Uncle Abe's words failed to ring true to me. God had his chance to intervene on behalf of righteous people, punish the wicked and keep me from going into exile. But he chose not to, and I wondered if my father, so relentlessly downcast and disengaged, would be comforted by this hollow prayer. Davey, who I thought God had chosen to do battle with injustice and who seemed so willing and able to serve in that role, now appeared lost, bereft of authority, and alone.

We left the house for the last time, the friends of the family to their cars, and Davey, Jesse, Uncle Abe and I, braced against the freezing wind, waiting by Uncle Jack's immense new Oldsmobile, hemmed in by two police cars with heaters going full-blast as Jack locked the house and pried loose a *mezzuzah* from the doorway.

Two of my friends, a Negro brother and sister from across the street, came out to say goodbye. Their eyes conveyed a sorrow and understanding none of my young cousins or other friends could express; probably, Uncle Jack reminded me, because their father had died just two months before, killed in an argument. Then I got into the front seat of the car, between Uncle Abe and Uncle Jack. Davey and Jesse climbed in back. Uncle Jack put on leather gloves, punched them to fit snugly and adjusted a fedora low over his eyes. Only I looked back as the caravan drove slowly away.

From inside his overcoat, Uncle Jack pulled a rolled-up fight poster and handed it to me. "This is the only thing Grandfather had in his safe." He shifted into second gear. "It's from one of your dad's rare fights at Madison Square Garden. Years ago." He tapped the graphic print with his finger. "Davey was on the undercard that night…six rounds."

Likenesses of the main-eventers were hand-drawn in each upper corner. But a head-and-shoulders photo of Davey had been placed in the center, a vivid representation of my father's handsome, chiseled face and smoldering gaze.

At the train station, the sergeant and an associate helped Davey and Uncle Abe load their luggage onto the train and accompanied them to their seats. Goodbyes were muffled and quick as three policemen alertly scanned the platform. Uncle Abe smiled and embraced me. Davey did the same, unintentionally rubbing the rough stubble of his unshaven face against my cheek. He eased his grasp when the conductor signaled departure.

"We'll make a new home, Danny," he promised. My eyes welled with tears. So did his. "You're the only treasure left to me, son. Remember that… no matter what." He glanced behind me and wiped his eyes. "Jesse has a surprise waiting for you as soon as you get to his house," he promised, forcing a smile onto his creased, tired face.

He reached out to shake Uncle Jack's hand. "See you in a couple of days."

"Soon as I tie up loose ends," Uncle Jack said, turning to nudge the others back along the aisle to the exit.

The locomotive's wheels screeched against rusty, frozen rails; then they caught, and the train lurched slowly into the night. Jack had one more chore to do that evening.

Chapter 4

A three-car cavalcade, equipped with tire chains, made its way from the train station along snow-clogged thoroughfares. We passed the city's center which only a week ago (but seeming like another lifetime) I'd appraised from the hilltop across from Meltzer's deli.

We passed the gutted site of my grandfather's store, the Armory and Central High School, and at the outer edge of downtown, the Paramount theater. We passed an intersection a mere three blocks from the western border of the Jewish cemetery, and we continued to that outer part of the avenue that was nearly deserted this time of night.

Blustery winds whipped snow across Uncle Jack's line of vision, nearly obscuring the red tail lights of the lead police car.

Nevertheless, with his headlights casting ahead like beacons in a fog, he steered the Olds sedan, tire chains clinking softly, along the lead car's rutted wake.

He drove wordlessly, nearly exhausted yet making a concerted effort to remain focused. The only time his head moved was to occasionally glance in his rear view mirror at Jesse and me.

Through a backseat window, I glimpsed only a few homes where holiday ornaments still glimmered.

When we stopped at a traffic light, Uncle Jack turned to Jesse.

"You doin' okay?" he asked. Jesse nodded.

Uncle Jack had never seemed comfortable with Jesse, a man his own age but who looked at least a decade older and whose hair, worn long and fastened with a rubber band and tucked discretely beneath his collar, had already turned steel gray. Uncle Jack couldn't understand why Jesse would want to live alone, in a cabin, on a decrepit 6,100-acre reservation. No one else in the family seemed to disapprove; in fact, Uncle Abe even praised his choice.

But Uncle Jack said Jesse was wasting his ability by living on the reservation, that a man who'd proved himself during war had now settled for so little. Uncle Jack held Abe in the same kind of contempt. Why would a learned man like him settle for living in a shabby apartment, studying the Torah and its commentaries, and working as a *shamus* at the synagogue?

Uncle Jack also had no interest in Abe's fascination with Iroquois and Jewish religions.

Jesse's grandfather had also been an Iroquois scholar, helping to transcribe—at the turn of the century—The Great Law ("Their version of the Old Testament and U.S. Constitution, put together!" according to Uncle Abe), and the Code of Handsome Lake, the Seneca prophet who, in 1799, instigated the revival that became the new Iroquois religion. Abe had likened The Great Law to the *Halakhah*, because it also didn't distinguish between the ethical and the legal.

But Uncle Abe most appreciated Jesse's skills as compiler of the Hiawatha traditions, a centuries-old epic of Biblical proportions in which Hiawatha spoke for Peace Maker, creator of The Great Law ("just as Aaron spoke for Moses!")

Uncle Abe said his own ecumenical leanings began with his under-standing of *Midrashic* legend: when God took clay for the making of Adam by gathering it from every part of the world and from every color of earth to ensure the brotherhood of the human race. Uncle Abe also believed that the *Mitnagged* and *Kabbalah* perfectly complemented the revelations of the Iroquois prophets: peace and unity among warring tribes and apocalyptic renewal through a redeeming messiah.

"Abe," Uncle Jack said one night in exasperation, "how do you square that stuff with the fact that we live in a 'dog-eat-dog' world? People kill each other over differences, remember?"

Of course, Uncle Jack had no interest in any of this. As a matter of fact, his recollection of Jesse was that he barely contributed to the garrulous camraderie at Burt Street pinochle parties.

"But you should hear him in the Council House," Uncle Abe retorted. "When he speaks, he's an orator."

By now the avenue had become State Highway 1, and we were passing the infamous Iroquois Tavern where many Indians (including, at one time, Jesse) drank themselves into oblivion.

At a forked intersection, the lead car veered right onto the unmarked Holley Valley Road, and we entered sovereign Iroquois territory, at this time of year a frozen, forested wilderness that seemed to supplant all traces of civilization.

The lead car pulled over because police jurisdiction ended at the entrance to the reservation, and they had to wait there until my deposit was completed.

Jesse anticipated Uncle Jack's need for direction. "The turnoff to my place is about two miles ahead, on the left."

Uncle Jack tightened his grip on the steering wheel and peered intently ahead. He flashed his lights. "My brights don't seem to make a difference out here, in this storm," he complained. "It's harder to see, not easier."

"Have you ever tried to drive at night without your lights on?" Jesse asked nonchalantly. "Especially in a storm?"

Uncle Jacked contemplated a response, but merely grunted. He probably figured that anything he might say would only amplify the gulf between them.

"Slow down; you're coming to the turn-off."

Uncle Jack could barely see five feet ahead. He decelerated to a crawl.

"See that gap on the left?" Jesse asked. "Turn there. But don't slow down."

Uncle Jack turned abruptly, thudding through a bank of snow made by a county highway plow. Then he glided down a slight incline onto a sparkling white road that wound into the woods.

"Just keep to the center of this road," Jesse said, evenly. "In a quarter of a mile we'll be right there."

Uncle Jack proceeded, seemingly afloat in a sea of snow, until he reached Jesse's cabin.

"It's best to back your car into my yard and aim back toward the main road," Jesse advised. "You could get stuck trying to take us straight up to the door. Between the two of us, we can unload the boy's belongings."

Even though the snow storm had subsided by the time he reached Jesse's cabin, Jack seemed reluctant to trust the Olds to idle independent of his intervention. He even revved the motor a few times before getting out.

Under veiled moonlight, a hoary cold enveloped him and clung to his overcoat, and his breath formed oddly-elongated, vaporous webs. Wind-swept snow drifts looked like waves that undulated beyond Jesse's yard toward a line of trees.

Uncle Jack glanced back at the cabin. Its front door swung open, hazy light spilling out. In the entranceway, a husky boy stood in silhouette and, just beyond, Jack could glimpse features of a by-gone hospitality he was anxious to avoid. He hurried to open the car trunk where Jesse hauled out his stenciled USMC sea bag, loaned to me for this occasion.

"That's Sonny, my clan mother's son," Jesse said. He waved to the boy. "He's been waiting, keeping the fires for us."

Uncle Jack nodded reflexively and reached into the trunk for a leather briefcase. He withdrew a manila folder containing my birth certificate and medical and school records. He handed it to me and told me to keep it in a safe place.

He also pulled out a large gym bag. "I put in two sets of sparring gear. Don't get rusty while we're in Brooklyn."

He said this with an enthusiasm meant to ease my transition, and he reached out to caress my head, awkwardly shifting my wool cap, forgetting my injury, but with the best of intentions—until I raised a hand to stop him.

"Sorry, Danny. I'm beat."

His handshake with Jesse was loose and brief.

"Soon, when things begin to get straight, I'll send money. Abe'll bring it when he visits."

He slipped and nearly fell returning to the driver's side, but he grabbed the open door, regained his balance and pulled himself behind the steering wheel. A pale, orange glow from the dashboard illuminated his face. Everything had taken its toll on him; he looked defeated. He waved at me, saluted awkwardly and pulled away.

Trudging behind Jesse, I struggled with my possessions, tightening my grip and directing my feet into his lead footprints. When we reached the cabin door, Sonny stood back as Jesse swung the sea bag inside, kicked his boots free of snow and entered. I did the same.

Sonny selected a log from a small stack and added it to a pot-bellied stove. I looked around. Flickering light from a fireplace at the furthest end of the cabin created an ethereal sense of expansion and dilation, almost like breathing and, in its sway, I searched the room for a place to anchor.

A movement at my hand startled me, and I pulled back. A muscular, short-haired hound sat at my feet, head erect, eyes bright with anticipation.

"This is Echo," Sonny said. "He's sort of a clan dog; he hangs out here most of the time."

So this was the surprise my father had mentioned. I'd never owned a dog before. I'd wanted one, but it would've never fit in at Burt Street. No one to walk it or pay close attention; we were all too busy. I removed a glove and extended my hand. Echo leaned toward it and accepted a novice pat between his ears.

A tea kettle atop the wood stove spouted steam.

"Show Daniel where he can put his things," Jesse said, "and where his bed is; then we'll have some hot chocolate."

Echo followed us across a plank wood floor. Alongside one wall, kerosene lamplight danced, illuminating articles hung for storage: several knitted and beaded wool sashes of various widths and decoration; a pair of snowshoes; three hand-carved hickory lacrosse sticks whose nets were wrapped in oilcloth; and, hanging from hooks by leather thongs, three large cups carved from wood which Jesse removed and placed on the table.

When I reached what was to be my side of the room, Echo sank gracefully next to a bed constructed in bent-wood style with curved head and foot boards. On top lay several wool army surplus blankets from Grandfather's store.

Jesse dragged the seabag next to the bed, then he shepherded Sonny and me to a table made of polished wood hatch-covers where he spooned heaping teaspoons of chocolate powder into cups which he then filled with hot water, evaporated milk and dollops of spooned honey.

Stirring and inhaling the hot chocolate distracted me from my initial appraisal of bleak exile. I imitated Jesse and Sonny and gripped my cup's oddly-toggled handle and slurped noisily. Jesse explained the layout of the cabin.

"We don't have electricity or indoor plumbing. You'll see the outhouse before we turn in. In the morning, I'll show you how to use the water pump, how to prime it. If we don't do it right, the water in the pipe will freeze.

"Also, whoever wakes up first in the morning lights the wood stove and puts water on to boil. I'll show you how that's done, too."

He gestured at Sonny. "He lives just up the road. You'll meet his mother tomorrow."

Smiling with guileless curiosity, Sonny asked. "You know how to box?"

Jesse raised a hand, braking him.

Waiting—tired and hoping to go to bed—I sat as distanced as possible, feeling obligated, but resisting this deliberate attempt to make me feel comfortable.

Outside, pine limbs keened in the wind, and from the fireplace, logs cracked and split. When we finished the hot chocolate, Jesse opened the stove door and stoked the fire. Reaching into a shirt pocket, he tossed a small bundle into the flames. Immediately, the pungent aroma of tobacco wafted into the room. He took hold of our hands so that we formed an intimate circle and in a calm, regal voice, he began to chant.

The chant seemed to possess such a familiar rhythmic pattern. Disoriented, I took it to be Hebrew. Even the tone seemed familiar: angular, discordant, muted; delicately-paced stanzas; repetitive refrains; an unfamiliar language. Still, the intent was obvious: consolation, companioned grief. Like *Kaddish*.

And there was something more: an incipient promise beyond mere condolence. I could feel it, but for some other reason the chant brought me to the brink of tears, and my body steamed inside my shirt. I ground my teeth so hard they hurt. Jesse turned directly to me, his gaze steady and kind, and he repeated the chant. Only years later did I discover its meaning:

> " *...you are mourning in the deep darkness,*
> *but I will make the sky clear for you and*
> *you will not see a cloud.*
>   *"And I will give the sun to shine upon you,*
> *so that you can look upon it peacefully*
> *when it goes down. And I hope that you will*
> *soon see pleasant days. This we say and do—*
> *we brothers.*
>   *"And another thing we say, we brothers.*
> *We will open your ears, and also your throat,*
> *for there is something that is choking you. And we*
> *will also give you the water that will wash down*
> *all the troubles in your throat. We will hope that,*
> *after this, your mind will recover its cheerfulness.*
> *This we say and do, we brothers."*

After Sonny had gone home and as the fireplace embers died, I burrowed beneath my blankets, balled my fists in the armpits of my sweatshirt and pressed my stockinged feet together, waiting for my forehead to stop throbbing and to fall asleep as quickly as possible.

But despite my best efforts, a cold draft crept down my back, denying me the deep sleep I craved. Instead, fitfully, I began to dream:

Gusts buffeted the roof of the cavernous Armory. I hovered helplessly over the bell while in a corner of the ring a man in a wretched mask shook free from Uncle Jack's grasp and drove my father into the corner stanchion. Across the ring, looming above their seats, three men tore off their overcoats and hats to reveal scarred and heavy brows and huge, bent noses. They stalked around the ring, glaring at me, their mouths agape, jeering. I slid into a seizure, gnashing my teeth and jerking in spasms. From his chair next to me, Grandfather called my name and steadied me in his arms. He told me he knew the dream and warned me there would be others in the nights ahead; visits, he called them. Some would be good, some would be bad, he said. But they would be only dreams. Finally, gratefully, I fell into a deep sleep.

CHAPTER 5

I woke at dawn's first light, exhausted, my jaws cramped and aching, pinned beneath layers of blankets. But my exposed nose burned, and a cloud of my breath hovered in a beam of light that bled through an ice-streaked window.

From a few feet away where he lay on his stomach—head propped on a pillow entwined in his arms—Jesse called to me.

"I'm afraid this is how a winter morning is around here. I keep my clothes rolled in bed with me; yours are, too, by your feet."

I watched while Jesse began to dress himself in bed, pulling trousers over long-johns and snaking them over his hips, pushing his arms into a heavy wool shirt then rolling out of bed and stepping into a pair of deerskin slippers. Standing cautiously, straightening his legs but not taking a step until both knees cracked. I'd never seen anyone do that or make such a sound.

"Watch what I do."

He walked to the wood stove, opened the grated door and shoveled sooty ashes into a cardboard box. Next, he tore sheets of newspaper and crumpled them into a half-dozen loose balls which he placed inside the stove and covered with kindling. From a box on a nearby shelf, he pulled a match and struck it and within minutes the stove's belly glowed bright orange. Soon my steamy breath disappeared, and I groped under the covers until I found the pile of my clothes where Jesse had placed them.

Prone and grunting, I dressed awkwardly, struggling with my trousers. When I finished, I walked to the table and faced a chair toward the stove. I sat as close as possible. Tired. Groggy. Contemplating the flames. Rubbing my hands together.

Echo padded over to where I sat and rested his muzzle on my knee, giving me a strange look that reminded me of the mourners at Hertzberg's. Jesse carried over several short oak logs.

"It's easier to build a fire when the wood is dry. Lay these across the kindling and when they catch fire put a bigger one on top. Then shut the door but leave the grate open. The draft of air keeps it alive."

As he performed the task, Jesse changed the topic. "What did you dream about last night? You had a bad dream."

I acknowledged this with only a silent, suspicious squint.

"I had similar dreams when I came home from the Pacific. If yours continue, maybe we'll try the healing ceremony during Midwinter. It helped cure me."

Of what, I wondered? As the room began to warm, Jesse pulled on his overshoes. "Now let's go to the outhouse. Then I'll show you how to pump water from the well to wash and to make coffee."

He cracked the door open. Sunlight flared from the top of forested, snow-covered hills surrounding the cabin. A lone, masked cardinal glided to a landing atop the wood pile as Echo nosed his way onto the porch.

With my bladder about to burst, I hurried to the outhouse ahead of Jesse, lifted the seat and pissed into a dark, foul-smelling hole that made me gag. At the pump, I studied Jesse while he primed it and coaxed water into several buckets. Back at the house he changed my bandage after applying an ointment. I let myself exult a little in front of the stove's dry, smoky warmth, the only comfort of the morning. After a while, the coffee boiled.

Jesse set the first steaming cup in front of me and added honey and evaporated milk.

"I remember you drinking coffee-milk with your mother one Saturday morning before she went off to work. This version is different, stronger; we don't have much canned milk today. I hope you like it."

I was yearning for something hot and savory to drink after my first night in this cold cabin, and I worked the spoon until the honey dissolved, then noisily spooned a sip, and another. I felt my ears tingle before the coffee seeped into my belly. I sipped faster then gulped the rest of it. Afterwards, I lay on the floor with Echo curled into me, his spine against my chest, and we basked in the stove's radiant heat. My headache seemed to subside.

From outside, Sonny called, then burst through the front door with news.

"What is it?" Jesse asked.

"Moore beat Maxim for the title!"

Jesse and I exchanged glances. I was stunned. In my new setting, I'd momentarily forgotten about the fight. Now the result hit me hard: the family enterprise, and the destiny they all believed in, and the title they came so close to attaining. So close. If it hadn't been for me....

"How?" Jesse asked. "Knockout?"

"Points," Sonny said. "There's already talk of a rematch in June."

Sonny took off his jacket and cap and sat down to breakfast: oatmeal sweetened with dissolving chunks of maple sugar. Sonny wanted to talk about the fight, what he'd heard from a friend of his father who'd come to the house that morning, but I ignored him and ate my cereal. Jesse changed the subject.

"Your school is just down the hill from here, south about a mile along the highway. After you enroll, we'll see if we can find *ga wa sa*...snow snake," he said, winking slyly.

The desolate setting and cramped and rough cabin seemed somehow appropriate, consistent with my down-in-the-dumps attitude. But, rather than being unnerved by the contrast with Burt Street, I was actually intrigued by it. So far, I had been able to behave without resentment and in accordance with what was expected of me because Jesse's manner was so like Uncle Abe's: instructional and peppered with little stories that showed a commanding and empathic knowledge. But I wanted to resist, do what I did best—receive advice and comply, but not really revere it.

Never having lived with a dog before, I was impressed by Echo. When he wasn't actively accommodating me, he remained close by, like a sentry—head erect, attentive, his forelegs crossed in gentlemanly repose. I couldn't get over how attached to me he seemed.

In front of the fireplace lay a bear-skin rug. Next to it was a slender wood and glass cabinet which housed a lever-action rifle and a long-barreled pump shotgun, with one box of ammunition for each. I was completely unfamiliar with guns; in my family they were never a subject of conversation. Hunting was an alien activity.

Horizontally-striped cement joints between pine logs gave the cabin an artificial sense of expanse, while above, ears of red and yellow corn—their dried husks woven together—hung decoratively from several rafters. In a kitchen alcove, deep storage bins with lids that could be used as cutting boards harbored iron skillets, several pots and a kettle. And along a wall, four long shelves held plates, bowls, jam jars that served as drinking glasses, cutlery, canning jars of green beans, turnips, and dried beans and smaller jars of spices.

What Jesse's cabin lacked were electrical appliances of any kind, a telephone, radio or victrola (a possession which Uncle Abe most prized, besides his books). There wasn't even a closet. Jesse simply stacked all of his clothing by category on pine shelves stacked on cinder blocks. All of his jackets and caps hung from hooks along another wall.

After breakfast, we left for school. It took me several minutes to adjust to the snowy glare all around. From atop Jesse's mailbox, the cardinal seemed to eye me warily, then flew away.

Flanking Jesse, protected by buckled overshoes, we pushed through deep powdery snow. When we passed the modest, rectangular Council House, its windows shuttered, several men were shoveling paths from the road. They waved and said a plow would come later to clear the road.

At the highway, Sonny and I followed Jesse along tire tracks made by Uncle Jack the night before when he'd breached the snow bank. Jesse glanced north and south, then led us across the road.

"Walk single file next to the snow bank," he advised. "You got to be careful walking this road, especially in winter."

From a distance, the school—with its steeply-pitched roof, bell tower and arched main entrance—looked more like a church. As we approached, I noticed an animated group of boys at play waving their arms in unusual underhand thrusts. Others, with jackets unbuttoned, stood nearby; Jesse said they'd just made a straight-line track in the snow by pulling a log about a foot in diameter down a grade 300 to 400 yards to the west.

A taller boy, hatless and with a prominent nose, walked gingerly through the track, smoothing it with his feet. He was followed by two others who ladled water from milk cans to form an icy crust from beginning to end.

Several boys clutched smooth, polished wood rods ranging in length from five to nine feet. The heads on each were rounded and turned up slightly on the underside and tipped with a band of lead resembling a snake's slit eyes—to prevent them from splintering, Sonny said.

"After you register at the school, Sonny will show you how to throw the snake," said Jesse, his eyes watering from the cold.

When I entered the school, I noticed that entire sections on the corridor walls contained painted images. Jesse called them murals and said they depicted Iroquois stories, which he explained to me. Some I vaguely recollected learning from my mother, told to me when I was first learning that a previous, mysterious world existed.

The first one was titled Creation. It portrayed the Iroquois other-world set in a wooded valley with a large "tree of life," a sacred fruit tree never to be disturbed, according to Jesse.

"There, the man who was caretaker for the tree got married. Soon after, his wife became pregnant. She yearned for delicacies to eat, as women do when they are expecting a child. She asked her husband for fruit from the tree, but he refused. Instead, he said he would provide her with other special foods, but the tree must always be protected."

Uncle Abe always gushed over this story, about how the Iroquois tree was "like the tree rising out of the Torah."

And that's when something inside of me boiled over. My face burned and I stalked down the hallway. Jesse was just working up another homily. I didn't want to hear it.

Near the principal's office, a second mural showed another woman lying on her back beneath the ground, arms and legs spread, with green shoots rising from her body to form corn, squash, beans, tobacco and strawberries. Above her, their backs against a tree, sat two young men. One smiled from amidst a garden, pointing to a large collection of land and sea animals, including a dog who resembled Echo, and birds in flight. The other, who scowled, sat in a landscape choked with thorny vines and populated by a serpent and hideous men with wild hair wearing grotesque masks. I peered close, recalling DiNardi's men.

Above them and in the center hovered the woman who fell from the sky-world and directly over her head, nine moons in phases, with the full moon in the center.

"This painting is about two brothers, Sky-Woman's grandsons," Jesse said, pointing, beginning a story I'd heard before and couldn't help but associate with similar ones I'd already learned in Hebrew School. I turned away.

How like Uncle Abe he was, and how bored I was with his stories. They only reminded me of my treachery.

In the principal's office, Sonny and I sat on a bench waiting while Jesse conferred with her, a petite white woman, and an older woman, Sonny's mother.

We waited, watching and listening to the precise movements of the office clock. After 10 minutes, Sonny broke the silence.

"I watched you box last year, at the Boy's Club and at summer camp; you're lucky to have your father teach you so good."

I looked into his shining brown eyes, not wanting to acknowledge him.

"I don't know how to box, but I'd like to learn. Would you show me?"

I looked back at the clock.

"I'll teach you how to throw snow snake, and in the spring I'll teach you how to play lacrosse."

Before I could respond, Echo's bark resounded from outside, and we sprang to a window. He was leaping and chasing after a snow snake that scuttled through the icy rut. It had shot way ahead of him to a distance of about 150 yards where a boy marked it with a stick. When Echo finally arrived, he skidded to a halt, barking and chomping at the snow with darting lunges.

Then he trotted back to the throwing area as the next boy, the one with the prominent nose, taller by a head than the others and long-limbed, took his turn. But before he threw, he rubbed the snow snake with a cloth.

"He's rubbing his snake with medicine," Sonny said, grinning.

I must've looked puzzled because he explained what he meant.

"He's using wax… or some kind of oil. Each family has a secret mixture. We use water milfoil—the plant—boiled in water."

Grasping the snake in his right hand and placing his forefinger in a notch cut into the tail, the boy balanced it with his left hand, stooped, and set his feet to sprint. Then he burst into a quick series of steps, leaped, and threw with a leaning sidearm motion.

Echo again raced off, yipping excitedly as he ran, but the snake traveled with the speed of an arrow, and the dog caught up with it only at the end where it was marked, 20 yards beyond the first throw.

Two more boys took turns. Some others jeered and shouted and generally tried to unnerve them. Echo waited about 50 yards down the track but, even with a head start, he could only harass the snake as it sped by him. After the boys had thrown all their snakes, they tramped down the side of the course to retrieve them.

The office door opened, and Jesse came out.

"The principal and Mrs. Hill would like to talk to you now."

With a feeling of dread ballooning inside my stomach, I entered the office, still at a loss for words and with a ringing in my ears like a high-pitched wind.

Both women stood as I entered. The principal smiled and introduced herself. "I'm Mrs. Cole and this is Mrs. Hill, the Wolf clan mother; she'll teach some of your classes." Mrs. Hill beamed as if she recognized me, but I couldn't recall ever seeing her before. It was just like when I met any of my father's friends and his acclaim brought me instant esteem. Her freckled, unlined face broke into a wide grin, revealing gleaming, gapped teeth. Beaded earrings dangled below a thatch of short, black hair. She took my hands and studied them.

In turn, I examined her. She wore a red and black Iroquois dress that was beaded and embroidered in swirling pink flowers and fringed with white shells. It covered a black-beaded and embroidered shirt and matching leggings and moccasins. She radiated a kindness that numbed my anxiety.

"Your people are well-known to us, Daniel, and we're very happy and honored to have you attend our school." The principal spoke. "We know that you have a grieving illness in your throat, so we'll tell your teachers that you won't be participating until it heals." She handed me a black and white marbled notebook. "We've had other students who've suffered throat sickness. This helped them join in."

I wondered why she talked about my inability to talk as "a throat sickness". It seemed like a childish thing.

"In every class, your two cousins will sit next to you and speak for you. Sonny will be one…." Mrs. Hill went to the door and beckoned. "…and Yvonne Logan will be the other."

A tall, serious-looking girl with thick, glossy pigtails, wearing wire-rimmed glasses, stepped into the room. Her eyes widened and her lips parted in a dimpled smile and another, different feeling filled my chest.

"It is our custom that cousins look out for one another. When classes begin tomorrow, you can speak through your notebook… and through Sonny and Yvonne. Your teacher will show you how."

Mrs. Cole asked Jesse and Yvonne to leave her office, and then she turned to me.

"Jesse told me about your family's trouble. There's a long tradition here of harboring people in trouble. As a precaution, you'll be enrolled as Daniel Isaacs, which was your Iroquois grandparents' last name and the last name your Uncle Jesse uses. The teachers and all the students—even the ones who knew you from the Boys' Club—will call you by this name."

I nodded. It made sense to grant me even greater anonymity.

Mrs. Hill returned to the office with two snow snakes, each about six feet in length.

"We keep these in storage; Sonny will show you how to use them. They're boned and waxed and ready to throw."

Sonny thanked her for both of us and nudged me toward the outer office where Jesse and Yvonne waited to take me to the snow-snake track.

"I'd throw with you today," Jesse said, "but I skipped work to bring you here and to go to the Council House." He said he was a "fire-keeper" which obliged him to attend a special ceremony three weeks before Mid-Winter or New Year's, "when people make peace with the Creator" by confessing and atoning for their sins of the past year. This had to occur before he could renew his life cycle.

A kind of *Yom Kippur*, I figured.

Smiling modestly, he turned and walked south along the highway with Mrs. Hill.

Approaching the snake throwers, Sonny advised me on the proper grip, run-up, and release. He also emphasized how important it was to keep the snake as level to the rutted channel as possible. The other boys stepped aside when we approached, as if they'd been expecting us.

Even though I felt awkward, my first throw had power behind it, but I angled the snake too sharply and it ricocheted out of the groove and sailed into the air, landing nose-first about 40 feet to the left. The other boys howled with laughter.

Sonny leaned close. "Don't throw so hard next time. Keep it level, like this."

He threw next and his snake sailed down the channel, lifting occasionally when it struck several uneven patches, but it came to rest about 160 yards away.

The second and third times I got off decent releases, but distance was sacrificed, as Sonny had urged, and I was distracted by a persistent headache. The others ignored me.

Sonny's fifth throw went a bit farther than the best throws of the other boys, to about 175 yards. The tall boy glared suspiciously.

"I'll bet you on the last round of throws," he proposed confidently.

Sonny retreated. "I don't have any money...."

Then an idea came to him. "But me and my cousin will carry you home if you beat me."

Everyone laughed at his novel proposal, which also relieved a certain tension.

Each boy took three throws; the farthest one would win.

My throws actually improved in form and distance, and before my final one I glanced at Sonny, then Yvonne, whose expression I couldn't make out because of glare off her glasses.

As the others hooted with derision, I unbuttoned my jacket, lay it in the snow, and limbered my throwing arm in windmill fashion. When I threw, it was with more of a motion recommended by Sonny, and as the belly of the snake entered the channel, more evenly than on any previous throw, I grunted. At the sound of my voice, Yvonne elbowed Sonny hard in the ribs, nearly knocking him off-balance.

Echo ran the length of the channel, past the boys holding markers, before he skidded to a halt. The tall boy eyed me warily and he, too, removed his jacket. He rubbed his snow-snake with a chamois and spoke to it under his breath, seemingly oblivious to the others' jeers. He took a longer run-up than usual and skipped deftly so that all forward momentum would shift to his planted foot. At that point, he whipped it underhand in the orthodox style. It whished down the channel. As soon as he released it, I knew it would easily surpass mine, and it did. To about 200 yards.

Sonny was last to throw. He was really casual about it, even keeping his jacket on. He also talked to his snake as he rocked back and forth in his stance, digging in for traction. He got a good start and gathered speed while maintaining stride in the trampled, slick pathway, skidded to a half-crouch, then thrust the snow snake across his body with a snapping release. His snake whacked into the groove and sped off.

By now the sun lay low on the horizon, and shadows cast by giant elms crept across the field. Sonny's snake ran furiously along the frozen track then disappeared in shadow for about 50 yards, only to leap into the air when it ricocheted off a slight bulge in the track near where Echo sat. The dog winced at its sudden trajectory out of the channel at about 180 yards.

All the way home, we kept falling in the snow because we couldn't control the sway of the bigger boy's body, especially when Sonny bumped my hips. By the time we reached the Council House, whose twin chimneys issued tufts of white smoke, he parted to go his way, seeming to forget his grievance.

When we reached the cabin, Yvonne set kindling ablaze in the stove and in the fireplace. Before she added logs, she studied my boxing poster tacked to the wall over my bed. When she looked back at me, it was with the smile she'd first given me, including her eyes, as beaming as I'd ever seen, and as undeserving.

CHAPTER 6

Including the dreams that plagued me, activities during the days that followed took on a customary cadence. Early each morning, I would sit near the wood stove and have coffee and oatmeal or cornbread and jam with Jesse, and Sonny and Yvonne would call for me, and we'd all walk to the highway where Jesse caught a bus or ride to work.

At school, Yvonne nagged me to write in my notebook. If she even perceived a hint of curiosity on my part about the subject being discussed, she'd raise her hand. Then all attention shifted to me. At first, I was uncomfortable with this, until I realized how relieved the others seemed. For even though they'd known each other and their teachers from previous years, their general demeanor was one of shy engagement.

In every one of my classes, whenever I asked a question, teachers seemed willing, even happy to respond. The way it worked was that after I wrote down questions or comments in my notebook, either Sonny or Yvonne would read them aloud. At first, teachers encouraged the students to try to answer my questions, even to the point of having them come up to the blackboard in math class to demonstrate a solution to a problem. This seemed to give the teachers an opportunity they never had before. And for this same reason, the students seemed to appreciate rather than resent the attention paid to me.

In addition, Mrs. Hill spent a portion of each morning going over that part of my notebook in which she wanted me to make personal comments. She seemed especially impressed—and occasionally taken aback—by the similarities I noted in Iroquois and Jewish teachings.

I'd compared Midwinter ceremonies of confession, atonement and renewal to *Rosh Hashana* and *Yom Kippur*; the rivalry between Sky Woman's sons to biblical rivalries between Esau and Jacob and Cain and Abel; the Peacemaker and the formation of the Iroquois Confederacy and the capitol at the Brant reservation to King David's unification of the 12 tribes to form a nation and establish Jerusalem as its center; the destruction of the Iroquois empire by the British and King George to the destruction of Israel and the temple at Jerusalem by Babylonian forces under King Nebuchadnessar; the Iroquois constellation of Seven Sisters to the seven planetary deities commemorated in the seven branches of the *menorah*; Sky Woman to Jeremiah's Queen of Heavens.

One day, during Mrs. Hill's language and culture class, while she was discussing the steep decline of the Iroquois empire due to broken treaties, disease, and war, I raised my hand. Mrs. Hill paused in mid-sentence. The others leaned forward in their seats and Yvonne read aloud:

"Daniel says six million Jews were killed by the Nazis during World War II, mostly in concentration camps. He calls it a ... 'hollow-cost'."

Mrs. Hill nodded somberly. What I noticed about her was that sometimes she thought hard about what she wanted to say. It often took her a few minutes to respond to students' questions.

"Both Indians and Jews are dedicating themselves to restoration—the Indians by re-discovering and honoring their traditions and returning to their homelands, and Jews by migrating back to Israel. And both Indians and Jews by marrying among themselves and having children to carry on those traditions."

Was this a rebuke? Poised over my notebook, I thought about my jumbled heritage. Even as a Jew, there was always some question about my total acceptance. I was the only child in my Hebrew school class from a mixed marriage.

I wanted to respond and began writing in my notebook again. Yvonne noticed and, before I could write it out, she raised her hand. But I changed my mind and quietly placed my pencil into the carved niche at the top of my desk. I really wasn't ready to explore that terrain. It might come out wrong. As I thought about it, really for the first time, there was probably enough Indian and Jewish blood in me to belong to either tribe. Yet here I was, bereft of faith in each.

Early one morning while I was drinking coffee and fingering the long scar that ran above my right eyebrow, a man's deep voice summoned Jesse to the door. Sonny, Mrs. Hill and a somber-faced man kicked snow from their boots and entered.

"Daniel, this is Yvonne's father, Mr. Logan; he's chief of the wolf clan."

Mr. Logan extended his hand. "Welcome," he said, ceremoniously. He wore dark blue corduroy work pants and a pale red calico ribbon shirt. Over his shoulder, and diagonally across his chest, he wore a broad woven sash with white beads strung in open places, fringed at each end and tied at his left side. Also on his chest was pinned a large, silver wolf. On his head, he wore a skull cap of tanned skin attached to a wood-splint frame bound at the rim with a silver band. A cluster of different-sized and -colored feathers were fastened at the top with two especially-long ones, one pointing straight up, one pointing backward.

Mrs. Hill wore the same outfit as the day I enrolled in school.

Jesse had dressed in identical fashion as Mr. Logan, and he, too, wore a silver wolf pin.

Mr. Logan placed a large object wrapped in cloth on a bench near the fireplace next to a similar one belonging to Jesse.

"Today is the first day of Midwinter festival," Jesse announced. "Mr. Logan is going to make the thanksgiving speech this morning. Then the False Faces will leave the Council House; they'll walk about and enter homes to stir ashes in people's fireplaces, sing songs of thanksgiving and treat sick people.

"Mr. Logan and I were made well by the False Faces when we came home after the war," Jesse explained. "So now we're part of the Society."

Mrs. Hill baked cornbread for us and served it with berry jam while we watched the men open their bundles and remove what seemed to me large, oblong wood bowls. From the hollowed part, each man carefully removed bags of tobacco and a large turtle shell rattle with elongated neck skin and dried heads at the end, bound in place by wood splints and leather thong.

As they unwound long strands of horsehair, the true nature of the objects were revealed to be masks—black, grotesque faces with deep-set eyes highlighted in tin, large bent noses, severely-arched eyebrows, wrinkled foreheads, and scowling, thick-lipped mouths.

"Look, yours is sweating!" Mr. Logan exclaimed.

"That's a sign someone here is sick," Mrs. Hill said, wearing a reserved, inward expression.

I moved closer, astonished, as Mrs. Hill anointed the masks with sunflower oil: they looked exactly like the faces in my dreams, like DiNardi's men.

At the Council House, I joined a line of men and boys waiting by a side door. I had missed *Chanukah* this year—the special songs and dances and games with a *dreidl*. I wondered what past event Midwinter marked, what rituals would be performed, what special foods prepared. I thought about the Maccabee victory over the tyrant Antiochus, and the recapture of the Temple in Jerusalem. But victory now seemed such a fleeting concept.

Like in an orthodox synagogue, Mrs. Hill joined a line of girls and women entering the Council House from the opposite side; many of them carried covered dishes. The separate groups, men and women, sat on plain wood chairs around stoves at opposite ends. But here the similarity ended. The Council House was so small and drab in comparison to the elaborately-decorated, domed synagogue and its rows of polished pews. Several men placed bundles of tobacco in the stove at their end, and Mr. Logan made a long thanksgiving speech. Out of habit, I tried to concentrate on every detail of the ritual. But my observance was purely out of a personal sense of obligation to Jesse in order to be polite. It had no real meaning.

Then Mr. Logan told a detailed story about creation, translated in a whisper to me by Sonny, about the Creator's gifts, and the Four Beings—messengers from the Creator who appeared to Handsome Lake—who helped protect the people, and Handsome Lake's message of remembrance of how the Creator wanted people to behave.

After several dances and another, abbreviated thanksgiving speech by Mr. Logan, women heated kettles and distributed containers of corn soup. Despite my acceptance into this setting, I still felt like an intruder at a family picnic.

When everyone filed out of the Council House, Mrs. Hill led Sonny and me and several adults to Jesse's cabin. A fire was lit in the stove only; the fireplace, begrimed with white ashes, was kept cold.

There was a knock on the door which Mrs. Hill answered. A half-dozen men wearing masks of the False Faces staggered in, pretending to be afflicted in some strange, grotesque way. They crawled across the floor, dragging blankets draped from their shoulders, demanding gifts of tobacco and food. They began to shout and shake huge turtle shell rattles, startling me.

After a few minutes, Mrs. Hill stepped in front of the False Faces. A man holding a small drum in one hand—no more than five inches across—began tapping delicately, accompanied by two others who swished cow horn rattles. To me, Mrs. Hill began to tell the origin story of the False Faces.

She summoned the tallest of the masked men, the only one who walked and gestured like a normal person. It was easy to tell it was Jesse, but she introduced him as *Hadui* and told me yet another long story, trying to convince me that Jesse was actually the mythic leader of the False Faces. I listened as patiently as I could, but it was all I could do to stand and take it.

She said he had the power to cure disease by blowing hot ashes, and when she finished the story the others were taken with it and seemed to breathe in unison with the gentle rhythm of the water drum and horn rattles, and the cabin seemed to expand and dilate, like on the night of my arrival.

I reached for my pad and wrote a question that had been plaguing me for days: *'Why do your monsters have the power to heal?'* It was a question Uncle Abe would answer more to my liking many years later, at a time when explanations came in a torrent. Mrs. Hill more or less repeated what Jesse had said.

"These False Faces represent the original ones. They take possession of *Hadui's* helping spirit to ensure protection from illness," she said, signaling the adult guests and children to lay small bundles and bowls at the feet of the False Faces who promptly reached out and pocketed the bundles and sat cross-legged, spooning soup through the openings of their misshapen, swollen lips.

"We have to honor *Hadui's* pledge by giving him offerings of tobacco and corn soup during our New Year festival.

"Now," she said, "are any of you sick, really sick enough to ask *Hadui* to cure you? Or do you know someone who should be visited by the False Faces to receive the ashes?"

Everyone stood motionless, then one hand eased into the air.

"Yes, Yvonne?"

Yvonne stood. "There's a boy here who can't speak, so I'm asking for him to be cured by *Hadui*."

My face burned with embarrassment. I stood frozen, staring at Mrs. Hill, whose steady, smiling gaze I knew was meant to reassure me. But I didn't even care to resume speaking. What made Yvonne think I wanted to be "cured," especially in front of all these strangers? I really had nothing to say to them or to anybody.

"Would you like to participate in the healing ceremony, Daniel?" Mrs. Hill asked, holding forth her hand. Yvonne gently grasped my shoulder from behind and I turned. She looked earnestly into my eyes. My heart thudded irregularly and sweat began to drip from my armpits. I wanted to resist her, but Yvonne pressed me forward.

Two False Faces stood and walked to the cabin door and assumed sentry positions with folded arms.

A singer stood next to *Hadui* and as the drum and rattles shifted tempo he began to chant. *Hadui* took a stick and stirred the ashes in the fireplace. He leaned in, grabbed a handful, blew chalky clouds in four directions and beckoned me closer. Yvonne had to nudge me.

Hadui stepped closer, dwarfing me, as he reached from under his blanket to produce a small handful of ashes into which he dipped the fingers of his right hand.

I stood erect, eyes fluttering. The great False Face slowly extended his fingers and gently massaged my scalp, jaw and throat. With a tremulous voice, *Hadui* joined the singer and, despite my misgivings, I began to feel a curious warmth, and my scalp and ears tingled, then my throat, even against my will, and I found myself beguiled by prayer.

The ceremony ended when the False Face sentries stepped away from the doors and opened them to lead a procession outside, followed by the drum and rattle group, the singer, and the rest of the False Faces, including *Hadui*.

Mrs. Hill hugged Yvonne, then me, brushing damp hair from my brow.

"The cure may take awhile, Daniel," she said confidently, "so don't try to regain use of your voice all at once. Rest it for now, but you might try it out on Jesse when he comes back home."

Mrs. Hill and Yvonne cleaned the cabin floor of tracked-in snow and ashes and left.

It was near dark when Jesse returned. I was sitting on the bear rug with Echo. Fires were going in both the stove and the fireplace, but I had drawn back into myself. Jesse removed his boots and coat and slipped into moccasins and, as he heated water for coffee, he glanced my way. I managed a wan smile and shrugged my shoulders, but he read the failure in my eyes.

"If it weren't for the False Faces, I wouldn't be around today," Jesse reminded me. I shrugged again and looked away.

CHAPTER 7

After Midwinter, Sonny and I often brought our snow snakes to school. We'd throw before class, during lunch break, and, for a longer time, after school. Eventually, I improved. On occasion, I even came close to Sonny's best throw, just under 200 yards, a maximum range surpassed only by the tall, hawk-nosed boy.

The tall boy was named Welcome Shenandoah. He was a year older than me and acted more like a young man, more purposeful than the rest. Although he was a cousin of Yvonne's on her mother's side, he cast such an intention upon her, guarded by a palisade of jealousy, that an intruder wouldn't dare to penetrate. And even though I hardly knew Yvonne, our arranged proximity seemed to take a bite out of him. Moreover, Yvonne's devotion to me, even though it was shared by Sonny, seemed more than obvious to Welcome, and it was the source of his grievance.

One day before school, during a particularly spirited game when my throws crept closer and closer to Sonny's, Welcome's competitive hectoring became more directed at me. To make the matter worse, I gave him an excuse to intensify it. I unintentionally interrupted one of his throws to shoo Echo from the track where he'd been sniffing and pawing at the tip of a protruding twig. During his run-up, Welcome stumbled clumsily to a halt and slammed his snake at his feet, disgusted with the wasted effort.

"Hey, dummy, get out of the way!" Welcome yelled.

I'd crossed his run-up path without looking when he was ready to throw. Instead of moving out of the way, I continued trying to wave at the dog.

Exasperated, Welcome set his hands on his hips.

"I said, get out of the way…dummy!"

I continued toward Echo, whose ears now stood straight up. But instead of moving as I urged him to do, he simply stood there with a puzzled expression, infuriating Welcome even more. Welcome's companions, who'd been polishing their snow snakes, fell in behind him as he strode toward me, cursing, his anger building with each step.

I situated myself in front of Echo.

Welcome laughed as he approached, and he thumped me in the chest.

"I'm talkin' to you, dummy, not the dog!" he shouted.

Sensing a fight, the others gathered around. Sonny tried to intervene. "Leave him alone; he didn't mean to get in your way. He was only trying to help."

"Shut up, Logan," Welcome spat. "I'm sick of these two dogs trailing around here. One's a bitch and the other's a chicken-shit who needs his hand held. And I'm sick of pretending he's an Isaacs. He's not one of us; he's a Jew son of a bitch."

The boys murmured with anticipation and circled tighter.

My stomach flip-flopped with panic. It wasn't just a fight I was facing. It was Welcome's willingness to renege on the Iroquois pledge of asylum. My mind raced to figure out a good response.

Despite the threat he projected, he was tall and lanky. Davey would advise me to duck low, get inside of him and wing a flurry of gut punches to take the fight out of him. But there was the bigger problem to contend with—no matter how I defended myself, he would still be my enemy.

Several of the boys moved directly behind me, edging Sonny out of the way, daring me to stand up to Welcome. As they closed ranks, Welcome, angry and buoyed by my passivity, again thumped me in the chest, forcing me back against the tightening circle. Then he cocked a fist and lunged. I leaned to one side. His looping punch missed and he sprawled face-first into an embankment.

He floundered in the deep snow trying to right himself, and when he finally regained his feet, tufts of snow clung to his face, masking his rage with a burlesque veneer. At the sight of him, his friends burst out laughing, which angered him even more. He charged me again, leading with a haymaker.

This time, I ducked, and Welcome's punch rocked one of the boys standing in a rank behind me, stunning him. The boy put his hand to his mouth. Blood seeped from a tear in his lip. Welcome sputtered apologetically, but the boy stormed into him, windmilling wildly. Welcome tried desperately to ward him off, but the boy burst through, and all Welcome could do was hold onto him. Together, they careened off-balance and fell into a snow bank, with the boy still wrestling for a clear punch.

Sonny quickly hustled me toward school and the other boys followed, leaving the melee behind, remarking on the turnaround:

"How did he do that...make him miss?"

"Did you see him duck at just the right time?"

"Did you see him fool Welcome?"

Sonny threw his arm around my shoulder. Apparently, it didn't matter that I hadn't fought back. Fooling him seemed even better.

"I really want you to show me how you did that," he implored.

Word of the fight—or near-fight—and a gossipy explanation of Welcome's motivation for challenging me soon spread. Yvonne was both angry and embarrassed. Angry, because while she liked and admired Welcome, she had never encouraged him in the way he intended, and she was furious over his betrayal. Embarrassed, because she hated the notoriety that came with even a hint of jealousy.

The incident made me realize that it was foolish to feel secure on the reservation, despite what Mrs. Hill had promised, and this prompted me to burrow further into my isolation at Jesse's cabin and further into the distraction of my schoolwork. But this strategy had the unintended effect of generating even more contact with Yvonne. After all, she was my tutor, and she took seriously her obligation. As much as I cherished solitude, I'd also become her principal devotion.

With a certain amount of enthusiasm, I reciprocated every day after school and on Saturdays by loading firewood onto her father's truck which he sold door-to-door. I feigned a bright and cheery albeit mute presence to make it seem not even like work; the logs weren't heavy at all, and doing this favor for her father helped me to develop a reputation as a worthy help-mate, something the Iroquois really valued.

Jesse learned about the near-fight from Mrs. Hill. She'd already spoken to Welcome's father, but only about his son's hateful comments. She asked the man to appear before the next Council of Chiefs to encourage him to reform the boy's attitude toward me, if only for the sake of honoring their asylum agreement.

For the past two weeks since Midwinter, in keeping with my effort to

satisfy my host, I dutifully built fires and set the table before dinner, with
Echo my prime company. The dry, smoky warmth in the cabin seemed
to ease Jessie's aching knees and shoulders and, after he changed out of
his work clothes, he prepared dinner. But my good deeds weren't going to
hold him back from what he needed to say.

"It's good that you didn't get angry the other day when Welcome
called you those names," Jesse said, spooning Dinty Moore beef stew into
an iron pot on the stove. "'Son of a bitch' is the worst kind of insult."

My face flushed and I reached for my notebook.

Jesse added salt and pepper to the stew.

"The way the fight ended, when he hit that other boy, that was a
good way for it to end, a just way, because he brought shame on himself."

I sat at the table and wrote a modest reply. *'It happened so fast, I could
only get out of his way.'*

Jesse walked to where I sat and looked over my shoulder.

"You weren't afraid of Welcome, even though he's bigger and older
than you?"

'No,' I lied. *'I thought he was going to hurt Echo.'*

"Good; you protected your dog," Jesse said, walking back to the stove.
"When you love a dog, you get *orenda*, great power. But would you've fought
him had he hit you and not the other boy by mistake?"

I looked toward the fireplace where a burning log broke in half.
Jesse ladled stew into two wood bowls and brought them to the table. He
ignored my silence.

"A steady warrior never loses his temper. Perhaps the Creator meant
for Welcome to humiliate himself the way he did in testing you," Jesse said,
stirring the stew in his bowl, adding more pepper. "But the Creator has
blessed you. You come from a long line of warriors. He wishes you to use
those skills with the greatest respect. Every warrior is responsible for his
own safety. If that means fighting back, you can do it."

I turned from the fire and wrote in protest. *'I'm not a warrior.'*

Jesse shook his head. With a sharp knife, he cut open a package of
bread, stacked slices on a plate and dipped one into his bowl.

"You're just a few years away from manhood. Sonny already hunts
for his family, and you already know how to fight. It's part of your heritage.
The games we play—snow snake and, in spring, lacrosse—the games we
all play, men and boys, they're more than mere games, more than just for
enjoyment. The Creator gave us these games to help us survive, to prepare
us for struggles, to honor the best in ourselves.

"Your father'd want you to remember that. Just as he'd defend himself and fight for his people, you must do the same. There's great honor in that."

I pondered the steam rising from my bowl. I reached one more time for my notebook.

'But look what happened to my family because of fighting. Where's the honor in that?'

Jesse breathed deeply, held it for a moment, then exhaled, slowly, measuring his words. He dipped another slice of bread into his bowl.

"Evil knows no limit; big or small, you have to fight it."

I watched Jesse eat. Then I wrote, *'How do you fight someone like DiNardi?'*

Jesse smiled. "Remember what Uncle Abe said: the Creator won't let that evil go unpunished. But we can help that come about sooner if we play hard and protect ourselves with the greatest effort. Sonny already knows this...that's why he wants you to teach him how to box, so he'll be a better warrior."

My stomach moaned with hunger. I had no appetite, but I lazily dipped my spoon into the stew. This uncle also held each person responsible for the fate of everyone else.

CHAPTER 8

In just a matter of weeks, I'd grown accustomed to a narrower, confined world where space and light and even the sounds of silence were profoundly different from the city. But at its core, life here with Jesse was really just the same as with Uncle Abe. just as remote, just as hard to understand, just as demanding.

What I missed most was the comfort that used to be provided to me. It was especially sweet to come home from my old neighborhood school, or the Boy's Club, or the Armory, and be greeted by my mother and be served cookies and milk and have at least an hour of conversation while she prepared dinner.

But on the reservation, throughout my first two months, a stark winter confined me to a ribbon of Pine Valley Road between Jesse's cabin and the Indian school. Then, in late February, on a Friday afternoon when a balmy thaw began that would last for several days, Jesse came home from work with news: we were going to accompany the Brant University coach, Ray Sammons, on his annual trip to *Akwesasne*—the island Iroquois reservation on the St. Lawrence River—to buy new, hand-made hickory lacrosse sticks for his team.

"We've been talking about it for a few weeks," Jesse affirmed, handing to me new editions of *Ring* and *Life* magazines where I sat on the rug with Echo.

"He asked me if I wanted to go along because he knows I need backup attack sticks in case I break my favorite ones in Red League games this summer." Jesse gestured toward several sticks wrapped in oilcloth hanging on the wall. "We're also going to buy a couple for you. Sonny and I are going to teach you how to play."

I raised my eyebrows in surprise.

"Uncle Abe is paying for it."

Jesse stoked the fire in the wood stove and removed from a military knapsack two cans of chile, a can of lima beans and a loaf of bread.

"Slugger—Ray Junior—is coming along. He's a pretty good player already."

The next morning, Uncle Abe arrived. Coach Sammons had invited him to make the trip, too. He slid out of the back seat of a taxi driven by a reservation Indian named Sid, a quiet, somber man with a shock of white hair who carried a carton of food from Meltzer's. We were going in Sammon's station wagon. Sammons' plan was to bundle all the lacrosse sticks in canvas tarps and tie them to the roof rack. The shorter attack sticks would fit behind the rear seat.

Jesse sat up front with Sammons and Slugger. Uncle Abe, Sonny, and I nestled in the back, next to the crate of sandwiches, potato salad, dill pickles, and cream sodas. The aroma proved too tantalizing, and I was the first one to dig in. We chomped halfway through our provisions by the time we reached the northern outskirts of Brant and headed past hundreds of acres of frozen wetlands studded with skinny, bare-limbed trees, skeletal loose-strife, burnt tufts of reed canary grass and long-leaf cat-tails tipped with cigar-shaped clusters.

As the station wagon's snow tires hummed along the two-lane blacktop, the coach and Jesse exchanged lacrosse stories, detailed and raucous descriptions of the annual, reciprocal games between the university team and the Brant reservation Red League team. The university team would host the reservation team in April, just prior to the intercollegiate season. They played field lacrosse rules and would "run the Indians into the ground." However, the return match would be played in June, prior to the beginning of Red League play—summer weekend games played among other Iroquois—on a much smaller, walled box lacrosse field, sort of like hockey on dirt terrain, with a very different set of tactics, including ferocious cross-checking.

"After the first year of this home-and-away series, I called a team meeting and told the boys it was our turn again to go to the reservation," Coach Sammons explained to Uncle Abe. "I asked for volunteers. Only the new players raised their hands. None of the veterans budged!"

He and Jesse erupted into devilish guffaws that set the tone of joking and self-effacing banter—all the way to the Salmon River—and it enticed Uncle Abe out of an uncharacteristically somber, distracted mood.

Slugger passed his attack stick to the back seat. He demonstrated with nimble fingers how to adjust the pocket at the stick's crook-shaped head to maximize more effective passing, catching, and shooting. And he dropped a hard, white rubber ball into the pocket. It nestled just under the bottom of the wood frame.

"Slugger shoots mostly sidearm," Jesse said, turning and hooking an arm over the seat. "He needs a deep pocket to keep the ball in the stick." He reached down to demonstrate how the ball rolls up and over the smooth path of strings at the tip. "If there's a ridge or gully created by the strings, they have to be adjusted."

The station wagon continued north on a pale concrete road free of snow. An unusually bright sun had poked above clouds banked on the eastern horizon. The rolling farmland of the St. Lawrence lowlands adjacent to the Oswegatchie River became hilly and broken, imprinting the windswept snowscape with variegated, folded outcroppings of rock and boulders. And as the sun burned off the late morning fog, a distant ridge of northern pine forest emerged.

"Tell Daniel the story of how lacrosse originated," Sammons urged Jesse, turning onto a stretch of highway parallel to the Raquette River which ran swiftly along terraced banks. Jesse began rather solemnly, describing how the Creator gave the game of lacrosse —*dehontshigwa*—to the Iroquois. He wanted them to play for his amusement and so his people could develop endurance, honor, team spirit, and courage in war.

"In the old days," Jessie said, "when an elder or anyone got sick, the medicine people would call for a game to be played, to provide extra healing power. By showing that we hadn't forgotten his gift—by playing very hard and well—the Creator would reward the players' efforts and not forget the sick elder." Uncle Abe nodded in agreement. He couldn't wait to tell Jesse how much he remembered about the story of Handsome Lake dying in his cabin in 1815, and how a lacrosse game was played to try to save him. To Uncle Abe, Handsome Lake was another Ezekial, a visionary who rescued his people from centuries of inter-tribal warfare and feuding. And this commonality launched him on yet another homily about how Indians and Jews both knew what it's like to be the victims of the most hideous scattering of tribes to far-flung, separate and distinct communities. Tribes who've lived life on the run, who've not had time over many generations to grieve or mourn or even bury their dead.

I tuned him out, reflecting instead on how many of his Jewish friends always claimed he was simply a hopeless romantic, and that his judgment about the Iroquois was being overly-influenced by the heroic romance between Mary and Davey, that these heathens had a history of vicious warfare with their traditional enemies, that they held slaves, that they craved empire just like the Babylonians. I couldn't wait for this trip to end, but I had to endure more lacrosse stories.

After we arrived at Chisholm's factory on Cornwall Island, I met a Menominee carver who told me yet another origin story: how the Creator gave the game to *his* people. And on the way back to Brant, Sammons told about the time he met a Cherokee at a bus terminal in Chicago who told him all about how the Creator's gift of lacrosse was meant especially for *his* people. All of these stories were about animals—bird and land animals—and each story ended with different sides defeating the other. And when Sammons finished his version, Jesse corrected him.

"That's not the Cherokee version; that's an Ojibway tale." They all cracked up at that response. Uncle Abe rocked me with the rhythm of his wheezy spasms. Tears of glee welled in his eyes. But I couldn't figure out why anyone would laugh about not getting their stories straight.

We arrived back in Brant well after dark, so I spent the night at Uncle Abe's Hill Street flat. After a light dinner, Abe sipped tea, encircled and consoled by floor-to-ceiling shelves crammed with books, dog-eared manuscripts, mementos and a record collection. He said the trip to Akwesasne and conversations with Jesse left him even more convinced that Iroquois and Jewish beliefs shared an ancient, common beginning. He kept going on about the *sefiroth*—the cosmic tree—and the great Iroquois tree of peace that connected God to man. He said that any concerns he might've had about how harboring me on the reservation might interrupt my spiritual development had vanished.

"My only lapse in judgment is that I wasn't forceful enough in prevailing upon your father to control his temper, to not revel so much in resisting the influence of Raymond DiNardi, to mix some deception into the family's strategy."

It was painful to listen to Uncle Abe dredge up his guilt and the end of my life as I had known it.

"As a family advisor, I always felt a nagging dread. Despite my ecumenical fervor, I tend to be an absolutist in many things, and I could never quite resolve an ambiguity between the family's quest to make a champion and charting safe navigation through corrupt waters in order to reach our goal.

"I always reminded your grandfather: 'When you try for the title, given the nature of boxing, you'll have to collaborate with the Philistines.'

"Of course, either your grandfather never fully understood that possibility, or I failed to adequately press the issue. Nevertheless, the goal had been nearly obtained. Glory began to emerge, after years of struggle. But, unfortunately, so had evil.

"The exact nature of collaboration lay within the sport itself. Your grandfather always tried to argue that he wasn't working *with* the syndicate that controlled the fight game; he claimed he was actively *resisting* them. 'Fer Chris' sake, Abe,' he'd rant, 'my boy's compiled a quality record; we hardly ever got to fight where the big crowds and big money were—New York, Detroit, Chicago. We were lucky to get into the Garden twice in the last three years. I practically had to kiss Mike Jacobs' ass. And sportswriters...! They ignored my boy. If it wasn't for Frank Graham of the Journal-American, Jacobs woulda never buckled.'

"'I'll concede that some of what he said was true. There are other good fighters and managers who tried to remain independent of the syndicate. But Davey toiled in the wilderness for almost all of his career. For one main event in Boston, the total purse came to only $32.50. Your grandfather's clothing store bankrolled Davey's career. There'd been only a few decent purses, and those had been earned when Uncle Jack had been able to promote locally at the War Memorial Auditorium, filling the 7,000 seats with dollar-and-a-half and three-dollar customers.

"The family's goal was to win the title, then rub it in the face of the syndicate. But the odds of that ever happening are decreasing each week. The story of our family tragedy hasn't even been carried that far by the press. And Maxim, so drained by his fight with Robinson that he's lost his title, is banking on Moore's gentlemanly promise to give him a re-match."

His brooding gave me a stomach ache. A phone call gave me an opportunity to go to the kitchen for a glass of milk. I stayed there until he was through talking on the phone, and he called me back out to the living room.

"That was your Uncle Jack, *qvetching* about life in Brooklyn."

He expertly mimicked Uncle Jack's voice in re-telling the story.

"'I don't dare go to the city, to Jacobs' Beach, to get work as a trainer,' he said, referring to the fight crowd's base on 49th Street near Madison Square Garden. 'I been to see Russ Armato down at the Gramercy Gym. But he's pretty much shut out of the Garden now, too, and he can't afford to hire me.'

"'Charlotte found clerical work at the office furniture store owned by our landlord. But she's the only one bringing in grocery and rent money right now.'

"'To help kill boredom, I've begun taking law school courses at night at Brooklyn College, investing a little of the family's nest egg for a possible career change. I've been thinking about it ever since I graduated from college, but Dad talked me into going into the family business instead.'

"'That's where I go to school. Davey's going to school at Nevins Bar and Grill, except for runnin' along the boardwalk at Brighton Beach when there's a break in the weather and handball at the Central Y. He spends most of the time with those Indians in his raising gang, drinking beer, watching television, and talking about what their job in the city is going to be like come spring. He always wears this black watch cap pulled down over his eyes and a ratty surplus Army topcoat. He's so down in the dumps, no one'd recognize him.'"

Uncle Abe changed voices. "So I asked him, 'Do you take him to *shul* every now and then to say *Kaddish*, like I told you to?'

"Jack says, 'No; I don't see no sense to it; I don't see it the way you do. It only makes him more upset.'"

Well, that went for me, too. Davey and I both failed to see the consolation to the bereaved in the mourning hymn. Instead, it all seemed to be about God, *his* greatness, *his* accomplishment, *his* kingdom and what we need to do to bring it into being. Even when I first moved to the reservation and Uncle Abe visited, he nagged me to say the prayer. I could never ignore it, never forget it. And here he was on it again, as if it could help.

"...so I told Jack, 'You've got to get him to go, get him to understand: every mourner wants to withdraw from the world; every mourner sees fatalism and despair. But there is a pattern to life and death in this world that God made; we've got to remind Davey that when he says *Kaddish* it's for *him* and it's got to be a daily ritual now, to re-dedicate himself, to bring God's kingdom into being. Not only is that the best revenge and the ultimate meaning of our existence, but also it's the only way to get him out of himself and back on track.'

"'Remind him that prayer is God's love because that's what's missing in his life right now, love and purpose and community. Those things are waiting for him at *shul*....'

"But Jack scoffed at me. 'He don't listen to me. Those Indian boys are his community. They look after him now. They keep him pretty deep in the booth.'

"'What do you mean?' I asked.

"Jack says, 'The Nevins can be a rough place and there's guys who know he's here, that he ain't right.'

"So he concluded the conversation by asking whether I could bring you to the phone to talk to Davey. 'It could be a three-way conversation. Davey can talk to the kid, Danny can write down what he wants to say, like they do at his school. And you can read it back. It'd be better for Davey than sending letters back and forth, and maybe that'd cheer him up enough to do as you say. We gotta do something more than we're doin' now.'

"I disagreed. I told him it's up to him to bring Davey out of his despair; 'Take him to *shul* like I said, take him to see Rabbi Montoya there.'

"Jack said he would. 'But keep those letters comin'; Davey really needs them.'"

I really hated it when Uncle Abe acted out conversations. I really hated it that I couldn't talk to Davey myself.

CHAPTER 9

In March, the deep cover of snow receded, radically altering my perception of a pristine, 6,100-acre Iroquois island nation and most of its simple, single-family farmhouses which dated from the mid-19th century. Walking from school, I now noticed classmates trudging along unpaved roads and into a skeletal forest to patchwork houses of tarpaper and plywood exteriors and sheets of translucent plastic in lieu of windows. They climbed rotting stairs to porches with fractured railings. Inside, smoke from wood stoves mixed with smells of mildew and dry-rot. Some entered battered trailers set precariously on unbalanced cinder block foundations. Cars which I thought had been merely parked for the duration of winter turned out to be discarded, rusting hulks.

One leaden gray afternoon when I walked home from school, I spied a disheveled man struggling south along the highway, crab-like, almost sideways in his stride, as if he were dragging himself to his destination, oblivious to the youngsters coming the opposite way. When he approached, we crossed the road, except for Welcome, who caught the man by the front of his jacket as he slipped on a patch of ice. I grabbed the arm of one boy, nodded in Welcome's direction, and worked a puzzled expression onto my face.

"That's 'Sidestep'," the boy whispered. "Welcome's father. He walks like that and acts like a cripple because he's a drunk."

Mrs. Hill made certain to keep me engaged during those first two months after the funeral and, in time, I got over feeling like a nursed patient. At school, I accepted the substitution of journal writing for speaking.

Most of my classmates felt sorry for my mute condition. I preferred it. Mrs. Hill even scheduled after-school sessions with me and Sonny and Yvonne, devoted as much to stimulating a kind of conversation as to matters of scholarship. And after these sessions, my cousins walked with me to Jesse's cabin, accompanied always by Echo who drifted in surreptitiously from the periphery, then away again, but never losing contact.

At the cabin, I let them help me light fires in the stove and fireplace. We studied together, and when that became boring we played checkers. Curious about my life before the reservation, they asked me questions that I could write answers to—what my house, my school, my neighborhood were like.

Sonny reminisced about our experience at YMCA camp, how it was a luxury for him because we were served meals like in a restaurant, could play in open fields and forests free of refuse, choose from a myriad of activities. Even the surplus Army tent we slept in seemed luxurious to him. But, by the end of each week, I'd have a long, falsely-cheery letter ready to send off to Davey, filled with details about my life on the reservation.

I also began to learn lacrosse. On a large rectangle of paper which nearly covered the table, Jesse first drew a diagram of a playing field, positioning checkers to represent opposing players, showing and explaining basic strategy and rules. On a shoveled patch of field near the cabin, with Sonny and Welcome and four other boys, I began practicing with my own short-handled stick, throwing and catching, scooping ground balls, learning how to dodge, shoot, pick-and-roll and feed teammates cutting toward a goal. As expected, while attempting to catch or pass a ball, I had trouble keeping it in the net of my stick. The other boys laughed and tested me like they would a wounded animal, bumping and cross-checking me, making me look foolish.

At the end of one of these practices, while we still had energy, Jesse surprised me by bringing out my boxing gloves and two pairs donated by Coach Sammons. He began this activity by ordering me to demonstrate stances, blocks, and punches—especially the jab. I half-heartedly obliged. He drilled the others on the jab and right cross: "one-two, one-two, one-one-two," and several simple blocks and counters. Then he paired us off.

After a handshake, we sparred for a timed minute then rotated to different opponents. For a change, this was something I was more expert at; boxing was as natural to me as snowsnake and lacrosse were to them. But rather than exult in the advantage, I chose strategic caution, slipping punches left and right like a mongoose avoiding a cobra's strike, While the other boys soon abandoned schooled orthodoxies, I continued to just jab and slip, jab again, and circle away from my opponents.

After several rounds, Jesse broke up the pairs and matched me with one other boy. He told the others to form a circle and watch. For one minute, they observed me skillfully box one wildly-animated but ineffective opponent who was badly-winded and leaning on his knees even before the minute was up.

Welcome, however, made up for lack of movement with his longer reach and was able to connect, snapping back my head and forcing me to retreat. After several of these flurries, he was emboldened to go all out. His reach was a problem for me, and because I didn't care, I failed to get a safe distance: I neither avoided the jab nor bothered to get inside to beat him to the punch. I could almost hear Grandfather stage-whisper:

"If you're gonna take a guy out, you're gonna hafta get inside. And if you're gonna get inside, you're gonna hafta go to work!"

For several seconds, I remained passive; I couldn't quite figure out what to do. Trying too hard to avoid Welcome wasn't working, yet I didn't want to attack him. The other boys hooted with glee that Welcome was able to do to me what they couldn't. One stinging right numbed my jaw.

I remembered that in one of my dreams, indecision had caused Grandfather to abandon me in disgust. Before he left, he yelled at me: *"Come on! What are you waiting for!"*

As Welcome set to charge, I tucked into the Mendoza crouch: feet parallel and close together, elbows pulled in tight, gloves at each side of my head. Welcome paused, a sneer crossed his face. This transition didn't make a bit of difference to him and he swung a roundhouse right. I ducked and hooked two hard lefts to his ribs.

As his guard came down and he leaned awkwardly forward, I began what would've been a hard right to his head. But halfway to the open target, I pulled the punch back. To avoid what he thought he saw coming, Welcome swiveled his head anyway and, just as in our first confrontation, he swayed badly off-balance, lost his footing, and fell.

"Just a slip," Jesse said, stepping between us. "It's getting a little spirited, isn't it? Maybe it's time to quit."

He turned it back into a lesson. "Just remember, if you go after someone that hard, don't get so excited that you leave yourself wide open. Somebody who knows what they're doing, they'll take advantage of that."

On subsequent days after school and on weekends, when the boys came by to practice lacrosse, they imparted their lessons to me more generously, although Welcome continued to stalk me with special vigilance whenever I had the ball, waiting for just the right opportunity to strip me of it or, better, knock me flat. I didn't mind; I figured I had it coming.

CHAPTER 10

On *Purim*, after the first day of fasting, Jesse brought Uncle Abe home with him after work, and they entered the cabin in a celebratory mood, carrying containers from Meltzer's filled with stuffed cabbage and *hamantaschen*, enough for the three of us and Yvonne and Sonny, too. As we ate, Uncle Abe recounted the story of an ancient war and gave us *groggers* to twirl, and we stomped our feet to drown out the name of Haman.

"The Jewish temple in Jerusalem had been destroyed," Uncle Abe said. "The nation of Israel was conquered, and the people dispersed to foreign lands. Haman, descendant of the tribe of Amalek, devised a scheme to kill all the Jews on a single day. And it almost worked…had it not been for Mordechai, a descendant of King Saul, who sensed the danger. Donning sackcloth and ashes…," here he paused and met Jesse's knowing smile, "…he went to the gate of the palace to rally the Jews."

A loud, persistent knock interrupted the story. Jesse scraped back his chair and went to the door. It was Mrs. Hill, her face pained with grief. She pulled him onto the porch, out of earshot of the rest of us.

What she told him was that Davey had been shot. All I could hear were a series of gasps as Jesse urged her to compose herself. Yesterday, she told him, a fight had broken out at the Nevins. Davey tried to stop it. Somebody had a gun.

She began to stammer, then cry, startling all of us inside. Jesse held her close, steadied her, and pressed her to tell him the rest of the story. We kids walked to the doorway to listen.

"None of our boys knew any of the people in the dispute, or at what point Davey got involved. They were all drinking and the next thing, the police said, was that Davey got into an argument. That's how it began. Then a fight broke out. He tried to break it up. The ones who did it got away."

I don't remember how I felt when I heard the news. I just remember waiting for what seemed like a very long time, walking back and forth between Jessie's and Mrs. Hill's cabins, receiving visitors there who brought us food and tended the fires. I was in a fog, just kind of shut down, like you would close a store for business if there was a very good reason. At least I couldn't be blamed for this loss.

Uncle Jack brought Davey's body back for burial, along with a copy of a police report and a handful of newspaper clippings. I slipped one of them into my coat pocket, a column written by Max Case, sports editor of the Brooklyn Journal-American and president of the B'Nai B'rith Sports Lodge there. It was a piece Uncle Jack hadn't included in the tribute scrapbook he'd placed next to the sign-in book at Hertzberg's. Throughout *shiva*, I pulled it out to read, over and over again, until it was committed to memory.

"*Would you believe*" it began, "*this great fighter had only six bouts in New York City over a 12-year period? The fellows in my fraternity have been strangely silent on this matter. You'd think that a fighter of his caliber could've been better matched. But the corrupt IBC runs Madison Square Garden and St. Nick's and God knows what else out-of-town. Through Mike Jacobs, they influence the promotions of the 20th Century Sporting Club. And Frankie Carbo runs the Boxing Manager's Guild. They're all in each other's pockets, but Davey Mendoza wouldn't let them into his.*"

Further in his column, Case referred to the impact of television and how the IBC-run weekly national hook-ups with 50 big-city outlets only made matters worse for independent fighters who, like Davey, were forced to find other means of support. The column ended:

"*We in the fraternity all know that boxing is corrupt, but we write about it and promote it to our faithful readers anyway. Well, here's a punchline to a story that very few of us will get to read: Davey Mendoza was killed by boxing.*"

What I couldn't understand, and what I found so condemning, was that if he could see the truth of it, why couldn't everyone else?

An 11-paragraph, inside-page news story from the same newspaper revealed what'd happened at the Nevins, but it didn't provide useful details. No one there could recall what started the dispute, or what men were involved, or at what point Davey came into it.

"*But the police said that Mendoza became involved through an argument which was instigated by three strangers against a group of Indians. When fists began to fly, he leaped in to try to break it up. 'He was acting as a peace maker,' said Deputy Inspector Robert Stampalia, a police spokesman.*"

The story continued, including the discovery outside the bar of a stolen 38-caliber revolver. Four shots from it had been fired close-up, hitting Davey in the back. He died before reaching the hospital. The police investigation of his death seemed as desultory as the one conducted after my mother and grandfather were murdered. No eyewitness, no traceable evidence, only a vague motive, no arrests, no convictions.

Davey was buried next to Mary and Grandfather, whose graves were, by custom, still unmarked. After the ceremony, Uncle Jack commented bitterly, "We'll probably hold a same-day unveiling ceremony of the headstone for all of them."

Several young fighters lingered at Davey's grave after the burial. Furtively, they squatted next to his grave, rubbing dirt into their hands. Uncle Abe explained that they were trying to absorb Davey's greatness, but I saw it differently, more like they were corrupting themselves, and I wanted to go home, to never return, to never grieve. Instead, in a seamless transition, I began to speak again, shocking everyone, even though I struggled with a stutter.

"Like Ezekial," Uncle Abe readily explained. "When Jerusalem and the temple were destroyed by the Babylonians, and he regained his voice."

Through the funeral and *shiva*, I ignored the rabbi's prayers. And while I searched the mourners for familiar faces, no sooner did I recognize one face than I cut off eye contact. Each familiar face carried an expression of pity which I disdained.

For some reason, I thought I might see Joey DeYoung, but Uncle Jack said he'd been out of town, tuning up for a non-title summer fight against his idol, Jake LaMotta.

The rabbi read a parable about the competition between wheat and weeds, a contest between good and evil. He assured the mourners that in the end God is like a farmer, clutching the wheat close and banishing the weeds.

The themes other speakers developed were similar: the brevity and capriciousness of life, and the maddening mystery of evil in a world with a supposedly benevolent creator.

I knew enough to doubt all of it. Where was God the night my father was shot? Where was he the day of the fire? The only answer that came to me was that God was an incompetent referee, and the only commandment that anyone should ever take seriously was, *Protect yourself at all times.*

At the cemetery, my gaze shifted to the sky. It seemed not to have changed at all since the previous burial: from horizon to horizon, nothing but flat, leaden gray, without a trace of color or cloud to give it dimension. Through a stand of naked trees, I could see a squirrel nosing in vain among dessicated leaves and broken branches, taunted by the mocking cries of muscular, hopping crows, while atop a distant hill a family of deer led by an antlered buck filed across in silent procession which, for some reason, plunged me into a deeper desolation.

In the car, on the ride back from the cemetery, I asked Uncle Jack two questions: "A-a-a-a-are you here to s-s-s-stay? W-w-w-will I c-c-come live w-w-with you now?"

He and his wife stared at me. In fact, Uncle Jack wanted to remain in Brooklyn. He said he was determined to finish law school, for the good of the family, and he insisted to Jessie and Uncle Abe that it was in my best interests to continue living on the reservation. I couldn't believe he was going to leave me there again.

Before he left, Uncle Jack gave me a box containing Davey's white satin boxing robe trimmed in royal blue. Uncle Abe called it a *zelem*, "a garment for the soul, woven from a man's good deeds."

I opened the box and unzipped a clear plastic bag. I smelled the robe, but any residue of Davey had been supplanted by the fumes of moth balls and dry cleaning chemicals. I closed the bag and covered the box and shoved it beneath my bed at Jesse's cabin. On the way out to say goodbye, I overheard Uncle Jack say to Uncle Abe: "Well, at least the burden of Pa's quest is off my shoulders. 'Blind folly holds up false hopes.'" I don't know where he got that idea, but I wrote it down in my notebook and, after some study, it seemed to sum things up for me, too.

But Uncle Abe muttered angrily under his breath.

"Others will have to do his part, or the *yetzer ha-rah* becomes stronger. The duty of correction now lies on someone else's shoulders who can't, in any way, evade or shirk his responsibility."

I just shook my head in contempt.

CHAPTER 11

In April, two ceremonies were observed on the reservation. The first was private, a Passover *seder* at the cabin officiated by Uncle Abe who was transported to the cabin by one of the reservation taxis. He again brought with him—along with his good nature—a box of ceremonial delicacies from Meltzer's. After he and I lit three candles, Abe conducted an abbreviated, ironic *seder*.

When it was my turn to participate, as the youngest Jewish male, I asked, in Hebrew, the first of four questions. For some reason, I didn't stutter when I spoke or chanted in Hebrew.

Abe cleared his throat as if he were stifling a sorrow and answered in a clear, loud voice.

"This night is different from all other nights because it marks the time the Lord our God delivered us from Egypt."

As I still remained in exile, the ceremony seemed a charade to me, just another ritual-as-habit, and I wondered why this supposedly unique historical precedent held so much importance for so many Jews, after all these years of Diaspora and mayhem. Even the new state of Israel, threatened on all sides by Arabs, seemed a delusion.

The second ceremony occurred after Easter, the All-Night Dance, a solemn occasion at the Council House attended by about 200 residents, including children. During the thanksgiving, Sonny, Yvonne, and I sat side by side, listening quietly. The ceremony droned on until, hours later, adults began to sing songs, including one to honor the dead, and to dance, accompanied by rattles and water drums. At 2 a.m., the clan mothers formed a circle and sang and danced some more. This evolved into a pathetically-modest give-away: socks and towels and aprons. Then a feast began, with corn soup, fry bread, rice, macaroni and tomato sauce, and cakes and pies. Very bland and unimpressive stuff compared to the gift-giving and sumptuous meals that I was used to.

Social dancing followed the meal and lasted until dawn. I watched Yvonne dance with the older women. She carried herself with a regality that seemed adept beyond her years. When she returned to her seat to rest, I gave her a slice of cake and a soda pop with a straw.

"How did you learn that dance?" I asked.

"I just did," she answered, taking a demure bite and catching crumbs with her free hand. Her eyes shone with a satisfaction that seemed oblique to my very real question.

Later in the month, a two-week Planting Ceremony included a children's day in which special dances and songs were performed at the Council House, and every child's name was read. Their English name and Indian name. When my name was called, I was shocked to discover that I, too, had been given an Indian name, He-Who-Listens-Quietly. When did this happen? I wondered. What part of what ceremony? Despite the language difference, how could I have missed it?

At the end of the school year, a graduation ceremony honored 12 students, including Yvonne, Sonny, Welcome, and me. In September, we'd be bussed two miles into the city to Pine Valley Academy to begin high school. For most, it would be their first off-reservation experience, and many parents were unhappy about it.

By the first of June, the glacial valley had transformed. There hadn't been much of a spring. Aside from the brief, illusory February thaw, snow drifts hadn't begun to dramatically recede until late April, revealing a bare, lifeless forest and flattened, brown meadows, while the seamless gray sky continued to cast a pall over dilapidated residences and a pot-holed, two-lane highway that traversed the reservation.

But on one extraordinary day, walking home after our last day at school in bright sunshine, Sonny and Yvonne were cheered enough by the visit of blue sky and swiftly-moving, billowing white clouds to identify for me as many emerging plants as they could find.

Elms, beeches, yellow birches, sugar maples, willows, hemlocks and poplars were all beginning to sprout tiny, green leaves.

Before May, the only sign of life had been contingents of over-wintering flies buzzing about fetid, yellow-green and speckled flames of skunk cabbage. Then, here and there, shoots of tender, edible cowslip began to unfurl, like miniature sails.

But within the past week, wildflowers had erupted from the floor of the gravelly, open woods, varied in color and riotous in abundance. Red trillum and blazing star, furry stalks of hepatica, bloodroot and buttercup beckoned us from the road, and we forged new trails along the pliant loam, pausing to trace patterns with the tips of our fingers in mossy tree bark and to squint at their breeze-rattled crowns, imagining the lush canopies to come.

Farther in the woods, we squatted by the fecund mud banks and swales of the swiftly-flowing creek that drained the valley, and we spied the first tendrils of ferns, green dragon, brome, and loose strife.

Climbing to high ground, we found tongue ferns beginning to sprout from limestone ravines and gulches that rimmed the valley. Nestled in the crumbling limestone talus were smooth rock cress, which they said would soon bloom with yellow-green bells, and red and yellow chandelier-like columbine. Clematis peeked over rock ledges like primeval banners.

In the meadows, Yvonne collected bouquets of blue flag, field pansies, and white and blue violets for us to bring home to our drab houses.

The creek became a favorite play area to explore, although we exercised caution because several children each year slipped from its banks and were lost to its swift current.

Soon, Sonny said, men of the reservation would be netting trout, and we sought glimpses of the species which were becoming rarer with each passing spring. In calmer eddies, younger boys bottled tadpoles. My favorite pastime down there was to race sticks along the bank of the creek, as far as they would go, until they became ensnared in the debris of fallen timber.

By the time we trekked out of the woods to the road to Jesse's cabin, the sun had passed the western ridge, but shouts from the lacrosse box lured us further along the road. A dozen boys scrimmaged, their long, ink-black hair flying.

With the end of school, the ground in the lacrosse box had dried and Sonny and I and the other boys played lacrosse every day, running and cutting and colliding in knee-deep clouds of fine dirt.

Of the men representing the reservation's Red League team, some worked construction since Yvonne's father was business agent for the

Laborer's Union local. Others worked high steel out of town, mainly New York City; they called it "walking iron." For them, lacrosse practice was pretty much out of the question. So on the weekend, when they played their games, they had to summon up skills that had lain dormant all winter.

The small arena—half the width and 130 feet shorter than a collegiate field, encircled by four-foot-high boarding and topped by another six feet of chicken wire to protect spectators from flying balls—was set apart in a clearing, just off the highway.

The day the Brant University team came to play, several dozen white spectators, knowledgeable fans, and a few athlete-friends sat in the stands with about 400 reservation residents. A group of women elders were among the most vocal supporters and during moments of heated play they would stand behind the boards, seizing and buffeting the chicken wire. I overheard one white man exclaim: "Their faces are like mud puddles."

The Brant team's bus driver had to be carefully-directed to the playing site because it was so hidden by the wooded terrain. Coach Sammons had to warn the driver to slow down to about 10 miles per hour or he'd miss the unmarked, dirt-road turnoff. The players who hadn't been on the reservation and who'd never seen the box and its environs seemed in shock as they stepped off the bus into "this different world," as one player put it.

Despite thorough counseling by the coach and a few veterans from the previous summer, the players mumbled with disbelief when they disembarked near the playing area which, to them, resembled an outdoor hockey rink.

An hour later, Indian players began filtering out of the woods, joking with anticipation. Two months previously, they'd been "run into the ground" on the much larger university field, "stretched out, made to suffer," as Sammons described it.

I had been practicing for only a few months, but I understood the challenge faced by the university players; it'd also been the main topic of conversation among Sonny's friends and among Jesse and his teammates. It was their turn to cause suffering.

Aside from the reduced size of the field, the biggest difference between the two styles of lacrosse had to do with how integral cross-checking was in box, similar to that in ice hockey, which made the game much more physical, like the difference between supervised boxing and an all-out street brawl. As in ice hockey, Indians played without helmets. But they did wear padding over the upper part of their torso. A university player, used to a demanding but relatively contact-free game except, of course, for the occasional foul, now had to contend with the continual stick across his back, ribs, shoulders, and arms. In addition, there was no rule for offsides. Any player could go anywhere in the arena. This led to a more open brand of play, including clean breakaway runs to the opponent's net.

Also in box, there were no specialists as in field lacrosse. Indians were capable of all facets of play, both offense and defense. And their famed repertoire of stick-faking and "heavy" shots was enhanced by a difference in the lacrosse stick itself—a narrower, rounder head and a leather pocket of unrestricted depth, banned in college play. As a result, it was very difficult to dislodge a ball with field checking techniques. And while an Indian player had to sacrifice release time because of the deep pocket, his more deliberate shot had the power to crack boards or penetrate wire.

Complicating matters further, the box goal was quite a bit smaller—16 square feet versus 36.

Coach Sammons' advice of greatest potential consequence for his players was to never get trapped against the boards. Before the game he warned them again. They listened intently because during warm-ups they'd been horrified to see the many splinters and protruding nails all along the surface of the battered boards.

He also reminded his players that while the Indians did not wear helmets, that didn't mean they weren't willing to take risks. That was apparent with many players: wide, blackened gaps where front teeth used to be.

Away from his boys, Coach Sammons chuckled with anticipation of the experience they wouldn't normally have playing the game. Outside of the box, he mingled with elders he'd played against in the 1920s when he was an All American defenseman, kidding them over "Indian time"—the two-hour difference between the scheduled and actual time to begin play.

When he re-entered the box, he called his players into a circle and in a confident, metallic voice, exhorted them.

"There's no cool and comfortable locker room to retreat to at halftime. We stay here, in the hot sun."

He nodded at the Indian spectators surrounding the box.

"It's their crowd; it's their scoreboard and it's their referees. There's no sanctuary.... But this'll be a good test for your stick and survival skills. Let's go out there and get 'em!"

At first, not unexpectedly, the Brant team played with a tentative awkwardness. They hadn't had time to practice the box version and seemed encumbered by the hard-shell padding worn on their arms, back, ribs and hips which they'd borrowed from the football team. One attacker looked stricken when the box door latch closed behind him.

But the coach chose his "volunteers" well: midfielders and attackmen and his top defenseman who were agile and who could pass and shoot quickly.

The Indian center, barrel-chested but with slender legs, won the first face-off, trapping the ball and flipping it to Jesse, one of his two forward attackmen. Jesse dashed downfield unopposed and beat the goalie with a triple-fake: near corner, far corner, near corner, then firing from close-in, a straight overhand shot just past the goalie's head.

Whoops and cries reverberated throughout the box, and the university players settled down into the relentless, aggressive style of play, responding as best they could to each other's spontaneity, like jazz musicians. They tried to meld within a desperately combative tempo, keeping the ball aloft as much as possible to avoid being clubbed, hacked, checked or slammed to the ground. The referees let everything pretty much go, but there were no blatant fouls and no fights, and a sense of prideful stoicism overtook the game.

Late in the final period, hoping to dent what appeared to be a lax, over-confident defense, the university team ran a set play involving fast, four-corner passing, and on the third go-around, Jesse over-played his man. He was slow in re-coiling his stick after a lunging cross-check and his man rolled away and cut inside for a slashing overhead shot that bounded down between the Indian goalie's legs.

But the reservation team still had a comfortable lead and, with only seconds remaining, Jesse scored the final goal. Sprinting hard toward one of the abler university defenders, but too tired to execute an adequate fake, he grasped his stick close to his body and bulled into the kid, shoving him back just enough to create an opening for a fast-rising underhand shot that sailed past the astonished goalie into the uppermost part of the net.

At the end of the game, players from opposing sides snaked toward each other, exchanging handshakes. Cases of cold beer appeared almost immediately for the players, but Jesse slaked his thirst by draining a quart jar of tea and lemonade, while in imitative aftermath we boys gamboled upon the dented terrain.

Over the rest of the summer, I witnessed an intensity of Red League play that seemed to me more like war, as ball-carriers were attacked by a variety of daring over-the-head and wrap-around stick checks and ferocious body checks. I witnessed every technical infraction a player could possibly inflict: slashing, tripping, holding, high-sticking; every possible attempt to prevent a goal short of tackling a man.

But fights rarely occurred; it was more a controlled mayhem in each game where one or more players were carted out of the box, some to an ambulance. In one game against a visiting Caughnawaga team, a burly French-speaking player named Baptiste molested every local shot-taker with an exuberance that strained the patience of the onlookers. After one particularly vicious cross-check from behind, Baptiste stepped on his man's head. And, after apparently reconsidering, stomped him again. For that he earned a five-minute penalty. As he settled into the penalty box, rolling his massive shoulders with irritation at the boos and catcalls cascading upon him, the victim's mother strode resolutely along the boards to where Baptiste sat. She tapped him on the shoulder, cursed him in a screeching voice and slapped him hard in the face.

Players were remembered for delivering or withstanding fearsome body checks, even from years ago, and the boys I played with imitated their elders. Once Sonny unintentionally knocked out another boy. He'd meant only to cross-check him as the boy charged. But, inexplicably, the boy ducked at the moment of impact and ran right into Sonny's knee.

Jesse, who bore a fresh scar across the bridge of his nose ("a badge of honor" he called it), spoke to me about this level of play late one afternoon on his porch as I watched poplar leaves glimmer in a gentle breeze.

"It's a tradition to play hard; that's the game's true purpose. The Creator's good feeling comes from the spirit of our play. It's the time and the place and your people cheering you on."

Jesse looked away to a distant ridge and beyond, to the massive, rolling green hills that seemed to stretch on forever.

"You know, there aren't too many ways a young Indian can prove himself. We give and take, but we don't hate our opponents. We don't mean to hurt anyone, by word or deed. And if we lose, we bear defeat with dignity."

Those words rang with familiarity; they were similar to what Grandfather and Davey said to me when I began to learn to box at the Boy's Club and in the Burt Street ring. But, I wondered, how far did God's pleasure extend? I'd become obsessed with violence. Not in the sense that I had earlier experienced it as part of my family's enterprise, but more as a constant reflection on man's desire to defeat another and, underlying that, the anger—inevitably, no matter what was said to the contrary—and the need to injure someone in the process. I reflected, too, on the inevitability of having to fight and deal with that fight's repercussions, and the seemingly preordained and nearly overwhelming anxiety about it all, despite my upbringing, that only I seemed to possess.

CHAPTER 12

With the advent of summer, Iroquois began showing up at "the dam," a small limestone pool formed after the time when glacial meltwater sought escape into the valley. Winter run-off had long since subsided, and now only a stream meandered through deeply-fissured folds of the eastern hills. A few volunteers had just finished repairing the dam which formed the pool by fitting layered, loose slabs of limestone across its lip.

At various times of day and early evening, people walked to the dam to bathe and shampoo their hair. Because it was across the road from Jesse's cabin, he or I could wait for a solitary immersion or join friends when they came by.

In July, an enervating heat crept into the valley. One day, by late morning, Sonny, Welcome, Yvonne and a few of their friends gathered at the pool to soak in the shallows, to talk and laugh and sprawl lazily on the sun-warmed flagstone.

Yvonne—her smooth, dark arms glistening—grinned into the eyes of her cousins as they joked and shared intimacies. But, toward me, she would cast only occasional, shy-smiling glances which I read but ignored.

Preferring to remain an outsider, I mostly listened to their talk, feigning interest just to remain in their good graces. I was reluctant to speak for another reason, too.

My father's death three months before, rather than adding duress, seemed like a weight off my shoulders, and with that relief my voice came back. But now I spoke haltingly, as if I had to learn to speak all over again. I didn't want to speak in front of people for fear of stuttering like a fool.

Toward the end of that year at the reservation school, I would seize up whenever teachers directed questions at me. A tension would grip my stomach, making it hard for me to breathe. Sweat would drip from my armpits, my face would burn, and my ears would ring with embarrassment.

During a history class, I had begun to anticipate the time when students would be asked to read aloud, one-by-one, row-by-row, and when it came close to my turn, I'd ask to leave the class to use the bathroom. And once I left, I'd be reluctant to return. Instead, I'd wander the empty, window-less hallways.

After about 15 minutes, my ears would resume ringing and, if I paid attention, the ringing would become voices, at first like the noise of a sporting crowd, then faint and indistinct but repetitious…and seductive. Against my will, I'd feel compelled to concentrate, and when a particular voice—a woman's voice—called my name, this unnerved me more than having to speak, and I'd retreat to the safer environment of the classroom.

Mrs. Hill discovered me wandering the halls several days in a row, well beyond the time it would've taken me to use the bathroom, and she escorted me back to my classroom and spoke discreetly to the teacher. From that time on, I was not allowed to leave a classroom unaccompanied.

No longer able to evade reading, I struggled to get through sentences, often pausing interminably because I just couldn't get the beginning letter of some words to pass my lips. At these intervals, teachers would usually speak the word and urge me on, and I would plunge forward, determined to read straight through to the end until another difficult letter, like "L", would hold me up again. Eventually, Mrs. Hill concluded that I was being exposed to a much greater scrutiny than journal-writing ever had. When she urged me to revert back to the pad and pencil, my classmates and I were relieved.

The stuttering also occurred in conversation with friends and with Jesse and Uncle Abe. It disappeared only when I sang, when I practiced my *haftorah*, or when I walked the forest paths alone with Echo and spoke quietly to him. The dog's steady kinship and acceptance of me, his genuine, adoptive friendliness, helped dispel my sense of wretchedness.

On a Sunday in mid-August, a day after Joey DeYoung suffered a brutal kayo loss to LaMotta and a week before the Green Corn ceremony, Jesse planned a surprise party to celebrate my 13th birthday. It would be a hot dog roast in the early evening after the big lacrosse game against visiting St. Regis. Mrs. Hill, Sonny and Yvonne, Welcome, Slugger Sammons and Uncle Abe were invited.

By noon that day, as he adjusted his pads and lacrosse stick pocket, Jesse glanced at us youngsters moping in the shade of his cabin porch. It was already muggy and hot, and not a breeze stirred.

"Why don't you kids hike over to Deep Lake?" he suggested. "Here's some money; you can stop at Camp's store and get some cold sodas to take with you."

Sonny grinned and scraped the change from Jesse's outstretched, callused palm, and the four of us sauntered down the road toward the highway.

As we left the forested portion of the reservation, I noticed a peddler's old truck creep past. Several women hurried from their houses, waving, so they could purchase tomatoes, corn, green beans, cucumbers and fresh peaches. I remembered stories about Grandfather and how he first earned his living peddling produce from the City Market, probably along this very route.

Just off the reservation, we stopped at Camp's store. It was owned by a beefy deputy county sheriff who was also a Justice of the Peace. We had just enough money to buy two sodas apiece. The first one we drank right away before leaving the store; the second one we saved for after the two-mile hike to Deep Lake, a round, 60-foot-deep plunge basin of a long-ago waterfall.

We were dressed in shorts and white, sleeveless cotton tee-shirts and, though our bodies were already deeply tanned, the hot sun burned red patches on our noses and bare shoulders, and we longed to hurl ourselves into cool, dark water.

By the time we reached the horseshoe-shaped, forested rim of the extinct cataract, we could smell fresh lake air. The limestone cliffs where we stood loomed about 200 feet above the plunge pool, part of the ancient glacial drainage system which, when it retreated, hewed gorges like this one across rocky ridges long before Niagara was formed.

"Wh-wh-wh-where are we going?" I asked, nodding vigorously to form the first word.

"Down there," Yvonne said, pointing to the dark maw at the base of the cliff face that suddenly filled me with dread.

Forming a single file, with Welcome in the lead, we followed a trail around to the opposite side of the wide crescent. Although Welcome was anxious to reach the cool refuge of our destination, he walked slowly and deliberately along the deeply-fissured ledge where once a deluge had hurled itself over the brink.

I felt relieved when Welcome veered onto a side trail behind the horseshoe rim.

"Let's look over here first," Welcome said, making his way through a network of paths that led to a series of dry, shallow basins and channels made centuries before by rapids racing to the cataract. But as Welcome circled the group back to the trail leading down to the plunge pool, anxiety gnawed at my insides. I flinched when Welcome cawed like a crow, and it eerily reverberated within the depths of the chasm. A vital part of me felt as if we were descending too rapidly and I began to hyperventilate.

I tried to mouth a plea for them to stop their descent, but I couldn't get a word out, and I skidded to a halt about a quarter of the way down. The others trampled excitedly to the lower pathway which encircled the lake, and when they hit that trail they took off at a sprint. Their whoops grew faint, then faded.

Dragonflies hovering above the placid, aqua pool darted away when a whorl of cooler air descended. A silver wolf-clan pin that Yvonne had presented to me and fastened to my shirt that morning suddenly burned like ice against my chest, and I shivered in the leafy darkness. I felt exposed and vulnerable so far away from my sanctuary.

I surveyed the woods and limestone ledges above. A tree trunk, then a boulder, then the path itself seemed to breathe. My ears began to ring. Panicking, I turned to run back up when I heard what sounded like angry shouts coming from where my companions had disappeared. I stopped and listened, but the ringing in my ears resumed and, just like in school when I paid attention, it became a voice, calling my name, distinctly a woman's voice, but more amplified. I realized it was Yvonne, and she was screaming, punctuated by a resounding slap.

Then all was quiet. I looked down again to the pond. Gusts of wind raked the surface. It grew darker in the cataract, and dead leaves wafted aimlessly.

I stood still, dizzy, facing downtrail. More wind-whipped leaves skittered past me. I flinched and nearly lost my balance but proceeded carefully ahead, reminding myself to remain alert, to search the trail as it opened into new terrain, to examine every inch of the forward ground which had previously seemed so alive before moving ahead, cautiously, 10-15 yards at a time. I don't know how long it took me to reach the bottom but, when I did, a glimpse of a white tee-shirt stopped me in my tracks. Instinctively,

I dove off the trail and dropped silently, letting my hands and feet absorb the fall. I landed next to an ancient, gnarled elm. Through an opening in a shrub hedge, I saw Welcome about 100 yards downtrail, kneeling, his hands clasped as if in prayer.

I crept beyond the tree in order to get a better look. Slightly past Welcome, in single file, also kneeling in supplication and facing the same direction—away from the pond toward a rocky knoll—were Sonny and Yvonne.

Bewildered, I squinted, trying to telescope the scene into clearer focus. A loud voice suddenly exhorted:

"You better pray harder, or I might not let you get out of here!"

Two men in olive green rain parkas shuffled menacingly into view. Parka hoods yoked their shoulders. Lank hair edged over their ears. Their faces were indistinct but not their features—dark and weighty brows, contemptuous smirks, prominent red noses. Their appearance seemed a recapitulation of previous indelible images: DiNardi's men, the demons of my dreams, and *Teharonhiawaka*, the Great False Face.

Dark clouds surged above the crescent, disappeared, then surged again, amplifying the phantasmic menace that rooted me to the forest floor.

The men seemed to be interrogating their kneeling captives and, after a brief exchange, they skulked closer to Yvonne. Sonny said something to her, and she pointed back up the trail to where I lay. One of the men swung a large walking stick in my direction and strode swiftly toward me.

Clawing crab-like, I bellied back through the shrub and into a small cave formed by a broken limestone ledge, concealing me from trailside view. As my eyes adjusted to the dark, I realized the cave was already occupied. Amazingly, Echo awaited me there.

When the man reached abreast of where I hid, a commotion arose back at the captive site. He turned and I peeked out. Sonny and Welcome had jumped the other man. They'd tackled him to the ground and were punching him repeatedly in the face. He called for help, but his cries were muffled by blows.

Yvonne sprang to her feet and ran along a pathway that led back up to the rim, directly across the pond from me. She could escape if Sonny and Welcome could subdue their captor, and they seemed to be successfully doing just that. Welcome had even wrenched free their tormentor's walking stick and continued to beat him, swinging through the man's raised hands.

The other man turned and ran back down the trail, raising his stick in the air, but Echo leapt out from the cave and chased after him. Without barking, he dashed up to the man and clamped his jaws onto a loose end of the man's parka, spinning him around. The man stumbled and fell, striking his head on a boulder which jutted from the shoreline. Sonny and Welcome backed away from their man and ran up the trail, after Yvonne.

Echo jogged to the second man and sniffed him where he lay moaning and cursing, then scampered back to the cave. He sat panting, seeming to wait for me to leave with him. But I shrank further into the cave. I sat with my back to the limestone wall, my arms clasped about my knees.

After a while, Echo came over to me and sank to the ground, vigilant, his forepaws crossed ahead of him.

Large drops of water began to fall, pelting the dust-covered elm leaves. They fell slowly at first, then—as the wind gathered strength and thunder rolled from a distance, sounding like an avalanche of boulders—they fell steadily in a downpour. Through a translucent curtain of rain, the only thing visible to me was lightning as it exploded into the cataract.

Cold sweat, which earlier had run in rivulets from my armpits, had turned to dried-up streaks of salt. My mouth felt parched, and I remembered the soda clutched in my hand. I popped the cap off with my belt buckle, took a long draught and gasped for air.

After an indeterminate time, the storm dissipated, and my cousins returned with Deputy Camp. Echo led them to me. The two men had apparently vanished, but I felt their presence nonetheless. I vowed to never again leave the reservation. No season, it appeared, was safe.

The storm lasted two days. Temperatures dipped into the 60s, even lower at night in the valley, cold enough to wear sweaters and to once again rely on the stove and fireplace. This gave me an excuse to remain sequestered. I was still too embarrassed to face my cousins. But tending Jessie's fires proved no escape; it only encouraged me to endlessly play over in my mind my most recent failure.

However, on the second day of steady, chilling rain, Deputy Camp received a phone call from the city police. They said they'd apprehended two hobos—penniless, scabbed, and rummy army veterans with surplus rain ponchos in their rucksacks. They'd been arrested in the basement of a downtown tavern where they'd been discovered drunk and passed out.

Apparently, they gained entrance by breaking a back window the night before and proceeded to sample variously-labeled bottles, then became too drunk to escape. In the morning, the proprietor found them prostrate amid broken glass and their own vomit.

The men were identified by Sonny and Welcome as the ones who'd bullied them at the lake. And after interviewing all of us, the police theorized that the hobos had probably hit on some vague, spur-of-the-moment scheme to hold the four of us, but their exact intentions were unclear. At any rate, the police said, the hobos were too derelict to carry out their plan and too addled to answer questions about it. In the short run, they said, it didn't really matter because the men were still going to spend time at the county's fortress-like penitentiary, built next to the quarry where its granite blocks were mined and cut.

Picturing them there helped me.

CHAPTER 13

W hen the storm ended, the valley experienced a lengthy spell of dry, hot days and cool evenings, a harbinger of autumn and a series of events when my narrow world seemed to re-open.

The first was a pow-wow at the reservation's athletic field. It seemed to me like an extended family picnic, one I believed I might never again experience with my own family. It was a vast pot-luck get-together. Relatives from other nations, even from far outside the Iroguois Confederacy, visited their kin. While women cooked and chatted, the men told stories and played horseshoes and organized races for the kids. On Saturday, we all watched Jesse lead his lacrosse team in a raucous Red League game against Cattaragus.

Ceremonial dances drew everyone. What fascinated me was how many performers wore regalia I'd not yet seen on the reservation. Some men even wore full, feathered headdresses instead of their more modest but traditional woodlands headpiece.

Several Kiowa—friends of Iroquois students attending college in Oklahoma—danced in buckskin. And a traveling troupe of young Hopi from First Mesa wearing skirts and capes performed a corn dance. They faced each other from two parallel lines, and their gourd rattles sounded like summer rain.

During games set aside for young men, Sonny and I finished one-two in a 100-yard barefoot race across a freshly-mown meadow.

The following weekend, during a solitary morning stroll with Echo, I stumbled upon an extraordinary transaction. From the back end of a huge canvas-covered truck which crept house-to-house, the reservation's Indian agent was distributing small, bound sacks. When I reached the cabin, Jesse had one, too. He explained that this give-away was an annual, free subsidy of eight pounds of salt guaranteed to each resident by a pre-Revolutionary War treaty. He said keeping up with the treaty provisions, even small, symbolic ones, was really important. He said something about it helping to preserve a larger principle, sovereignty, which I didn't understand or even try to pursue.

To me, sovereignty meant having power over your own life, and I couldn't see how that could be obtained if the Iroquois were so poor and beholden. It seemed to me that the Iroquois, like the Mendoza family enterprise, simply didn't recognize their true condition.

The final, end-of-summer Green Corn ceremony had private and public aspects. At noon, 18 men—many dressed in non-traditional apparel including several in feathered bustles of a sun-burst western design—danced on a wood platform at the edge of a large cornfield. Among the many observers were several hundred white volunteer firemen. They and their families had been invited by their reservation counterparts to help promote a long-standing practice of mutual aid among nearby towns and villages.

The crowd grew to about 2000 people because dances were repeated every two hours until 7:30 when Wayne Schramm and His Ozark Mountain Boys took over for several hours of bluegrass and country music.

I didn't pay much attention to the music, but it seemed to make Jesse nostalgic. One song about leaving the Eden of the family hearth for the cold world outside also seemed to resonate with other Indians as the musicians lingered over details of misery. Jesse glanced around at the undulating, green hills cradling his valley, his face both sad and noble. To me, the lyrics and music only conjured up memories of pain and resentment, memories which I knew were best to forget.

Distracted, I roamed with my cousins around game and food booths whose earnings went for our fire department's upkeep. And we watched the final Red League game of the season against St. Regis.

Before the game, four Iroquois chiefs escorted a tall, dark man resplendent in a traditional chief's deer antler headdress to the center of the dirt field where he was introduced to a quietly-appreciative crowd murmuring their admiration. When I asked who he was, Yvonne exclaimed: "He's a movie star! He's been in movies like 'Drums Along the Mohawk' and

'*Western Union.*' And he's from here!"

Earlier in the day, my cousins and their families had gathered at the Council House for a ceremony acknowledging the beginning of yet another cycle of life.

After a prayer of thanksgiving, Mrs. Hill—her head covered by a carefully folded and untied scarf—led a women's dance chant. Nine women of varying ages wearing calico dresses trimmed with narrow velvet ribbon over leggings and moccasins and smiling demurely, shuffled onto the center of the floor in a deliberate, slow pace, as if they were massaging the earth. They sang in a low pitch; one woman carried an infant in her arms.

Yvonne followed Mrs. Hill, bearing a basket containing corn, beans, and squash: the "three sisters" which flourished from the body of the daughter of Sky Woman.

At the conclusion of the ceremony, Jesse asked me to accompany him with the False Faces as they trekked house to house to conduct healing ceremonies. Wearing a new pair of beaded moccasins made for me, I carried Jesse's large box turtle rattle, and we walked single file along narrow and shaded paths that wound up to the valley's eastern plateau. As we climbed, I fastened my attention on the root-clogged path and on the ragged blanket that shifted behind Jesse's legs.

"Are your dreams the same as before?" Jesse suddenly asked. "You still fighting DiNardi's devils?"

My stomach tightened with anxiety and my throat began to constrict; I didn't know what to reveal and conceal, and it was even harder to talk while climbing the hill.

"Sometimes I'm a-a-alone and sometimes I-I-I'm with my father. A-a-and Grandfather is shouting for us t-t-to do r-r-right."

"Where are you when the dream begins?" Jesse asked in a voice that reverberated more deeply in the forest.

"Running behind Davey through hallways, in the dark, r-r-running through a tunnel at the Armory, away from voices."

"What are the voices like?"

"Angry, and all around us, calling m-m-me toward a lit-up ring and a shouting crowd."

"And when you get to the ring, are the devils there?"

"S-s-some are in the ring and others a-a-are in a c-corner, shouting and c-c-cursing us. And Grandfather is in the opposite corner w-w-with a towel over his head and he's d-d-dodging objects being thrown from the crowd. He's shouting at us, b-b-but we're not ready. M-m-my gloves are split and coming apart. I'm going to have to fight in street clothes and heavy winter boots. D-Davey can't undo his robe…. It's choking him."

"What is Grandfather yelling?"

"Instructions."

"Why?"

"Because we can't fight back. We're being hit and p-p-pushed in all directions. They're hurting Davey, and he's mad, he's c-c-crying. And I can't g-g-get angry."

"What does Grandfather say?"

"He yells to me: 'Stop holding back your p-punches! Keep your hands b-b-busy! Jab, straight right, hook!' But I'm…winded; I can't…catch my b-b-breath and so he yells again: 'Hold on, hold on to him! Grab those arms and push!'

"But they're too b-b-big for me and I'm…grabbing around their legs and they kneel and fall on me and I…can't breathe."

I managed this last part only with great effort because of the climb. I was nearly out of breath and light-headed, stumbling on the trail. I also felt wretched talking like this.

"Aren't there other dreams?"

There were other dreams, especially about my mother, vivid but ordinary shared domestic experiences from my childhood: me struggling to keep up with her on shopping day as she strode briskly through the farmer's market; she embracing me in the kitchen after taking my first baked apple pie out of the oven, my face pressed against the lap of her flour-dusted apron; me seeing her look of satisfaction in the barber's mirror when he finished my haircut, as if I were a gift.

"No." I didn't want to describe any of that. Jesse stopped where the path veered along a swiftly-flowing stream that fed the dam below. The others went ahead. Drawing his blanket over his knees, he squatted on the bank of the stream and gestured for me to sit beside him. He cupped water from the stream and drank.

"Go ahead; you take some."

I placed the mask on a tufted mound of grass so that it stared straight up to the sky pocked with puffy, swiftly-moving clouds. I cupped my hands and dipped into the stream, but most of it escaped. So Jesse cupped water for me, and I took his hands and drank that way. Then he wet my brow and stroked my hair, so long now that it reached below the nape of my neck.

"Do it yourself," he urged. "Keep your fingers close together, one hand slightly overlapping the other."

Jesse formed a deep cup with both hands and dipped into the water.

His silver ring reflected the sun.

This time I succeeded. I took a drink, then another, repeated the process, took another. I hadn't realized how parched I'd become.

"Chew this," Jesse ordered, pulling a plump, tan root from his shirt pocket. "We'll just sit here awhile, sit quietly and drink more from the stream."

Like chewing gum, the tangy root stimulated saliva flow in my mouth. After a while, it splintered and began to disintegrate.

"What is…this? W-w-what am I chewing?"

"It's called heal-all; it's mostly for sickness caused by grieving, but it also provides athletes with great strength. We chew it, spit on our hands and rub it on our arms and all over our muscles before we play lacrosse." He said, "When you're finished, spit it out and cover it with dirt. Then drink some more water."

I did as I was told. Jesse sat cross-legged and looked out, admiring the valley and the green hills beyond. He seemed to be hardly breathing. I grew restless in the silence, anxious about anticipating correct behavior in this situation, anxious about what was coming next and what changes in my behavior he expected from me.

"Just sit still," Jesse said, his gaze fixed on the horizon. "Relax. Breathe in from the water and out to the clouds, like this." He demonstrated, as if he were praying. "Try to be as still as possible." When I began, my breathing was shallow and rapid and high up in my throat, the same as when I was climbing, the same as it always seemed to be.

"Press your hand to your stomach. Make the breath come from there."

It seemed impossible to force this process lower, but pressing on my stomach helped me at least become aware of how far I had to go and, surprisingly, my breath did move lower, but only from my throat to my chest, no further. It slowed somewhat, too, almost imperceptibly, but I didn't have the faith to persist and bring it down further. Almost against my will, the process seemed to inch back upward. It took more concentration, more desire, than I could muster; I couldn't share this moment like Jesse wanted me to.

Seeing me struggle, Jesse pointed to my reflection in the stream. I looked so much darker now and thinner. With my long hair, I looked Indian. I searched the stream as it raced across its limestone bed, struggling to breathe deeper and slower like Jesse, but to no avail. My vision blurred and the stream became a river of tears, so deep did it cut into my composure. Jesse's gaze shifted to the rare-blue sky and towering, white clouds slowly roiling as they drifted past. He seemed rooted to the spot, quietly exultant, as if he had discovered some profound meaning right within his reach. His condition reminded me of what Uncle Abe used to call his "*via mystica*," a sort of trance-like state he could attain when he prayed before a certain stained-glass window in his flat—an elaborately-patterned zodiac containing smaller circles mingled with hexagrams and Hebrew letters—and he looked inward and into words. Here, Jesse looked out, to the same effect. But my mind, instead, only turned round and round.

Just before High Holy Days, Uncle Abe asked Jesse to get me ready for synagogue services. He sent along a white shirt and tie and neatly-pressed trousers that'd belonged to Davey. But on the morning of *Rosh Hashanah*, just moments before I was to be picked up by the family's police confidant, I absent-mindedly stepped into my moccasins.

Uncle Abe met me at the side entrance to the synagogue. He was somewhat taken aback by me, thin as I was and tanned and with my hair below my ears. Before the service began, he took me to the men's room, dampened my hair, and pulled it back and fastened it with a rubber band. It was the solution to fitting a white, silk *yarmulke* on my head. When he looked at my feet, he just shrugged.

As Uncle Abe, the synagogue's *shamus*, escorted me to a front row, heads turned. My face burned from the attention I drew and, when we sat down, I pulled my feet well under the pew and tried to distract myself. It was easy. Above and around me, painted on the oval ceiling, were large pastel murals depicting the 12 tribes of Israel, festivals, and stark moments of God-contact featuring prophets of the nation.

When the service was well underway and as organ music and choral singing filled the ornate tabernacle, I shifted my gaze to the elegantly-dressed men and women sitting near me. Some of the women sank back against the pews and fanned their faces with folded programs, looking bored.

At one point, the service was interrupted by a lengthy speech and plea for donations to help Jewish refugees re-settle in Israel. Pamphlets showed them at desert settlements among big, black tents. They were brave pioneers, the speaker said, leaving the Holocaust behind them to face yet more enemies who wanted to destroy them as they tried to make a new life in the Promised Land. Dark-suited ushers collected pledge cards.

After the service, we returned to Uncle Abe's flat. He was in a bad mood. At first I thought it was because of me, how I looked. But as he took off his shoes and put on his slippers he complained about "once-a-year

Jews" who like to get dressed up "to impress everyone." People who, Uncle Abe said, "sat through services like mannequins, bored, as if seeking God were a necessary consolation, whether they believed in him or not. The real meaning of the holiday is more profound."

Uncle Abe sat next to me on an aging, fading davenport that had lost its resilience but had absorbed all the aromas of his existence.

"Wh-what is the real meaning?" I asked.

"In a general way, it's that we all come together to affirm our commitment to *mitzvoth*—righteous behavior. But it's more than that—it's three things."

Uncle Abe, like Grandfather, Uncle Jack, and Davey, liked to enumerate when he lectured. He began by holding up a fist, raising a thumb.

"Step one is remembering, looking at what we've done and what we've become during the past year."

He unfurled his index finger. "Step two is measuring what we've done and what we've become against the highest of who we should and could be."

He unfurled his middle finger. "The third step is *teshuvah* or repentance—determining what we are going to do differently in our lives, taking into account those things which might deter us or interfere with us reaching our goals."

Uncle Abe gazed at me. I sat unconsciously knitting my fingers, looking so unwilling, a victim of deep regret. Sighing, he stood and stretched his aching back and went into his kitchen. He came back with two glasses of cold tea, fresh-cut lemon slices bobbing amid a blizzard of dissolving sugar.

"Atonement doesn't confine itself to owning up to one's personal wrongdoing. Even if one hasn't committed any grave sins, somebody else certainly has. You are a righteous and blameless person, Daniel, but if you can atone for the transgressions of somebody else, you help redeem the standing of everybody."

What was he getting at? It was enough to give me a headache.

"A great tragedy has ruptured our family. Your grandfather—my brother—was at the center of every one of our activities, but now he's gone. The family enterprise is … gone. Our champion—your father—gone. And the light of our life—your mother—has also been taken from us.

"We have all suffered as a result of these evil deeds; you especially. But, believe it or not, this is a test, put forward by God. We can't allow that evil to prevent us from using all the attributes that we possess, created by God, to fulfill God's intention for us: to serve his purpose, to live righteously, to unite with him. We can't just be carried along by events."

His eyes moistened with sincerity. I felt myself growing agitated.

"But wh-why did God create a world where evil people c-c-cause innocent people to suffer and th-then get away with it?"

Uncle Abe reached for a manuscript on the coffee table. He opened it to a page that contained the *sefiroth*, the tree of life. He traced the hierarchical pathways from the world to God, ascending the tree.

"When God created the world and human beings, he withdrew a part of himself in a shattering explosion of his divine light. Sparks of that divine light flew either back into its divine source or downward to the earth. God had to exile himself in order for creation to occur. But an accident of great cosmic proportion happened, and elements of the lower lights broke away from the divine and became the powers of evil. These powers are opposed to existence and cannot survive on their own. In order to be, the evil powers must derive spiritual force from the good, divine lights.

"In order to unify all existence, God created man to make righteousness victorious, to bring forth the downfall of Satan and all of his realm. When men do evil, more divine lights are brought down, evil becomes stronger, and the victory of good over evil becomes even more difficult. The world could be destroyed in this way.

"Our task is to fix the world, *tikkun*, through a constant effort of raising the holy, scattered sparks to their divine source. It's a tough fight, but living a life of *mitzvoth* is the way to bring this about.

"God made evil in order that man can achieve a righteous state without any outside assistance, against maximum odds, requiring maximum efforts. What God wants is for us to make the maximum possible effort to reach the heights we are capable of. Without evil, that would be impossible to achieve."

Uncle Abe summarized the abstract, cosmic theology until I begged him to stop.

"Why? What's the matter?"

I just couldn't absorb it. "You're m-making my head hurt."

I reviewed in my mind all the stories of good and evil that I'd learned: Esau and Jacob, Cain and Abel, the grandsons of Sky-Woman. The distinctive differences between these pairs of individuals seemed to me to be insurmountable. How could one forgive the evil of the other? Why should we be responsible for repairing the world? God didn't get the job done and we're supposed to make it right? And me, too? A kid? It made me sweat. Moreover, the worse things seemed to get, for Indians and Jews, the more they clung to God, while I released my hold on faith. Uncle Abe shrugged and took my empty glass, then returned from the kitchen with two more glasses of tea. If he was disappointed in me, he didn't show it. In fact, he was already looking ahead.

"Five days after *Yom Kippur* is *Sukkot*. Jesse's going to help me build a *sukkah* in the clearing next to his cabin, a beautiful one, the best, adorned with all of the fruits and vegetables from the countryside. What better place to see the stars and to affirm our commitment?"

Suddenly, and with a dread that ballooned in my stomach, I realized that the charge to Uncle Jack on the day of Davey's funeral to "do his part" wasn't meant solely for him. It was on my shoulders, too, and neither Uncle Abe nor Jesse would let me off the hook.

Jesse, Sonny, and I built the *sukkah* under the direction of Uncle Abe. We drove sharp-ended hickory saplings a foot into the ground and rigged a large, square, open-ended frame on which we lashed sweet-smelling hemlock branches. Uncle Abe had us arrange these so that the sides and back would be covered but the roof partly open so that we could see through to the stars. We decorated the outside with locally-harvested vegetables: braided ears of corn, squash gourds, and stringed beans. Inside, piled in corners, we added small baskets of corn, green peppers, radishes, potatoes, and tomatoes, and even apples from a nearby orchard and some grapes and plums and miniature pumpkins.

In the center of the *sukkah*, on a large, woven reed mat as prescribed by Uncle Abe, we placed four species he imported: the *lulav*, a single palm branch; two willow branches; boughs of myrtle; and the *etrog*, a citron.

Over the next several evenings he hosted modest feasts, preceded by prayers of thanksgiving and for God's blessings. To those curious bystanders who wandered over—including the Hill and Logan families—he told stories about the 40 years in the Sinai desert when Jews lived in make-do shelters and, afterward, when they'd reached the Promised Land and lived in *sukkah*-like structures during harvest time. These stories and his giveaways of fruits and vegetables were a welcome respite from the somber mood of the Days of Atonement and the unyielding burden of greater commitment.

Many of the older Indians remembered Uncle Abe from the days when he accompanied Grandfather on his peddler's rounds. Many were still mourning my mother's death but accepted his gifts in a joyful spirit. Many, too, had never tasted cantaloupe and enjoyed Abe's spontaneous servings of the special melon he brought, eating it the way he recommended, with salt and lemon.

Uncle Abe also taught those who came by before sunset the ritual waving of the four species in all directions, signifying that God is everywhere. At first I was embarrassed by his enthusiasm, but I lost my self-consciousness when Jesse mimicked this directional ritual by scattering sacred tobacco, and when Uncle Abe led children on a parade into and out of the *sukkah* and around the yard as he sang ancient songs about God's generosity.

Toward the end of the holiday week, Welcome strolled by with his father on their way to the dam to bathe. They peered at the *sukkah* and at smoke rising from a bed of coals where Jesse cooked unshucked corn. Uncle Abe waved to the boy and his afflicted father. "Come join us!" he yelled. "We have way too much for just family."

The night of *Simchat Torah* was uncommonly warm and muggy and Jesse, Uncle Abe, and we three youngsters lay on mattresses in the *sukkah*, gazing through openings in the branches at a veil of stars twinkling and adrift in the new moon sky. Uncle Abe retold the Jewish stories of creation and the Tree of Life and reiterated his theory of commonalities between Iroquois and Jewish faiths. And he tried to summarize the meaning of *Sukkot*, "the season of rejoicing, of prayer for well-being, peace and harmony among all nations."

But he also went beyond the ideal notions, to the strangely mystical.

"This festival marks the marriage of the feminine part of the divine emanation, the *shekkinah*, to the masculine, *tiferet*; and so the *sukkah* represents the bridal canopy for this conjugal occasion. By building it each year according to specifications outlined by the Torah, we get to participate in this momentous wedding."

In the silence that followed, I realized that no one quite understood what he meant. But they respected his sincerity, and as we lay in the *sukkah*, a star shot across the sky, its filament lingering for as long as it took Yvonne to exclaim. And she edged closer to me until our shoulders touched.

My *Bar Mitzvah*, the final event of the Indian Summer, occurred two weeks later. It was a modest affair, performed before the usual sabbath congregation augmented by only a few close friends and cousins who were notified by phone or word-of-mouth. Uncle Jack and *Hadassah* contributed money to cover expenses, including a reception in the temple auditorium, featuring food by Meltzer and a lively dance band that filled me with a rare sense of satisfaction. But, before the celebration, there was the daunting test of appearing on the dais before 140 souls, both anonymous and very familiar.

While I'd found the Hebrew fairly easy to learn and could read it well and chant in perfect pitch and steadfast tone my selected portions of Torah and *haftorah*, I had trained in the seclusion of Abe's flat or Jesse's cabin, with only them and Echo as my witnesses. For me, the most urgent aspect of my *Bar Mitzvah* was to be able to chant and speak as competently as was expected of any *Bar Mitzvah* boy and to avoid the humiliation of stuttering.

Both Jesse and Uncle Abe coached me on breathing and careful enunciation. And as my voice hadn't yet cracked in the transition from childhood to young manhood, and because I had an ear for music, I wasn't concerned with the chanting part of the performance. It was my speech to the congregation—in English—that had me most dismayed.

With only solitary rehearsals under my belt, I would be standing at the dais, side-by-side for the first time with a rabbi and a cantor I barely knew. For added pressure, Sonny and Yvonne would be sitting in the front row. This time, I was on my own.

Uncle Abe selected a singing portion from the *haftorah* that he said reflected a prophetic paradox of hope and despair. From Ezekial, he picked a chapter written after the destruction of the Temple, when the prophet's dumbness was removed and he could speak freely of a new world in which the Jews were exiled. In the passage I would chant, Ezekial teaches them how to live in that world, where the glory of God would roam, saving them from purposeless despair until their return to the Promised Land.

The portion that he chose from the Torah, he said, contained the essence of that work's wisdom: a passage from Job when God speaks to him out of a whirlwind, answering his questions but, more important, revealing himself.

Uncle Abe said his most difficult task was helping devise my speech to the congregation, one that emerged from and provided a connection to the preceding chanted portions. He believed it was important to help define where I should stand in relationship to the idea of my own emanation, and to impress upon me the need to both resist and deal with an oppressive world. In addition, he wanted to furnish me with a contrast to my crippling sense of shame by helping me to spread a message to others, via a lofty *Kabbalist* metaphor, that would both strike deeply and elicit great praise.

Uncle Abe also hoped that by repetition through practice, and by giving me a glimpse of these sustaining ideas, I might be able to absorb, over time, their meanings. Of course, I was just not capable of the deep immersion into text or spirit that Uncle Abe hoped for. The best I could do, to my way of thinking, was to at least go convincingly through the motions of making a personal and spiritual commitment.

At sunrise that day, Jesse took me to the stream on the hill. We chewed heal-all and rubbed it on my body and sat quietly until the sun poked over the eastern hills. In addition to the wolf pin that I would wear in the lapel of one of Davey's re-tailored suit jackets, I also received from Jesse a miniature False Face mask to carry in my pocket. And before we left to go to the synagogue, we drank a commemorative cup of hot chocolate with Sonny.

Yvonne presented to me, on behalf of Uncle Abe, a slender gold chain. Dangling from it was a gold-bordered amulet fashioned from Psalm 130, embellished with the name of the angel *Taftafiyyah* in the center of a star of David.

But at the synagogue, with each step up the stairs and across to the dais, I felt that morning's dedication leak from my limbs. I peered over the massive reading stand to expectant faces in the congregation: Sarah and her husband and the men in his construction crew, Ray Sammons and Slugger, Mrs. Hill and Mr. Logan and several of my classmates from the Indian school including Welcome and Sonny. Sarah marveled again at my appearance; later, she said I was a recognizable reincarnation of Davey. My hair was cut short again and I had on my feet Davey's gleaming cordovan oxfords. His own prayer shawl with blue and gold trim lay delicately over the shoulders of his blue serge suit. I was almost six feet tall.

Uncle Abe carried the heavy, scrolled Torah to the reading stand where it was kissed and placed in front of me. The cantor in his tall white hat and flowing robe and prayer shawl nodded. It was time to begin. Sweat began to drip from my armpits and I grew dizzy. For one anxious and mute moment, it appeared that my worst fears might be realized. The reassurance that I'd been given that morning seemed to just evaporate during that awkward silence, and my heart beat with an ever-increasing, maddening syncopation. Suddenly, Uncle Abe chuckled. He leaned against me and whispered in my ear. "Look to your right, behind the stairwell."

I turned quickly and the movement caused me to nearly lose my balance.

Standing out of sight of the congregation, Yvonne beamed at me. She was kneeling, holding a white *yamulke* on the head of a grinning dog. It was Echo, buoyant, anticipating my practiced speech. While on the surface his appearance didn't convince me of anything other than thinking Yvonne's tactic was a considerable long shot, he steeled me nonetheless. A sense of balance and lucidity of a kind that I'd all along hoped for, even nearly prayed for, surged through me, and I turned back to the congregation. I began with a blessing.

By the time I arrived at my speech, my friends in the congregation were beyond shocked at my bravura performance and, instead, were riveted to the sophistication of Uncle Abe's words, words which I was more intent on speaking correctly than embracing with conviction.

"...the Torah can best be understood as being concerned with a basic problem: man's withdrawal from the source of his existence and his withdrawal from himself. And God is always trying to overcome that estrangement. Exodus is concerned with making our way back to the Promised Land, from desolation to the haven we grieve for. But it is also an allegory of great personal significance.

"Escaping from the bondage of Egypt is also a search for personal freedom and development. Crossing the Red Sea is going beyond the point of no return, and the exodus becomes a living reality, as one starts on the journey through the desert towards the land of spirit.

"Carried out over a number of years, man gradually matures his potential, and he comes to the place where it is possible to come into the presence of the Lord and to become familiar with his ways, to enter and experience the world of creation, where man has a crucial role to play.

"Each of us has a task to accomplish in this world, to carry out the work of creation, to carry out any task God may assign us to further mankind's progress toward final perfection.

"So as you leave here today, think again about the holy books we have been given to study, and think of them not solely as a history of our people who have just now reached the actual promised land; think of them as a metaphor that applies universally to us all—that God wants us to reach our full potential and that each of us is responsible to all.

"On this day, I promise to begin my commitment to myself, to the people of Israel, and to you all: 'Holy, Holy, Holy art Thou, King of the Universe, Thy Glory fills all the worlds.'"

CHAPTER 14

Despite that promise, I failed to overcome estrangement during the next three years that I lived on the reservation, even with the constant rounds of rituals urged upon me by Jesse and Uncle Abe. I really didn't care to cultivate the basic premise that rituals would enable me to align with divine and right intentions.

Complicating things further, Uncle Jack's financial support had dwindled. As he explained in a letter to Uncle Abe, getting through law school and trying to make ends meet on just Charlotte's store clerk wages was proving too difficult. He could send some money to Jesse from savings derived from the sale of the Burt Street house, but in order to keep possession of his new home in the suburb east of Brant, he implored Abe and Jesse to pick up the slack. He said that after he graduated and returned home he would assume full financial and parental responsibility for me. I hoped that the end of his letter contained that promise, but I settled for just waiting to see if it would come true.

On a positive side, threats against my personal safety seemed to subside after the incident at the lake. I attended public school for a year without any adverse circumstance, and Jesse said he thought it was okay for me to venture off the reservation, as long as I was accompanied by someone trustworthy.

Some days after school, I went with Sonny by bus to the city's small downtown area. Not to explore the commercial center of department stores, shops and cafes, but to roam its margins, which somehow seemed more compatible to his sense of adventure and my lingering apprehension.

On one seedy block, we discovered an old second-floor pool hall and luncheonette owned by a paunchy, retired journeyman fighter named Nate Pesco. In 1935, when Mickey Cochran retired and the middleweight rankings were in a chaotic state with governing bodies quarreling how to determine his successor, Nate got his big chance. After a final elimination bout he won by split decision, he briefly held the American version of the title before losing it in an overweight match to another journeyman two months later. A few months after that, he retired and never again set foot in a gym.

He told me he thought he'd seen a ghost when Sonny and I first passed through his turnstile.

"You look just like a young Davey Mendoza!" he exclaimed gruffly when we approached and asked if we could play.

When we began visiting every day, he relented and let us play a little, despite being underage. Then he so warmed to our visits that he served us free lunches, mostly thin burgers or grilled cheese sandwiches with bowls of Campbell soup. He seemed flattered that we considered his drab, lonely pool hall a place where one acquired character.

Among the regulars at Nate's were active and retired fighters with odd hours and spare time on their hands, including the after-school hours of 3–6 p.m. Sonny took to sketching profiles of them at the lunch counter. He included in each profile small scenes of fighting poses, copies from their own scrapbook photos. Impressed by the results, Nate bought each one for $10 and framed and displayed them in a makeshift gallery by the cue rack.

When several visiting tavern owners saw in Sonny's sketches an opportunity to decorate their walls, Sonny had a part-time job making copies for them.

Some of Nate's customers recognized me right off. Jewish men whose nicknames I recognized from Burt Street stories: Moishe Lusticoff, Winky Lerman, Obbie Slutsky, Itchky Shestak, Tabor Bernstein. They'd approach me after a hushed conversation with Nate. Men with angular immigrant faces, creased and dented by what seemed like centuries of hard times.

"You're Davey Mendoza's boy?" they would ask.

Because I evoked memories of their relationships with him, they acted reverential toward me, as if I possessed his own qualities. Each man told me a version of a story I'd already heard at home—a personal recollection of Davey's indomitable courage, sense of humor, kindness—something they had witnessed and found remarkable.

I marveled at the way their faces lit up when they talked about him and the value they placed on his friendship, on his accomplishments. And now this value was transposed to me, automatically. Davey's light belonged to me and mine to them.

They wanted to know all about me, my life with Jesse and Uncle Abe as my mentors, my interest in a sports career, whether I would leave town and join Uncle Jack in New York or stay on the reservation with Jesse, who they also admired for his own legendary exploits. I could barely spend a dime for a cup of coffee in their presence. One of the men who owned a bowling alley invited me to come there anytime and bowl for free.

After we nagged him enough times, Nate taught us the games everyone played: straight rotation, nine-ball, and billiards. But we could play only with him and only during certain hours on certain days.

"If a cop comes in, the story is 'you're my nephews and I'm baby-sittin' you after school.' "

We emulated the pensive and deliberate nature of the veteran players, their stylized renditions of breaking, shooting, bridging, toting score with a cue by pushing beads along an overhead wire, and chalking up, especially while carrying lit cigarettes or puckering them at the sides of our mouths and squinting, just so, through the smoke.

One afternoon, Joey DeYoung came by, his features waxen and his step unsure, clutching a small bottle buried in a paper bag. When he noticed me, he turned and slapped back downstairs, acting like he, too, had seen a ghost, but not in the same light as the others.

Nate also got me a part-time job as a stock boy at a women's apparel shop on Main Street owned by his girlfriend, Marie. My actual duties were more janitorial because the stock was primarily lingerie and intimate apparel, and a Negro girl, Frankie, already handled that. For two hours after school, I'd move boxes for her, then clean and vacuum two floors and a flight of stairs. Frankie was a boyish, slender girl with delicate features and a knowing smile who wore a work smock over slacks and a tee-shirt. For a while, my employment status seemed considerably less prestigious than Sonny's.

But that changed one afternoon when Marie approached and asked me to shut off the vacuum cleaner and hand-dust for a while.

Behind her, waiting impatiently, stood a blonde stripper from the Chez Ami, wearing a suit that barely contained her, and carrying a champagne Yorkshire terrier, accompanied by a well-dressed man, poised to begin a shopping spree.

The man looked familiar and a chill crept up my spine. Well-dressed, blond hair combed straight back, and when my presence caught his eye he looked at me as if I were going to steal from him. Then I recognized him. Raymond DiNardi. It was all I could do to keep busy. His dark, menacing glare made my heart rise into my throat and I began to sweat. I turned and squatted and began dusting a low-slung table. I hoped he would see me as only a boy-nuisance and not a mirror image of a man he'd plotted to destroy.

He never came back, and I began to realize something else: I had never seen such an alluring woman or others like her who also frequented the shop. Marie catered to this clientele, and their quest for glamorous apparel sparked an enthusiasm in me that carried over to my dreams and these new dreams jockeyed with the predominantly-bad ones and brought me a secret, shocking pleasure.

When I told Sonny about the stripper, he began showing up at at my quitting time, waiting anxiously outside and eager to glimpse what I'd begun to regularly experience. However, Marie began to notice my heightened interest in lingering on the upper floors which were too immaculate for my own good and finally, per her instructions, I was banished to the basement. Working for Frankie only inflamed my arousal as she teased me and flirted with abandon, even trying on lingerie to model for me.

One afternoon when I opened the door to the basement, the harsh florescent light had been turned off; the staircase was barely illuminated. I descended warily, searching in vain for the light switch. I called for Frankie. No answer.

Alone and aroused to a breaking point, I locked myself in the bathroom and pleasured myself while simulating the vague, sensual experiences of my dreams and my imagined encounters with Frankie. From then on, it became an obsession.

One gray day, I received my final pay envelope. Marie said she wasn't displeased with my work. In fact, she said with a knowing smile, she liked me very much. But, realistically, there didn't seem much at the store for me to do that couldn't be done by one of the other girls working there. She said she had to let me go.

To compensate, Nate let me become his janitor and once again I joined the company of men. Away from temptation, my life returned to normal, except for the occasional erotic dream which always ended in delirious but embarrassing spasm. I didn't see Frankie again until three years later.

CHAPTER 15

When it came to school, Sonny and I slacked off. We felt trapped within a vocational track, and all he really wanted to do was draw and paint. I just wanted to avoid all aspects of being in a classroom. Fortunately for us, we were never singled out for our lack of diligence. Most of the boys from the reservation were passive participants and little was expected of us, so we were allowed to hide.

Except in English class. There was nowhere to hide. Our teacher—a diminutive, silver-haired but no-nonsense woman who always wore a black dress and carried an unusually long key chain over her shoulder like an Indian sash—devoted herself to drilling us in grammar with maps and diagrams I couldn't comprehend. It seemed she expected us to know what she was talking about, but it was all new to me. Not only wasn't I able to identify parts of speech, but also I stammered badly whenever she called on me. To her, my stuttering must've seemed like a clumsy evasion, and she kept at me every day until she became, in the process, even more frustrated and sharp-tempered. In turn, I became more hapless, diffident and, finally, withdrawn.

The ultimate travesty occurred one day while she paced back and forth in front of class, hectoring us during a sentence-diagramming drill. I sat in the front row, an over-grown novice, daydreaming. She tripped over my outstretched feet and fell in a heap. From that day on, her wrath was even more pointed and impassioned.

Shop classes were no respite. In metal shop especially, I had no interest. I faked involvement in a lathe project. Deception was easy because the teacher stayed remote, spending most of the time at his desk cramming on his own, studying to be an administrator.

The metal shop was located in a screened-off section of a larger industrial arts department, and it shared space with an auto mechanics shop. Here, several older boys held sway. They worked, unsupervised, on their cars—mainly older model Fords and Mercs. Welcome, who'd found a part-time job at an auto junkyard, insinuated himself into this group and conformed to their fashion: turned-up shirt collars, dungarees, and bulky work shoes. They wore their hair in D.A. style: long and pomaded on the sides into a duck's tail in back, flat brush-cut on top. They took cigarette breaks outside, far from the rest.

One of the shop class regulars was a 15-year-old named Donny Reed. He didn't own a car but worked on an old shop model. He was the most furious fighter in the school, and he patrolled our territory like he owned it, drifting into other shop classes when compelled by proprietary interest.

One day, accompanied by Welcome and two others, he approached me as I pretended to work the lathe.

"Hey, Mendoza, how old are you?" he shouted.

Jolted from my task, my stomach ballooned with trepidation. "I-I-I-I'm f-f-fourteen," I said, nodding hard to finish, meeting Reed's blunt stare.

"You're p-p-p-pretty b-b-b-big for f-f-f-fourteen." His mimicry drew peels of laughter. I found it difficult to breathe.

"Y-y-you g-got a f-f-funny name. Wh-wh-where are you f-f-from?" he asked coldly.

In lieu of a reply, I froze and looked askance. Welcome seemed greatly satisfied, as if he shared a secret about me and Reed was going to be my inquisitor. Instead, after a few swollen moments of silent intimidation, Reed turned and walked away, followed by the others.

From the periphery, I felt the watchful, disapproving stares of my classmates, while the teacher at the far end of the work area remained hunched over his books.

When the bell rang, I followed my classmates as they filed out to the corridor. But waiting there were Welcome and one other boy; they beckoned to me. When I approached, Reed sprang from behind, bare-chested, his shirt tied around his waist. A scowl clouded his face.

My classmates bunched just past the doorway and stared at us. Reed grabbed a fistful of my shirt. I smelled his acrid cigarette breath.

"Why didn't you answer my question?"

I stiffened but kept my expression impassive, as if that could placate his coiled anger.

"You're a punk!" Reed shouted, slapping me hard. I tasted blood; Reed glanced at the others then slapped me again, trenchant with rage.

I remained rigid but unresisting. In disgust, Reed wheeled and strode down the hall, indignant, his arms held slightly away from his body as if a great heat needed venting. His companions followed him, chatting like seconds, and when they reached the end of the corridor, Welcome cast back a look of disdain.

None of my classmates said anything as I walked past them to the bathroom to wash blood from a cut inside my lower lip or later when we took our seats in the next class. Some ignored the incident because it reminded them of their own craven encounters with Reed; others gossiped about it. I just carried my humiliation with me into English class where degradation had become a daily affair.

Fifteen minutes into the class, I excused myself on a pretext of seeing the school nurse about my cut lip. Instead, I wandered the halls haphazardly and, when student monitors appeared around one corner, I ducked into the library. When they entered after me, I picked up a newspaper, feigning some kind of academic enterprise. On the front page was a boxed story headlined, *Boston Massacre: Fighter's Beating Stirs Outcry.* The account of the fight began:

"In one of the most reprehensible mismatches in modern ring history...."

It was the story of a lightweight boxer, hospitalized after being knocked to the canvas 10 times in a championship bout televised nationally from Boston Garden. It took one of the fighter's cornermen leaping into the ring for the referee to stop it in the fourth round, the article reported. Several members of Congress were quoted as calling for reforms, especially some sort of maximum knockdown rule.

On a hunch, I turned to the the card catalogue. Under the heading "boxing," I found a book, *The Morality of Prize-Fighting,* written by a Catholic priest. One chapter was titled, "Moral Principles in Relation to the Problem." Its premise was that boxing was prohibited by the commandment to not kill. The priest quoted from the Catechism of the Council of Trent. It described mutilation and any other injury to the body as *servata debita proportione,* deriving from St. Thomas who asserted that fighting was not a sport because it was done "in a spirit of rancor or hatred with intent to inflict and harm the opponent.

"To take pleasure in the unnecessary sufferings of man belongs to the vice of brutality or savagery." The priest called this an emotionally perverse form of pleasure because it violated the true spirit of competition, which is undertaken to "give pleasure to those who participate." He called the virtue which regulated play, *eutrapelia*. It reminded me of Jesse's affirmation, which he likened once to 'counting coup.'

"You know, to make coup is when you approach your enemy and tap him with your coup stick. Of course, sometimes that tap can be a good whack," he said, laughing, "but there's a big difference between the brave act of counting coup and…what other people do."

The priest wrote that play was undertaken for the sake of pleasure and that gratification came from competition, the spirit of rivalry, keen desire for success in the contest between opponents, "…by fair and honest striving." He also noted the importance of bearing defeat with dignity.

Citing St. Thomas again, the priest defined the conditions for justifiable infliction of bodily harm: *"(1) It is not wrong to inflict moderate bodily hurts, if the other person is not unwilling and there is a reasonable purpose, such as exercise or training in the arts…. (2) There must be sufficient reason for the harm done. (3) There must be moderation in the harm or pain inflicted. (4) There must be sufficient authority; i.e., the head of the family has limited coercive power; other persons may punish or restrain only in case of urgent necessity."*

It seemed to me that those who set themselves up as God's arbiters didn't really understand his rules, or his game.

CHAPTER 16

The following summer, Sonny underwent a test of his own, one that he accepted without the slightest hesitation. Just before an end-of-season Red League lacrosse match against St. Regis that had title implications, he was asked to fill in for our goalie, an ironworker who'd fallen off a building and broken his leg.

A good stick-handler, built low to the ground, Sonny had shown courage in the crease where most of the collisions between shooter and defender occurred. And he was "quick as a cat," Jesse said, who could be a "stick goalie," one who rushed out to meet the ball when an attacker bore in. But one of the St. Regis players looked too much for Sonny to handle—Thomas George, who'd recently returned to play after being temporarily banished for hitting and killing a player with the force of his "heavy shot."

I sat behind the team bench and witnessed play that at times was downright vicious. Several players were clubbed unconscious and the body count mounted as the game pressed toward the final minutes with the score tied 6-6.

I overheard one onlooker who worked as a guard at the penitentiary say, "I've been attacked by inmates with broom handles, dead weights, even metal cots. But this game is more barbaric than anything I've ever experienced at work."

Sonny had caught, blocked, or kicked away about 30 shots and, after a penalty face-off, George finally got his best chance. He charged down the box at Sonny but instead of angling in close as he had tried to do, unsuccessfully, all afternoon, he dug in for an underhand shot from about 25 feet away, even as several of our players tried to cut him off. His shot came faster than Sonny could react; it hit him in the side and he collapsed into the net.

The game had to be delayed fifteen minutes, until Sonny could stand. Later, the doctor at the hospital said he'd suffered two broken ribs and shouldn't have stayed in the game, since he could barely stand or move laterally.

But he stopped George's shot. The pain hadn't mattered, to him or anyone else. If anything, it was an act of honor and it carried greater weight with the men than the final score and, in the waning moments, no one made a move to take him out, even as St. Regis fired four easy goals past him.

He said later that stopping George's shot felt like being hit with a baseball bat. But he was a hero. At 15, he'd already crossed over to join that pantheon of Iroquois players who'd withstood the most fearsome blows.

While he lay bedridden for a week and sat for most of another one encased in plaster, visitors flocked to his house to pay him homage. When he could walk, he and I were invited to join some other boys by the creek. We met at dusk, and they had a case of long-neck beer standing in the water and, under a fast-rising moon, we chased sips of PM whiskey. Within an hour, Sonny's pain had subsided, and I discovered a completely different sensation, one that—without expending any effort at all except for consuming unsavory potions—allowed me to digress and forget.

I drifted into and out of a number of conversations, so garrulous and animated that I took everyone by surprise. Usually in a group like these boys, I preferred to be a bystander because I still felt compelled to act deferentially, and I was unwilling to risk embarrassment because of my stutter. But drunk, I became a true confederate: joking, laughing, arguing, even declaring verities. Euphoria took hold of me and I just wanted the moment to last. The only reason we quit to go home was because we'd invented a profound over-arching truth about life that even I helped build and, once we accomplished that, our parley dissolved; there was nothing left to keep us intact and awake.

It began to come together as we discussed it—crudely, hesitantly, in fits and starts and certainly not in lofty language but, rather, piecemeal, worked out, probably, over several hours—a theme common to many movies we had seen in which torture had been used to wrench information or confessions from heroic characters like soldiers, cowboys, Indians, musketeers. Information and confessions that would most likely harm others or even one's country.

How foolish it was to suffer for that, one older and more experienced boy argued, or to die, when such "heroic" behavior was self-destructive.

"The most important thing you can do in this dog-eat-dog world is to look out for yourself," he said. "If giving up secrets means staying free and alive, that's what matters."

While that sentiment didn't jibe with the stand-up valor that Sonny had previously cherished—being accountable, what Uncle Abe and Jesse always preached—for us, that night, a new and better truth had dawned. Valor—at least in the face of torture or death—was only for suckers, even if it meant informing. Whoever said, *"no man is an island,"* didn't know jack shit. You had to keep a cool head to carry out this mission, like only a few characters in the movies. Mike Hammer, for instance. And even he went soft at crucial moments. And paid for it with a good beating, our friend reminded us. What we discovered that night was the truth, a new, bold way to go. It brought us together, and we marked the moment by burning the back of our hands with red-hot tips of cigarettes.

The next day, however, we had only ugly blisters and throbbing pain to show. Of our profound insight, neither Sonny nor I could recollect a word of it.

But I enjoyed staying out all night with these older boys, drinking and laughing and sharing stories around a smokey fire that kept most of the mosquitos, and my troubles, at bay.

Jesse hated it.

"You violated one of the four major wrongs," he told Sonny and me as we sat in the shade of the porch, sipping coffee and trying desperately to summon to the surface the wisdom we had, the night before, anchored so confidently beside.

"The reason you can't remember is because *oneka* causes the mind to split. Maybe last night you found some truth, but 'the mind-changer' brings great misery and hardship, even as you enjoy it."

After his angry lecture, Jesse made us pledge to never touch booze again. But my pledge was half-hearted. How could I not embrace this pain-killer, this ill-tasting but magical elixir that so enabled me to explore, no matter how briefly, speech, freedom, joy and wisdom?

A week later, Uncle Abe was just as furious. We showed up at his flat after a night of carousing in cheap downtown bars where proof of age was never checked. We drank 7-7's and rum-and-cokes for 50 cents apiece and smoked cigarettes and sang along to the jukebox and befriended nearly everybody. It was the best time we ever had and, after the last call, we paraded toward Uncle Abe's house, exhilarated.

We picked up a new companion who we met at The Open Door, a long room of a saloon with doors at each end. He called himself "Sugar Ray" and he did bear a resemblance, especially his sad, canted eyes. But Ray wasn't a fighter; he was a drunk and a raconteur whose greatest delight was teaching Sonny and me lewd Negro slang and a way of walking he called "the pimp limp," where you dipped one side of your body—the side you chose to keep stiff-legged—to a kind of rhythm of a silent melody he carried.

When we first met, outside the bar, he ordered us to walk back and forth for him so he could test whether or not either of us were "turn-ins." He wouldn't associate with anyone who was queer, he said. We passed the test, whatever it was. At that point, we hadn't even the wit to ask.

Later, when a woman wearing a skin-tight skirt walked by, deliberately swaying her high, rounded buttocks at him as he cat-called, he shouted: "Look at the *jaws* on that chick!"

And when we walked by a Negro tavern, The Tippin' Inn, he taught us that a "tipper" meant someone who was unfaithful. Sugar Ray re-worked everything we said on the way to Uncle Abe's, drilling us until we correctly copied his vocabulary, intonation, and limp. We bantered and hollered and laughed all the way to Uncle Abe's street, parting reluctantly. But it was awfully late, 4:30 in the morning. Still, we made him answer his doorbell.

When he saw us in our drunken state, he raged in both English and Yiddish and a kind of Spanish he only rarely ventured into. He called me *boracho*.

"You better get over this in a hurry," he warned. "What about the 'commitment' to yourself that you promised to begin at your *Bar Mitzvah*? You said you would climb the tree of life, not leap from it! Have you forgotten your *Bar Mitzvah* speech already?"

His question cut deep; my face flushed with shame.

He slapped his forehead. "Where do you keep your speech?"

"In the box with Davey's robe," I coolly replied

I didn't say how far that box was pushed beneath my bed, and that I didn't intend to open it any time soon.

He shot me an accusatory glance.

"Maybe you oughta give that robe to me...for safe-keeping."

"And you!" he shouted at Sonny. "I hate to say this, but what do you want to turn into? The proverbial drunken Indian?" He told us we could sleep there but only on the porch.

"You reek of alcohol and cigarettes!" And in the morning, we had to leave his house without coffee or breakfast. "If you want to punish your bodies, seek your own replenishment. If I feed you, I'll feel like I'm validating your sin."

Another time, later in the summer, we got drunk at The Open Door again and became sick riding the bus back to the reservation. We were kicked off two miles away from the turn-about, in a strange neighborhood. Unable to walk, we crept onto a house porch to sleep. At sunrise, we staggered back home, vowing to never drink again. But secretly, sick as I was at the time, I abjured. I just needed to figure out what was the right amount of beer or liquor to drink to get to the euphoric level of drunkenness but not get sick or lose my balance and physical dexterity, because I liked how I felt and who I became when I drank. I gabbed, I met people, including older women who wanted to dance close and kiss.

Throughout that summer, besides lacrosse, I also learned to catch a football. At 15, I was eligible to try out for the school team. Sonny believed he was still too weak to even try out. By the time I first touched a football, I had grown to be 5-11, 165 pounds and had become a fast runner; I looked forward to early training camp.

Several older boys, three varsity quarterbacks, praised me for having "good hands" but especially for making catches far down the field while running full speed.

"Farther!" they would yell, waving me out. I envisioned playing a sport in which I only caught spectacular over-the-shoulder passes like the ends for the Cleveland Browns, Dante Lavelli and Mac Speedie, who I'd read about in magazine articles, and whose action images Sonny traced and sketched for me that vied with the fight poster for space above my bed.

But the training camp planned by the Valley Academy coach proved vastly different from the run-and-catch ballet I'd foolishly projected.

The first two days were devoted to endless conditioning drills and running: dozens of sprints and laps around two baseball fields. From the shade of a huge elm, Sonny and Uncle Abe watched me and a few other debauched candidates suffer as we struggled to respond to the coach's commands. As I plodded past them, Uncle Abe leaned on his cane and shouted encouragement. He seemed older with the change of seasons, more fragile and bent, ankle deep in rusty, dead leaves.

In addition to the punishment of rigorous training, my toes and heels blistered badly from new high-top shoes. Pads chafed my shoulders and hips. And while I was issued an old, cracked leather helmet, most everyone else received gleaming plastic ones complete with face-bar masks.

Along with other rookies, I was introduced to dozens of difficult and bone-jarring drills that entailed blocking and tackling, aspects of the game I naively believed would be required of others, not speedy pass-catching ends with "good hands." The only time I touched a ball was at the beginning of each day's double session practice, when everyone who wanted to be a back or end ran out for passes.

I didn't know any of the patterns called by the starting quarterback, a tall, confident senior, so I simply ran straight out then turned my head to look for the ball. He kept waving me farther and farther until he finally let go a long spiral to a point where I had to sprint full-speed to catch it. I was exhilarated. I believed that he really appreciated my ability and wanted to test his arm strength, rehearsing how well we'd team-up together this season. But what he was really doing was part of an overall pattern of hazing first-time candidates. One long run after another. I'd race afar in perfect stride, arms outstretched as the ball descended with an alarming velocity. But I caught every one, and I was so far downfield that I never saw him laugh about it with everyone else.

Moreover, passing the ball was a very minor element in the coach's scheme. His teams relied primarily on a conservative, T-formation running attack, featuring two halfbacks and a blocking fullback. The only passes in the playbook were simple swing passes out of the backfield; ends were expected to block and play defense and only rarely catch a short pass, usually on a trajectory across the field rather than straight ahead. For this coach, players had to be hitters. My great practice catches were not only irrelevant, they were considered downright mutinous.

At his game, I was inept and illiterate. I also violated one of his unspoken, cardinal rules on the first sweltering day of practice when I broke away from laps to get a drink at the water fountain. I felt sick, overheated; salt streaked my blue practice jersey.

"Mendoza!" he barked. "Where do you think you're going! Get back in file!"

Several players, including three from the reservation, wouldn't take his abuse. They quit and walked home. But I took seriously the scrutiny from Sonny and Uncle Abe. And though they knew what my pre-practice expectations had been, for them you had to chew what you bit. That was a rule.

The most difficult drill, the coach's favorite, entailed two-on-one blocking. A defender had to fight off a double-team block and tackle a ball carrier. To make it more difficult, the coach stood behind the defender's back to signal to blockers which way the play would go. Only the most skilled and determined defenders got to the ball carrier. Everyone else got pounded into the ground.

Late at the end of one morning session, with the sun blazing nearly overhead, this drill had gone on for about a half-hour. The coach seemed to want to involve every player and everyone knew that this drill, over all the others, was a major factor in his winnowing process.

A few inept candidates, like me, were largely ignored. We were already considered marginal, junior varsity candidates. The coach wanted to test only his most viable players. From the shade of the elm tree, Sonny and Uncle Abe beckoned to me; the practice session was about over. Sinking to one knee, I waved back and concealed myself behind the milling, sweating players. I was staring at three young, proud marines dressed in tan tropical uniforms talking to an assistant coach. I asked a guy standing next to me who they were and he told me it was a team tradition for boys at Valley Academy who weren't going on to college and who were uncertain about their path in life to enlist in the Marine Corps, usually in early June so they could return to fall practice after they'd finished boot camp.

I never even heard my name called; a teammate alerted me and the other players parted, like flanks of a Roman legion, and I jogged lead-footed to the drill pit, feeling my stomach lurch upwards to my throat. Ahead of me, I saw two senior linemen kneeling in the dirt. A slender halfback stood 10 yards behind with the ball tucked lazily in his arm.

"We haven't seen you yet, Tommy Tel Aviv!" the coach rasped. I winced. A sun-bleached cap shaded the coach's eyes, but I could make out his cruel, thin-lipped smile.

Modeling others, I faced the two big linemen and took a four-point stance. They assumed low, three-point stances, balled their free hands into fists and glared at me through their plastic face bars.

From behind, the coach yelled. "SET!"

I readied myself: low on my haunches, my face exposed, sweating. "HUT one! HUT two!"

On the second count, the tackle to my right lunged. He slammed a forearm into my face, driving me off my stance and back a few steps. His confederate finished me off, clubbing me into a sprawl. The slender halfback trotted past. I tasted blood and dirt and I fingered numb lips to see whether my teeth remained intact.

"Not good, Tommy!" the coach shouted. "You need to stay low to ward off that first block, then spin away from the second! Let's try it again!"

An airplane droned overhead. Although the two tackles bristled with enthusiasm—hustling back and digging into their provocative, fist-clenched stances—a grim silence descended on the other players.

"SET! HUT...!"

At the first count, as I warily eyed the right tackle, the one to my left slammed his forearm into my face and, when I tried to spin away, the other one dove below me, cutting me off at my feet. Again, the halfback trotted nonchalantly past.

Shaking his head with feigned disgust, the coach fumed.

"Let's try it again! I'd like to see you at least put a hand on the ball-carrier before we break for lunch!"

We lined up a third time. The coach barked signals. This time both linemen hammered me onto my back. When I rolled from under them, blood seeped from my nose and mouth and beaded in the dust where I knelt.

I glanced up. Through a haze of stinging sweat, I glimpsed the running back standing exactly where the play had begun; he hadn't even moved.

"Do you want to quit, Mendoza? Like some of your buddies?" the coach shouted.

Several players looked away. Uncle Abe began to hobble onto the field, but an assistant coach I didn't know intervened.

"I want an answer! Do you want to quit?"

Dizzy, I leaned in the direction of the coach's voice and crept in a semi-circle until I believed I faced him.

The coach shouted in mock disbelief. "Do you want to make this team, Mendoza? Or do you wanna quit and go home?"

There was a familiar ringing in my ears, a kind of siren voice that I strained to decipher, above the noise of a cheering, whistling crowd, like the high-pitched voice of ringside announcer Johnny Addie giving an introduction.

In the shimmering distance, Uncle Abe resembled Grandfather. And the siren voice became his: *"Sometimes you need to be hit to know you're in the game!"*

I gave in to what was expected. "Sh...sure; let's do it again," I mumbled through split and swollen lips which then pursed involuntarily into a grin as I pondered whether I was giving God the pleasure he craved.

My old-fashioned leather helmet sat slightly askew and I could feel tears and sweat streak through the debris caked on my face. The heedless grin which stretched my swollen, blood-stained lips only complemented this mask of idiocy. Even my foes took no pleasure any longer. Now when we lined up, they averted their eyes.

On the command SET! I shot out of my stance and knifed between my startled opponents, bellowing, charging low, head-first, aiming toward the inert halfback's belly and when the ball popped free I scrambled after it, crab-like, sweeping it into my arms as I rolled into a fetal position. From the semi-circle of observing players came whoops and shouts, whether of celebration or derision I couldn't tell.

The coach threw down his cap and strode, red-faced, into the pit. "Shut up!" he yelled to the others. "You cheated!" he screamed at me and tried, without success, to yank the ball from my arms.

"You went before the count! That's an off-sides penalty against the team! You cheated! You hurt us! That's gonna cost you!"

While the other players withdrew to the distant locker room, I jogged penalty laps around the baseball fields, carrying the ball tightly in the crook of my right arm, spitting blood onto the trail etched by other punished players.

As I came closer to Uncle Abe, he seemed drawn into himself. Closer, it dawned on me: he'd been moved to tears. And when I passed Sonny standing next to the three Marines, he mirrored my idiotic grin as if he believed that what I'd desperately improvised meant that I'd finally reconciled with the warrior's true inclination.

The next day, before morning practice, the assistant coach who'd restrained Uncle Abe from hobbling onto the practice field during my ordeal approached me outside the locker room, carrying a new plastic helmet with a face bar.

"Some guy's girlfriend got pregnant and his father made him quit the team to get a job. This is yours. You earned it."

From a distance, prior to today's introduction, this coach had looked vaguely familiar. Now, face-to-face, I remembered him: Joe Aquilino, one of Sammons' Brant University boxers, a heavyweight and, like me, a Sephardic Jew. I'd seen him before at the Armory and once or twice at the synagogue.

I thanked him for the helmet and slipped it on. He helped me adjust the chin strap.

"You handled yourself good yesterday," he said as I stared at the dew-slick practice field, already in full sun at 9 a.m.

"Coach Andrews shows some temper when he's testing a person, but don't take it to heart. He liked what you did. Not necessarily beating the snap-count, but solving your problem and taking after that ball-carrier."

"I don't have set duties yet," he continued. "I'm here because it's part of my practice-teaching assignment.... I really don't know much about this sport, but Mr. Testa, the line coach, he's a good one. He'll teach you all you need to know."

He looked briefly at the ground, hesitant, then at me. I was stunned by the sincerity in his eyes.

"Mr. Testa and I...we both admired your dad...."

He cleared his throat and shifted his gaze to players strolling onto the field, while I lamented the onset of yet another punishing double-session.

"Mr. Testa also liked what you did yesterday. He told me he saw the type of young man he could take under his wing."

And beginning that day, Coach Testa did. He taught me how to come out of my stance, to charge low and use my forearms to drive defenders off the line of scrimmage, and on defense he taught me how to fight off blocks and dive into tackles. When I executed these maneuvers with requisite ferocity, he was enthusiastic with his praise, unlike Coach Andrews who maintained an aloof presence and dispensed relentless insults.

Mr. Testa tried to motivate me with an almost fanatical enthusiasm, even, on occasion, jumping into the fray to demonstrate how he wanted a certain technique performed. If I appeared tentative or lacking in enthusiasm for any facet of playing my position, he'd subtly summon forth memories of my father so accurate and vivid they sent chills down my spine. He awakened me to a level of intensity that he knew would appeal to Coach Andrews, and while I didn't completely buy into it, I did everything he asked in order to please him.

Of course, Coach Andrews' tantrum strategy also worked on me. He humiliated me one afternoon during a scrimmage when I was put in as defensive end. I mis-played a halfback reverse he planned to perfection based on my consistently-incautious charges into the backfield. I thought I was helping to chase down a pitch-out to the other side when a diminutive, speedy halfback passed me going the other way, ball tucked under his arm, his eyes wide with expectation as he tore upfield, untouched.

With mocking laughter, Coach Andrews delighted in ridiculing me for my mistake in front of observing parents and Uncle Abe, who came every day to watch practice. His shaming strategy worked; in spite of my conviction that nothing about this game really mattered, I vowed to never fail like that again.

The paternal enthusiasm of Mr. Testa combined with the scrutiny of Mr. Acquilino and Uncle Abe—measuring me against my father—and the derision displayed by Coach Andrews, worked to erode my deep sense of apathy. I became a willing practitioner.

Within a few weeks, I improved so much I was promoted to the varsity as a special teams' player on kickoffs and punts. We had a weak, small team and an unimaginative style of play, but we were well-schooled and though we lost most of our games, they were never by lopsided scores. Every day, I drilled and scrimmaged against the first team, giving what was expected and taking a pounding, too, which I actually enjoyed because it seemed deserving. In games I was put into, I crashed with reckless abandon into blockers like a human bowling ball and raced to tackle receivers as soon as they fielded a punt or kickoff.

In the last period of the final game, with our team ahead by two touchdowns and our final offensive drive looming, Mr. Acquilino inserted me for one pass play that he believed was a sure thing. He'd noticed a substitute defensive back wandering around, trying to figure out his team's proper alignment.

My heart pounded with that old feeling of trepidation, but I was too tired to worry about succeeding. On the snap, I ran a simple but precise come-back pattern, sprinting straight out then planting and rushing back into a zone so empty of players I felt like I was in a spotlight.

In what seemed like slow-motion, the ball arced my way, a perfect spiral, and after I pulled it in, I lunge-faked toward the sideline, pivoted, and as the defender clipped my shoulder and fell to the turf, I bolted upfield, heavy-legged but euphoric, past a lunging safety, and I sprinted 30 yards to the end zone. Several players, including the quarterback, ran and crashed into me, exulting. Jogging off the field with the crowd cheering was my happiest, most transcendent moment of the entire season, one that gave me a sense of hope.

At the end of the season, Nate gave me an advance on my pay so I could order a blue varsity jacket. It came with my number embroidered on each shoulder and a bright-red football on front, and Valley Academy printed on the back in big block letters. I wore it to school every day, and it seemed to confer upon me a new status of worthiness. To all, that is, except my English teacher, who continued to torment me.

CHAPTER 17

One day the following spring, while riding a bus home from Nate's, I met Peggy O'Neal, a cheerleader for LaSalle, an all-boys Catholic school whose football team had been city champions since 1949. She was a sophomore at their sister school, All Souls Academy, a perky blonde with a dimpled smile who wore a uniform of blue plaid skirt and blue crewneck sweater with a rounded, white collar. Surprisingly, she kept our conversation moving, even when I stuttered.

Just before her stop, about two miles before mine at the end of the city line, she told me about an open house, a school-sponsored dance every Friday night. Would I like to come?

I went the very next Friday with Chad Call, the quarterback who'd thrown me the season-ending touchdown. After a confidence-building game of pool and dinner at Nate's, we walked to a spired red-brick church which housed her school and followed the sound of music to a vestibule where we encountered the open-house chaperones: a priest and two nuns selling tickets and stamping hands with the school's insignia. They seemed surprised to see Chad and me, gazing alternately at our faces and rival school jackets.

Peggy and a girlfriend greeted us in the foyer, and we danced every song, fast and slow, and chatted through every intermission.

At All Souls, slow dancing was practiced with restraint because the nuns patrolled the dance floor, obliging everyone to bridle their ardor and dance at arm's length. But Peggy knew how to steal an intimate moment and, during one slow song, she guided me to a shadowy pocket in the middle of the throng and pulled her body closer. This gesture and the fragrance she wore thrilled me. Trance-like, shuffling awkwardly in a sweet embrace, I closed my eyes, and everyone else faded into an obscure periphery.

On every Friday night through the end of the school year, Chad and I met Peggy and her friend at her open-house dance and afterward we'd walk the few blocks to the late-night diner, Poodle's, for cherry Cokes, burgers, and fries, then catch the last bus out to the valley.

After the final open house of the year, we were among the last to depart, strolling out from the darkened alley. But under a street lamp, defiance etched in their faces, four boys in LaSalle jackets waited. My stomach roiled with dread.

The girls recognized them—football players who previously hadn't paid us any heed—and spoke first, a friendly greeting. But the boys were in a different mood.

"Hey, Peggy," one asked, "what're you doing with a Christ-killer?"

Peggy's eyes widened. "What are you talking about? These are friends of mine." She glanced anxiously behind, measuring the distance back to the church entrance. But the boys pushed past Peggy and her friend to confront me and Chad. Light from the street lamp amplified the pinched anger in their faces.

"What's a Jew doing at our dance?"

I met their menacing glare with as neutral an expression as I could muster.

"I invited him here," Peggy volunteered, her tone adamant. "He's been coming for weeks. You don't even know him. His name is Mendoza. He's…Spanish…or something. He's very nice and now we're going home."

She took me by the arm and made to go, but the most-fervently-offended boy blocked our exit. He mimicked her voice in an exaggerated whine. "He's a nice guy, and now we're going home." Then he reasserted his manly voice.

"We don't much care who you invite to our open house, but no Indians and no Jews from Valley."

Peggy's anxious expression turned quizzical. She searched my face. The LaSalle boys moved closer and Peggy, sensing a fight, ran back to the church. They ignored her. "You're not getting out of this alley, you Jew bastard!" the leader shouted. He peeled off his jacket.

I stood stock still.

Chad spoke up. "Look, we're just friends of the girls, having a good time. We're not interested in bothering anybody."

"He's bothering me," the boy said, still glaring at me. "His being here is bothering me, bothering all of us. He's not welcome here and neither are you." He stepped forward to swing a roundhouse punch. I blocked the blow with my arms, but the others jumped in, and our melee of scuffling shoes and shouts and punches pervaded the alley.

"Boys! What's going on here?"

It was the priest, sprinting toward us, followed by Peggy.

"Nothing, Father," the lead boy said, breathing heavily. "We're just kicking this Jew and his friend out of here."

The priest was young and fit and pushed into our entangled group, separating bodies and creating an open pocket where he inserted his authority.

"Does 'this Jew' have a name? Do you know who he is?"

I tried to respond but couldn't push the words out of my mouth.

"His name is Daniel Mendoza. I'm Chad Call. These girls are our friends. We've been coming here for weeks, just to dance and have fun."

"I know," the priest said. "I recognize you." He turned to me. "You related to Mendoza the boxer?"

I nodded. "My father."

The priest bristled and he confronted the others.

"You boys." He hooked his thumb to the church entrance. "Go back and wait inside for me." He stepped closer, studying my face again as the LaSalle boys retreated down the alley.

"I apologize for them. We don't condone this behavior, although wearing your Valley Academy jackets here is probably a bad idea. They're your rivals is all. I'm sure that's what they're actually puffed up about; nothing more than that."

The priest looked at me as if he were trying to place me in some scheme of things. "Your mother was Mary Isaacs, from the West End, right?" I nodded. "From an Irish Catholic family?"

"P-part Irish, p-part Iroquois," I answered. "C-catholic before she married my dad. She kept her mother's name."

Peggy hooked her arm through mine.

"...I remember...," he said. "Go with your friends, Peggy, wherever you were planning to go."

The priest turned back into the alley and walked toward the boys waiting at the door. "But he's a Christ-killer," one blurted as he was herded inside.

We walked in silence for several blocks.

"Assholes!" Chad grumbled.

We came to another street lamp. I could feel Peggy staring at me.

"Mendoza...? I thought that was a Spanish name, or maybe Italian."

I laughed.

"How come you don't go to East Brant High? That's where all the Jew...Jewish kids go to school."

"I don't live there; I live in the v...valley."

"I know. But, where, exactly?"

I paused. "On the reservation. I l...live there with my uncle."

Peggy stopped in the middle of the street we were crossing. She shook her head in disbelief. "I don't understand."

Over burgers and fries and cherry Cokes, I told them about my family. They sat riveted, Chad included, because he'd never heard my complete story.

"D-do you see all those ph-photos?" I asked, gesturing at the framed photos of celebrities ringing the booths. "That's my dad, over there."

Peggy rose from our booth to examine the photo, a replica of the one from the fight poster that Uncle Jack had given me. The rest of us followed.

"You look just like him!" Peggy exclaimed when we returned to the booth. She hunched over the table. "But I still don't get it; I see the Jewish star on his trunks, but 'Mendoza'? Why Mendoza if your family came from England?"

"The Diaspora."

Peggy frowned, uncomprehending. "The Di—what?"

"D-I-A-S-P-O-R-A. In 1492, wh-when Columbus...."

Peggy cut me off. "I know about 1492, Daniel," she said peevishly. With this first flash of impatience, I could feel the beginning of a separation.

"I know you do," I responded, "b-but it was also the time of the Inquisition. Spanish Jews either c-converted or they had to l-leave the country. Th-that's when my ancestors went to France, then sailed for England."

In a hushed voice, Chad asked: "How did Jews get to Spain in the first place?"

I glanced at Peggy. Her expression hadn't changed. "Diaspora." It was all I could think to say. Chad's pained expression signaled he was having difficulty comprehending. "An earlier one, the exile of the Jews around

600 B.C. After the…Babylonians destroyed the temple in Jerusalem."

Chad seemed on the verge of asking another question, but Peggy beat him to it. She glared at me "It's in the Bible, Chad."

"I don't recall reading anything like that in *my* Bible," Chad replied.

Peggy glared at him, too. "The *Old* Testament, Chad. If you went to Catholic school, you'd know all about it." An uncomfortable silence ensued. We finished our meal, but then we argued about how to share the check. Finally, we settled it and left.

Later, alone with Peggy on her front porch, she remained cool. Instead of unscrewing the porch light bulb as was her custom so that we could kiss a long, private goodbye, she let it burn bright.

"I probably won't be seeing you for a while."

My chest tightened. She could read my disappointment.

"It's got nothing to do with tonight. My family is going on summer vacation, to Indian Lake."

"I could hitchhike out to v-visit."

"We'll see. But I'll be involved in a lot of activities my parents want me to do. I'm not going to be that free."

The porch light seemed to grow brighter by the minute. My heart skipped, and my armpits dripped sweat. I could feel our connection wither.

"Next fall, then. I'll see you at the LaSalle game." I smiled wanly, humiliated by her sudden dismissal.

"Right," she said, without brightening, looking at me as if I were standing in her way.

"Okay, g'night," I said, hoping against all hope this final word might soften her.

"Good night," she said and disappeared into the darkened doorway.

Dejected, I turned away and walked down the hill from her house. A breeze carried a sweet scent, but it failed to revive my sunken spirit and through naked tree branches pregnant with buds, a near-full moon glared as bright as Peggy's porchlight. I walked past the bus stop and for block after block until my hips ached, along the same street I'd traveled with Uncle Jack and Jesse three winters ago, all the way to the reservation.

CHAPTER 18

That summer, I resumed my friendship with Sonny and, together, we devoted ourselves to playing with the reservation's Red League lacrosse team. We practiced in the early evenings alongside Jesse and other older players. Sonny and I were coached to work as an attack tandem, with me the feeder, and Sonny the shooter. I enjoyed the concept of team play: blending in, colluding with others in set plays. But there was quite a bit of improvisation, too. Most of all, however, tribal leaders like Jesse played the game as if it were some kind of holy endeavor that might rub off on us younger ones and cure us of our lapses.

Just carrying the ball in this physical game was a challenge. It placed a premium on one's ability to quickly assess situations, change direction, bump or get bumped without having the ball jarred loose, and maneuvering one's stick out of reach of aggressive defenders.

While boxing helped contribute to my agility in positioning my body and moving fluidly in the eddies and swirls of deep play, it was football that prepared me for the fearsome shoulder and forearm contact of Red League lacrosse. The greatest challenge was leaning into a defender at the moment of impact, spinning free, changing direction, sidestepping or leaning into yet another intrepid defender and bounding into a clear spot where I could pass off to Sonny or another shooter.

Defensively, Jesse taught me how to crowd a ball-carrier, poke and slap the man's bottom stick hand and arm, forcing him to move his stick away from his body, then try a dramatic, leaping swipe or wrap to dislodge a ball from deep in the stick's pocket.

I became a good passer, finding Sonny where he stood or leading him as he angled to the crease where he would brake, wheel, and shoot. From the crease, Sonny employed a variety of multiple fakes before shooting: high, low—at the goalie's feet—then high again. He could score at any point in this series of moves, wherever the goalie gave him an opening. Against Cattaragus in July, he used three quick fakes: low, high, and low again, and as their goalie dropped his stick on the last fake, Sonny flipped it nonchalantly over his shoulder.

I developed a powerful underhand shot from outside, but—more frequently—I set up Sonny, skipping and cranking as if to shoot, then, when defenders committed, hitting Sonny through a vacated seam as he darted from behind the goal.

I gained greater confidence during the annual match with the university team, drawing a double-team, then executing passes I'd seen only the best Indian players try. After one face-off, I broke for the goal then skidded to a shooting stance. But when defenders swarmed, I spied Sonny alone behind the goal and passed to him, high. From there he dove into a defender and hooked it one-handed around the front of the goal.

Desperate to score and keyed up after a series of humiliating Iroquois fast-breaks featuring no-look, behind-the-back shots on goal, a university player sprang to his feet after I back-checked him into the boards. He went to slug me, but I leaned back and he sprawled face-first into the dirt.

Then Sonny closed in. He scoop-passed the loose ball to me. I freed myself from a swarm of defenders, spun away, and passed the ball right back to Sonny who snatched it on the run. At their goal, he double-pumped, wheeled, and swept it in under-hand. Off-balance from the second pump-fake, the goalie collapsed in front of the net.

Based on that fluent improvisation, Sonny and I made the trip to Tonawanda to start in our first Red League game.

Their boxed playing field stunned me: a snow fence instead of chicken wire, tacked onto warped, weathered boards which were, in turn, braced by junked cars. These were strewn in angled heaps, like iron tumbleweeds, and players had to climb over rusted hoods and roofs just to get in. My shock was apparent to Jesse. "Aren't you happy to be here?" he asked, grinning. The other players, all of whom cultivated a steep sense of irony, just laughed.

For this game, Jesse outfitted Sonny and me with hard-shelled hockey pads. In addition, he tucked *Life* magazines inside our football rib pads.

Most of the Tonawanda players were older; big men fitted out with hockey pads, too, but, as usual in Red League, none wore helmets and most owned gaps where their front teeth had been knocked out. Before the game, I dosed heavily with heal-all. But it proved harder than ever to avoid these opponents, despite their size. They knew the game and their places in the box and covered space so well that by the end I was exhausted and battered. I lost track of the score. One man who defended me shook my hand afterward. "You take a good beating," he said, smiling, his own face cut and knotted. *Anything for the Great Spirit*, I thought.

Sonny scored three goals, but only one of them came through my assistance. We won, 5-3. Despite the protective padding, I had welts all over my aching body. As I changed into my clothes, someone handed me a locally-brewed beer; it tasted awful, but draining several bottles dulled the pain.

During the long drive home, I wanted badly to sleep, but a heated and prolonged conversation among Jesse and two others kept waking me up. Something about the government having to condemn the homes of 130 families in order to flood 9,000 acres of the Seneca Reservation and build a flood-control dam on just the right spot along the Allegheny River.

Jesse and the other men shared the conviction that the loss of ancestral land and the bulldozing of sacred sites such as cemeteries and the old Cold Springs longhouse by U.S. Army engineers violated the 1794 Canandaigua Treaty with the federal government. They called it "another theft of land" similar to the expropriation of 1,260 acres of Caughnawaga reservation land to begin the St. Lawrence Seaway project. And New York State's expropriation of thousands of square miles of Iroquois land in the central and western parts of the state via treaties that were never confirmed by the federal government.

They vowed to fight it for however long it took. It puzzled me to hear the ex-marine I knew who wore his medals and paraded every Memorial Day speak so vehemently against the government and President Eisenhower as enemy, so willing to fight to thwart its intentions. At one point after that, I slept. But I had a disturbing dream about my father, unique from the repetitive dreams in which he and I were attacked by men in grotesque masks.

In this dream, my father lived apart from my mother, alone, deeply anguished, and worse, inward and mute. When I tried to console him, he silently demurred. Instead, he shot me a look of mistrust. Out of what sense of deep shame or, possibly, disappointment, I couldn't tell. It was a vivid and deeply-troubling dream, and I awoke from it sweating profusely, with a headache, and in greater bodily pain than ever. I passed the remainder of the drive home staring out the side window trying to figure it out, taking in mile after mile of forest and rolling farm land.

For a long time afterward, my fear was that Davey blamed me for everything: death, exile, the end of the family enterprise and his own burning quest. It was a misery I wanted to bury.

The fluency I gained through playing lacrosse, and the physical punishment I absorbed in the process, seemed to beat the stutter out of me. Occasional binges helped to diminish much of the frustration I felt about my dreams, school, constant scrutiny, and the seemingly-willful chasm Yvonne had created between us since the beginning of high school. Avoiding opportunities to spend time with me other than those which were dutiful or ceremonial, she appeared to lose regard for me after the summer of the hobos.

To make matters worse, I was continuously experiencing a yearning as intense as when I worked at Marie's. Almost as if the scant and abbreviated opportunities with Peggy or with drunken women at low-life bars were driving me toward some inevitable breakthrough.

But my hopes weren't high for a true reckoning, confined as I was to the reservation with no telephone, no access to a car. Plotting a seduction eluded me, since I couldn't even figure out what that might entail.

But at a party that Chad hosted toward the end of summer, I vowed to be alert for any opportunity, no matter what. From what most of my age-mates had claimed or implied, I was one of the few who hadn't yet "gone all the way." Chad hung out with a mostly college prep crowd, but he invited a wide circle of friends to his party, both from school and beyond, including a few of us from the reservation.

Yvonne's father drove her to the party just before sunset. I watched her wave goodbye to him then walk tentatively around the side of the house to the backyard, seeking the source of the music and laughter. She wore a ruffled, long-sleeved white blouse and long, tight black skirt, slit along one calf. Beneath a shadowy curtain of bangs, her face was lit with anticipation.

Our party was a first, a celebration of classmates about to enter their junior year. A few of them, like Chad, were already talking about graduation and a college life beyond. Yvonne, too. She had abandoned the home economics track school administrators selected for her, and she aggressively pursued college prep courses, planning to attend an Indian college in Oklahoma. Sonny was ready to drop out now. He wanted to be an artist, keep doing what he was already doing to earn money, only on a grander scale which he hadn't yet determined. He didn't think school was necessary to realize his goal. I was also anticipating the end of school, though for no particular reason other than to be free from classroom humiliation.

Yvonne had always been quiet and studious, absorbing everything, while Sonny and I just went through the motions. Outside of school, she studied ballet at a teacher's home studio just a block from the reservation. But I'd never seen her in this type of situation. Chad was first to spot her, hailing her with a fresh enthusiasm. "Hey, Yvonne, you know everyone, right? C'mon, better get some of this punch before we drain the bowl. Then let's dance!" he exclaimed.

It had been one of those July days when people normally sought shade or just stayed indoors. Chad planned the party with care, knowing he would have the house to himself, that his parents wouldn't be home. On a picnic table, a big block of ice sat in the center of a huge glass bowl that he filled to the brim with a blend of fruit juices and a barely detectable two fifths of vodka. It was so hot and humid and the punch tasted so good, everyone kept re-filling glasses. Within an hour, we'd become transformed, irrepressibly gregarious.

By nightfall, it was still hot, but everyone was loose and dancing. Except me. I could still barely move; it'd been only two days since the game at Tonawanda.

Instead, I stood at the periphery and watched. Yvonne was one of the dancers who knew all the latest steps. When she spun and dipped, her dress accentuated her well-formed legs and she radiated happiness dancing with Chad, mouthing lyrics to every song. Periodically she'd return my gaze and smile. But I assumed a cool distance, sipping my drink with nonchalance at the punchbowl, pondering how to maintain that elusive balance between slaking my thirst and remaining functionally intoxicated. Finally, when Chad went inside to mount a new stack of 45s, Yvonne drifted over. I offered her a glass of punch. She shrank back slightly before accepting it.

"Daniel? Your arms are so black and blue! From Sunday?"

I nodded. "Sore, but I'm feeling no pain."

Yvonne smiled, but her eyes searched mine with suspicion. Nonetheless, she accepted the glass of punch and drank it down, let me refill her her glass, and finished that one, too, innocent of its potency, scrutinizing the patio as a spectator and taken somewhat aback by the growing level of uproar.

"It's too bad you're so beat up; you can't dance!" she shouted.

My pain had begun to fade as the punch kicked in.

"I can dance slow," I said, subduing a sly smile that worked at a corner of my mouth.

Yvonne averted her eyes. In the darkened yard, fireflies flickered against dense, bordering shrubs. She sighed deeply, anxious, it seemed, for Chad to return.

I sighed, too, and ran my gaze from her mascaraed eyes to the beads of perspiration on her upper lip, the pulse at her neck, her arms disapprovingly crossed but pulling the fabric of her blouse tighter against her breasts.

A slow song came on that had been a favorite of Peggy's last spring. I reached out and grasped Yvonne's arm. She stiffened.

"This isn't a church dance," I blurted thickly, unthinking.

Her eyes flashed angrily. "How would I know?"

Most everyone else took the cue from the music and the dimmed patio lights and paired off once again, entwined in each other's arms, with an economy and focus of movement the nuns at All Souls would've never allowed.

I tugged on her arm and Yvonne yielded but kept me at arms' length consistent with our estrangement. When I tried to pull her closer, she tightened her defensive grip on my arms. I winced.

"I'm sorry!" she said, sliding her hands higher to my shoulders, ready to thrust me away at any moment but closing the distance ever so slightly. I loosened my grasp but continued to corral her with footwork. When Chad returned from the other room, he seemed astonished to see Yvonne in my arms.

Gradually our movement became less strained. She took to the intimate suggestion in the lyric of the slow song being played, and then another, from a string of 45s so well-stacked by Chad that no one parted, even during the brief, mechanical segues.

Most of the lyrics contained a desperate, urgent quality made for the moment, a moment Yvonne seemed now willing to accept. I could tell by the way she clung to me, on tiptoe, seeking the same places I sought. Exhilarated, I lost all sensation of pain. The slightest whimper escaped from her but then, alarmed, she pulled away.

I tried coaxing her back, wordlessly. To no avail.

"No. Don't...."

She staggered backward and nearly tripped turning away from my outstretched arms, perplexed at her sudden lack of ability to walk a straight line to the punch bowl. She braced herself against the table and in the process inadvertently kicked something underneath. An empty vodka bottle skittered onto the dance area. Her face flushed with anger. She glanced back at me then retreated into the house toward a telephone, picked it up, then realized there was no one to call. I followed her, regretting an opportunity slipping away, but she ran out the front door. By the time I reached the front lawn, she'd disappeared.

I turned back to the house, to Chad's darkened living room, cursing my bad luck until I realized someone else was in the room, slouched across a big easy chair, smoking a cigarette.

"Hi," the smoker said. "You're Daniel Mendoza, right? My name is Phaedra, Phaedra Moore. I'm a cousin of Chad's. I know you, but you probably don't remember me."

"I can't even see you," I said, deep in my gloom. But I remembered meeting her, with Chad, at a downtown lunch counter. She lived in a section of the city I'd only heard about, Elm Hill; in the fall, she'd be a senior at Central High.

She rose from the chair and walked toward me.

"How long have you been here?" I blurted. "I haven't seen you yet tonight."

I could see her face only when she drew on her cigarette, a sardonic smile.

"I just got here. You leaving already? Looks like you're not having a good time."

I backed away as she took a few steps closer.

"What did you do to chase Yvonne away from the party? It's pretty quiet on that back patio; I didn't hear an argument."

"I don't know…a misunderstanding. We haven't seen each other in a long time."

"I get it: You're in the mood, and she isn't, right?"

I had no answer for her boldness. She laughed.

"I'll dance with you, even though I haven't seen you in a long time."

Her confident, metallic voice with its mocking tone seemed strangely familiar to me. She strode to the patio, waving her cigarette for me to follow. Everything about her was different, including the alluring, leisurely roll of her hips. She wore a form-fitting sleeveless sheath and low heels. Her straight, shiny, blonde hair was cut to just above her shoulders and after she worked her way to the back of the patio and turned and opened her arms, her shrewd grin abated, her knowing eyes closed halfway, and she folded expertly and willingly against me.

Where Yvonne had resisted, Phaedra came so eagerly into my arms that, within seconds after we began to dance, she pushed herself closer, and I felt the filminess of her dress between my legs. Her cheek burned against mine and she began to kiss my neck. No sooner had my lips brushed hers when she opened her mouth and slithered her tongue rhythmically against mine, sending a shock wave through me.

We slow-danced that way for a long time, stopping only when it was certain the music had stopped for good. I realized my eyes had been closed all that time, and when I opened them it was as if I had awakened from a nocturnal dream, too choked from desire to speak. Only three couples remained on the dark patio, pensive, weak with longing. Phaedra broke the silence.

"Why don't we go to the quarry?"

Chad led a caravan of cars to an abandoned, flooded quarry several miles away. I had no idea of the direction or of his intention, locked as I was in a continuous embrace with Phaedra, our hands kneading places of pleasure. The car we were riding in stopped somewhere along a dirt road.

Phaedra led me to a ledge overlooking a large pool. We smoked and drank beer and laughed as first one couple then the rest of us threw off our clothes and plunged into the water. We swam only a few strokes before resuming our dance-embrace. The others stole away among the limestone ledges, but Phaedra led me back to Chad's car. We used my shirt to dry off and I followed her into the back seat. She squirmed onto my lap, kissing my neck and shoulders. She placed my hand on her breasts and began a rhythmic sway, a kind of skirmish, a sequence she commanded which I readily followed.

We could hardly breathe as we finished a long kiss. She sighed and whispered, barely audible.

"Are you ready?"

"Ready?"

I was lost in novice uncertainty.

Later, we all regrouped, collected our clothes, and prepared to leave. Chad and another guy clinked beer bottles in a silent toast of boastful prowess. I could only simulate the cronyism they toasted.

As Chad drove us home, I held Phaedra's hand but she sat apart from me, staring out the window most of the way, lost in thought. When I walked her to the door, I sensed I had let her down and half-expected a rejection scene similar to Peggy's. But she kissed me as intently as the first time.

"Call me some time," she said, smirking masterfully. "We'll try it again."

I nodded, amazed at her bravado, forgetting for the moment that I had no phone, no car. Wondering how, the next time, I could be better prepared, more in command. I didn't know yet; I just wanted it to happen soon.

CHAPTER 19

Under a pre-dawn sky burnished pink, an oppressive humidity smothered the reservation, a carryover from yesterday.

"Wasn't it a great night, Danny?"

Chad took credit for the party and all that had ensued while he steered his sedan along the narrow gravel road to Jesse's cabin, a half-filled beer bottle tucked between his thighs, windows open, the squeal and crunch of his tires rousing nested songbirds. I nodded absently and gazed out my window at clusters of fireflies that flit within the darkest hollows where meadow met forest, corralled by meandering fingers of fog.

The implication was that I had "won my spurs" due largely to Chad's intervention. His braggadocio hadn't waned in the slightest since departing from Phaedra's house a half-hour earlier.

"I can't get over how you two hit it off. You lucky guy; I've had the hots for her since second grade, but somebody's always beaten me to it. I should've figured this would happen. I could tell last winter."

I glanced at him, intrigued.

"You remember? That time we had lunch at Schenker's Café? She stopped paying attention to me the moment you walked in. Not knowing her, you didn't notice. But when you left to go to Nate's, she asked me lots of questions. That is, until she found out where you lived. Having the hots for you is one thing, but Phaedra's a practical girl."

"Of course, maybe all that's changed after tonight and my magic party. Who knows? She's got her eye on you, bud. And now that she can drive her daddy's car, and you phone her like she asks? Maybe she'll make a house call."

Chad laughed, mocking my dilemma.

"Speaking of cousins, what happened to Yvonne? I thought I had it all set to move in on her. I turn my back to stack some records, next thing I know you're bird-doggin' her. Then she runs off, and you're with Phaedra. I had to move fast on Pam Bell; otherwise, I'd have been odd man out. Not good for the host to be solo when everybody else is getting some."

I kept silent, not only about my motivations and actions and errors, but about Chad's intentions. The only way to shut him up, I figured, was to not fill him in on anything he'd missed.

But he persisted. "Oh, Danny, a coupla drinks and you start messin' with your own cousin."

He drained his last beer and placed it clinking against the other empties on the floor in back.

"Hey, how about inviting me in for some of that cowboy coffee you brew up? Fry bread for breakfast."

I begged off. "Uh-uh. Too tired. I'm going to feed the dog and get to bed, sleep late. It'll be quiet today. Jesse's gone to visit his cousin at the Lake reservation for the weekend. To fish."

He was disappointed. He expected me to agree with any caper he imagined: skip school at the drop of a hat, hitchhike to Indian Lake, get drunk, build a bonfire, break into cars and steal blankets and sleep in the sand dunes that hugged the shoreline. He expected every invitation to be irresistible.

What he probably really wanted to do was hang around the cabin, catch a glimpse of Yvonne. Fat chance after last night. Funny how he never mentioned his interest in her before today. I wondered how long he'd been cultivating it, and what kind of confidences he'd never share if he was as desperate as me.

He stopped the car. I got out and trudged up Jesse's path. Despite being tired and hung over, a part of me still clung to the memory of the opportunity Phaedra had presented to me. I felt a reservoir of longing along with a curiosity about her unexpected familiarity. But whether that desire belonged to something in the past or the future, I couldn't tell. I could only hope for further encounters.

Chad's eyes seemed locked on the next pressing issue as he backed into the yard, turned around, and drifted down the rutted gravel road to the highway. The beams from his headlights bobbed against the Council House.

With only a few strides remaining before I reached the cabin, I lifted my gaze from the path and stopped in my tracks. Yvonne was sitting on the porch with Echo, squinting anxiously behind her glasses, wearing shorts and a man's shirt, sleeves rolled up to her elbows, hands clasped tightly about her knees, barefoot. Her worn tennis shoes lay strewn on the landing.

"Where've you been?" she demanded, in a mock scolding tone, signaling, to my amazement, that she was no longer upset with me. I sat on the step next to her and leaned against a railing.

"We stayed late."

"I guessed that, Daniel. Where did you go afterward?"

I stared into the gray dawn, at the mist in the meadow that seemed akin to the stupidity clouding my mind.

"What do you mean...*afterward?* How do you know we went somewhere?"

"I hung around and watched."

I wondered what she had seen.

"We went swimming."

"At the quarry? Skinny-dipping?"

"Yeah."

"With who, Chad?"

"Chad. Pam Bell. Tony Micelli and Louanne. Chad's cousin, Phaedra."

She rolled her eyes.

"You were with her?"

"What do you mean, 'with'? We all just went together."

She looked askance, her glasses catching a glint of pink from the rising sun.

"You were with Phaedra. I know all about her. She had an abortion, you know."

I stood up; her scolding tone had turned authentic, biting too deep.

She buried her face in her hands then straightened and flicked back her mane of hair.

"I'm sorry, Daniel. We hadn't talked in such a long time. Then...last night. Now...I sound stupid...jealous."

I tried to absolve her with the wave of a hand. But to no avail.

"It's not right," she said, seeming to assume all of the blame.

Then her tone became angry, confusing me, breaking new and, I thought, unrelated ground.

"It's not fair. You have the best of both worlds."

To avoid her scrutiny, I began to gather kindling to build a small fire in a dirt pit next to the porch. She continued to scold me as I went into the cabin for matches, coffee and a fire-blackened pot.

"You might as well make some for me; it's almost daylight."

While I primed the pump and drew water, she went on.

"You get to venture out on your own, with Sonny and Chad. You boys. *And* have a good life here. With Jesse as a father when you need one, him and Uncle Abe to make sure things are all right for you. Some of my friends have also become orphans. But they have to live in an institution miles from here, in another world."

I returned to the porch to let the fire burn down to red embers. Not really getting her point.

"I hardly ever leave, except to go to school and to dance lessons. I'm not even allowed to take the bus downtown or do much of anything on my own. The party last night was important to me; the first one, really, of my high school years."

I guessed now she'd changed her mind and I was going to be berated for ruining her evening. But that wasn't it either.

"You can do what you like. But I'm bound by rules.... A lot of rules."

I put the pot of water on the fire and retrieved the wood mugs from inside.

"Do you know why I left the party?"

I shrugged and guessed an answer.

"Because of the spiked punch. Because of...me."

She shook her head, looked down, then back at me. Tears welled in her eyes and she tightened the grip around her knees. My stomach sank.

"Why her and not me? I was so glad to see you.... After such a long time"

Tears spilled effortlessly as she spoke, but her expression remained calm. I'd never seen anyone cry like this before.

"Oh, I hoped we'd dance. Or at least have some kind of reunion.... But you've changed from the boy I knew. You prefer a stranger, that kind of girl, over me."

I looked down, confused by her confession yet ashamed of disappointing the ally who'd most helped me. She was right in a way, but it was even worse because I'd kept cautionary distance from a demanding world ever since I could remember, avoiding proof of trust even before my troubles began. Yet, at Chad's party, there I was ready to take advantage of her. With Phaedra, it didn't matter. She would give me what I wanted without the belief that comes before trust.

Intuitively, Yvonne grabbed my hand.

"No. It's not that. You're still the same.…"

The water in the pot came to a sudden boil, jarring its lid. I slid away and removed it from the fire, throwing in a small handful of coffee to let set for a while.

"It's me. And you don't understand."

I ran my hand through my hair; an uncomfortable tension was becoming almost unbearable.

She confessed now, tears falling. She didn't even bother to remove her glasses, just wiped the tears from her cheeks with the backs of her hands.

"I've loved you so much, but we have no chance." She paused, probably to see if I had anything to say, but nothing was forthcoming. I felt locked and speechless, afraid anything I said would give away my incapacity and another greater betrayal.

"With your people, it's different. There's no restrictions. You had tribes once, but not anymore. You can marry anyone, Jewish or not, even distant cousins."

My mind raced to sort out what she saw in our relationship, what 'cousin' really meant to her over the years of our friendship, which actually had occurred on the cusp of adulthood. And in the ethereal light of morning, there was all this emotion and confusion. Nothing was making sense to me.

"What do you mean, 'marry'…'cousin'?"

"We're cousins because we're in the same *clan*. Cousins from the same clan can't marry. That's why Welcome felt so sure about me. He's not Wolf; he's Eel."

I poured us coffee, using a banged-up strainer to keep out grounds and stirring in honey and canned milk. I took one sip and poured another cup. I couldn't believe how far she'd thought all this through. "Oh, some clan members marry. But not my family. We're very traditional. Orthodox, you might say."

Something compensatory needed to be done or said, but I felt inept.

"That's why I've stayed away from you; why I ran away last night."

Echo rose from the porch and sought Yvonne's lap as she sipped her coffee, relieving me. But I had to say something, something that wouldn't condemn me.

"I thought you were mad because of the punch. Chad spiked it quite a bit."

"Oh, I didn't care about the punch. It was perfect how we met last night...how we danced. I wanted it to last forever. But I got scared."

She put aside the mug of steaming coffee and fanned herself by repeatedly tugging on the front of her shirt.

Echo ambled off the porch but paused and turned his head halfway down the path. "He wants to go for a walk," Yvonne said, urging a smile through her tears, not waiting for a reply, running after him instead. The coffee had revived me, but only reluctantly did I follow them down the path. Echo darted across the road to the dam. By the time Yvonne reached him, he was already barking and lapping at the water, and when I climbed the slate cliff wall, Yvonne was wading in, knee-deep. She looked back briefly to see where I was, then waded in further, to her hips, shirt tails floating behind her like water wings. She looked back again.

"Come on in!" she ordered, in that joking/scolding tone, then held her nose and sank out of sight. I strained to see how far she'd gone under, not really wanting to go in myself, when something else caught my eye through the trees. A patch of man-made color, about 300 yards away. A shirt, somebody moving this way through the field. It was Chad, with Welcome leading the way. Heading toward us.

Yvonne finally surfaced, laughing, holding onto her glasses and pulling her hair back away from her face. The shirt, now translucent, clung to her breasts. They were larger than I'd imagined, and her nipples stood erect.

"Come take my glasses?" she pleaded, holding them out to me. "Keep them for me if you're not coming in?"

"Ssshhh," I whispered. I stepped across the boulders to the lip of the pool to retrieve them, but she switched hands, grabbed me by the wrist, and pulled me in.

I submerged beside her, and when we surfaced, she rose against me, sputtering with laughter until the water had drained from our faces. Drops clung to her eyelashes. Her lips the color of plums. I looked down at her breasts and they rose higher as she climbed into my arms. Just then, Echo barked sharply, once. Voices reached us. Yvonne's arms stiffened.

"Chad and Welcome are heading this way. I saw them through the trees when you first jumped in."

Yvonne began wading toward the bank, glasses clutched in her hand. "I don't want them to see us. Let's go back to the cabin."

If we moved quickly, there would be no trace of us by the time they arrived. Echo seemed to read my mind and dashed ahead of us. When we got to the cabin, I brought the pot of coffee and mugs inside. Yvonne closed the door and ran to the window and peered from behind a curtain.

"They're going for a swim. Welcome has a six-pack of beer."

I took off my wet shirt but stopped when she walked back to the center of the room. The points of her nipples still showed against her clinging cotton shirt.

"Daniel, can you give me something to wear?" she said, shivering. "I'm getting cold.".

I reached beneath my bed and opened the box that contained my father's robe.

"Here. It's silk, but it's big and if you wrap it around you tight and tie it, it'll keep you warm."

From a hook on the wall, I also handed her my towel, and she turned to get out of her wet clothes. I shed my trousers for sweat pants and reached for a towel of Jesse's to dry my hair. But I stole a glance at Yvonne, naked, muscles rippling beneath her browned skin as she placed the wet shirt on the back of a chair and unfurled Davey's robe.

"Oh, this feels fabulous. Daniel, are you sure it's all right?" she asked, tying it close and shaking her wet hair free of the robe's blue-trimmed cowl. She stood looking out the window as she dried her hair and her glasses, putting them on and peering out, carefully, to keep from being seen.

"I don't think they'll come up here," I said. "I told Chad when he dropped me off that I wanted to sleep late and not be bothered. He wouldn't expect to find you here anyway, which is what he really wants."

"I'm not interested in him," she whispered earnestly, turning away and pulling a chair to the hatch-cover table where we'd drank coffee-milk and hot chocolate just a few years ago.

"I'd warm up the coffee for you," I offered, "but the boys would notice smoke and come over here."

She waved me off. "Do you have some wool socks I could wear, Daniel? My feet are still awfully cold."

I withdrew a pair from my stacked storage boxes. She put them on, trying to keep her head erect so the towel would remain wrapped around her head. But as she jammed her toes in the heel of the sock, the towel tumbled to the floor. When we both reached for it, the robe fell open and I could see her breasts, tawny like the rest of her, with small brown nipples.

We stood staring at each other until she untied the robe and stepped closer, mouth defiantly raised. I kissed her, softly at first, then, as she gave way, my kiss became insistent and searching, the way I'd learned last night. She clung tighter and, wordlessly, we staggered to my bed. She took off her glasses, clasped my hands, and sat down, still staring at me. She pulled me close.

"Give me another chance?" she pleaded.

Yvonne began to cry as I took her in my arms and we settled onto my bed and began urgently seeking each other. I held my breath, startled by her emotional outburst but more so by the sound of a car rolling slowly on gravel, pausing, backing up, and halting in front of the cabin, just as Yvonne began to open to me, oblivious.

The car pulled into the yard. I pulled away, rolled off the bed and ran to the window, pulling up my pants. Just past the curtain, a big sedan nosed up to the fire pit. For a tantalizing moment, its windshield caught the glare of the sun, but then the driver's side door swung open.

"What is it, what's going on?" Yvonne exclaimed where she lay, frantically folding and tying the robe back into place. "Is it…? Has Jesse come back?"

"Be quiet," I whispered. A burly man slid out of the car, removed his sunglasses and peered this way. He'd gained considerable weight since I last saw him.

"It's my Uncle Jack."

Panicking, fearful of an embarrassing intrusion, Yvonne sat bolt-upright and swung both feet to the floor. Her wide-eyed stare implored me to take command. But, whether due to my true nature or to some oblique glimpse into a potential change in my destiny, the only response I mustered was to urge her toward the only available exit.

"See if you can climb out the back window."

I peeked again through a gap between sill and curtain. As a dog might, Uncle Jack cocked his head: first right, then left, then at alternating angles, trying to detect signs of life. Here in the middle of nowhere, this time of the morning, I feared that the slightest noise might encourage him to barge right in.

"Hello! Is anybody in here…anybody home?" His booming voice sent shock waves through my gut. Tentatively, he approached the front porch steps, head cocked, eyes squinty, yet confident that someone would be home to answer his call. I stepped away from the curtain, gathered Yvonne's wet clothes and tennis shoes and pulled her toward the window.

"If I don't open the door and stall him a bit," I whispered, he might just...." That was all Yvonne needed to hear. She slipped out of Davey's robe, threw it on the bed and hooked one brown leg through the open sash. I extended a hand to help her; she pushed me away, eyes flashing.

Somehow, she managed to contain her exasperation but hissed one final reproach. "I can climb out; just hand me my things."

Nimbly and delicately, she eased herself down the notched log siding to a bare patch of ground and peered back at me as I leaned to pass her damp, crumpled mound of clothing. Her final look was crimped with anger, shock, and regret, but mostly anger.

A loud knock drew me back into the room. But before I could advance, the door swung open and I stood there, frozen to one spot on the floor, heart pounding in my ears, face burning, weak-legged and bedraggled, tee-shirt half-tucked in, arm pits stained with half-moons of sweat, trying to breathe as if nothing untoward had occurred. But I needn't have worried. To Uncle Jack, the sight of me was all that mattered.

"Daniel!" He crossed the floor and smothered me in a bear-hug embrace. I could barely reciprocate and, instead, tried to get a grip on my rattled emotions and a crisis so mishandled as to probably gain me Yvonne's eternal enmity.

"My God," Uncle Jack marveled, thrusting me to arm's length. "Look how you've grown! You look just like Davey at the same age...."

Then his expression changed, as if he had a second thought. "Did I just wake you? You look like you just hopped out of bed." He didn't wait for my response, just glanced in disbelief around the cabin that always seemed to him so incredibly primitive.

"I almost can't believe you've had to live here for three years! Was it tough for you? Even with the money I sent?"

Before I could answer, he noticed Davey's robe strewn haphazardly on my bed. He walked over, stared at it a for few pensive seconds, lifted it from the rumpled sheets to his face, then cast a glance of wrinkled, puckered disdain my way.

"What's that smell?"

I stood mute, groping for an explanation for so long a time that Uncle Jack just let it pass.

"You been wearing this?" he asked, incredulous.

I shrugged.

"You wanna be careful, Danny, taking the robe out of the garment bag like this. When you take it out, put it on a hanger, and when you're through, put it back in the garment bag. With the mildew in this place, it'll get ruined if you just let it lay around too long." He paused thoughtfully, seeming on the verge of tears.

"It really belongs in a showcase," he said, tremulously.

I improvised, giddy with a dawning lie. "I got it out last night to show a friend of mine, a white guy from school. My, uh, quarterback. He drove me home from a party and stayed for a while. We had coffee…he wanted to try cowboy coffee."

Stupidly, I picked up the fire-blackened pot. "Want some?"

He stared. "'White guy?'" He shook his head. "'White guy?' Jesus Christ, Danny. You been living here way too long."

Saying that to me, so full of implication, swept me from my panicked state like a buoyant wave, lifting me from a storm-tossed sea and onto the shore of a promised land, a situation I'd longed for but which seemed so implausible after years of exile and, with what I'd just done to Yvonne, drowning in disgrace.

Still speechless, I gestured again with the coffee pot.

"Coffee? Forget about it; I'm taking you home for breakfast!"

He cupped my chin in his hand, a gesture Grandfather used on me a long time ago. "You look so good! I can't get over how you've grown! And I swear, you're the spitting image of a teenaged Davey!"

The reunion with Uncle Jack displaced every gloomy thought I'd held about my reservation confinement and my loss of preferred identity that the deaths of Grandfather, my mother, and Davey seemed to make so permanent. In spite of Jesse's and Uncle Abe's best intentions to repair my spirit and teach me devotion in what they perceived to be a sanctuary, I felt more confined than counseled, more palisaded than sheltered, trapped in the old-world orthodoxy they both cherished.

Granted, after all that'd happened, and my deception and lack of heart, exile was what I'd deserved. But before the deaths in my family, deep down, I had believed in a deserved legacy. Since those deaths, however, and because I blamed myself for most of what had happened, I'd doubted that Uncle Jack would ever return, let alone reclaim me.

While I hadn't been completely abandoned, as Yvonne reminded me, I'd certainly felt like I inherited a wretched existence. But now I was thrilled by the portent of change in my fortune; my ship had finally come in.

"I'm home for good now, Danny," he said, confirming to me the promise he made on the last day of *shiva* for my mother and in letters he wrote to Uncle Abe about me.

"I'm glad," I said. "I'd begun to lose hope."

A twig cracked outside the back window, followed by the slight rustling of leaves. A solitary footfall, but nothing more. Uncle Jack didn't even hear her. Had Yvonne overheard this conversation? It really didn't matter now. My life was about to change in a dramatic way: Uncle Jack had returned, and my exile was over.

My mind was already racing ahead in anticipation of escape. Even though Jesse would expect me to remain here at least until Sunday when he would return, I couldn't wait to leave the reservation. Anyway, Jesse must've known Uncle Jack was returning for me; why didn't he tell me?

"Soon as you pack, we can leave. Me and Charlotte and Victor just got back from Brooklyn yesterday; we opened our new house. I'm sorry to get you up so early today, but we're anxious to have you moved in. Charlotte says to tell you, 'We're waiting until Uncle Jack brings you home before we can really celebrate coming back to Brant.'"

Home. This was really going to happen. I really was being reclaimed. Yet, even as I buzzed with elation, I still tamped down my excitement for fear of jeopardizing my good fortune. "But Jesse's gone for the weekend, until Sunday," I revealed. "Shouldn't I at least wait? He expects me to look after things here."

As soon as I said this, I regretted it. Every instinct in me wanted immediate reconciliation; why should I risk losing it out of some sense of loyalty to Jesse?

"Jesse didn't tell you I was coming? Uncle Abe knew; he was supposed to relay the word, get you ready."

"Uncle Abe is in the San again," I said. "For tests. They wanted him to stay over a few days because he's been coughing blood."

He acknowledged with a shrug. "We'll just leave Jesse a note. I passed the state bar exam last week. I got a job with the D.A.'s office here; I'm an assistant prosecutor," he said, self-congratulatory.

This unexpected news excited me. He would pave the way to my legacy, to the life that was promised to me when the family enterprise was poised on the verge of realization.

I could feel Uncle Jack studying me as I stuffed my clothes into Jesse's seabag and gathered up my other belongings, sizing up my potential. When we left the cabin, I didn't even pause to say goodbye to Echo. He merely lay on the porch of the cabin and watched us pack the car, paws crossed, head erect. His usual stoic repose.

CHAPTER 20

I spent the rest of the summer learning how to drive, shopping with Aunt Charlotte for my "new fall wardrobe" and getting used to living with electric lights, a refrigerator, flush toilet, hot running water, washing machine and dryer, garbage disposal, window air conditioning units and a TV which we sat around and watched after dinner. I felt like I'd been ushered out of the Dark Ages and into the civilization where I belonged, a big step up from what I'd previously experienced even on Burt Street so long ago. With new clothes and a haircut and bagels every morning for breakfast, I no longer felt reduced and deprived, and when I looked in the mirror, I no longer saw an Indian face there.

The only drawback seemed to be that I had to share a bedroom with my cousin Victor who resented my presence. He hadn't changed much: still thin, introverted, uncoordinated. On a regular basis, despite his medications, at night or in early morning about every three or four days, Victor suffered epileptic seizures, falling out of bed, writhing on the floor, fists clenched and arms flailing as if fighting demons, a strange noise coming out of him like a truck that wouldn't start. I was trained to look after the poor kid. Mostly that meant covering him with a blanket, checking to see whether or not he was cut or bruised or choking. Ordinarily, when the seizure passed, I'd clean the spittle from his face and neck, carry him to bed and tuck him in. When he awoke and recovered his composure, he got dressed without acknowledging me. I completely understood his embarrassment and how my coming to live with him and sharing his room wasn't such a good deal for either one of us.

Uncle Abe came out of the San later in July, looking wan and pale, relying more on a cane to get around, but with clear lungs. On his birthday, Uncle Jack hosted a cookout in our yard behind the tree-shaded, sprawling brick house, a family picnic. But it was a one-sided affair since Jesse hadn't been invited, and it was just as well for me because I still felt embarrassed by my quick departure.

Driven to our house by Charlotte, Uncle Abe began quarreling almost immediately with Uncle Jack, but out of earshot of the rest of us. A certain tension between them lasted all through dinner and, afterward, he insisted on going home by bus, even though it meant walking to the end-of-the-line shelter a half-mile from the house. He even refused to let me drive him ("It's still Jack's car!"), but he insisted that I accompany him.

A humid haze made the sky one-dimensional, except for a white-hot sun that burned through, baking the newly-paved asphalt road that ran by our house. The sun drew from the paved road waves of shimmering heat; its vapors still reeked of tar which must've seemed suffocating to Uncle Abe.

Stubbornly hostile, his breathing and stride encumbered, he labored to distance himself from the house, pausing to rest only when we were so far from the house that a line of curbside trees blotted it from sight. Then he wiped his brow with a white handkerchief, and when he resumed walking, took hold of my arm the remainder of the way. We passed a firehouse, crossed the road to the bus stop and waited under a dense canopy of twin elms. What was going on, back at the house, between him and Uncle Jack? Once he regained his breath, he had plenty to say.

"I'm not sure it's in your best interests to live with Uncle Jack. If it was up to me, I'd rather you live back at the reservation, with Jesse."

I asked him why. What would be the point? Wasn't I now rescued, as had been originally intended?

"One: Living there would keep you tough and humble, which is where you need to be in order to receive and act on religious instruction. Jack is a totally secular man. You're *Bar Mitzvah*? That's the end as far as he's concerned.

"Two: Jack is disappointed with his own son because there's no opportunity to reflect credit on himself. Your Uncle Jack has a manager's mentality. He basked in your father's limelight, and now he's got you to take his place."

"How?" I asked. "And even if he did, why is that so bad for me?"

Uncle Abe stepped into the road, craning to see if the bus was approaching. It took a while for him to respond, and then I could tell he was reticent.

"Three: Because what's good for him might not necessarily be what's good for you."

I couldn't help but devalue Uncle Abe's concerns about plans Uncle Jack might have for me. After all, wouldn't they be more in line with what was originally expected of me, rather than the kind of tutoring and testing I'd been subjected to? So far I had no complaints. Uncle Jack had been very generous, had made me feel comfortable and at home in what he so obviously considered my deserved place, compensation for my three years on the reservation. I felt like I was on a long-overdue vacation. I didn't even have to mow the lawn; a landscaping crew did the work.

"Out of necessity, you were placed in the hands of religious zealots," Uncle Jack had told me. "Both of them deluded idealists, living in the past, denying the present, as if that was a proper way to build somebody's future. With me, I'll help you obtain what Davey would've wanted for you."

I believed him. Out here where we lived, I was far removed from the fray of pressure, of tests to pass, of fears to motivate me to go beyond mysteriously-ordained thresholds where I felt I didn't want to be. Nothing but the ordered calm of comfortable suburban prosperity, the smell of mowed lawns and newly-paved asphalt, the family's goal attained. At night, out here, even the cicadas sounded relieved. And Uncle Jack was willing to work hard to achieve success for the rest of us. Having him as a benefactor—that's what he called himself—felt to me like a long-delayed victory. Uncle Abe's and Jesse's ways seemed more like a kind of boot camp, with no guarantees of making rank, and advancement was always predicated on sacrifice and based on a principle greater than my own happiness, which to me seemed long overdue.

Uncle Jack quickly won me over when he talked about being self-sufficient and "working the system." He confessed that he really hated the fight game and had chafed under Grandfather's master plan because it meant "going against the grain rather than with it." And those risks far outweighed the rewards.

The first thing he did when he passed the bar was file a civil suit against the estate of Charlotte's obstetrician. As Uncle Jack explained it, the night she'd been admitted to the hospital to give birth to Victor, the doctor was being honored at a retirement party, and he directed that nurses provide her with rectal ether over a 12-hour period, until he could deliver the baby.

After Victor was born, they both remained hospitalized for 12 days. Uncle Jack made the case that rectal ether had caused his son's brain damage and subsequent seizures. He said he stood to win a substantial settlement. In fact, this incident had motivated him to go to law school in the first place, he said. The fruits of this suit's settlement would help make up for the family's tragedy and inability to gain just compensation from an untouchable Raymond DiNardi.

"The world will never change. There's a system that has power over just about everything," he taught me that summer. "And once you learn that you can manipulate it to your advantage, because you have the training to do that, you never buy into anything else. You just play it for what it's worth. For you, personally."

His wisdom mirrored exactly what I'd discovered that night two years ago by the creek, an epiphany perfectly aligned with Uncle Jack's advanced way of thinking, and I looked forward to being the son he always wanted.

I felt sorry for Uncle Abe, leaning heavily on his cane and on his obscure spiritual foundation, waiting spitefully in the oppressive heat for a bus to take him back to his dingy flat, in the same way he waited for the world to be reformed. Still, there was a question I wanted him to answer, too.

"Why didn't you tell Jesse that Uncle Jack was coming back to Brant?"

"I didn't want you to leave; neither did Jesse. But when I got sick and went to the San there wasn't any way to get news to him of the exact date of Jack's arrival."

An empty bus pulled into the roundabout and slowly circled and stopped. The passenger door rattled open. I helped Uncle Abe climb aboard and sat with him while the driver readied for the next round-trip.

"Is Jesse mad at me?"

"No," he replied. "Just disappointed that he doesn't see you anymore. He says your cousins miss you, too. I told him when you learned to drive and got your license you'd come by to visit, maybe even help the team before Red League season is over."

"I don't want to play war anymore, Uncle Abe. Get the crap beat out of me for nothing. I want to enjoy my freedom, at least for the rest of the summer."

Uncle Abe held my hand. "Don't give up the fight, Daniel. You've got a lot of work to do to help make this a better world."

I didn't want to hear anymore about fighting to make a better world, or to hear his and Jesse's justifications for the relationship between the one and the other. Still, I realized I had to let him down gently.

"I'm just not ready now, Uncle Abe. I need some time to think about all this, about what's the right thing to do."

I felt secure in resisting his exhortations to choose the path he wanted me to take, a direction that seemed so contrary to my nature and my best interests.

"Don't put it off too long, Danny," he said with unstinting conviction, releasing my hand and patting me on the leg. "We'll talk more about this when you can come to my place for longer visits. With a little more life experience and instruction, I think you'll come around to make the proper decision about things."

The driver turned to us, ready to depart, and Uncle Abe nudged me to the exit.

"Danny, just remember what Rabbi Hillel said about waiting to get ready to engage correct behavior: 'If not now, when?'"

That night, as I lay in bed in my air-conditioned room, the radio playing low, I could pick up faraway stations, even Philadelphia and West Virginia—jazz and country music at my fingertips. I could call Phaedra on my own phone, and she'd come pick me up. I had never been so satisfied or so filled with expectation.

CHAPTER 21

One evening after dinner, some boys wearing identical blue gym shorts and carrying a football came to the front door. With a flourish, Uncle Jack welcomed them into the house and introduced us—a new set of friends, working-class Jewish athletes from East Brant High School.

Their leader was a senior quarterback, Jacques Lorbeer, short, dark, and wiry, a war refugee from France adopted by one of Uncle Jack's friends, a kosher slaughterhouse butcher. Another was a 6-2 senior lineman, Billy Pearl, whose father was a barber and who was bigger than any high school athlete I'd ever met, probably 250 pounds, with a shy grin and calf muscles that bulged like softballs. If he gained any more weight, his shorts would split. The third was a smirking, burly center/linebacker with a thick neck and sloping shoulders, Freddy Kaplan, who my uncle advised to study pharmacy then take over his father's business. Freddy demurred; he said he wanted to join the Merchant Marine and see the world. Reluctantly, I allowed myself to be delivered into their hands. Uncle Jack beamed like a proud father.

Jacques drove us to a nearby park where he led us in laps and calisthenics. Then we talked, seated in an approximate circle. Or, rather, Jacques queried me while the others listened, evaluating our exchange. He first wanted to know what was it like to have Davey Mendoza for a father and Jesse as an uncle; had I been taught to box, and what was it like to live on an Indian reservation and to play Red League lacrosse. I realized I came equipped with a legend, and that it gave me an instant, first-dose cachet.

Not recalling my presence at the game against them the previous year, he wanted to know my history at Valley Academy. I told him of my futility of "going deep" every day at practices, and about my unimaginative drill-sergeant-for-a-coach. So he tested me short and deep, to each side of the field, nodding emphatically as I jogged back to take yet another of his passes. Soon, other boys drove by, parked, and got out of their cars, enough of them for what I imagined would be a game of touch. But, without any announcement to the contrary, we began a rough-house game of no-pads tackle. I feigned nonchalance and pretended to mimic their level of fool-hardy physicality, the only test that ever mattered.

I made my greatest impression as a receiver. East Brant didn't have one as skilled and agile as I was proving to be, and I comported myself to the best of their wildest expectations, delivering myself to this semitic cohort as my Uncle Jack had most likely promised them: the great Davey Mendoza's boy, his athletic heir-apparent, the prized recruit—a refugee, too, returned from his protective exile.

I out-ran and out-faked anyone who covered me, snaring balls long and short and, afterward, in front of everyone, Jacques praised me, in a nasal European accent that reminded me of my childhood neighbor, Remson.

"Wait'll I tell the coach about you. You'll fit right into our plans."

Jacques revealed that, as fate would have it, several good, key players were transferring from other schools to East Brant, a fine school academically, but at the bottom of the ladder when it came to sports.

"Last year. LaSalle beat us 52-0. Now…? We've got a completely different team. Maybe even give them a run for their money."

I felt put upon, again, to fit in, to rendezvous every evening at the park with these ambitious, aggressive Jews who Uncle Jack praised as "the new generation." Not only were they capable athletes and smart but, like Davey, they were desperate enough to prove their worth through sport and to make it pay off in college scholarships and the possibilities that lay beyond.

Sometimes we ran laps and played football; other times we played basketball or tennis, games I was unfamiliar with, finishing when it got dark when we went to the pharmacy Fred's father owned, straight to the soda fountain for free shakes and ice cream.

I found myself repeating a familiar pattern—doing everything I could to ingratiate myself, using my ability to intuit proper, skilled behavior as I had done in every relationship I could recall, in order to be deemed worthy. And, again, I was a success. They even promised me membership in their Jewish fraternity once school began.

"As an athlete, you'll probably be wooed by the two *goyim* fraternities," Jacques said. "But they'll offer only a 'social membership' because you're a Jew. It's been offered to some; but for us, that's not good enough."

Other days, I caddied with them at a new Jewish country club, a job arranged for all of us by Uncle Jack, who'd become a founding member. We made good money working 36 holes a day, and after work we were allowed a brief swim in the pool.

Nights I could evade them, I spent with Phaedra. We'd go to a drive-in or a country tavern with a big Wurlitzer and dance floor where teenagers were catered to. Or we'd swim at the quarry, capped each time with a bold foray into what I most looked forward to. I became more adept at what she expected of me, more deliberately attentive to giving her pleasure. This gave me stature and continued access. I repressed the obvious—that she had been initiated but abandoned by someone still very much on her mind. And I tamped down the nagging jealousy about being less-admired because being with her allowed me an opportunity to define the imprecise yearnings that haunted me.

I had to ignore Phaedra's moodiness that could come on toward the end of an evening when she would just pull away, satisfied yet sullen, and drive me home, depriving me of our usually steamy farewell. I tolerated her blue moods as just another test to pass. A day or two later, she would phone, drive over to pick me up, as brimming with charm and enthusiasm as ever. The only drawback was her parents' disapproval of me. Her father, one of the most prominent gentile morticians in Brant—an Episcopalian—preferred she not date a Jew. Until now, he was the only man I'd ever met who failed to appreciate that I was my father's son. And even though Phaedra defeated him on that issue, there was always a certain tension in the air on those rare occasions when she brought me to her house.

Then there was Phaedra's mother. In the middle of the third week in August, just before Phaedra's departure for her family's annual Cape Cod vacation, she provoked Phaedra in my presence: was Eric, that nice boy at Princeton, spending summer at the Cape again? Eric, the "legacy enrollee" whose father was a surgeon in New York City?

Phaedra never answered in my presence, but the tactic was discouraging, as if her mother's question and Phaedra's reticence were part of a conspiracy. I spent most of the time she was away yearning for her return. But getting ready for a new football season gave me plenty of distraction. In her absence, I had no excuse to not spend each evening with my ordained companions.

One evening, much to my surprise, Donny Reed showed up at the park, more muscular and grim than ever, chauffeured by a weaselly companion. He stalked onto the basketball court where we were playing. Unshaven, wearing an oil-stained, sleeveless tee-shirt, he didn't want to play, just stand and glare menacingly, his eyes made darker by brows and cheekbones hammered in the forge of fury. Occasionally, he sipped from a small bottle in a brown paper bag, looking somewhat like a vagabond gunfighter entering a frontier saloon. During one full-court fast break, he stepped unexpectedly onto the court and with one hand shoved Jacques off-balance and onto the asphalt. We all stared at him, incredulous. He puffed up and shook a fist.

"I'm patrolling the parks of this city looking for Jews like you," he announced. "Who the fuck gave you permission to play here?"

I couldn't believe his audacity. Was he drunk? Fred was the first to step forward. Reed confronted him, standing within inches, head and chest thrust forward, snarling contemptuously, veins bulging in his neck, fists clenched, daring Fred with insults and curses. Fred glared back, dangerously angry but contained and, without a word, in the middle of Reed's bombastic hectoring, crashed a punch to Reed's jaw, dropping him like a Jewish Paul Bunyon might fell a tree with one mighty swing of his axe. Standing astride Reed, he reached down and grabbed the front of his shirt. He lifted him and punched until blood began to smear Reed's face. The more Reed bled, the greater Fred's rage became, infuriated at this attack on his closest friend.

Jacques and Billy yelled for Fred to stop, and when that failed they rushed in and dragged him away. Then Jacques, in a tone of voice reminiscent of Grandfather when he told off DeYoung's entourage, yelled at Reed's friend, who had backed against the chain-link fence, white-faced and disbelieving, to get him off the court. Reed's skinny friend helped him to his feet and across the street and back into the passenger seat of his chopped, lowered, primer-coated '49 Ford, then drove away.

"Where'd he come from?" Jacques asked. "Anybody know that guy?"

I told Jacques about him: the bully of Valley Academy, conveniently leaving out, of course, the anecdote about my own cowardly encounter. He just shook his head.

"Demented shmuck. Imagine; he'd try that with Fred and Billy and you here." Then he barked instructions and the game resumed as if this momentous drama had been nothing at all. An aura of trust permeated the basketball court the rest of the game; they carried a genuine personal sovereignty that I could only pretend. I hoped with a fervor very close to prayer that circumstances would never unmask my real condition.

One Friday night when the boys came to pick me up, we went to the house of someone I'd never met before. His name sounded familiar—Prado—but it didn't really sink in who he was until I entered his living room and noticed family photos displayed on various tables and a fireplace mantle. His father was Max Prado, one of the contractors who'd attended Davey's final sparring session and who faced off against DiNardi's men; his mother was Sarah, the statuesque, peroxide-blonde who I'd met that day and who sat next to me the day of my mother's funeral.

Prado—his first name was Robbie—led us into a dining room lit by an overhead chandelier. A large, polished wood table was laid out for playing cards.

"You play poker?" Jacques asked me.

"I only watched card games at home, at my father's house. And they only played pinnochle."

Prado asked who I was. When Jacques introduced me, Prado's eyes got big, then narrowed.

"I always wondered whatever happened to you. I remember you from the Boy's Club. I was at your *Bar Mitzvah*. My dad played pinnochle with your father. We're actually distant cousins."

He looked me over, approvingly.

"I hear you're gonna play for East Brant this year.... You're transferring?"

I nodded modestly.

"So, where have you been the past three years? My parents said we weren't supposed to talk about it."

I told him that I lived on the Iroquois reservation the past three and a half years, for protection, with one of my mother's relatives.

"Out of touch, man!" he said, inflecting like a Negro, making me wonder if he'd somehow also met the slang-talking Sugar Ray. "Where you living at now?"

"With my Uncle Jack. He just got back from Brooklyn where he went to law school. Now he's got a job in the D.A.'s office."

Prado nodded approvingly.

Jacques sat at the head of the table.

"Alright already, let's start. Mendoza, you can learn by watching. This is serious poker. You got any money?"

Totally unprepared, I shook my head. I'd thought we were going to the park. I never carried more than $5 in my wallet. Everything I earned caddying went into a bank account. When he knew I had a date with Phaedra, Uncle Jack would peel off a few dollar bills, but only enough to pay for a movie, a couple of cokes, popcorn, or burgers and fries afterward. If we went to the country tavern to dance, Phaedra would pay for our drinks.

"Where's your mother and father?" I asked Prado.

He laughed. "My father has a card game of his own; he'll be out all night. My mother tends bar on Fridays; she won't be home until real late, like 3 or 4 in the morning."

He joined the other boys setting up chairs around the table as Jacques took charge, telling everyone where to sit. I was placed at one end, next to Prado. As he pulled out a wad of bills to pay Jacques to distribute chips and to deal the first hand of cards, I blurted out: "Your mother tends bar?"

I couldn't imagine the elegant, statuesque Sarah working behind a bar, at least the bars I'd known.

"It's my father's place, Café Jake," said Prado, fanning his cards. "But my mother runs it."

"Where's Café Jake?" I'd never heard of it. "And why the name 'Jake'? That's not your father's name."

"You wouldn't have heard of it," Jacques announced. "It's a *schvartzer* bar on South Lafayette Street, about eight blocks from the city center, in the heart of the ghetto."

"And 'Jake' is a liquor made from Jamaican ginger," Prado added. "It's also a Negro slang word; it means how you get paralyzed from drinking." He smiled at the logic of it.

Jacques chimed in again, in a joking way, as if to mock Prado, but also to show his awareness.

"You take your life in your hands if you go down there."

"C'mon, it's not that bad," Prado protested. "Granted, there's a scuffle every now and then, but if you want to hear the greatest music in the city, you gotta come. My mother's partner, Eugene? If he knows you're good people he'll take care of you."

Jacques, this time needling me, said, "You think Nate's pool hall and The Open Door and those joints you been to downtown are something? Wait'll you see Jake's."

"When do you go there?" I asked, bored with the prospect of watching a card game but curious about seeing Sarah again behind her own bar. "Weekends?"

"Hardly ever!" Fred volunteered, laughing, asking for more cards.

"Okay, Mendoza; forget about Café Jake," Jacques ordered. "I'm teaching you how to play poker."

But once the boys began to play in earnest, my tutorial was over. It was too distracting to them to explain hands when the point was stealth and concealment.

I watched but ignored the mechanics of the game; only their interaction held my attention, taking me back to Burt Street: a lot of joking, bragging, and story-telling. But with the money involved, there was also a serious, competitive quality I'd never noticed at home, where a card game was a distraction from the everyday business of training. Soon I became a non-entity, so I wandered into the kitchen. At one end of a counter top were piled bags of popcorn, potato chips, pretzels, and peanuts-in-the-shell. Reflexively, I opened them all and placed large portions into plastic bowls I found in the cupboard.

I opened Prado's refrigerator and searched through the remaining cabinets, then returned to the archway that led back to the dining room.

"Are you guys thirsty or hungry?"

That drew a jubilant response, but no one wanted to think hard about preferences or move out of their chairs, so I brought out the bowls, glasses filled with ice and a wide tin tray containing bottles of various sodas and a pitcher of iced tea that had been sitting in the refrigerator. It was surprising to see everyone smoking cigarettes, although without the practiced nonchalance of the guys at Nate's. Jacques pretended to inhale, puffing his cheeks after a shallow drag and carefully blowing the smoke overhead. Freddy whooped with joy. He won the first hand.

I turned the knob on a large, square window fan and watched it draw away their pall of smoke. The conversation eventually turned to the purpose of the card game, winning money. It astounded me to watch several pots build up to nearly $30. I also learned that Jacques and Fred had older brothers, college students, who were working that summer at Catskill resort hotels. Between their earnings and playing cards with well-heeled guests, they'd impressed, they'd won enough money to join a stocks-trading club. I was surprised how much Jacques and Fred and Prado knew about ways to make money grow, including buying gold. And they all joked about the primary advice their fathers had given them about moving up in the world: marry a rich girl. Finally, I fell asleep on a couch in the living room until Jacques, a grin splitting his face, woke me. It was 2 a.m. The bulge of bills in his front pocket was twice as large as when he'd arrived.

CHAPTER 22

The following Friday marked the beginning of the final weekend of Phaedra's Cape Cod vacation and the end of the summer. Monday, I'd begin pre-season football training. Jacques and Fred drove south for one last spurt of vacation and to visit their brothers. I was at loose ends until Prado phoned me in the afternoon.

"Hey, Daniel; wanna have one last fling before the torture begins? Come down to Café Jake with me tonight; we'll have a real good time."

He said since the band didn't even begin to play until the Negroes came out, around 11 p.m., we could go downtown, see a movie, grab a snack, and shoot pool at Nate's.

After our last game, we washed up, combed our hair, and walked the mile and a half into the heart of the East Side ghetto. Prado called it "The Ward." He reminded me that it used to be part of the Jewish neighborhood, like Burt Street.

It was still hot and humid at 11 p.m. When we arrived at Café Jake, a group of well-dressed men and women were lounging outside a lit-up, raucous bar—a simple one-story square-brick structure with a flat roof, inconspicuous neon sign, and small rectangular windows along the front and side. I got the impression that a lot of people must've walked here from their homes because there was plenty of empty space in the back parking lot and along the streets nearby. During the time we stood in front, several taxis pulled up, discharging more well-dressed patrons. Most of the men wore high-waisted, pressed slacks and short-sleeved dress shirts or colorful suits and expensive shoes. The women wore patent leather high-heeled pumps and party dresses.

We walked around back to a door Prado had a key for. When we entered, the place was smoke-filled but lit as bright as a school room, and people shouted and laughed and argued while a four-piece band on an elevated stage played with a gusto and expertise that was thrilling. I'd never heard a live rhythm and blues band, nor had I heard the kind of music these men created: sassy, syncopated, joyful. And they weren't even professionals; the leader worked for the city's sanitation department and all the others had full-time jobs. But they were on fire and perfectly synchronous and it was contagious; the patrons were already in a delirious state of celebration, consuming beer and liquor in every variety of concoction and color and glass imaginable.

Sarah worked the three-sided bar with a tall, slender, scowling Negro man who paced and served drinks in front of a huge shelf-mound of liquor bottles—a tabernacle of various hues and colors, all back-lit. Sarah barely had time to look beyond the customers who sat and stood two-and three-deep shouting drink requests that punctuated several decibels above the crowd noise and music.

Everybody seemed to know young Prado and shouted greetings to him. Some men slapped his hand in a kind of handshake I'd never seen before. A waiter named Wilbert brought us short-necked baby bottles of beer—Champale—which he covered with over-turned glasses still dripping from the wash. He served us at a half-circle booth near where we entered, jammed in with four other people, exactly diagonal to and hidden from the front door.

"Keep low," Wilbert warned. "If the police looks in, they won't see you."

The Tippin' Inn, the only Negro bar I'd previously visited with Sonny and Sugar Ray, was positively staid compared to Café Jake. And while The Open Door had a level of excitement at peak hours when the juke box roared and the bartender played spoons on the bottles, Café Jake was a unique experience. The place reverberated with an energy and noise that was like being inside of a big, unruly bus hurtling down a highway, too crowded to even dance. The booth was actually the best place to be because people on the floor bobbed and bumped so recklessly that novices to the club were stalled in their tracks or pushed into a corner or out the door.

I craned to get a look at the band I'd heard so much about: Si Simpson and the All Stars, three men in dark suits playing organ, sax, and drums, swaying with verve and passion, their ebony faces shining with sweat. A guest musician, a guitarist, sat in front, poised on a stool, playing with a saintly smile.

Suddenly a dark, slender woman with close-cropped hair and ruby-red lipstick blocked my view. She waved and pushed closer through the sea of bodies, smiling brightly and looking directly at me.

It was Frankie, the woman I worked with in the basement of Marie's lingerie shop. She pulled me to my feet and gave me a big hug. I looked around, embarrassed, but nobody seemed to notice.

She stepped back, holding me at arm's length, gripping tightly, looking me up and down, then circled me as if I were the subject of an audition.

"Look at you!" she shouted. "A big boy now. I seen you the minute you come in with Prado. Took me all this time just to get over here. How you doin', honey!"

Just then, one couple got up from our booth and snaked their way toward the bandstand. Frankie pushed Prado and me back into the booth. Her almond-shaped eyes gleamed. There was something there, a glassy intoxication, but her movement and speech were precise, something I'd never seen before.

When I asked her if she was still working at the store, she flashed a look of disgust.

"Nah. I got me a department store job now. Still workin' in the basement doin' stock, but...." Her eyes rolled. It was unimportant compared to the moment and she talked to me like a long-lost friend, through several rounds of drinks and into the band's first break when we didn't have to shout anymore.

A steady stream of men and women passed us on their way to the bathrooms and exits. Frankie held my arm, but no one paid us any attention. Then she jerked a look toward the patrons filing rapidly outside. A woman was waving.

"Listen, honey, I got to go outside for a while. Someone I got to talk to. But save me a seat; I'll be back for the second set."

She left, the last one of about three-quarters of the crowd to squeeze out the door. I went to the bathroom. On the way back to our table, Sarah stepped from behind the bar, pushing a loose strand of hair back into a tightly-piled French twist. Her greeting mimicked Frankie's: surprised to see me, scrutinizing me, a big hug. She introduced me to Eugene, her partner, and his face opened into a grin for the first time since I'd seen him.

Again, the value of being my father's son was all I needed to make a good impression.

But Sarah lectured. "No more Champale for you or Robbie. You can stay and listen to the music, but from now on it's only ginger ale."

Sarah and Eugene returned to the bar where they began washing dozens of glasses for the second set's customers and re-stocking beer into the cooler. She handed me four quarters for the juke box and a list.

"Play these for me, will you, dear?"

By the time her songs ended, the musicians filed back into the bar, followed by a stream of old and new patrons just as lively and excited as before. Frankie entered, too, with a young couple in tow whose smiles seemed just as bright as hers. They elbowed their way back to our corner booth.

"Remember these guys?" Frankie asked.

I studied their faces: a guy somewhat older than me, darkly hand-some, with a prominent jaw and pouting mouth and the brow of a boxer, and a younger girl whose mocha-toned face was framed by straight, sleek hair that fell in bangs to her eyebrows. Except for the difference in skin tone, they looked enough alike to be brother and sister and, in fact, they were.

"Brenda and Lonny Starr. You remember them," Frankie insisted. "They lived across from you on Burt Street."

Lonnie's smile softened.

"Last time we seen you it was winter. Three years ago. You was leaving home wit' a police."

"Never to return," Brenda added. "Cousins of ours bought the house from your uncle."

An image of the two of them standing downcast in a freezing wind saying goodbye to me because their father had died only a few months before brought back a moment in time, incongruous with the nearly-hysterical gaiety of the present. Excited to see me, they shook my hand across the table, and Wilbert brought a fresh round of drinks. We owned the booth and as the band struck up another set, we reminisced about our old neighborhood. Sweat dripped from my armpits with the excitement of this improbable reunion, so far from my most recent worlds.

When the band finished their second raucous set, Frankie leaned closer.

""Let's go over to my place, make our own party."

In order to get there, Sarah generously let Prado use her car, consider-ing he'd been licensed only three months. Eugene would drive her home, she said. But she was eye-to-eye frank with Robbie regarding its return.

"Just come home at a reasonable hour. I want you in bed before daybreak. And no alcohol. Promise me."

I couldn't believe how liberal she was. Uncle Jack wouldn't even let me drive alone during daylight hours. Of course, I had only a junior driver's license, but still.

The five of us piled into Sarah's car, a big Olds like Uncle Jack's, and Prado drove toward my old neighborhood. Frankie lived a few blocks east of Burt Street in a downstairs flat she shared with her mother, who was herself arriving back from her night on the town with several friends bearing large containers of barbecue pork ribs and chicken, potato salad, and jello laced with marshmallows. It was agreed that she and her friends would confine their revelry to the kitchen, and we could take over the living room where stacks of 45s lay waiting to be put to good use. But if we wanted food, she said, come back down the hallway and help ourselves.

"Just be willin' to share what you-all got," she said, laughing and flashing us a knowing look.

After Frankie stacked records and set the turntable in motion, she sat on the edge of a davenport and pulled a small container from her handbag which she emptied onto a coffee table. Pinching from a small pile of what looked like shredded tobacco, she dropped a thin line onto a sheet of cigarette paper and rolled it in a way I'd seen done only in cowboy movies. My first reaction was that making cigarettes this way was unnecessarily primitive and time-consuming. But she painstakingly repeated this task, then licked each thin, finished cigarette and laid them on the table to dry.

Prado pulled my head to his and whispered emphatically. "I told you we'd have us a great celebration."

A wry, knowing smile spread across his face that accelerated into a high-pitched cackle.

"Why smoke these kind of cigarettes," I asked, "when there's an unopened carton of Pall Malls on the table over there."

Lonnie slapped me on the back. "Because this ain't no cigarette, man; this here is *boo*."

Brenda took one, lit it, took a big drag and, without exhaling, passed it to Frankie.

We all sat cross-legged on the floor near the coffee table. Robbie leaned to snatch the cigarette from Frankie, took a deep drag then passed it on to me. But I couldn't manage the pass, and it fell onto the carpet.

"C'mon honey," Frankie said, passing me a new cigarette and lighting it for me. "S'gonna take you a while to get the hang of it. Me and you'll split this one."

From its smoldering tip, a spiraling filament of smoke floated lazily toward me. It smelled pungent, like burning grass.

"Don't take too big a hit," she cautioned, speaking in a pinched whisper as she held her breath. "Otherwise it'll make you cough. And what you take, keep it all in. That's what gets you high, keepin' it all in."

I glanced at Prado, his grin now slightly askew.

As directed, I took a modulated drag, a slight inhale, but even that had me coughing and, within a few minutes, Frankie had three cigarettes circulating, each supplanting the previously-lit one. When we finished, I didn't really feel anything like what I was expecting. But there was no time to judge because music started to play and the girls stood up to dance.

During the first slow song, Frankie folded into my arms and buried her cheek in my neck. I closed my eyes and moved with her and began to feel an elation I'd never felt before.

Frankie's mother and friends and a white girl, blonde and lanky who, like Prado, spoke in slang and with a Negro inflection, joined us and we began a kind of spontaneous trading of partners. All of the women who danced with me held me the same way, earnest and provocative but in a way that was more integral to the style of dance than amorous. And, after awhile, I followed them into the kitchen to devour the leftover barbecue with an astoundingly-heightened sense of taste until it was finished and the sauce all mopped up with bread. Then we moseyed back into the living room for coffee and cigarettes and subdued conversation that just picked up where we'd left it at Café Jake.

Brenda and Lonnie pressed me about the deaths and exile on the reservation I'd experienced, and they also revealed more about their father. He'd owned an after-hours club—Midgie's—featuring dancing to recorded music and, sometimes, live bands on weekends. But his mainstay was running a numbers operation and managing a network of card rooms around the East Side ghetto. They said he was considered a big man in the community, a prudent manager of his businesses and well-liked, even idolized, for his unique success, stylish apparel, pale yellow Cadillac, personal magnetism and generosity, who only occasionally had to be ruthless in response to some rare betrayal and, then, only with his fists.

There were, they said, no long-held grudges, no competitors, no rivals angling for his businesses before he was shot down in the street after closing the club early one Sunday morning. The police investigation into his murder proved just as frustrating and inconclusive to their family as the one involving mine. Their mother now ran the club on weekends, with the help of some friends, but it brought in barely enough to pay living expenses and rent. Brenda lived a couple of blocks away, with an infant daughter, on welfare, in a two-bedroom subsidized apartment. Lonnie had just begun to box professionally as a middleweight, training at a small, storefront gym in the neighborhood. He lived with his girlfriend and their child in the same subsidized project as Brenda.

"So, who runs the other family businesses now?" I asked.

"Raymond DiNardi," Mrs. Starr said, without a trace of bitterness or loss. "He got the whole city action now."

A knot formed in my stomach.

They shared their stories with me as matter-of-fact rather than melodrama, as if fate had dealt them not unexpected hands. They were all on their own now, and Brenda and Lonnie, at 16 and 17, had to make it as best they could. I wondered how they could celebrate with such abandon.

Later, at home laying in bed in a dream-like state, listening to early birds sing and watching the gray light of dawn break outside my window, I marveled how smoking their stuff had affected me.

For one thing, I'd momentarily lost all anxiety—that over-alert state I seemed always to operate within.

Then at Frankie's house, I really felt like there was nothing external to distract me, no sense of fault or vulnerability, and I really heard everyone's story and the significance of some record lyrics that previously hadn't ever seemed profound.

My stammer, which had already receded, completely disappeared as every speech and every scenario seemed to slow down. And deep within, displacing every anxious edge, I felt a sense of astonishment.

The shared ritual of smoking went way beyond the camaraderie of a drinking experience; I felt somehow wedded to everyone—sharing a secret, a desire, and a feeling that all hurtful debts had been satisfied.

And during all that time not even Phaedra entered my mind. And I began to wonder, before sleep and memory overtook me, just what kind of chance I had in my new world to enter into that state again.

CHAPTER 23

By the next morning, chance became a non-issue. Even before I finished my coffee, a car horn sounded from the street. There, sitting in a bright-red 1939 Chevy coupe convertible, brimming with bravado, sat Jacques, Billy, Fred, and Prado.

"Come on, Mendoza!" Jacques, the driver, yelled. "Today's the day you pay for your misdeeds!"

I knew he meant my so-called wild weekend, but a second meaning held more sway with me. I grabbed a banana and my football cleats, said goodbye to Aunt Charlotte who glowed with satisfaction at my new life and her role in securing it, and slid into Jacques' back seat.

I was the last of the boys to be picked up because Uncle Jack's house lay on the farthest outskirt of the city, at the end of a radius marking the range of social classes among Jews on the East Side. Jacques had first called for Billy, who lived across the street from him in an identical two-family house just seven blocks past Café Jake. Fred was next, nine blocks farther out. He lived in an apartment above his father's two-chair barber shop. And two miles beyond, next-to-last, was Prado, whose father had recently built a Spanish-style bungalow on a vacant lot just inside city limits.

From Uncle Jack's house, we drove through tranquil, hilly, suburban streets shaded by giant elms, maples and occasional weeping willows. I was glad for the breeze that riffled through my hair because already the sun was hot, and this would be my last respite before the first grueling morning practice of a double session pre-season training camp.

Racing the engine and double-clutching, Jacques turned abruptly, causing the back-end of the jalopy to drift into position before the driveway of the expansive East Brant High School parking lot. He down-shifted to first gear, revved one final time, popped the clutch, screeched toward an open parking spot, slammed on the brakes and skidded to a ceremonious halt before a half-dozen cheering teammates trudging up a trail to a bluff behind the school. There, on a perfectly-manicured practice field, clusters of boys meandered among blocking sleds and tackling dummies. Others played catch. A handful—rookies and low-down subs—sat pensively along a low-slung wooden bench.

Due to coffee and a case of nerves, my bladder felt ready to burst. Inside the school, once my eyes adjusted to the dark, cool corridor, I strolled past a spare, pathetic trophy case with carefully-spaced bronze plaques for cross-country, tennis, and soccer teams, and pushed through a swinging door into the boys' lavatory. I was the only one there, and the only sound was that of my steady stream against the porcelain urinal.

It was only after I finished that I became aware of adult male voices speaking from the other side of the wall. I stood quietly and listened. Two coaches were talking, appraising the team's potential. One voice sounded familiar.

"...well, Frank, as you say, you're set at several positions. No doubt Jacques will be a great quarterback this year. He's a natural field general: quarterback, point guard on the basketball team, third baseman in baseball.... He barks orders like a drill instructor and the others love him."

"Right," a deeper voice replied. "I've taught him a lot, but he brings stuff you can't teach. He knows how to lead, how to inspire, how to intimidate to make things happen."

"Then you've got those two transfers from out-of-county schools," the other coach said. "Big, experienced linemen. And the bruiser from Scranton who's used to playing before crowds of 10,000."

"They'll definitely take the pressure off Billy and free Fred to roam and plug the secondary. He's a real hammer, that kid. I'm looking for him to have a banner year. But, tell me, what about that junior from Valley Academy, the one Jacques is high on, what's his name...?"

"Mendoza.... Danny. He's a good one, considering what he's been through, losing his family and all. You remember, the boxer's boy?"

I imagined the other coach nodding thoughtfully.

"He's the one who'll take the pressure off your fullback, Cerio. He's

fast, has great hands, and can really take off and run with the ball once
he's in the open field. Now you've got a real good target for your passing
game. He's a tough kid, too. Played Red League lacrosse for the reservation team. Best of all, he's settled back in with his family, his uncle. Good
people. He should really blossom now, after all that adversity."

I finally recognized the tone and cadence of that voice, the way he
knew me. It was Joe Acquilino.

"This could be the year I've been waiting for!" said the other coach.
"I'm so glad you're here to help."

On the field, the coach called all the players and candidates around.
Mr. Federov was a calm, reasonable-sounding man compared to the tyrant
who was my last coach, and he was gracious enough to take into account
last year's veterans who he introduced, along with his new assistant, Mr.
Acquilino. He praised their 5-3 record, the best in recent school history.

Then he shifted his stance. "I don't want to dwell on our losses—most
of them came against tough teams, and we played them close."

Then his face darkened. He raised his voice, inserting a tone of
disgust. "But that 52-0 debacle at the hands of LaSalle! That was abso-
lutely unacceptable."

Players stared gloomily at their feet as he resurrected their inglorious
past.

"I still don't know why—we had success against some pretty good
teams, and we finished tied for second place in the conference. Maybe
you let their record cow you into submission. Seven city championships
and 49 straight wins.... OK, that's impressive. But, believe me, fellows,
they're only flesh and blood, just like you. And God, contrary to what
some may think, is not on their side!"

This last remark, while spoken in sarcasm, caused Fred to drop to one
knee and slam his helmet into the turf. Something deep and humiliating
was gnawing at him.

"I don't want to say anything more about that now," Mr. Federov
said. "But I do want to remind you that you can be a very capable team. I
won't single anyone out right now, but we've been blessed by the addition
of several transfers who're probably going to start. We could be the surprise
team of the conference."

Here, the coach launched into an "adversity-builds-character"
speech, how important it was not to wilt in the us-against-them test, taking
on, again, those teams we'd beaten and, ultimately, defeating even the best.
He closed by telling a war story, in a voice constrained by emotion but
pregnant with implication regarding the sacred relationship of sport to

life, about racing across a deserted air-strip on Tarawa with what was left of his Marine Corps platoon, just seconds ahead of the pursuing enemy. Exhausted, without food or water or ammo, out-running the Japs until they reached a drainage ditch, met reinforcements, had barely enough time to re-load and fix bayonets and turn the tide.

"Remember, boys, the average man runs until his breath gives out...."

His voice caught and dimmed before the punchline, and we strained to listen

"...but the champion never quits."

He might not have been a tyrant, but such heart-felt expectations made my heart sink. I would have to proceed with extra caution, more than ever before.

I made it through that day and the grueling weeks that followed, shining when I wanted, dogging it when possible, willing to be a pass-receiving end who team-blocked with Billy on off-tackle slants and shielding running lanes past the line of scrimmage, but laying off on defense and letting another player, a stolid senior who attended the same church as Mr. Federov, assume that task. I was, after all, a junior, excelling at a part-time job, placating everyone.

Only Phaedra was unhappy with me. She'd returned from Cape Cod moodier and more discontented than ever, willing to give me only one night a weekend, claiming she had to study harder during this final year if she was to get good enough grades to be accepted to Wellesley: what her parents wanted. Like a fighter in training, she maintained an incorruptible distance. The fact that her car was being repaired made it even more difficult, so after practice one Saturday, I took a bus to her house.

She met me outside and suggested we walk to a park in her neighborhood, a long, exhausting walk that had an air of finality to it, as gloomy as the gray flotilla of clouds that crowded overhead. I tried to steer her toward conversation that might draw her out of her indifference, but Phaedra seemed intent on smothering every one of my attempts.

Fortunately for me, a timely thunderstorm intervened, catching us exposed on a hillside meadow, and we had to run all the way back to her house for our only real cover. No one was home. Wordlessly, she led me upstairs, first to a linen closet stacked with bath towels, then to her bedroom where first Phaedra, then I, stripped off our cold, wet clothes. In the near-dark, she came into my arms. Our towels slid to the floor, and we moved together in an erotic dance.

After the past week, during what seemed like an interminable denial, her new-found willingness jolted me like an electric current, and the familiarity of her scent and whispered implorings thrilled me. Her hands swept over me, searching, reassuring. When she reached my chest, I let out an audible moan, overjoyed with expectation. Then suddenly I staggered backward in pain, as if stabbed, when she pinched and twisted one of my nipples. I blocked her arms and cupped my hands protectively.

"Hey!"

She quickly retreated, walked into the hallway, stopped and looked back. I could see only her silhouette. From an overhead skylight, swiftly-moving storm clouds created patterns over her body that made her seem to disappear then become whole again, and in a moment of complete clarity her face came into view, a mask that conveyed both contempt and conniving invitation.

A chill ran down my spine that made me shudder. She laughed and beckoned with an outstretched arm. I followed her into the hallway, entranced by the patterns of light and shade that danced over her body. Wordlessly, she welcomed me into her arms again, into the heat and dampness of her body.

We kissed and resumed the nuance of enrapture, gently at first then gathering a momentum that reached the brink of incaution made even more precarious when Phaedra hooked a leg around me. I reached behind her to steady us against the wall, to keep us from tumbling to the floor. Instead, she pulled backward so that she thudded into it, crying out in pleasure. Astounded, I tore from her grasp, and she embraced herself in a paroxysm of ecstasy.

I waited until enough of the moment had passed then reached out to her. But instead of acquiescing, she kneed me on the point of my thigh. I rolled away, doubled over in a blinding flash of pain. She tore her fingernails down the length of my back, ran to her parents' bedroom and stopped just inside the doorway.

The lights had been turned on in that room and in contrast to the shadowy gloom where she had staged this dance-skirmish these lights burned with an acute vivacity like spotlights on a stage. Blue-black bruises covered Phaedra's belly and hips. She turned. More bruises marked her back, below a tan line.

"How did you get so…beat up?"

She wouldn't respond except for a peculiar, defiant smile, and she crossed the floor, past an unmade bed and stood with her back against a wall, her arms outstretched in supplication. This time I didn't respond. She moved away from the wall and disappeared from view. I waited, confused, filled with trepidation that I was witnessing a transformation I wouldn't be able to accommodate. Suddenly she appeared again, in the same place, wearing a pale blue silk robe, applying a lustrous pink lipstick with one hand and touching herself with the other. I edged closer to the room, alert for any sounds of an approaching car, doors slamming, or footsteps on the stairs, but hearing only the crash of thunder and wind-driven rain raging against a window.

Hostility borne of frustration welled up inside of me. She smiled provocatively. "Don't be mad at me. Just come here. I'll give you what you want."

She was taunting me, taking pleasure in my confusion and disadvantage, rousing my anger to the surface, to a point of danger. But this was what she wanted, and as I crossed the room her eyebrows lifted with a dare, knowing she could shape my anger into a force of her own.

When I confronted her, she pulled me against the wall, pulling and thrusting against me and I thrust back, driving her into the wall, searching, frenzied, until I entered her and then impelling the breath out of her with each thrust, rocking and shouting until she cried out at the point of no return where she had led me so many times before. For the first time she was ahead of me. Her legs slid off me, and she slumped, scraping against the wall, to the floor. She pulled me down beside her—battered, bruised, lipstick smeared, but exultant.

Breathless, she could hardly speak. "Now you know."

"Know? Know what?"

"Who I am, what I like."

I rolled away from her and flung an arm over my eyes, to cover myself, to hide, my mind racing to cope with an alien mix of emotions, of torment and desire, empowerment and repulsion.

Without an awareness of her, I felt the pressure of her hands, wanting me to follow her lead, savoring me. And then Phaedra sat astride me, rocking gently. I opened my eyes. Tears streamed down her cheeks and splashed on my face and chest, bringing me to where she had just been, crooning, crying, choked with remorse.

"Oh, Danny...you're so good, you're so good."

I carried her back into her room where we lay together in her bed for a long time in the dark, listening to the rain. When she fell asleep, I slipped from under the covers, dressed and let myself out of the house. I caught a bus downtown, transferred and took another bus home. A note was waiting for me on the kitchen table, propped beside a covered dish of meatloaf and potato salad. Uncle Jack and Aunt Charlotte were having

dinner at the country club and would be home late. I should help myself.
At that moment, I didn't know quite what it meant, nor did I think I could
even pretend.

CHAPTER 24

Once the school year began, I was also expected to study hard, especially to overcome my poor record of the past two years so that I could fulfill college prep requirements, including math and science. Had it not been for a tutor hired by Uncle Jack to prod me—two hours after dinner every weekday—I would've whiled away my time listening to the radio in my room, sleeping, doing as little as possible to match my state of mind.

No mentor or friend could help me with the Phaedra dilemma, and the more I tried to resolve my conflicted feelings over her, the more frustrated I became. I longed for the carefree days I spent with Sonny taking the bus downtown after school, shooting pool.

Maybe if I could've had the relief of Café Jake at least one night on the weekend, that would've helped, but Café Jake was off-limits. At least, Prado said, until the end of the season. Some of our games were scheduled to be played on Friday and Saturday nights anyway, but even if they weren't, Sarah gave orders to not let us in the door. My lethargy extended to the football field, but the pressure to perform and the scrutiny that came with it was unrelenting. Coach Federov's ambition drove us to work hard, and he and Mr. Acquilino brought the team together, like chaplains before battle.

Before the start of City League play, we dominated two high-caliber, non-conference teams in controlled scrimmages. The reconfigured line performed as expected, allowing Cerio to blossom as a running back. He had already proven to be the most talented player on the team: a tall, slashing runner who also handled all the kicking chores.

Jacques ran the split-T offense to perfection. He was an exceptional play-maker and excelled at the option roll-out when he often broke away for long runs or hit Prado or me in the open with short bullet passes. The team became so good, playing was easy, and near the end of the season, Cerio, Jacques, Billy, and Fred were being touted for All-League honors, and I had the second most receptions among all ends: 25 for 470 yards. We were all hailed as heroes at one school dance and at nearly every all-school assembly. Moreover, we were undefeated.

There was only one game left to be played and that was LaSalle. As usual, they were also unbeaten, and now we were tied for the lead. Between the two coaches and Jacques, the pre-game scenario was expertly dramatized. Throughout the final week of practice, they reminded us—in groups and singly—about how we were traditionally perceived by LaSalle players as privileged suburban boys who, when presented with a daunting challenge, had neither the stomach nor the backbone to persevere.

But the overriding resentment having to do with our unworthiness was that we were a team dominated by Jews. This was always the last resentment mentioned, after listing the others, so that every player on the team was bound to be offended. But the way Coach Federov and Mr. Acquilino handled it, we were all equally branded with the same epithet: Jews were inherently cowards who even contributed to their own demise. And though we may have created some measure of success, these victories came because of an attribute that no other team possessed: cunning bordering on deceit, growing out of a nefarious moral transgression dating back at least 2000 years, a powerful motivating doctrine.

For most of us, of course, such a doctrine was manipulative propaganda, an exasperating screed that our coaches hoped would whip us into a frenzy. It was true that among the starters six were Jews: Jacques, Billy, Fred, Prado, me, and our Scranton import, the freckled red-head, Mickey Gale, a guard who was built like an extra-large fireplug. But the others included an Italian, a Greek, a Negro, a Syrian, and an Irish Seventh-Day Adventist—exemplars—the coaches told us, of the true American melting pot who, working together, could conquer the post-World War II world.

All of them took the LaSalle slander to heart. It worked for all of them but less for me because deep within I knew it carried a kernel of truth.

But the day before the game, the pressure was beginning to get to me.

Not only the coaches' propaganda, but also speeches at home by Uncle Jack, exhortations over the phone from Uncle Abe, all the fathers showing up at practice. They were all reminding us of our obligation to prove the LaSalle Hornets wrong.

To make matters worse, Pappas, the defensive end, suffered a badly-sprained knee at our final practice. Horsing around near a drinking fountain, his cleats skidded on wet pavement and he went down hard. By the time he was carried to his father's station wagon, it had swelled to the size of a grapefruit, and no sooner had the car pulled away than I was tabbed to take his place. Because of this extra duty, an added incentive was announced: I would be the third co-captain to take the field Saturday night, along with our permanents, Jacques and Fred. At the instant of the announcement, I went from very nervous to sick with anxiety while I was brought onto the field to walk through every possible defensive challenge.

As it turned out, my personal responsibility was to defend against LaSalle's strong side. For seven weeks, I had watched Pappas staunch successive opponents by thwarting multiple blockers, stuffing running backs, rushing passers. He played with the stealth and verve of an assassin.

The coaches relied on Pappas and groomed him for LaSalle because they ran a single-wing formation. Exclusively. They were the only team left in Central New York to use it, and opposing teams defensed them poorly because they had only a week to prepare.

What was expected of me was, first, to defend against the sweep which came in the form of a gang of blockers escorting the wingback or tailback. I also had to be cautious for a wingback reverse or end-around. Essentially, this meant I had to stand my ground, force whatever came my way to the inside into the waiting arms of Fred, our Hebrew Hammer, or push it to the outside without conceding any territory. Or, like Pappas, cut down the stampeding wedge of blockers and runners like a bowling ball.

Then there was the pass/run option, performed expertly the past four years by their All League tailback who, as I learned from newspaper photos, was the lead assailant that night a year ago at the end of All Souls' alley.

But the Hornets' pìece de resistance was the Statue of Liberty when the tailback faded back to pass, drawing onrushing linemen to him while cocking his arm, only to have it expertly picked off like a stolen loaf of bread by a wingback circling behind. They ran that play every game and Jacques, who backed me up on that side, berated me about it after one terrible lapse during practice when I let up and allowed a junior varsity halfback to sprint past me.

"Don't ever leave me out there like that again!"

For all those reasons and more, I couldn't sleep the night before the game. Uncle Jack said we often need extra incentives to perform up to expectation. I agreed, but what he didn't understand was that the two biggest incentives—fear of disappointing those for whom ordinary effort is sacred, and the fear of humiliation, of being unmasked—were add-ons I couldn't handle.

At dinner before the game, probably because he knew it wasn't in my nature, Uncle Jack gave me one last piece of advice: "Turn on the switch when you have to play defense." His conduit metaphor implied I needed to create mayhem, torpedo the Catholic dreadnought, which seemed so out of my realm of possibility, so contrived. For guys like Fred and Billy, and for my father, all they needed to do to burn with a fierce incandescence was to merely lift up the lampshade.

Just before the game, I lay on the training table. So quiet in the locker room. All I hear is the slap and tear of tape being applied to my ankles, the cleated shoes of some armored player clicking along the corridor to the bathroom. The silence accompanies me as we board the bus to take us to City Center Stadium, but it's a silence of determination, not despair.

"I can feel it," Prado whispers as he sinks into our shared bench seat. "Can't you?"

Jacques strolls the aisle, imparting final words of wisdom and encouragement, slapping shoulder pads. I dread his confronting me, seeing the fear in my eyes. He tousles my hair.

"I'm glad you're with us this year, Danny," he shouts, spit-flecked lips startling me. "It was terrible to be under-manned against them the last time."

I slump in my seat, feeling weaker than if I had a disease. Jacques stalks to the front of the bus to stand in the stairwell next to the coaches. He thinks we share a secret knowledge and a chill runs up my spine, triggering a body tremor I can't constrain, like how I used to stutter. Prado doesn't seem to notice.

The stadium is lit up when we arrive. A luster fills the jet-black sky. Competing bands are blaring fight songs as we exit the bus, and I shrink to the back of the milling group. Suddenly, they burst ahead of me through a tunnel. I follow, sprinting to catch up. After a clamorous interval, we erupt onto the field.

My lungs fill with cold air and it's as if I'm possessed.

I sprint through all our pre-game drills and pass patterns, way past where balls spiral into the turf. When I race back to the huddle, Jacques yells at me: "Slow down, goddamnit! You're over-running every pass. You're not even looking for the ball!"

The Hornets are at the other end of the field, two separate squads running single-wing plays out of the end zone, dressed in yellow and black, their helmets gleaming. An All Souls cheerleader walks the sidelines staring my way, shading her eyes from the overhead lights like a frontier scout. Her presence has no effect. My pulse is pounding out of control.

We run off the field for our final instructions and a prayer. We huddle together and clasp hands. I lean in. To extend my hand far enough to make contact, I turn my head toward the East Brant sideline. In the bleachers right in front of me, eye-level, stands Uncle Abe, waving. I believe I can see tears in his eyes again. Next to him is a guy wearing a Marine Corps field jacket and a black knit cap pulled low over his brow. I see steam escape his mouth as he shouts. And next to Jesse, in a shimmering line, sit Sonny, Yvonne, the Prados, Uncle Jack, Aunt Charlotte. Waving like crazy. The East Brant band is blaring 50 feet away and the effect is dizzying.

I take one last look as our team breaks away.

A woman is leaning on Uncle Abe's arm, clutching him, wearing a Navy pea coat and matching scarf. Mother? I look harder but I can't focus, my eyes brimming. I can't be certain. I want it to be, but it's just not possible.

Someone is clutching me from behind and I turn to swat him. It's Mr. Acquilino.

"Danny! Jacques and Fred are waiting for you! It's time to flip the coin!"

I don't move. "You don't have to do anything! Jacques will call it. Just get out there!"

"Danny!" I turn in the opposite direction. It's Uncle Abe waving me over to the fence in front of the bleachers. Phaedra is with him, smiling, calm, her face framed by a blue scarf. It was her. I glance beseechingly at Mr. Acquilino. "Yes! But hurry it up!"

I run over to the fence. Uncle Abe grabs me by the shoulder pads, pulls me to him, shouts in my ear. I stare at Phaedra. His encouragement reverberates inside my helmet and down my spine.

"After the Patriarch won the championship, he toured England, Scotland, and Ireland! Squire Fitzgerald said he was a dirty Jew bastard who wouldn't stand up to him and fight! Said he was a coward, a sneaky fighter. But the Patriarch thrashed him! Held the title for another year!"

Brimming with an urge to explode, positioned between Fred and Jacques, hemmed in by their poise, it's all I can do to keep from staggering as we jog out to the center of the field. I keep my helmet on, hoping that the Hornet tailback, McCarthy, won't recognize me and swell with confidence. Even when we're introduced and shake hands, there is no sign of recognition; he sizes us up, stares at our numbers, calls the coin as it's flipped into the air. No smile when he wins. He just licks his lips. I notice slightly-crossed eyes, steam rising from his buzz-cut scalp. We shake hands one final time, turn, run off the field.

"He don't look like much, does he?" Fred murmurs, adjusting his chin strap as we approach the bench.

"Forgetaboutit!" Jacques snaps. "He's a fucking genius! Starting tailback since freshman year! All League ever since!"

I take my position way at the end of the kickoff team's phalanx, wanting it not to occur, praying for a power failure to knock out the lights and cancel the game. I feel like I'm standing on the deck of a ship at sea, awkward and off-balance, conscious only of a deep sense of dread roiling in my stomach, of warm urine running down the insides of my thighs, my ears ringing.

Cerio plants the ball on the tee, glances to the sideline, raises his arms. Drums roll as he and our phalanx approach the ball like the release of a bow string; cymbals clash, and urgent screams from friends and foes explode as he kicks it end over end, high into the black night sky, and I'm off, racing down the sideline. I feel like I'm off the ground as my legs churn. The diminutive wingback waiting for the ball behind their advancing phalanx is out of kilter in my field of vision, so fast am I running. He flexes his knees slightly, one leg in front of the other, waiting, waiting.

At the first sign that LaSalle defenders are forming a wedge up the middle, I accelerate…against my will. One Hornet peels away to meet me, but I have the accumulated momentum and though he reaches me, it's all he can do to just leap and hurl a forearm, a glancing blow against my shoulder, further jarring my field of vision, but not slowing me down, and I continue racing to the spot where I believe the wingback is waiting.

He comes into view only when I am on top of him, running full-speed. At the last second, I try to rein in, but I can't, and I'm afraid he hasn't yet caught the ball. A collision sends me sprawling. Bodies thud, and there's a blur of movement continuing in the same direction. Hysterical cheering.

Fred leaps over me. Teammates hoist me to my feet. I look to the sideline. Others on the bench are throwing off their parkas and waving in ecstatic celebration. Mr. Acquilino races down the sideline, yelling at me and pumping his fist, waving me off the field. It's only when I reach the sideline and Jacques' outstretched hand that I discover what's happened. The wingback fumbled. I ran face-first into him just as he caught the ball. Prado recovered and sprinted into the end zone.

We huddle for a brief conference.

"Can you do that again?" Coach Federov yells, his face alive with joy.

I don't know how to respond as we take the field and line up to kick off again. This time, three players peel from the center of the field and knock me out of bounds. But they've left a gap in the middle, and Fred and Billy pour through, trapping the wingback deep on his own 10-yard line.

Coach Federov shouts over the band and cheers and screaming fans. "We've got the lead, so bottle up their running game! Force McCarthy to pass! I want an all-out rush against him!"

I line up on the wing for their first offensive series. McCarthy sends his fullback up the middle for no gain and on third down he fakes to the middle once again. I freeze until Jacques, from his position behind me, yells, "Pass!" I sprint belatedly into the backfield right into McCarthy as he spins to set his feet. I lower my helmet at the last second into his ear-hole and there's a terrible crraackk! He goes down between my legs, clawing at the air. An avalanche of bodies hits me from behind and when we unpile, Fred is holding the ball in one hand, screaming, pushing it into my face.

I look to the sideline again. Helmets sail into the air. Mr. Acquilino, arms akimbo, is running in place, pumping his knees to his chest. Players race off and onto the field. Jacques clutches my jersey to keep me in place. We huddle.

"Off-tackle slant, 26, on three. Ready...break!"

I line up. On the snap, Billy and I burst low and drive a LaSalle lineman back into the center of his formation. Cerio breaks off our block and sprints into the end zone. When we regain our feet, the LaSalle middle linebacker leans over one of his despondent players. He stares into my face, questioning some deep-held truth. Another one of them from the alley.

We kick off again. They make some progress with a mix of runs and short passes to about midfield. But, on third down, their first wingback reverse, I'm waiting and drive him out of bounds where I collide into several Hornets and a young priest wearing his collar, black topcoat and fedora. He, too, stares at me as I break away from his embrace.

At halftime, it's bedlam in the locker room. A student manager passes around pieces of orange to suck on. The sweet acidic taste tingles in my ears, but the rest of me is numb. I'm aware of flecks of blood on my pants, across the padded thighs, nothing more. I'm still wound up, trying to control my inner tremors, fists clenched. I don't want to go back out; I want the game to be over. Is the emotion, the terror, the fear of failure great enough to sustain me for another 30 minutes of play?

In the second half, we protect our lead with a time-consuming and risk-free running game. But at some point, when they score after a long drive, Jacques demands that we retaliate. He repeatedly pounds Cerio off-tackle, runs a draw up the middle, calls sweeps to the outside. Steadily we move downfield. On another off-tackle slant, I help Billy drive the Hornet tackle to his knees. He's just as big as Billy and very strong and they've been hammering each other throughout the game like two unyielding bulls. When I walk back to the huddle, I make my only comment of the game.

"We could run that play all night long."

Billy gives me a look of disdain, doesn't even have the energy to chastise me. He's in the fight of his life on every play, alone, and now that I've helped him bury the big man, there will be hell for him to pay.

At their 7-yardline, Jacques calls a timeout, dashes to the sideline, dashes back.

"Huddle-up! Huddle-up!" he screams.

Our waterboy trudges off the field, and we return to formation. The Hornet linemen are on all fours, silently digging in; defensive backs close-up behind them.

"All right! They're wounded!" Jacques screams, scanning our faces. "Now let's make them bleed a little bit more!"

Three straight running plays fail. A fullback draw is stuffed. Jacques rolls right but just barely makes it back to the line of scrimmage before he's hounded out of bounds. They stuff our right tackle slant. My legs are cut out from under me, and I'm trapped at the bottom of the pile.

Because I'm so exhausted, I feel like I can make deliberate moves without losing control of my body. Jacques is given the okay to run one final play, a fake belly drive to Cerio and jump pass. The linebacker who covers me plunges head-first into the center of a pileup. I release from a double-team on the tackle and sidestep quickly into the vacated seam. Jacques leaps up, pumps, lands, and waves me further along the seam, across the widest chalk stripe. He sprints away from the final onrushing lineman and launches the ball high. I leap, one hand outstretched, tip the ball forward, reach out, clutch it to my chest and tip-toe the back end-zone stripe—chalk dust bleeding into green—before sprawling out of bounds.

In the final quarter, they're desperately trying to close the gap and I'm still driving off the ball into the Hornet backfield, re-possessed by an unremitting, mechanical zeal. Jacques senses that I'm out of control and he directs me on just about every play. When he shouts "Pass!" I sprint to McCarthy, barreling inside the blocking wingback. Twice I'm penalized for roughing the passer.

On one play, when it appears McCarthy is pitching it wide, I stall. Then Jacques pushes me from behind. Perhaps it's too late. McCarthy is setting up to pass. He looks like a statue. I sprint to make up for lost time and collide with two players, McCarthy and his wingback circling behind.

When I think they can't come at me again, just before the end of the game, us ahead, 28-8, McCarthy decides to once more test my side, escorted at full, raging speed by his fullback, wingback, and a pulling guard. Without even thinking, I roll into them just as Pappas would've done, only from the ground I reach out and grab an ankle, stalling McCarthy. Stuck, attempting to break away, McCarthy's hit from behind by Fred, pursuing, bellowing all the way to the point of collision. McCarthy, who throughout the game stood with sleeves rolled up, expressionless and supremely willing, now lays in a crumpled heap, one foot still digging into the turf as if trying to outrun the pain.

After that, Coach Federov pulls me out of the game, a gesture to honor my last play. Except I'm not coming off alone. Jacques and Fred have me by each arm. Several teammates closest to the sideline where I exit hold their hands out, aghast, as if to catch a valuable piece of china before it hits the floor. Mr. Acquilino embraces me with a parka to wrap around my shoulders. I look down. My jersey is spattered with blood. As I'm escorted past the bleachers, robust cheering gives way to respectful applause that ripples all along the sideline.

In the locker room, a man gingerly lifts off my helmet. A thick strand of blood pulls away from the jagged ends of a broken face bar. I rise to look in the mirror, suddenly weaker in the knees. Blood covers my mouth and chin and my nose is sliced and bent to the side. I'm taken aback by the mask that used to be me.

Later, after a doctor has washed, stitched, re-set my nose and bandaged it, Jacques hands me my aluminum cup protector, dented nearly flat. His eyes are wide with admiration, for the first time at a loss for words.

He and Fred help me into the shower room to scrub the rest of my game away. We pass a group of sportswriters questioning the LaSalle coach.

"Your highly-regarded defense allowed a season-high 382 yards of total offense, coach," one stated. "Cerio rushed 31 times for 204 yards and two touchdowns. What happened?"

When we finish showering, he's still explaining, nodding in our direction, hatless, sweat-plastered ringlets of hair curled around his balding dome.

"We couldn't get the ball moving because their defense was so good. Their middle linebacker and defensive end were so quick and strong we couldn't get them blocked."

My teammates' whooping and hollering on the bus ride back to school made me realize that I'd participated in winning a championship title, the first-ever in football for East Brant. I felt like I'd had to climb out of my skin to help achieve it, and I wondered how extraordinary the experience was for others.

Jacques and Prado kept me company in the back of the bus and kept others from pummeling me with overflow gestures of appreciation. So I sat mute and stiff and numb but still reverberating from the impetus that'd overtaken me. Helpless. Wanting it to stop because every quiver, in addition to every pulse beat and every shift in the bus's movement rushed currents of pain into my head.

As our bus lurched to a stop in the school parking lot, the band struck up a fight song. A mob of cheering students swept forward when we emerged and followed us into the corridor decorated with hand-painted banners, balloons, and streamers. It was all too much for me, and I sought the furthest reaches of the locker room. But like a wave rushing into a secluded cove, well-wishers sought me out where I stood leaning against a sink. In a mirror, as I examined my blackened eyes, I could see them burst through a door, all smiles, heading my way: Uncle Jack, Aunt Charlotte, Uncle Abe, Phaedra, escorted by Jacques, his hair still spikey-wet from a hasty shower.

"See, I knew you could do it!" Uncle Jack raved. I cowered before his bear hug.

"Leave him alone, Jack! Can't you see he's in pain?"

Aunt Charlotte caressed my shoulder.

"Jesus, honey, you were terrific out there. We're so proud of you; your father would've been so proud." This sentiment moved her, and she began to cry.

Uncle Abe took one of my hands and kissed it. Phaedra stood behind him, looking simultaneously stupefied yet proud. It was a moment of supreme adulation, but I was still too displaced to comprehend it. Then

Prado ran in.

"Come on out, Danny. Coach Federov is making a speech. He wants us all there."

We filed back out to the corridor. From amidst a group of teammates, the coach waved me over.

"And here's the one who started it! Our most valuable player tonight...."

Students and parents cheered.

"For a guy who didn't play any defense all year, he did a pretty good job, don't you think?"

More applause and cheers. He took my arm and raised it. I smiled through the pain.

A few minutes later, Aunt Charlotte pulled me aside. She held out a cup of water for me and pressed two white tablets into my hand.

"Here's some pain-killers the doctor gave me, sweetie. Take these right now and you'll feel better. We're going home, but you can celebrate with your friends. We told Phaedra not to keep you out too late."

She hugged my shoulder; Uncle Jack shook my hand.

"Congratulations, champ."

I gave him a surprised glance. "Sounds good, doesn't it? Another season like this one and you'll have college scouts beating down our door. I heard one sportswriter say tonight's game was the best in City League history."

Phaedra and I left the victory celebration, joining a small cavalcade of cars, Prado leading the way. We were on our way to Café Jake.

By the time we arrived, though the pain had diminished, I remained in that same game state of mind, still fighting the tremor that had taken hold of my body. Phaedra took one of my hands in both of hers as if she understood and tried to calm me, while Prado transported us from one riotous scene to another.,

We entered the cafe in the middle of a set—a wild, rocking, sax-honking blues/camel walk number with people strutting along the aisles, locking one foot behind the other in what looked to me like a mimed disability. From behind the bar, Eugene spotted us first.

"Did you win?"

I nodded.

"The reason I ask is 'cause it's hard to tell...with that face you got. You okay?" He waved Wilbur over. "Get this boy a table. A big one so all his friends can join him."

Though loud and raucous, the music didn't grate on my nerves. Even as it amplified the pain, it also carried an indescribable joy. Wilbert brought a tray of Champales, eight bottles covered with glasses, for Prado, Billy, Fred, and me and our dates. Gene held aloft a glass of milk and scotch and toasted us from the bar. He was working alone tonight.

Phaedra tugged at my hand. "That bartender knows you. You've been here before?"

I looked at her and nodded and pointed to Prado. "His father owns the place."

She didn't appear fazed at all. In fact, her eyes lit up with a new admiration. Besides Prado and his girlfriend, however, the others looked pretty uncomfortable.

I felt something hard knock my knee under the table. It was Prado passing me a pint of Peppermint Schnapps. Under the table, I poured some into my glass, took a deep draught, poured some more, took another. I nudged Phaedra, but she smiled, rejecting the offer. I took one more, passed it back, and chased it with a glass of Champale. It tasted good, and when Wilbur came back, I ordered another round. I felt as if I needed to quench a great thirst as well as mute the force that still burned within me.

The more I drank, the better I felt. At one point, Phaedra pulled me to my feet to dance, a slow blues number. But with the saxophone wailing and with nowhere to move, and she pressing her body into mine, this wasn't what I wanted. I broke away from her and pushed my way through the crowd. People complained, but when they caught my bandaged face and blackened eyes, they opened a pathway to the door and to the cool night air beyond.

I stepped outside, walked through a knot of people pressing to get in and rounded the street corner, taking the cool night air deep into my lungs, blinking tears out of my eyes, but I walked smack into someone coming directly toward me who refused to alter his line of direction. I pushed him away. Angered, he came right back at me, cursing. I braced myself and thrust hard with both hands, palms open. The blow struck him in the chest and he fell to the pavement.

He looked up at me, momentarily puzzled, then angry again.

"Mothafucka! You jive-ass mothafucka! Ahm 'onna cut you up!"

He scrambled to one knee and reached into his waistband. Out came a switchblade knife, sprung open. I kicked him in the face, once, then once again until he landed sprawled on his back. I continued kicking him, up and down the length of his body, denting him like a punching bag. Somebody grabbed me from behind and pulled me away. I turned to hit him, too, but then I recognized him. It was Lonnie Starr, with his girlfriend, Enid, and Brenda. He grabbed me and pulled me away.

"Man! What happened to you?"

He took me by the shoulders, face to face, shaking me a few times until I dropped my hands. Then the pain returned with bold, pulsating spasms. I was surprised at how stupid and slurred my voice sounded.

"I got my nose broke."

He laughed. "I can see that, my man. But, how?"

"Tonight. A few hours ago. We beat LaSalle."

"No shit! Congratulations!" He embraced me. "And you still got a little fight in you, huh? What'd this brother do to deserve this?"

"Nothing. He just bumped into me when I walked outside and turned the corner. I…."

He shook his head, squatted, picked up the man's knife. "You all alone, or is Prado with you? Man, you could get yourself killed fuckin' with dudes like this. He's a bad-ass, hear what I'm sayin?'"

He turned me around and quickly escorted me into the alley behind the cafe.

"Danny! Danny!" Phaedra ran up behind us. "Where are you going? You're not leaving?"

I put my hand out to her. Enid introduced herself, then Lonnie, then Brenda.

"We're just going over here and get our man together," Lonnie said.

The guy I knocked down staggered by.

"Where's that white motha*fucka?* Where's my knife?"

Everybody closed ranks, hiding me. Lonnie turned around, closed the blade with a click and handed it to him.

"He's gone, man. Hey, let me get you a cab. You need some stitches."

The man jerked away and staggered off down the street, cursing and dabbing his face with a handkerchief.

"What happened?" Phaedra demanded. "Did you get into a fight? You?"

"Just a little scuffle, is all," Lonnie responded, chuckling. "The man here is still a little wound up from his game."

Phaedra nodded anxiously and took me by the arm.

"Well, why don't we go back inside? He'll be all right there."

"Don't worry, honey," Enid said, in her faux-Negro patois, "we will; we jus' wanna bring him down a little."

She reached into her purse and pulled out a pipe, opened a small medicine bottle and poured some its contents into the bowl. Then she tamped it down with her finger.

"Gimme a light, honey," she ordered.

Danny flicked open a Zippo. She took a few puffs until the bowl glowed red, then handed it to me.

"Take some big hits, baby. It's all yours."

Drunk now, I didn't cough. I took a big drag, held it in, let it go; took another.

"Give some to your girlfriend; you probably scared the shit outa her," Enid said, laughing.

Phaedra glanced around, then defiantly grabbed the pipe. Lonnie lit it for her. She also took a big drag, coughed, then sputtered.

"Okay, girl; take a break and try again," Enid advised. "But keep it quiet, you dig? You don't wanna get us busted."

"No," Phaedra whispered conspiratorially.

Lonnie re-filled and lit the pipe, and she tried once more, this time successfully. He and I finished it off.

Jacques and Fred and their dates met us at the door as we went back inside. "Hey, Danny," Jacques announced, looking surprised to see the company I was in, "we're going over to Poodle's to get something to eat. You, uh, sticking around or coming with us?"

"Yeah," I mumbled.

"Yeah, what?"

"He's stickin' around wit' us," Lonnie said.

"Probably for jus' one more set," Brenda explained.

"Okay," Jacques, agreed. "Prado is still here, too, he'll... ."

"Don't worry, man," Lonnie said, "we'll get him home, one way or another."

"I have my car," Phaedra announced.

"All right!" Enid exclaimed giddily. "We all set."

We barged past Jacques holding the door.

Inside the raucous club and back at our booth, Prado sat sandwiched between two heavy-set women laughing hysterically. He waved us over.

"Hey, where you been, man? You haven't been cuttin' me outa somethin', have you?"

Enid passed him a full pipe as she slid into the booth.

"Why 'on't you take a walk, Prado. You a champion, too."

A huge smile creased his face. He glanced around, then back at Enid.

"All right! I shall return. Save my seat!"

When he came back, bobbing to the rhythm of the band, we finished the schnapps and another round of Champale. Our booth rocked. We danced from the waist up, swaying, snapping our fingers, and as word of our momentous victory got around, people who knew Prado came by to offer congratulations. Phaedra learned the Negro code handshake—slapping palms. I'd never seen her so animated, so garrulous. She couldn't get over the band and didn't want to leave until the end of the last set, and when she drove me to my house, she thanked me profusely, something she had never done before.

"What a great celebration! That was the most fun I've ever had...I mean it."

She soothed my brow and rested her other hand on my thigh. "You look terrible, sweetie. Is there something I can do for you?"

I shook my head. Fighting nausea and with the cumbersome bandage on my face, I didn't even feel like kissing her.

She licked her lips, pretended to kiss me, and moved her hand over me, softly.

"Oh, I think there is; I think there might be some life in you yet."

Once again she surprised me. I knew I was back inside myself when I tried to leave her car. I was bent over with pain, and it took every ounce of strength to walk up the path to my house and climb the stairs to my bedroom.

I collapsed on my bed fully clothed.

CHAPTER 25

I lay in bed all the next morning. Aunt Charlotte woke me at 1 in the afternoon and gave me more painkillers with my orange juice and waffles and sausages smothered in maple syrup that she served me on a tray. Uncle Jack brought the Sunday newspaper. Our game was headlined on the front page of the sports section. One photo showed Cerio diving for a touchdown. I couldn't remember the play. Another showed me dragging down McCarthy from behind on one of his roll-outs. I couldn't believe the amount of coverage, or how I was represented: "...*stellar performance by last-minute sub...one of the most impressive defensive interdictions in East Brant scholastic history, especially coming as it did against the vaunted LaSalle Hornets, with only a week to prepare....*"

I even got a separate sidebar: "*Mendoza Clips Hornets' Wings*" read one headline. I skimmed the story, stopping at a line of bold type, a quote from Coach Federov: "*Mendoza inherited his toughness from his father.*" I shook my head with disbelief.

"Now we need to get your grades up, with what's left of the semester," Uncle Jack said. "Dr. Berman's coming out to check on you. Your tutor will be here at 4 but for only an hour and only for chemistry; you got a test on Wednesday."

Uncle Abe was right; Uncle Jack was my manager, but now it seemed like he was looking out for my best interests.

When Dr. Berman examined me, he said my nose would heal just fine. "There'll be only a small scar along one side, a 'badge of honor.'"

I looked into Dr. Berman's hand-held mirror. Perhaps the new scar would cancel out the badge of shame, the scar that still dented my eyebrow.

The following Monday, Coach Federov approached me in the hallway as I headed to the cafeteria for lunch. "Come on to my office," he said, barely suppressing a conspiratorial grin. I followed him into the tiny cubicle adjacent to the locker room that he used for an office.

"Sit down," he said.

I sat in his slatted swivel chair. He handed me a typed list, broken down to three team lineups and a long paragraph of names with positions in bold print.

"These are the All-City football teams—first, second, third, and honorable mention, an advance copy for coaches; it'll be published in the newspaper tomorrow. Congratulations."

I was flabbergasted and just stared at him without looking at the list.

"Don't look at me, look at the list," he insisted, laughing.

Along with Freddie Kaplan (center/linebacker), Billy Pearl (tackle), and Peter Cerio (fullback) of East Brant High, I was named to the first team, one of only two juniors.

"What about Jacques?" I asked, still dumbfounded.

"He made second team behind McCarthy. I don't think I can quarrel with that selection; it's McCarthy's fourth year in a row. He'll probably make the All-Upstate team, too."

My disbelief wouldn't vanish, even though there it was, in black and white.

"How are these teams chosen?" I asked.

"By the coaches. You were a unanimous selection, although it was probably your work in the LaSalle game that clinched it for you."

"I still can't believe it." This was something I had never considered, even in my wildest imagination.

Coach Federov extended his hand and pulled me up from the chair. His other hand grasped my shoulder. "You deserved it. I hope you'll deserve it next year, too. But it'll be a tough challenge; we have to rebuild again."

The following Saturday, Uncle Jack hosted a party at his home for the entire team, a buffet catered by Meltzer. We all received identical championship trophies. I won an extra one for making All-City. After dinner, we watched game-film highlights until we could barely keep our eyes open.

With the help of my tutor over the remainder of the semester and a lot of studying, I averaged B overall and scored As in English and history. I couldn't wait for Christmas break.

The first thing I did was have an obligatory lunch with Uncle Abe at Meltzer's after Saturday synagogue services. We fortified ourselves against the chill of an early-winter snow storm with bowls of hot barley soup, and we split a plate of stuffed cabbage. Then we took a bus downtown to see a boxing movie, *The Harder They Fall*, with Humphrey Bogart. I'd missed it when it was first released the summer before because Phaedra had already seen one boxing movie with me, *Somebody Up There Likes Me*, the life story of Rocky Graziano, and despite my enthusiasm, she didn't share it. But I liked the movie so much I also read the book and even wrote a report on it for my English class.

I'd already known a lot about Graziano from articles in *Ring* magazine. That he'd had a Jewish manager, for example. But I didn't realize he'd married a Jewish girl, Norma, and that she'd inspired him to become a middleweight champion. There were some funny parts in the movie that had me in stitches. In one scene, a goofy Rocky—played by a new actor, Paul Newman—auditions for his future manager Irving Cohen at Stillman's Gym. Cohen tells Rocky to go into the dressing room where he'll be given shorts and a cup. And in his typical, clownish way, Rocky answers, "That's okay, Mr. Cohen; I'll drink out of the bottle."

Uncle Abe told me the movie we were going to see was roughly based on the story of Primo Carnera, a 6-5 former circus strongman dubbed "Satchel Feet" not only because his feet were so enormous, but also, as Uncle Abe pointed out to me, "he couldn't move them worth a damn."

"You know, Daniel, this movie is actually based on a novel by a very famous Jewish writer, Budd Schulberg," he said with great pride.

"Anyway, Carnera had a rock-hard body—muscles upon muscles— and could take almost any body shot," he continued as we rode the bus downtown, "but he wasn't a skilled fighter, and he had a glass jaw.

"Italian gangsters first saw his potential and took him on a circuit through Europe beginning in 1928 when he was 22 years old, arranging 18 bouts with paid-off boxers or boxers of low caliber. After he beat them all, the gangsters brought him to America and, after three more years compiling a 64-3 record, he fought Jack Sharkey in 1933 for the heavyweight title.

"Sharkey outweighed him by 60 pounds, went down in the sixth round from what some called "an invisible punch." But, obviously, the fight had been fixed.

"A year later, after two bouts with nobodies, Max Baer, one of the last fighters besides your father to wear the Star of David on his trunks, gave Carnera a savage beating and took the title, knocking him down 12 times until the ref finally stopped the bout in the 11th round."

"Is this what the movie's about?" I asked.

Uncle Abe's expression soured. "More or less," he said, cryptically.

I wondered what he meant, but I already knew the theme of corruption lurked in the plots of so many boxing movies and figured maybe that was it.

I helped Uncle Abe off the bus in front of the Strand Theater. We paused before a movie poster and read the promotional blurb: *the only thing that's on the square…is the ring itself.…* Inside the lobby, Uncle Abe gave me enough money to buy a Coke and some popcorn, and out of the corner of my eye, I saw him strike up a conversation with someone I couldn't see. Then I realized it was Sonny, and Uncle Abe had invited him to join us.

"It'll be good to see a boxing movie with someone else who really appreciates the sport," Uncle Abe said, trying to ease any tension between Sonny and me. He knew it'd been a long time since we'd seen each other.

I nodded to Sonny, but words escaped me. I was still chagrined about my rude and unceremonious departure from the reservation.

But before we even took our seats and the lights dimmed, the gulf between us seemed to fade as we started talking eagerly about other boxing movies, two of our favorites, *Gentleman Jim*, with Errol Flynn, and *Champion*, with Kirk Douglas. We agreed that *Champion* captured the brutality of boxing, especially toward the end when Douglas, battered to the canvas, his face a bloodied and distorted mask, still had the determination to get up and defeat his opponent. But we also agreed, along with Uncle Abe, that the boxing scenes in *Gentleman Jim* were choreographed more realistically, capturing true boxing skills rather than slugfests with very little attention to defense.

The Harder They Fall opened with the fictional Carnera character, Toro Moreno, arriving in New York harbor by boat from Argentina. Like Carnera, he's huge and he sports a Dempsey-style haircut, shaved tight around his ears. Soon, Eddie—a weary-looking Humphrey Bogart in his last film before dying of cancer—is introduced. He plays a sportswriter down on his luck after the newspaper he works for goes under. He agrees to publicize Toro when Nick, a syndicate-backed promoter played by Rod Steiger, offers him "an open-ended, tax-free expense account."

Eddie recognized that he's got his work cut out for him when a trainer, played by Jersey Joe Walcott, takes Toro down with a simple one-two combination to his jaw. However, he has no compunction befriending Toro and promoting him as the South American heavyweight champ, "the Wild Man of the Andes." Eddie proves so valuable to Nick that he becomes a managing partner for 10 percent of every purse Toro wins as Toro campaigns for a title shot by knocking out a string of syndicate fighters willing to take dives.

The blatant level of corruption makes me wonder how Grandfather had managed to guide Davey through this terrain. Could sportswriters really be so dumb not to see what was going one? Or were they all like Eddie, too involved with their own livelihoods to even care?

Eddie's wife, played by Jan Sterling, is disgusted with his hypocrisy, selling out to the syndicate and betraying all of his principles. And she's disappointed that Eddie's messing around on the road with other women at one hotel room party after another.

Sonny becomes riled over the next scene. An Indian fighter too proud to take a bribe changes his mind when Eddie suggests he put a small piece of chicken wire in his mouth. That way, Eddie tells him, when Toro hits him, he'll bleed so badly and so convincingly that the fight will have to be stopped. Then he won't look like he's laying down. The Indian accepts and any pride, any honor, is stripped away. Sonny's disgusted.

Eddie couldn't be more of a hypocrite. He castigates six managers who cheat their fighters, but he just stands by while Nick takes all of Toro's money.

After a tour of 25 more fixed fights, Toro ends up in Chicago where he's to fight Gus Dundee, who's recently lost his title to the new champ, a real brute played, ironically, by Max Baer. Dundee had been pulverized in the title fight and he shouldn't be allowed into the ring, even to fight Toro. But the Chicago Athletic Commission okays the fight anyway.

I wonder: are they in on the fix, too?

With a no-talent lug like Toro, even Nick wonders whether Dundee can make a fight of it. Sure enough, one powder-puff punch sends Dundee to the canvas in the third round. He has to be carried out of the ring while fans boo loudly, figuring it's a dive.

Later, Nick tells reporters with fake piety, "If there's a God in heaven, then I'm sure he'll be in Gus's corner tonight." An unforgettable quote, but later Gus dies on the operating table.

Eddie's wife, who's joined him in Chicago, pleads with Eddie to quit his involvement with the syndicate. But he won't listen. Fed up, she leaves him after he tells her: "Money…if you don't have it, you're a bum in anybody's book."

Maybe that's the most significant line in the movie; my ears start to burn.

Next, Toro signs for a title fight with the Max Baer character, Buddy Brannen, who resents Toro for getting the credit for killing Gus Dundee. He insists he's going to "butcher" Toro from the get-go. Knowing Toro has no chance, Nick secretly places large bets *against* his fighter.

Here's where Eddie regains his conscience and tells Toro the truth— that he's a terrible boxer and all his fights have been fixed. Toro doesn't believe him, so Eddie calls the Jersey Joe character into Toro's hotel room and tells him to hit Toro. They square off and Jersey Joe K.O.'s Toro with a hard right. When he regains consciousness, Toro asks Eddie in desperation, "What'll I do?"

"Jesus," Sonny whispers to me. "The poor bastard."

Eddie tells Toro that Jersey Joe will coach him to make the fight look good, so he can go back to Argentina with a lot of money instead of broke. "Use your reach and jab, stay away from Brannen; clinch when he hits you; go down as soon as you're hurt."

But in the fight, it's as if Toro hasn't heard anything. He doesn't jab and doesn't clinch and Brannen knocks him down three times in just the first round. Brannen looks like he's intent on killing Toro. Plus, he fights dirty—rubs his laces across his face, hits him after the bell. Toro is too prideful. Like the Indian, he cares about his reputation. He insists on giving the match his best shot. But he's already a bloody mess.

Sonny groans. "Oh, shit; he's gonna get it now."

The bell rings for round three and in under a minute Brannen pounds Toro face-down to the canvas, knocking him senseless and breaking his jaw.

After the fight, Eddie asks Jersey Joe why Toro took the God-awful beating.

"Some guys can sell out; others can't."

What a line, it brings tears to my eyes. Eddie looks crushed.

Afterward, Eddie goes to Nick to collect his share of the purse, $26,000 in cash. But that doesn't sound right to me if he was supposed to get 26 percent. More cheating going on?

When Eddie asks for Toro's share, Nick tells him after all of the meticulously-accounted percentages and expenses, Toro's share is only $49.07. What's worse, Toro's contract has already been sold to another manager, so the manipulation will continue.

Then with a pang of conscience, Eddie quickly heads for the hospital where he plans to sneak Toro out and whisk him to the airport and back to Argentina. He gives Toro his own cut. Toro responds by saying it's a lot of money and that he'll buy his mother a new house and take his father to Buenos Aires where he'll buy him many new pairs of shoes. Eddie puts him on a flight and Toro is gone.

The movie ends with Eddie reconciling with his wife and Nick threatening him: "You open your mouth, we'll shut you up."

But Eddie tells Nick, "You can't scare me or buy me."

The movie ends with Eddie sitting at his typewriter as his wife brings him a fresh cup of coffee. He beings to pound out a title, *The Harder They Fall*. Then he writes the opening line:

"Boxing should be outlawed in the U.S. if it takes an act of Congress to do it."

We sat quietly as the screen credits scrolled and the house lights came on.

"Reminds me of *On The Waterfront*, also written by Budd Schulberg, a real *mensch*," Uncle Abe offered. "Like a documentary. The truth, instead of a made-up story. The crooked world of boxing, and the crooked world of the longshoremen's union."

Sonny and I both wanted to know more, and Uncle Abe was happy to enlighten us with scholarly detail. But what I first wanted to know about was the line in the movie that Eddie wrote about the government banning boxing, and how he could've managed to escape retribution from the syndicate and their thug promoters, like Nick.

"The chairman of the New York State Athletic Commission said the same thing in an article he wrote four years ago in *Life* magazine. Robert Christenberry said either boxing should be wrested from those who control it, or it should be outlawed.

"Those columns could've been written, Danny. Some writers are so courageous, so widely-read, they can't be touched."

"Oh, yeah?" A man in front of us had been eavesdropping. He turned and faced us. "What about Victor Reisel?"

"Who's he?" Sonny asked.

Uncle Abe sighed with frustration. The man answered for him.

"A crusading labor columnist for the New York *Post*. Syndicated in a lot of newspapers, including our own."

"So what happened to him?" I asked. I really wanted to know.

"Acid thrown in his face last April, blinding him," the man answered. "Only an hour after he'd finished a radio broadcast criticizing the leadership of a Long Island local of the International Union of Operating Engineers. Then the guy who did it was assassinated so he wouldn't squeal on higher-ups."

The man snorted in disgust, got out of his seat and left.

This revelation was almost too terrifying to pursue, but it rang true to me, considered what happened to my family, and it made me wonder why Uncle Abe wasn't forthcoming about it when he had the opportunity, why he claimed courageous writers couldn't be touched.

"So, if writers have been writing about it and then there's this movie, what's going on in boxing today?" I asked.

"What's portrayed in the movie, Danny, is still going on," Uncle Abe admitted. "Those people have so much power, they're too big to be stopped so easily. The State Athletic Commission investigated, held hearings; the government has sued the International Boxing Commission as a monopoly under the Sherman Anti-Trust Act and won, but he IBC has appealed. Now it's up to the U.S. Supreme Court to put them out of business, and I'm betting they will."

"What does the IBC have to do with the syndicate?" Sonny asked, still taken aback by the vastness of the corruption.

"We can talk more about it at my house," Uncle Abe suggested, pushing himself painfully from his seat. "I've got some fresh chocolate macaroons and I'll make some tea. You want to, you boys can stay over."

It was pitch black by the time we got back to Uncle Abe's flat; the macaroons and tea felt soothing in my belly. Uncle Abe pulled a thick manila file from a shelf of books, opened it, and took out two magazines: a *Life* dated May 26, 1951, and a *Ring* dated June 1953. I recognized the cover, but I'd missed reading that one because I'd lost interest in boxing since the fire and my father's murder.

Uncle Abe rubbed his hands together vigorously. "Okay. First let's take a look at the article by Christenberry."

He sat on the davenport between Sonny and me and opened the magazine to a dog-eared page, "*My Rugged Education in Boxing.*" Above and below were captioned police mug shots: Frankie Carbo, "*a lowly gunman who rose to become overlord of boxing's underworld....* Frank "Blinky" Palermo, "*...most active stable of fighters now in the business.*"

I always wondered about the word "stable," as if these managers owned race horses. In fact, in the article, Christenberry likened these managers' ownership of fighters to race horses: buying them, training them, making money off them, selling them.

It seemed DiNardi was just part of a pattern, syndicate managers who not only controlled the fate of two-thirds of all American boxers, but who also got away with all kinds of crimes, including murder. The IBC encouraged a small group of crooked managers to form an organization, the International Fight Managers Guild, supplanting an independent guild and squeezing out managers like Grandfather who opposed them. More importantly, the IBC also controlled all gate receipts and film, radio, and television rights to fights.

"According to the lawsuit, the IBC staged or controlled 81 percent of all championship fights," Uncle Abe pointed out. Then he opened *Ring* to an article by Dan Parker, "*I Say the Boxing Business Smells.*"

"This is one of the courageous journalists I was talking about."

The article detailed Carbo's influence over managers and promoters and fighters, some of the biggest names in the sport, including, at the bottom of one paragraph, Raymond DiNardi.

I felt like I was inside a secret vault and drawers were being opened, one by one, and until that moment, I'd never realized the power of the written word.

It was Sonny who opened the last drawer. "So that's why your dad fought in all those small towns all over the country, or here in Brant, and was rarely on TV; that's why he waited so long to get a title shot, waited so long to get a decent ranking."

Uncle Abe pointed to the end of the Parker piece: "*...boycott of managers outside the IBC guild kept many talented fighters from earning their just desserts; for example, Davey Mendoza, a fabulously-talented light heavyweight deserving of a title fight after laboring his entire career in the hinterlands. He could've been on TV every month if his manager—his father Jake—had agreed to cut some of the vultures in on some of his earnings.*

"*His big break finally came in December 1952 because of his astounding popularity, capturing the hearts of fans all over the country, including a few prominent sportswriters who badgered the authorities for a shot against Joey Maxim.*

"*At first, the IBC—which holds the rights to Maxim—objected. They wanted their man to fight another IBC chattel, Archie Moore. And they received the usual backing from Christenberry, who wanted to see the title fight broadcast from Madison Square Garden.*

"*However, the IBC finally capitulated and agreed to "partner in' on the venture when they were secretly approached by the fighter's trainer and business manager, his brother, Jack Mendoza. It seemed the Mendoza braintrust's determination to stay free of the IBC had to come to an end in order to give Davey the fight he so handsomely deserved.*

"*Subsequently, Christenberry agreed, too. But just weeks before the bout, tragedy struck. In a fire of uncertain origin, Jake Mendoza and the fighter's wife, Mary, died when they were trapped inside Jake's clothing store. Debilitated by grief, Davey backed out of the fight and Moore, who subsequently signed, defeated Maxim for the title. Then, a few months later, Davey was shot and killed by unknown assailants during a barroom brawl in Brooklyn.*"

Up until now, everything fit together, made sense. But this last part of the story had me confused.

"So why would DiNardi set fire to Grandfather's store? Why would he have my father killed if the syndicate and IBC agreed he could fight Maxim?"

Uncle Abe yawned, shook his head. "I'm not sure, Danny. I've been puzzling over that for a long time. Maybe the only one who can shed light on it is your Uncle Jack. But be careful how you raise it with him. I'm sure it's a delicate topic he'd rather not visit."

We were all exhausted by this time. Uncle Abe made a bed for Sonny on the floor with cushions from his easy chairs. I took the davenport. But as tired as I was, it took a long time before I could get to sleep.

CHAPTER 26

By morning, it had stopped snowing. Uncle Abe called a taxi to drive Sonny home, then served us a breakfast of oatmeal with brown sugar, bagels and jam, and coffee. As he ate, Sonny invited me to help prepare the new snow-snake course.

"You're on vacation. You can stay with me or Jesse for a few days. This is the perfect weather to begin building one."

Uncle Abe smiled and nodded his head like he was *davening*. I was afraid that if I accepted Sonny's invitation to the reservation so close to Midwinter I would be obliged to participate in some of the rituals I had no affinity for. It also meant foregoing the luxuries of home, especially during this brutally-cold onset of winter. I wasn't enthused about using a privvy or making a fire just to have a cup of coffee in the morning. I got up from the table to look at Uncle Abe's calendar. The new moon would rise January 1st, so preparations for Midwinter could begin any day now.

"What a great opportunity to see Jesse and your old friends," Uncle Abe encouraged.

I gave in, mainly because I didn't want to disrespect Sonny. And my conscience nagged me. I probably needed to mend fences with Jesse because of my abrupt departure.

"All right," I conceded, suppressing my resistance. "Let me just call Aunt Charlotte, make sure it's okay with her and Uncle Jack."

"How long will you be there?" she asked, a note of exasperation in her voice.

"I don't know, a few days."

"Won't you need a change of clothes?"

I covered the mouthpiece and asked the same question of Uncle Abe.

His eyes grew big, and he raised an index finger.

"Aha! I've still got boxes of brand-new long underwear and socks from the store. You can take a couple of my wool sweaters; they're big."

"Uncle Abe has some stuff in boxes here for me to take, Aunt Charlotte, stuff from Grandfather's store; I'll be okay."

"What if Phaedra calls?"

"Tell Phaedra to drive over to the reservation. Chances are I'll be at the snow-snake course near the Council House on Holley Valley Road. If I'm not there, tell her to ask anyone how to get to Jesse's cabin. It's close by."

I thought of Phaedra and me alone in the cabin, the fireplace going, and it kindled a burst of focused enthusiasm. She'd probably like that.

Building the snow-snake course turned out to be fun. Welcome Shenandoah was there with some of the boys from Indian school days, and he treated me like a long-lost friend. I also think that wearing my East Brant letter jacket gave him comfort that I was no longer a rival, just a visiting celebrity from another world away.

It was so cold, the course was ready for play the day we finished making it. Everyone was throwing well beyond their old marks, and this time the sense of competition was friendly. But I had the vague sense of something missing, and I couldn't figure out what it was. I looked around, re-orienting myself with familiar landmarks: a line of towering pines marking the edge of the forest; the old school, late-afternoon sunlight glinting off its windows; the freshly-turned roll of snowbank at the roadside.

Then it hit me. I tugged Sonny by the shoulder.

"Where's Echo?" I remembered him chasing snake along the course, happy to be part of the game, dashing through the snow, yipping in a high, excited voice. I felt a pang of conscience, of wanting to make up for another of my lapses.

Sonny's wide smile collapsed. He seemed to be searching for words.

"Echo's...gone...."

"What do you mean?"

A premonition hit me in the gut, and my face burned with shame before he could respond.

"You mean, he's…dead?"

Sonny nodded.

I blinked rapidly to prevent tears from welling. I swallowed hard and took a deep breath so that I could get the words out.

"When? What happened?"

"A farmer shot him. Said he was bothering his cows."

My legs went weak, and I passed up my next throw of the snake.

"A white farmer? The guy who owns the apple orchard down the road? How did Echo wind up on that guy's property? Why would Echo chase a cow?"

"No, it was our neighbor, Mr. Johnson. Remember that field where we used to play? He turned mean in his old age, just shot Echo without warning one day last summer while we walked through his pasture on the way to the lacrosse box."

"What did you do?"

"I went home, got my 20-gauge, and shot one of his cows."

I must've looked incredulous.

"The Council met about it," he said evenly. "They said it was a fair exchange."

"Where is he buried?"

I thought immediately about visiting his grave, although there would be no stones to find in all this snow to leave my mark of remembrance. How callow I had been to not say goodbye to him when I left with Uncle Jack, to not even pause to think about thanking him for all the comfort he gave me when I was in such terrible shape. My new-found enthusiasm for snow-snake drained out of me.

"You feel bad?" Sonny asked. He seemed surprised.

I nodded.

He held out his snow-snake to me. "Throw it in his honor."

My knees buckled as he passed me his snake; I felt so unworthy, so overwhelmed with self-loathing and hypocrisy that I vowed I would stay on the reservation until the rite of confession. I needed to unburden myself before I could return to Uncle Jack's. And maybe something would happen to help change me from the miserable wretch I had become. Parading about in my letter jacket as if I was somebody important. Just because of one game I didn't even want to play.

But, at the same time, I questioned staying and making a stupid show of my remorse, my repentance. What good would it do to go through such a public ritual, especially here? I was only one-quarter Indian anyway; it wouldn't be sincere. Worse, not believing in God, I didn't even feel Jewish anymore. After all, I hadn't yet visited the graves of my grandfather, mother or father. And the first time I recited *Kaddish* at the synagogue was just the other day, at Uncle Abe's insistence. I never once went to synagogue or recited *Kaddish* on my own since moving in with Uncle Jack. Even though I had a prayer book and looked at the words, I still couldn't make myself pray.

I took the snow-snake. Everyone backed away. A feeling of crippling solitude swept over me; disgrace eviscerated my strength. I could barely grip the polished wood shaft. I trudged reluctantly toward the open channel, and my weight sank into my hips so that when I picked up speed I wouldn't slip before completing my release. I ran up, planted, and torqued my arm with an inconclusive might. And yet, despite my lack of sincerity, an almost emitic fling sent the snake speeding down the track with a force much greater than I thought I could muster. It ran straight and true, farther than any one of my previous throws.

What happened? Where did that come from?

It was in that moment of despair and wonderment that Phaedra found me.

"Danny!" she yelled, fording through an opening in the snowbank. I turned. A white plume of exhaust billowed behind her from a car parked on the highway. I walked to meet her.

"What are you doing here? My God, you look miserable. Are you sick?"

I had no sense of being so transparent, no sense of anything, really, except blinding white snow. I didn't want her to see me this way. Her arrival seemed an intrusion of sorts, as if this place and my despondency were, in fact, sacred. I was on the verge of dismissing her and ruining the fantasy that in the back of my mind I'd planned for the two of us.

We spoke for only a few moments; I handled it badly. "I have to stay here," I said with vapid yet insistent finality.

"Then why did you send for me?"

I had no answer, and she stormed off, exasperated. Disgusted with myself, I turned and walked back to the group of engrossed, yet expressionless, boys standing bare-headed, waiting for the game to resume.

The next day, Jesse led me through the rite of confession at the Council House. It began with recitation of the Code of Handsome Lake—the teachings of the prophet. A string of wampum was placed on a bench, and he and I joined a line of men and women. It was a simple ceremony. Each person picked up the wampum string and stated what he or she ought not to have done, replacing the wampum on the bench when finished. But even in light of the candor with which each person confessed their regrets, all of a much graver nature than mine, it was difficult to level with those beside me.

I tried to contain my emotions. It was as if all the unmentioned sins of my past, never revealed during all those *Yom Kippur* services I attended as an anonymous, silent worshipper, gushed forth in my simple statement to the strangers gathered before me. Simple as it was, I still had to write it out the day before while sitting on the floor of Jesse's cabin, in order to actually speak it.

"I left Jessie Isaacs' cabin unguarded, to return to the city with my uncle, without thanking Jessie for giving me a home when I had no place to go. Just as bad, I left without saying goodbye to Echo, the dog who gave me the gift of *orenda*, who was entrusted to me in order to help heal me when I was in great distress. Because he's dead, there is nothing I can do now but to say how sorry I am."

A murmur of acknowledgment rose from those gathered; it was simple and simultaneous, like an amen, and as soon as it was uttered, a great weight seemed to rise up from the pit of my stomach where so much travail seemed to collect. Now it was just the husk of my being that still seemed so brittle.

Mrs. Hill approached me and shook my hand, followed by her husband, Sonny, Welcome, and a few others. And suddenly, emerging from behind another group of worshippers, wearing a fringed and beaded shawl wrapped tightly around her, Yvonne came forward. She nodded solemnly. I bowed my head, chagrined. She held out her hand as if she wanted me to take it. But it was balled into a fist. Then her fingers unfolded, palm-up, revealing a silver wolf pin.

"You left this behind at Jesse's the day your uncle came for you. You should take it back."

CHAPTER 27

I stayed on at Jessie's for a few more days, following Sonny on one occasion when he supervised a group of children dressed in old clothing and masks—the Beggars—who went house-to-house collecting tobacco to be used later in certain invocations, and witnessing for him a specially-requested rite of dream-guessing.

Sonny had left Valley Academy at mid-semester after a series of arguments with some teachers. He had been foiled in his attempt to study art; instead, he was forced to choose among a series of vocational-training courses. There was also an irresolvable dispute with Mr. Andrews, the football coach who also taught U.S. History, that turned out to be the final straw for him. One day in Mr. Andrews' class Sonny insisted that the Founding Fathers learned the concept of a federation of unified colonies from an Iroquois chief, Canassatego, modeled on the Iroquois Confederacy.

According to Sonny, Andrews scoffed at such a claim. The U.S. government derived from Europe, he insisted, namely the Greeks and Romans. Plato had sketched out the ideal government in *The Republic*, and Aristotle analyzed different constitutions in *Politics*. He told Sonny to look at photos of the architecture of Washington, D.C. if Sonny wanted further evidence of the classical European influence on the Founding Fathers. But Sonny persisted, reiterating stories he'd heard from tribal elders. That's when Mr. Andrews required proof.

"Myths do not count," Mr. Andrews said. "Come back when you have proof, documented evidence; then we'll see who's right, once and for all."

The day Sonny returned, he approached Mr. Andrews at his desk and asked him if he had a dollar bill.

"What's that got to do with anything?"

Sonny persisted. Mr. Andrews took out his wallet, withdrew a dollar bill, and pressed it out on his desk.

"There. So what does this prove."

Sonny pointed to the Seal of the United States. "See the bundle of 13 arrows clutched in the claw of the eagle?"

Mr. Andrews put on his reading glasses and peered closely. "So? Those arrows represent the original 13 colonies."

"Why an eagle? Why arrows?"

Mr. Andrews shrugged.

"There's a mural on the wall of my grammar school that shows the Peacemaker and his messenger Hayenwatha standing on the Tree of Peace. The Peacemaker holds a bundle of five arrows that symbolizes the Five Nations Confederacy and carries the message that strength comes from unity. A vigilant eagle of peace sits at the top of the tree. What kind of branch do you think that eagle on the dollar bill holds in his other claw? Where do you think the Founding Fathers got the ideas for these symbols?"

"The eagle is a traditional European symbol...."

Then Sonny opened his notebook. Copied neatly onto one page was a heading: *The History of the Five Nations* by Cadwallader Colden, 1727, followed by text. Another title appeared on the second page, *League of the Iroquois* by Lewis Henry Morgan, followed by more text. On a third page, a third title, *Democracy in America* by Alexis de Tocqueville, 1945, followed by text. And, finally, on page four, *Notes on the State of Virginia*" by Thomas Jefferson, 1779, followed by several final paragraphs of text.

"Where did you get these?" Mr. Andrews demanded.

"A friend of mine, a scholar by the name of Mr. Abraham Mendoza. He found these for me at the Brant University library."

"These parallels don't mean anything; they're just coincidental."

That's when Sonny quit school.

At the beginning of the dream-guessing ritual, Sonny said to me, "Since then, I've been having this dream about my future. You're in it, too. I'd like some help in finding out what it means."

This ritual was attended by only a few persons: Sonny's parents, Mrs. Hill, Jessie, myself and a few older people. Uncle Abe had been sent for, too, because of my appearance in the dream; he arrived by Iroquois taxi carrying a large tureen of beef and vegetable soup prepared by Meltzer. I thought Mrs. Hill, our former teacher, would be upset with Sonny's decision to leave school. Instead, she seemed to support it.

After the burning of tobacco and stirring of ashes in the fireplace at Sonny's house and everybody had settled into their seats, Sonny described the details of his dream. They seemed sketchy and perplexing, almost like a riddle.

In his dream, he said, he finds himself in an encampment, similar to the palisaded Iroquois settlements of old. But, instead of being away hunting or traveling, all the men are at home, and it is the women and children who are absent. Moreover, he recognizes no one, save me. In fact, we enter the encampment simultanously, and together we train to become warriors. But, suddenly, the dream changes, and instead of going to war, we're playing games. The competition is keen among the players, but the games we choose to play are not the same, and we become separated. And the play, he says, is endless.

There is a respectful silence afterward. It is apparent we are all trying to make sense of his dream, but no one appears to have a discerning angle.

"Well, it's possible you're both attending a college where Sonny plays lacrosse and Daniel plays football," Uncle Abe guesses.

"Except Sonny has left high school," Mrs. Hill advised.

"And I'm not going back."

"Maybe it means that you're both going into the Army," one older man suggests. "That would account for the settlement populated only by men, training to be warriors."

"Except they wouldn't be playing games, would they?" Mrs. Hill asks Jessie.

"Well, it's possible," he answers. "The military loves its sports teams. Sonny's been boxing long enough now to compete on a service team. Daniel could play football."

"But what would be the point?" Sonny asks. "Don't you join the Army to fight or learn a trade?"

"The war in Korea is over," one white-haired man said. "Is there some other country we could be fighting next?"

"I don't think I want to join the Army," I offer. "I want to stay in school. I could earn a college scholarship next year."

"It wouldn't be the Army anyway," Sonny says in an admonishing tone. "It would be the Marines."

"Then that definitely leaves me out!" I say, to a sudden eruption of laughter.

I can't imagine myself in an outfit like the Marines, with its fierce harassment of recruits, or having to put up with a drill sergeant like Coach Andrews. I can't imagine Sonny volunteering for such torment either, especially after what he's already endured at school.

So the dream-guessing ends inconclusively. I'd expected solemnity, but this ritual has been light-hearted, concluding with a mini-feast of soup and cornbread. Uncle Abe tells me later that the purpose of it probably isn't so much to guess the dream as it is to console the dreamer.

"Sonny's at a crossroads in his life now; he has to make a choice soon about his future, and his options may be limited. He can't make a living selling his boxer profiles. He's too young to join the Marines. Winter has just begun, so he can't get a construction job. There's not a lot he can do, but there is a lot for him to think about...and maybe even worry about."

Before nightfall, we said our goodbyes. It had been only three days, but I felt like my stay had lasted much longer and that I'd gained a new appreciation for the reservation; I knew I would return and that I had friends there who really cared about me. I was especially relieved there were no hard feelings about my abrupt departure last summer, and I vowed to be more thoughtful of others and never take sanctuary for granted.

Fate seemed to have drawn me there. Even the similarities that'd fascinated Uncle Abe but seemed so far-fetched to me were nudged closer by coincidence: a grainy photo Uncle Abe noticed, cut and pasted into a simple wood frame that leaned against the kitchen counter at Sonny's house. It showed an Indian named Wovoka, the Paiute prophet of the Ghost Dance, wearing a long black suit coat and high-crowned hat so similar to that worn by Orthodox Hasidic men. It was a close-up of him standing on a street corner, staring at the photographer. But it had the effect of him staring at me, standing like a statue, dark and resolute.

Perhaps I was neither Indian nor Jew, lacking blood of one and faith in the other. But I had experienced such a profound sense of bereavement and self-contempt, leaving me so suddenly and irrevocably adrift, that I yearned to feel remorse. And the reservation —everything that placed me there this time—seemed to bring me to the brink of what I could only call opportunity, that I could start over again if I wanted with a clean slate. I just had to acknowledge that.

I vowed to never forget the onslaught of shame that began with the insight of how I'd abandoned Echo, then branched out to include my other past sins. And now, when I looked at my scars, including the older one on my hand from the night I got drunk and burned myself with a cigarette, I would think of Echo and this past week instead of the wisdom I thought I'd obtained.

When we left Sonny's house, his father was taking down his False Face mask to prepare for another Midwinter ritual. It reminded me to ask Uncle Abe why a monster's image would be called upon to heal. Evening fell quietly over the reservation, made pristine again by the early winter storm, and our taxi crept slowly toward the lights of the city.

"Remember when you asked me about the meaning of Yom Kippur— the Day of Atonement?" Uncle Abe began.

"Sort of; can you remind me what you said?"

"I told you that atonement for an innocent child like yourself couldn't be about owning up to your own wrong-doings but for the transgressions of somebody else; that by doing so, you help redeem the standing of everybody.

"That led you to ask why God created a world where evil existed and caused innocent people to suffer. I commented on the *sefiroth* and how God created man to make good victorious over evil and that without evil it would be impossible for man to achieve a righteous state, albeit through maximum efforts.

"Well, the Iroquois—and other people, too—have a belief about the co-existence of good and evil, only with the beneficent twist: their creator has vanquished evil but allowed it to continue to exist in the service of mankind. So now, when a man like Jessie who has come face-to-face with the evil of war resolves his inner demons, he assumes the False face of *Hadui*, one of the evil twin's creations. He uses evil to banish evil by literally frightening away the evil of disease.

"What's amazing is how common this phenomenon is, from Asia to Melanesia to America. If you have time this vacation, I'll take you to the university library and show you photographs and paintings of gods-as-monsters."

As the taxi crept closer to the city center along a snow-clogged thoroughfare, I still didn't understand the mystery of good and evil, or how the mask of a monster had the power to heal. But I was beginning to appreciate the willingness of people like Uncle Abe and Jessie to immerse themselves in this belief, to understand it to the point of explaining it and practicing it in the service of others. In a sense, this alone was comforting to me. It would undoubtedly be hard to explain all this to Uncle Jack, beginning with the movie, *The Harder They Fall*, and through to Sonny's dream.

CHAPTER 28

More than anything, telling him about the movie irritated Uncle Jack.

"You gotta remember, Danny, a movie is not a documentary like Uncle Abe says it is. It's based on a novel, a made-up story. Granted, it's a story based on real-life situations, but it's one that's stitched together, like pieces of a patchwork quilt. The actors' lines are made up. The story demands a contrast between good and evil, good guys and bad guys, and boxing is a perfect subject to do that because it's a crooked sport. But you gotta take it with a grain of salt. And you gotta remember what I told you about Uncle Abe: he's a religious zealot. He sees things in black and white. Life is just not that way."

What he said made sense. But I wondered why I accepted it just as easily as I accepted the food from his table. The movie rang true for me, too, based on what I knew and what Uncle Abe had shown me, and I accepted it. Was one meal just as good as another to a guy with an empty belly? I worried that I could be so easily convinced of the truth of one thing, then later just as easily be disabused of it. Perhaps I just didn't know enough or know how to weigh contrary ideas methodically.

At any rate, it was a bad idea to ask Uncle Jack questions about the Maxim fight over a hurried breakfast on a morning he had to go to court, especially because I'd already agitated him by my actions over the past few days. I decided to put it off until another day. He stared at me over the brim of his coffee cup.

Trying to make amends with Phaedra was another matter.

"I thought you wanted to spend time with me over the vacation," she complained when I phoned her. "It's bad enough you weren't even around at Christmas, but to miss our date for New Year's Eve, the biggest night of the whole year? That is inexcusable."

Her tone softened, but the effect was the same. "Now I have to go back to school, and it's my last semester, and I really have to study hard and get good grades. I don't understand why you went back to that reservation. I thought you weren't going to go there anymore. You told me you couldn't wait to escape."

I tried to explain to her, like I'd hoped to explain to Uncle Jack, about how it all began with a date to go to the movies with Uncle Abe, meeting Sonny, going back to Uncle Abe's house, the invitation to Midwinter, learning about Echo. She didn't want to hear it.

"You and boxing; it makes me sick. And snow-snake? C'mon, isn't that a child's game? When I saw you, you looked like you were having a nervous breakdown. You got that worked up over a dog?"

Now my frustration boiled over. I felt like I couldn't apologize, nor could I possibly admit how depressed I'd become due to Echo's death and what it meant to stay and try to absolve my debt to him and to Jessie and Sonny and even to Uncle Abe and, in the process, rid myself of an accumulated and crushing burden. I couldn't even explain it to myself. And the more I tried, the more hesitant and tongue-tied I became. I just wanted to distance myself from the whole thing.

"Look, isn't there any way I can make it up to you? We have this weekend before school begins; we could...go to the movies."

"Oohh!"

Not the right thing to say.

"Even if I wanted to—and I don't—I can't now. A friend of our family, a boy from Princeton, came to visit us on New Year's Day. My mother invited him, so he's our house guest, and I have to spend my remaining free time with him."

"Is that the one your mother talked about last summer when you went away?"

"Yes," she said, her voice edged with satisfaction. "And he's invited me to Princeton's Winter Weekend; he's on the hockey team. And my mother wants me to invite him to my senior prom. Especially if I'm nominated to be queen."

From her perspective, whatever crisis I'd gone through compared little to the disappointment I'd caused her. She had her mind made up. There didn't seem to be anything I could say or do now. I was also certain her mother saw my absence as an opportunity to wedge him between us, and the awkward silence from my end made it even worse.

"So what will you do tonight?" she asked, petulantly.

"I don't know. Call Prado, maybe shoot some pool at Nate's, go down to the Café Jake. Why?"

Click. She was obviously perturbed at my answer, as desperate and truthful as it sounded to me. Café Jake was to have been one of our stops on New Year's Eve, along with several parties, especially a big party at Brenda Starr's house. Phaedra had been looking forward to going where none of her girlfriends could go, somewhere especially exciting. The All-Stars would've been rocking.

I called Prado. He sounded tired.

"I'm still recovering from New Year's. Where've you been, man? Why didn't you come down to the club? You really missed a great one. People were asking about you."

"Who?"

"Eugene, mom, Frankie, Brenda and Lonnie Starr. It was fabulous, man. Some other musicians came in from out of town. I've never seen anything like it. And the Starrs had a ton of food at their party; some of the best baked ham I've ever had in my life!"

"So, what did you say when they asked about me?"

"I said I didn't know where you were, that maybe you went to another party, that maybe Phaedra took you to her country club. You're pretty famous now, you know."

"Funny, very funny. Phaedra won't even talk to me because I missed our date."

"Well then, where the hell were you?"

"It's a long story, Robbie. I can't tell you over the phone."

"Okay. I got the car tonight. Let's go to Nate's, shoot some pool. Later, we'll hit Café Jake. The All Stars are playing again tonight. Maybe some of those cats who sat in New Year's will still be in town, too."

Not only did Robbie understand my story—and it was a long one—but about a quarter-way through, during a game of snooker—he just laid down his cue.

"I can't listen to this in here, man; it's way too intense. Finish telling me at the Open Door. I need a drink!"

At the bar, we started with glasses of beer and shots of schnapps, and as I talked he just sat and stared at me, shaking his head at certain parts.

"This shit is unbelievable!"

The more beer and schnapps I drank, the more wound-up I became. I expected the opposite effect, like in the old days. Instead, telling Robbie my story dredged up the same kind of confusion and internal quaking I'd experienced the night of the LaSalle game. My stutter returned, my armpits dripped with sweat, and the intensity of telling my story and the shared intimacy fueled our drinking. When I finished, he stood and lifted me off my barstool and hugged me.

"Danny! You're unbelievable, man!"

Right at that moment, three tough-looking guys entered the bar wearing long overcoats of a kind I remembered only too well. Prado turned to face them.

"Heeyy Prado!" one of them yelled, a grin of recognition spreading across his face.

Prado's intonation shifted from Negro hipster to working-class Italian. "Heeyy Steve, Phil, DeLuca; what're you guys doin'? C'mon over here and have a drink."

We shook hands all around. I recognized two as football players from Northside Genoa High School: Dickie DeLuca, a big lineman about Billy's size and with a reputation as a street-fighter; and Steve Breschi, a slender halfback who I recalled pass-blocking me with a ferocity that belied his size. The other had a cherubic face but manic eyes. He wore his straight blond hair in a D.A. And was introduced formally: Ray DiNardi Jr.

DeLuca said they were working their way around downtown bars. They joined us for shots and beers and reminisced about our past season. Too wound up, confused and afraid to stutter, I let Prado do the talking. There was a surprising camaraderie between him and the Northsiders, guys who I'd heard were notorious territorial gang-fighters. I remembered seeing a carload pull up near Valley Academy a year ago to do battle with Donny Reed's gang, replete with chains and baby baseball bats and tire irons. DiNardi kept his eyes on me throughout the conversation. Finally, during a lull, a light of dawning recognition broke his disquieting stare. He began politely, with a deference that was disconcerting.

"Are you in any way related to Mendoza the boxer?"

I nodded.

"His father," Prado said.

He referred to his father as R.D.

"R.D. knew him good."

I carefully measured his tone as he spoke, searching for any hint of sarcasm or belligerence and worrying about how I should properly respond.

"Mendoza...your dad...used to spar with one of R.D.'s boys, right? Joey DeYoung. They were friends, right?"

I nodded, taken aback by his assertion and his suddenly-sunny disposition. I couldn't even begin to address this line of conversation and tried to shift the focus. I managed to do this without stuttering.

"How is Joey? I haven't seen him.... I mean, I haven't heard about him since the LaMotta fight. What was that...about two, three years ago?"

He shrugged. A sneer pursed his lips.

"Losing to LaMotta in front of the home crowd as badly as he did...that was inexcusable. R.D. says it took everything out of him. He fought a coupla more times. Won one, lost one. But he hasn't trained in over a year. Matter of fact, he's been workin' as a bouncer at R.D.'s place, the Chez Ami. He keeps talkin' about makin' a comeback, but... ."

He shook his head, disgusted. His criticism of Joey seemed too irreverent to me, but I kept quiet, hoping for the subject to change.

"You should look him up some time; he'd probably really like to see you. Any friendly face from the old days. Matter of fact, we're goin' down there later for the last show. Maybe you'll meet us; we'll share a table."

I nodded, but my face burned.

"Jack Mendoza. He must be your uncle, right?"

Prado shouted for the bartender to pour another round of shots, trying to staunch the flow of repartee. The Northsiders demurred. "No more for us, Robbie," Breschi said, smiling. "We gotta meet my brother, Tony, and some other guys up the street in about... ."

He checked his watch. "...shit, five minutes."

But Prado signaled the bartender to pour the shots. Good-natured posturing, an insistence on generosity. Finally the Northsiders threw them back.

"What the fuck. Keep the chill off, right?" DiNardi said, wiping his lips. He started to say something more to me, but DeLuca took him by the arm.

"C'mon, Ray. We'll see these guys another time."

After a final round of handshakes, I made for the men's room where my piss ricocheted off stacked cakes of deodorizer. At the sink where I washed my hands, I peered at my reflected image in a cracked mirror and tried to replace the anxiety with blank disregard. But I couldn't even convince myself. When I returned to the bar, Robbie rolled his eyes and shook his head.

"How do you know those guys so well?" I asked.

"My father plays cards with their fathers, makes a few bets." He shook off my sour glare.

"A lot of Jewish guys from the old neighborhood know the Northside Italians," he said, defensively. "You notice we never have a beef with them like we do the assholes at LaSalle? That's because there's been a relationship for years between Jews like my father and some of the Italians. Billy and I have played hooky to visit them at Genoa; they've cut to visit us at East Brant. We've dated their girls; they've dated ours. Christ, I've been invited to Breschi's house for Sunday dinner with the whole family after mass. Drank a ton of his old man's wine. Even helped crush grapes one time, with our bare feet.... Washed, of course."

Prado enumerated on the fingers of one hand the similarities among our fathers' generation of Jews and Italians.

"They all came up in the Depression.

"Family is everything.

"Their fathers were peddlers, too, and they hung around the central market together.

"And they all liked to gamble."

"There weren't any Italians in our house," I countered, "except for maybe Joey DeYoung."

"Well, I don't know why not. My father and yours and Uncle Jack and all the fathers from the old neighborhood were friends. Unless it was the DiNardi thing."

"Does your father know DiNardi?"

Prado peered at me over the rim of his beer glass, then set it down on his paper napkin, seeming to measure his response.

"Only in the sense that they traveled in the same circles sometimes, like at sporting events, BU football, pro basketball at the War Memorial, playing the horses at Pompeii Raceway, they hit some of the same watering holes; late-night meals at Poodle's."

"What about my Uncle Jack?"

"In the old days? Sure. Today? I doubt it. They're on opposite sides of the fence.

"C'mon," he cajoled. "You just told me your uncle tried to make the fight with Maxim. He'd have had to deal with DiNardi for that to happen. That's how the fight game works, right? Obviously, something must've happened at the last minute. Your uncle must've backed off. My father says nobody really knows."

"What trouble is DiNardi in?"

"He helped plan a big syndicate meeting that the police found out about and raided last summer. Remember Apalachia? One of the biggest mob stories of the decade. A lot of the big shots got caught. DiNardi got away. Jumped out a window and got lost in the woods. Supposedly he was lost for three days. Until some hunters found him."

"Ever since then, they say he's been a little nutty. Burying his slot machines, shutting down a lot of his operations. My dad says he's been drowning himself in Chivas because the state police are after him, and the syndicate is mad at him."

Robbie pushed my shot glass closer; it skated across the bar on a water slick.

"C'mon, man, drink up. We need to relocate this party. Let's go to Café Jake; it's about time for the first set."

I remained on my stool, elbows on the bar, staring into the mirror that ran from one end of the bar to the other. And what appeared to be an optical illusion had my mirrored image staring right back, framed by columns and racks of liquor bottles in all sizes, shapes, and shimmering colors. Ignoring Prado, I studied my frozen image which, in turn, seemed to be studying me, possessed by a drunken steeliness. My ears began to ring as the blank disregard I'd tried to represent in the bathroom turned to revulsion. Stunned, I leaned forward and gripped the curled edge of the bar. I could feel Prado slip away to the bathroom.

"Hey, kid; you okay?"

The bartender/proprietor, a retired boxer everyone knew as Kid Firpo, called to me from behind the bar where he plunged dirty glasses into a sink, massaging them over an erect brush, rinsing them in an adjacent tub, then letting them stand to drain. I ignored him. Instead, I gave in—utterly—to this surge of anger that just immobilized me. The longer I stared into the mirror, the image stared back: angry, immobile, accusing. As if it had developed a spirit of its own and was hypnotizing me. All peripheral vision vanished.

Even when Prado returned from the bathroom and shook my shoulder, the only image I could see in the mirror was a masked version of my own.

"Hey. Danny." He tried to snap me out of my trance. "Hey, man; what's wrong?"

When I didn't respond, his voice took on an edge of alarm. "Danny. Danny! C'mon! Let's get outa here. Don't get strange on me."

He pulled me gently toward him. It seemed to me that he was deliberately trying to distort my vision and I couldn't let that happen. I whacked
his arm. He tried again. I flung him back into an empty booth.

"What the fuck is wrong with you?" He tried to right himself.

"Stay where you are!" I bellowed. "You touch me, I'll kill you!"

The few patrons—middle-aged men and women who made the
Open Door their second home—swung around their barstools in disbelief. Gripping a police baton, Kid Firpo raised his bar gate and stepped
swiftly toward us.

"Both a ya: get outa here before I call the cops," he said, with
conviction.

"You won't do that," I responded, suddenly alert to the dynamic of
the situation. "You're serving minors; you'll lose your license."

"Wise guy, huh?" He took a few quick steps and raised the baton
above his shoulder. Prado made a move to push out of the booth. I turned
and he sat back down. He sighed and banged a fist on the table. "Danny.
Let's...get...out...of here."

Between Prado's dismay and Kid Firpo's raised baton, I glimpsed my
own futile madness and just let go of it. I realized that the option of going
berserk and fighting Prado was pointless. There were, I supposed, other possibilities. But they remained unfocused. I just knew they existed and that
was enough. I shrugged, a helpless gesture, and a convulsive sob escaped
from between my clenched teeth. Prado just sat there, not knowing what
to do. Kid Firpo set the baton on the bar. It rolled off and onto the rubber
matting behind the bar as he made his way over to me and took my arm
and led me to the door, waving Prado out of the booth behind me.

"Take it easy, kid. We got us a whole new year ahead of us," he said
in a soothing, doctor-to-patient voice as he held open the door. "Come
back when you feel better, when ya feel like ya wanna have some fun. The
Kid'll play spoons for ya; just for you. Whaddya say?"

I looked into his rheumy eyes and at his furrowed and knotted forehead and tried to imagine what ferocity he'd brought with him into the
ring so many years ago.

I walked outside. The heat of my wretched anger vaporized and swirled
away in the cold wind. Prado kept a certain proprietary distance.

"Are you ready for Chez Jake? Or do you wanna go home?"

I looked at him, suddenly embarrassed at the tears that streaked my
face. He raised his hands forgivingly.

"Hey. Either way is okay with me. But, ya know? I think we should
stick to our original plan...catch some good music...see some friends. Be

good for you."

He pulled from his back pocket a large workingman's handkerchief and handed it to me. I wiped my eyes and blew my nose and started to hand it back to him.

He laughed out loud. "Hey, man; keep it. I got it at your grand-father's store."

He started down the street and I staggered after him, impressed with his good grace.

CHAPTER 29

I could tell by the dreamy looks of satisfaction and pride on the faces of the crowd at Café Jake that the All Stars—well into their first set—had already fulfilled expectations and lulled them out of the troubled rhythms and discordant idiom of their own ordinary lives. The pitch of excitement was that of a first set, too: loud, crisp, enthusiastic, but not yet transcendent. Customers were still calling for drinks, yelling out name brands and concoctions, rudely demanding to have their fuel with their music and no delays. Jockeying for positions closer to the bar, squeezing into extra chairs at tables, cramped in their seats but snapping their fingers, lighting cigarettes with a flourish, arranging glasses and ashtrays and napkins just so.

Wilbert, the young waiter, eyeballed us from the back of the room and waved us over to a single empty seat at his end of the bar which was, of course, the farthest from the front window where the police liked to look in.

Café Jake possessed an entirely different atmosphere from the gloom that had burdened me at the the Open Door. Here, one literally stepped into joy and bright lights, although at times the excitement seemed almost too much for some people to bear, and they went off in a different direction of expressing themselves. As a matter of fact, Prado told me that the bar was kept brightly-illuminated at night to better allow Eugene to pick out the troubled ones before things went too far. Knives and razors were known to come out during a provocation, and Eugene wanted to be able to leap over the bar and separate the combatants before damage could occur, or at least reach out with his night stick and club the weapons loose from their grasps.

Prado wedged me up against the wall to help keep me erect. He put a Champale in front of me and poured it halfway into a glass. He grinned reassuringly.

"Here. Relax. You'll be okay. And even better after Lonnie gets here."

The floor plan of Café Jake included a horseshoe-shaped bar with high stools and standing room, booths along the side walls, and a dozen or so cocktail tables in front of the bandstand. It allowed patrons to view the live entertainment from any location. But no mirrors. It was the kind of lively bar that discouraged morose introspection; Café Jake was a place of celebration. Rich, raging, spell-binding at times. But it didn't register with me that night.

Intoxicated, wedged between Prado and the milling, dancing, finger-popping patrons and a brick wall, I continued to nurse the sour mood that I'd been carrying since we left the Open Door.

Prado tried to lessen the risk of any further outburst on my part by plying me with drinks, ordering shots of schnapps for a jovial Negro with a dark, shiny face who connived to tip them discreetly into my beer glass.

I stared at my hand that held the glass. The burn scar reminded me not of Echo but of the night I stood by a fire three years ago with my compatriots of the moment, discovering in the dead of night the wisdom of avoidance, of not caring, of going it alone, of being free of obligation, of cutting oneself adrift. Of course, that didn't solve anything; it was just running away. Running away, not running until one's breath gave out. But what was the good of solving anything? It's not only too hard, but it's also too risky, too costly.

Prado grabbed my wrist. I looked up expecting him to be yelling something in my ear, but he was gazing at the front entrance. I lurched away from the wall to get a better look. Phaedra stood just inside the doorway, unwrapping a scarf, shaking loose her blonde hair, laughing, snuggling inside the arm of a broad-faced guy wearing a toggle-button greatcoat who carried himself with a kind of brave discomfort at having to follow her into a completely alien setting. Paired with him, she gave off a debutante aura, exalted yet basking in the moment of notoriety. A hurtful, sinking feeling pierced my chest, accompanied by a rush of blood to my face.

She glanced around the room, waved at Eugene, pushed her way boldly to the front of the bar, squeezing between two men eager to make her acquaintance, and claimed a just-vacated barstool. Eugene made a big show of welcoming her, toweling off the bar where she sat and sliding two napkins into place, alternatively beaming at her and scowling at the two men until they backed away and snaked around to the other side of the bar.

Phaedra's date slid into the space next to her, dipping his shoulder in order to angle up to the bar. Eugene asked him what he wanted to drink, but before he could respond Phaedra shouted the order and Eugene reached into a cooler for two Champales and set them down on the bar along with two clean glasses and napkins. The boyfriend picked up the bottle, studied the label, took a sip, glanced at her, nodded approval. She flashed a perfect smile at him; I sank further into despondency.

She lurched closer to him, grabbing him by the shoulder, wheeling around on her barstool, urging his attention in the direction of the band which was in full swing now, breaking into a series of improvisational solos, beginning with Sy himself wailing on his saxophone, dipping, swinging, his eyes wide with all the attention on him.

I used a bar napkin to sop sweat from my brow and took another sip of sticky-minted beer. I could barely get it down past the bile that was rising from my stomach and nearly choked. Prado turned to me, flashing a questioning look. Sarah finished serving a man who'd mounted a demanding refrain: "Sarah! Two S'litz! Two S'litz!" and came over to me, casting the same look of concern.

The boyfriend from Princeton drained his beer and yelled to Eugene for another. He glanced around the bar, smirking at the merriment that was his principal source of entertainment, then turned to Phaedra and grabbed a fist-full of the front of her coat and pulled her close. He seemed to be yelling something in her ear, but he wasn't; he was sticking his tongue there. She tried to push him away just as the guitar player began his turn at the break. But the boyfriend grabbed her by her wrist and torqued it until she faced him, and at that moment she found me. Her expression—a mixture of annoyance and fear—changed to one of triumph. Prado caught it, too.

"Oh, oh," was all he said.

I pushed off the wall, brushed past Prado's outstretched arm and wedged my way through the crowd standing two-deep along my side of the bar, impelled by betrayal just as the guitarist's solo ended and the crowd responded with a rousing, cheering ovation. As the band swung into the

final chorus, growing louder with a surge of finality, I bulled my way around
the bar, aggravating nearly everybody in my path. Phaedra's laughing eyes
followed me all the way, and when I stood before her she sidled seductively
closer to her escort. Their tongues swam in each other's mouths until she
pushed him roughly away. He swayed drunkenly, eyes half-closed, mouth
still clownishly puckered.

"Well, well; look who's here!" she shouted, her lips swollen and
contorted from smeared lipstick, glistening wet, ugly, tempting. "Danny
Mendoza. The boy I told you about, Eric?"

Eric regained his masculine composure. He had chiseled, high
cheekbones, ruddy from being out-of-doors. A smile of superior disdain
broke across his face. He nodded.

"Aren't you having a good time, Danny?" she asked.

Her mocking tone cut right through me. I stood there, speechless,
the applause winding down now as Sy introduced the band at the end of
the set.

"...and ladies and gentlemen, on guitar, the very wonderful, very,
very exciting Marcus Curry...Marcus...."

A man accidentally bumped me from behind trying to get by the knot
of uncordiality blocking his way to the exit, causing me to spill beer onto
the front of Phaedra's coat. In reflexive recoil, Phaedra bumped a woman
behind her who, in turn, spilled her own drink, spattering the shoes of
a man standing next to her and setting off a chain-reaction commotion.
Each aggrieved person competed to vent their displeasure, but only one
was directed at the source.

"You clumsy jerk!" Phaedra screamed at me.

A strange thing happened, so clear in my mind that it transformed
into a vision. I was meeting her for the first time: the confident, knowing
Phaedra who'd chosen me to be the focus of her amusement, and I reached
out to her. When she batted my hand away, her expression changed into
a mask of loathing and reproach, a visage of an aged crone. Startled, I
pushed her away and she fell off her stool onto the woman who'd previously
spilled her drink. Our little contingent was on the brink of chaos now, and
Wilbert tried to intervene. Eric reached in to separate Phaedra from the
other woman, and in a moment of panicked chivalry, he elbowed me into
a cocktail table, tipping it and a collection of bottles, glasses, and ashtrays
onto the floor. I lost my balance and fell into the back of Phaedra's legs.

"Eric! Get him off me!"

Eric grabbed the back of my jacket, choking me, and I rolled into his
knees, bringing him to the floor where I sat astride him, punching him in

the face with ruinous abandon, bellowing half-formed obscenities as if I was speaking in tongues until I was lifted from behind. Someone strong bear-hugged me under my arms and compressed my ribs until punching became futile and our contrary efforts choked the breath out of me. It was Eugene, pushing and steering me from behind, over broken glass, slipping and sliding out the front door, bouncing off bodies until we hit a patch of ice and careened into a snowbank where the determination of his body buried me into submission. Even so, he maintained his grip, breathing hard but speaking calmly and directly into my ear, cajoling, reasoning with me to quit even though I felt like I hadn't even started.

Once I appeared to calm down, Prado and Sarah took over.

"You handle the customers, Eugene," Sarah said. "We'll get him out of here."

They escorted me to her car. Sarah, wearing only a cardigan sweater, shoved Robbie in back with me, got behind the wheel, started the engine, turned on the heater and reached back, clasping my hand. Prado just stared at me. I sat silent, gripped by torment.

"He started acting strange about an hour ago," he volunteered.

"Where were you before you came here?"

"Shooting pool at Nate's," he said, sheepishly.

"And then where?"

He didn't answer.

"C'mon, Robbie; look at the shape he's in. This didn't come from just shooting pool. You must've gone somewhere afterward. He only had one beer here, and he was nursing that one when all the trouble started."

"We had a few...," he mumbled.

"A few what?" Sarah shot back.

"Beers...and schnapps."

"How many?"

"...I don't know."

"So, where?"

"...the Open Door."

Exasperated, she shook her head. "So, what happened there that he started acting 'strange'?"

"It's hard to say."

She grew agitated. "Well, think! How much did he have to drink? What happened while you were there? What was said or done that might've upset him?"

Prado synopsized my story about going to the movies with Uncle Abe, meeting Sonny, spending the night discussing corruption in boxing.

"Then what?"

"Then some guys from Genoa came into the bar, football players I know. We talked a little bit, just ordinary stuff."

"What guys from Genoa?" she persisted.

The car heater was making me a little sick. I wanted fresh, cold air.

"Breschi, DeLuca...." His voice shrank. *"Ray DiNardi Jr."*

Sarah bit her lower lip. "So, was anything said? Did DiNardi start anything?"

"No, ma. You know those guys. They like me. They respect Danny, respect all of us...because of the LaSalle game. It was just a friendly conversation," he said, preserving my deeper motivation.

Sarah pulled on my hand. "Okay, Danny, what made you go 'strange'?"

I shrugged. Prado interceded.

"Okay, he and Phaedra also had a fight earlier about him going back to the reservation with Sonny over New Year's, not telling her about it, not showing up for their date. The guy she came with tonight is staying at her house...a guest...a family friend ...from Princeton."

"Prince-ton," she said, in mock disapproval. "Okay, I can understand that. But, Danny, you don't get into fights. It's so unlike you. I can understand jealousy. But the way you went after that boy tonight? You hurt a rich kid like him in my place, I'm in a lot of trouble."

She pushed up a thumb to enumerate. "One, if the police are called because of a fight, they vacate the premises and report it to the Liquor Board who could suspend my license. Two, serving drinks to minors; that's a definite suspension. I've been good about letting you kids come in here to listen to the music, but you have to respect my situation. You come here, you stay out of the way, you remain on good behavior. Three, that kid gets hurt? His father sues me. Now I'm really in trouble." She tugged on my hand. "You don't want that to happen, do you?"

I muttered an apology. She let go my hand.

"Robbie, take him home. Better yet, take him to Poodle's and get some coffee into him, something to eat. Don't bring him home right now, not while he's in this state. I do not need grief from his uncle."

A shadow passed by the side of the car. Somebody knocked on the window. Prado rolled it down and Lonnie Starr leaned in.

"Mizz Sarah...Robbie.... How he doin'?"

"He's okay, honey. Just a lovers' quarrel. Robbie's taking him out for coffee. Why don't you go with him? How's everything inside?"

Lonnie laughed. "Phaedra be hot. And that boy she with, he be even more hot. Bloody mess, cussin' 'n' shit. Eugene told Phaedra to leave because the police was probably on their way. That got him. They both cleared out a little while ago."

He slid into the back seat. Sarah gunned the motor and got out of the car. Prado moved up front.

"After you take him home, come back. I need to pick up your father. We'll all go home together."

Prado backed the car into the street; shifting gears, he drove hurriedly past the café, its lights blazing. He exhaled a long sigh of relief.

"Man, I can't believe my mother took that so good. It's all on account of she likes you so much."

I met his reassuring glance with a half-smile, but it masked the confusion and conflicting urges that continued to churn within me. I didn't want a diversion, didn't want a cup of coffee. Everything was changing, had been since the movie, and tonight something happened that pushed me beyond caution, beyond reticence, like nothing much mattered, and I discovered an anger that'd been buried for a long time, waiting for the just the right provocation to force it to the surface. Funny thing, but now that I had it, it didn't feel strange at all. It felt good, liberating, so I could do as I pleased, even dig for things I'd been pushing away, pushing away for a long, long time.

I waited until Prado braked at a traffic light on Main Street to tell him where I wanted to go. I wouldn't ask him to drive me there—the opposite direction of Poodle's. I would just get out while we were stopped. I looked at the dashboard clock: 11 p.m. Plenty of time to walk the six or seven blocks and arrive before the midnight show. I'd never been inside the Chez Ami before, but I guessed tonight they'd let me in. I was wearing a suit of Davey's that Aunt Charlotte had re-tailored for New Year's and a topcoat over that. If I borrowed a cigarette from Lonnie, I'd pass.

"I'm getting out here." I opened the passenger-side door.

"Whaddya mean, you're getting out here?" Prado asked, stunned. "Where do you think you're going?"

"The Chez Ami."

"Chez Ami?" Lonnie asked, equally stunned. "What for?"

"I want to talk to Joey."

Shocked, Prado turned and stared. I laughed. He reminded me of myself.

"Don't worry, I'm not going to cause any trouble. I just want to get in there and talk to him. I've got some questions maybe no one else can answer."

Prado just sat there, stymied, working his mind.

"Let us go with you," Lonnie said.

I shook my head. "Go to Poodle's. When you finish eating, if you want to, drive over and get me. I'll be done by then. You can drive me home."

"You're going right into the lion's den," Prado said. "What for? What if *he's* there?"

"I just want to talk to Joey. I'll be careful, catch him when he's alone. He used to really like me when I was a kid."

A horn blared behind us. Prado pursed his lips, gripped the steering wheel with both hands and swung around the corner.

"All right," Prado agreed. "But when we finish eating, we're coming right over. Shit. I've never even been inside the Chez Ami."

Lonnie grabbed my arm as I started out the door. "Save us seats, man."

I got out and slammed the door, lowered my head and walked into a stiff, cold wind, smiling at its resistance.

CHAPTER 30

The lit-up marquee was the only sign of life at that end of Main Street. I joined a line of men standing in front waiting to buy tickets from a bored-looking young woman in an enclosed booth who'd over-decorated her eyes with mascara and blue eye shadow and a dark rouge highlighting her cheekbones. I lit a cigarette when it was my turn to purchase a ticket, but when I approached, she startled me with a dramatic change of mood and I recognized her, a classmate from East Brant High, a Sephardic member of my synagogue, Ninette Pascal.

"Well, hello, Daniel," she said, coyly. "You look really nice all dressed up. Your first time?"

Her expression changed just as quickly when she read my look of bewilderment. In a forgiving gesture, she reached out and touched my hand. "I mean, have you ever been here before? My father is the stage manager; I work here weekends." Then she brightened. "Wait inside until the box office closes. You can share a really good table with me."

I nodded, unable to keep from staring at her enhanced beauty.

"Over there, the chair in the lobby. Take a seat. I close the booth just before midnight."

I must've look bewildered again. She looked at her watch and smiled.

"In about 10 minutes."

Grateful, I nodded and forced a smile. "Okay."

The customers ahead of me and a group streaming in from behind made their way to a bar at the other end of the lobby, opposite the velvet-roped entrance to the nightclub. It was at the bar—crowded with garrulous, self-conscious men waiting for the strip-show to begin—where Joey sat, holding court. Ninette's offer to sit with me seemed really opportune: I needed time to adjust, to sort out a plan, and it would be stupid to approach him just now.

Instead, I could sit inconspicuously with Ninette at one of the little tables situated in a darkened area mid-way to the stage, barely illuminated by a tiny cocktail lamp. My first thought after sitting down: *I'll stay put until the bar clears out.*

Ninette wore her hair up, earrings that sparkled, a tight sheath dress and high heels. At school, she was one of the most quiet and studious girls, anonymous. Here she seemed swanky and confident, a practiced charmer.

When a waitress approached, I lifted Ninette's burning cigarette from the ashtray, attempting to look sophisticated. Ninette and the waitress chuckled, but politely, admiringly, while exchanging knowing glances. I got it: my adventure here was going to work out for Ninette, too, as she accrued a kind of status.

"What would you like to drink, Daniel?" Ninette asked. "It's on me."

I thought of the rarest, most sophisticated drink I'd seen ordered at Café Jake.

"Scotch and milk, please. Make it Chivas."

The waitress cocked an eyebrow and wrote on her pad.

"Coffee for me," Ninette said.

The stage curtain opened, revealing a seven-piece band. All the musicians wore tuxedos; their leader sat at a white piano.

The headline stripper was preceded by a comedian. I recognized him, Dick Tobin, the ring announcer from the War Memorial who'd introduced me and Davey several years ago. Wearing the same tux. It was eerie to see him in this setting.

The more the announcer joked, the more I regressed into past memory, one triggering another, each one piquant and dream-like.

Ninette broke through. "Did you come here to see Candy?" she asked after the waitress returned with our order. I didn't know how to answer that, so Ninette continued to carry the conversation. "She's a really great stripper, maybe the best."

I nodded, smiling with as much sophistication as I could muster, although my scotch and milk tasted chalky. She talked about Candy all through the comedy routine until the announcer told his final joke, took his bows, and exited to a crash of cymbals and a smattering of unenthusiastic applause.

Then the lights softened and the band segued into a sumptuous bump-and-grind fanfare, and from backstage stepped the most beautiful woman I had ever seen, a perfectly-proportioned honey blonde whose confident, sublime eroticism summoned the last of the bar patrons to their tables around the elevated stage, their eyes alert with arousal.

My throat tightened and I had to fight to remember my resolve. I muttered an excuse, grabbed my topcoat, and forced myself to my feet. My legs felt as if they were about to go numb. Ninette looked betrayed, but I turned away and forged my way against the flow of the latest group of arriving devotees, awkwardly weaving my way toward the bar. Inside, alone and slumped in a booth clutching a highball, sat Joey DeYoung.

CHAPTER 31

A lone now, his mood seemed vastly different. He looked preoccupied, tired and wan in a pale gray/green double-breasted suit with shoulders so squared and heavily-padded that the jacket appeared one size too big. His shirt was unbuttoned at the collar and his tie was askew, and he stared morosely at the highball glass fixed between his thick thumbs and fingertips, displaying his big hands and prominent knuckles, like Davey's, the hands of a fighter. He didn't even react when I entered the bar, didn't even notice me until I stood directly in front of his table. Only then did he look up, irritated at being interrupted.

But his irritation disappeared and was replaced—over a few mutable seconds—by a studious, suspicious squint, followed by disbelief when it dawned on him who I might be; then his face became ashen. Reflexively, he shifted a few inches away from me.

"Joey," the bartender said as he approached with two clean glasses and bar napkins, "you look like you seen a ghost."

Seeing the fear and disbelief in Joey's eyes took the edge off my trepidation.

"I'm not a ghost," I said. "I'm just wearing Davey's suit. You haven't seen me since I was 12 years old."

But Joey, seemingly unconvinced, maintained his distance, and the bartender retreated diplomatically.

"Danny? How...how old are you now?" he asked, attempting to calculate the years.

"Not quite old enough to be in the Chez Ami, but here I am."

Joey nodded at a space across from him. "Take a seat. Jesus, kid, you gave me quite a start," he said, relenting, searching my face, making mental comparisons, sizing me up. "You...you're the spitting image of your old man. You even look like a boxer. How'd you break your nose?"

"Playing football."

"Oh, yeah?" he said, buying time, calculating the circumstances of my arrival, adjusting his disposition. "Which school? How'd it happen?"

"East Brant. I got kicked in the face making a low tackle in the championship game against LaSalle."

He nodded, still studying me. "You had a good year? I don't follow high school sports."

"Well, like I said, because of that game, we won the title. I made All-City...end"

"Fantastic. Fantastic. And how'd you get the scar over your eye?"

"Four years ago. When my grandfather's store burned down."

His evaluative nodding stopped, and he shifted his gaze back to his hands and the highball glass, empty now except for the few ice cubes he rattled around, like shards of regret.

"So, you come to see the show? To visit me?" His gaze lifted. He had regained his composure, but there was still a trace of suspicion. "Or what?"

"To visit you."

He gestured to the bartender.

"You know, this isn't a good place for you. And now's not a good time for you to visit, either. Your timing is not good. I'm expecting R.D. any minute now. He would definitely not be pleased to see you here."

The bartender returned.

"Bring us coffee," Joey said, looking around, looking at his watch and at the front door. "Like I said, kid, I can't spend too much time with you. What's on your mind?"

Summarizing quickly, I told him about going to see *The Harder They Fall* with Uncle Abe, about our conversation afterward, and the articles he'd shown me

He nodded, noncommittal and impatient. "They got that movie right. It's a rotten game, the fight game; no doubt about it."

"Are you glad you're out of it?"

He held up his thumb and index finger and pinched them nearly together. "I came that close to a title; that close," he said obliquely.

The bartender placed two steaming mugs of black coffee in front of us, with pitchers of cream and sugar and spoons. He smiled and walked away.

"If I'd stayed with Jake, your grandfather, who knows?"

Joey's hammered brows and cheeks seemed softer, less burnished now that he'd retired. I wondered if, as a bouncer, he could rely strictly on his reputation, or whether he had to resort to force when troublesome drunks acted up. Or was it the other way around: was his reputation, his mere presence, a lightning rod, so that he could never escape trouble, never really relax. I searched his eyes, but they weren't showing much.

"I had a lot of respect for your grandfather, your Uncle Abe; especially Davey," he exclaimed.

"You could've fooled me, that day at the Armory."

But, actually, on this point, I believed him. After every fight I'd ever seen, either in person or on film, every losing fighter embraced his conqueror, even before a decision was announced, unabashedly, like a lover.

"I didn't have nothing against your father. He was one of the best: clean, tough, a really skilled professional. But my career was on the line that day; I was ordered to rough him up," he said, matter-of-factly, unapologetic.

"Anyway," he said, glancing again at his watch and the front door, "I paid for it in the end. I lost the best trainer I ever had, the only one who had my best interests at heart."

I nodded, conceding his point.

Then he gestured, circling his hand in the air, urging me to more pointedly reveal the purpose of my visit. "So…?"

Sweat trickled down my armpits. "What do you know about how my Uncle Jack arranged the Maxim fight?"

"Are you shittin' me?" Joey rolled his shoulders and snorted through his dented nose. "Why don't you ask your Uncle Jack? Have you asked him yet?"

"I will. I just want to hear your version first."

Joey squinted with disdain and the scars around his eyebrows deepened.

"I'm not sure you want to hear what I got to say. It's not complimentary. Your uncle is bad news, Danny. Right now he's trying to destroy R.D."

I took a sip of coffee and pushed it aside, frustrated at his evasion, wondering how to get him on track.

"DiNardi had my family killed. If my Uncle Jack is getting back at him now, it's only because it's taken him this long."

He laughed. He wasn't going to take me seriously.

"He's getting even, all right. And if he goes as far as I think he wants to, even I may be out of a job."

I persisted. "What do you know about how the fight was set up? The articles I read said Uncle Jack paid the IBC Combination a fee to get Davey the fight with Maxim. If so, what reason would DiNardi have to be mad at my grandfather? Mad enough to have Davey injured just days before the fight? Mad enough to burn down my grandfather's store?"

Joey shook his head. "There's some things you're better off not knowing, Danny. Believe me," he said, left hand over his heart, the right raised, glancing at the door. "I speak from experience."

I couldn't tell whether he was mocking me or just being dismissive.

"You don't understand, Joey. I'm in the dark about certain things having to do with my family, things that are hard for me to even think about. I try to put the past behind me because it's too painful, but now I feel like my Uncle Abe is trying to steer me to you…."

"Abe is? What for?"

"…to find out about this one thing. And now I have to know. If there's anything you can tell me about my family regarding that fight, please, just put it out in the open…. I need to see it. I don't hold anything against you…. If you still have any consideration…."

A loud noise startled us both. The front-entrance door had swung open, banging hard against a rainbow-hued Wurlitzer, knocking a record off its track. Ray DiNardi Jr. walked toward us, followed by Breschi and DeLuca. He was distressed and, now, surprised.

"Ray, what's up?" Joey asked.

DiNardi was out of breath, angry, but his voice rose with each sentence.

"I just got done talking with my mother on the phone. She's hysterical. She went to church, to confession, then had dinner at Aunt Theresa's. But when she came home, the house was ransacked. My father's car was gone. Is he here?"

"Not yet," Joey said, cautiously, trying to read the situation, stay in control, glancing at me, then at his watch. "He's a little bit late. I expected him before the start of the last show."

DiNardi slapped his forehead and paced back and forth, agitated.

"Calm down, Ray. He'll probably make it in before we cash up. He never misses."

DiNardi turned his frustration on me. "You.... You better get outa here; I gotta talk to Joey."

Joey and I exchanged glances. He tried to signal me with a barely-perceptible shake of his head but, stupidly, I tried to explain myself.

"I just want to find out something important. Joey's the only one who can help me. I may not get another chance."

Joey started to say something, "Kid, I owe you, but not now...," when Ray lunged at me.

"Help *you!*"

He grabbed me by the shoulders and dragged me out of the booth and onto the floor. I held up my arms to protect my face from his raining blows.

"You asshole!" he screamed as he winged punches. "My father's life is in danger on account of your uncle!"

In the blur between DiNardi's punches, I could see two others enter the bar and race over. Lonnie and Prado pulled DiNardi off me, then Breschi and DeLuca joined the fray. Joey, me, and the bartender tried to separate everyone. A chair was swung overhead and crashed into a light. Glass rained down. Joey grabbed the most persistent combatants and threw them across the room in different directions until he had everybody separated.

"Cut it out! Lay off this shit! Danny, you and your people get outa here. Junior, Breschi, Luke, sit down over there. We don't need this right now. We gotta figure out how to solve a problem, not make things worse!"

Lonnie wiped the back of his mouth. I checked myself in the mirror behind the bar. No blood, just a bruise beginning to swell high-up on my cheekbone. Nobody else seemed to be marked, unless you count the gash at the shoulder seam of Prado's sport coat where it had separated in the melee. The floor was a mess of debris: broken glass and cups, ashtrays and napkins scattered everywhere. Ninette, her father, and several waitresses barged in from the nightclub. The lights were coming on behind them, the show had stopped.

Prado, Lonnie, and I backed warily to the front door. Joey held it open, nudging us while gesturing like a traffic cop for the others to remain where they were. I was the last one through the door, and he followed me out to the sidewalk.

"Call me tomorrow afternoon," he whispered. "Maybe we can meet for coffee. But first ask your uncle what you asked me; *then* I'll tell you what I know."

He shook his head. "But keep in mind: things could change dramatically, depending on what happens tonight."

His handshake was slack, perfunctory, so typical of a fighter who has nothing at all to prove to anyone, and who treats his hands with the regard of a violinist. But in the process, he also palmed me a matchbook.

CHAPTER 32

Prado pulled his car to the curb in front of my house. He put his arm over my seat.

"If something happens tomorrow? Like you need a ride or a place to stay or some help? Call me or Lonnie."

As he drove away, I walked to the front door, searching inside my overcoat pockets for my front door key. Then my suitcoat pockets. Then trousers. Nothing. It must've fallen out during the fracas at the Chez Ami or earlier when I was shoved into the snowbank. I rang the doorbell. A long minute later, footsteps creaked down the staircase, and the vestibule light switched on. Then the porch light. The door opened. Uncle Jack stood in his bathrobe and slippers, his eyes swollen with sleep.

"Sorry, Uncle Jack. I lost my key." His eyes focused more acutely. "How'd you get that lump on your cheek?" I walked past him, down the hall into the kitchen, turned on a light over the sink, poured myself a glass of water. He followed me.

I said, over my shoulder, "I got into a tussle."

"Tussle? Who with?"

"...with Ray DiNardi."

His eyes widened.

"...Junior," I clarified.

"Where'd you run into him?"

"The Chez Ami."

He pursed his lips. "You certainly have developed quite a repertoire of night spots, haven't you?"

He stood opposite me, behind the kitchen table.

"What do you mean, 'tussle'? Were you alone? And what were you doing there?"

"I went there alone. Later, Prado and Lonnie Starr met me. I went to see Joey DeYoung. To talk to him. And right in the middle of our conversation Ray came in, upset. We had a brief misunderstanding. Nothing really came of it. Joey broke it up."

"Tell me about it," Uncle Jack said, nonchalantly.

He opened the refrigerator, took out a bottle of orange juice, poured himself a glass.

"You want some?"

I shook my head. He cracked open an ice-cube tray. "Here, put this piece of ice on that bruise so it don't get black and blue."

We both sat down in the semi-darkness. I accepted the piece of ice, wrapped in a paper napkin, and held it to the bruise.

"So…?"

"I wanted him to tell me what he knew about the Maxim fight, the one you made for Davey."

Uncle Jack pulled a cigar out of his robe pocket, bit off the end and licked the length of it several times before lighting up.

"First tell me why Ray Jr. was upset. You know, a grand jury we summoned is very close to indicting R.D. on charges that could put him away for a long…a very long time. Is that it? Is that why he attacked you? To get back at me for what I'm doing to his father?"

The ice began to burn my cheek. I put it on the table. Uncle Jack picked it up and began to gently press and move the swelling as if he were ironing fabric.

"Ray said his mother had come home from church to find that someone had ransacked their house, and that his father's car was missing, and that he hadn't been seen by anyone, either at his tavern or at Chez Ami, all night."

"*From church….* I like that," Uncle Jack said, smirking, his eyes self-righteous slits.

He scraped his chair back from the table, leaned back, and grabbed a phone off the counter, swinging the trailing wire over his head. He glared at me while he dialed. Almost immediately, someone on the other end picked up.

"Murph? This is Jack Mendoza. Find out if anyone's called in tonight about 'Rotten Raymond' being missing. Yeah…the rotten man…right…. I'll wait."

Uncle Jack propped the phone between his ear and shoulder, freeing his hands to pour another glass of juice and re-light his cigar.

"No? Well, something might be up. Put out a call to look for his car. We need to know where he is. Phone me right back if you hear anything. Yeah…at any time…. What do you mean, 'What am I doing up this time of night?' Having a little talk with my nephew. He's the one who told me. He found out from Ray Jr…. Never mind; I'll tell you later."

He hung up but kept the phone on the table, staring at me.

"Why now? What prompted your interest in this ancient history now?"

I told him about the movie, reading the articles in Uncle Abe's apartment.

"Abe the historian, heh? Okay, what he read to you is essentially correct. We—your grandfather, Davey, me—we decided to go over DiNardi's head, directly to Christenberry. Everybody wanted it to be this way. Even though it cost us a fortune—$25,000—it was better than cutting DiNardi in for a percentage…for the indefinite future. But for *him*, obviously, it was the last straw. That's all I can figure. He was totally insulted by losing out on a big deal…and, you know, by Davey…pushing him the way he was."

He studied my eyes.

"Look, Danny; we're dealing with a crazy person. He's just a mob underling in all this. His life isn't worth a pile of shit right now. I've been working with a joint federal, state, and local organized-crime task force to get him indicted. Everybody knows it. There's a very good chance that people want him shut up before he's called to the witness stand. We've finally got him where we want him, where we've wanted him all these years. He's going to pay now for what he did to our family, to you."

He dragged on the cigar several times until the tip glowed red, then he let off and exhaled and rubbed his forehead with the heel of his hand.

"Abe has a bug up his ass. I don't know what his problem is. As for Joey DeYoung? Stay away from him. He's too close to DiNardi; he'll only poison your mind. And for all I know, he could be a marked man, too."

I finished my glass of water.

"Lemme see your face."

I leaned over the table. He turned on the overhead light and peered closely.

"Don't worry, the swelling's gone down. You know," he chuckled, "you keep this up, you're gonna look like a regular roughneck."

I forced a smile.

"Anything else you wanna ask me?"

I thought a few seconds. It all seemed pretty cut and dried. Everybody was in on it; so, what went wrong? I shook my head.

"Look, Danny; we all thought we were taking a really big risk dealing with the top people, the people who controlled DiNardi, and obviously nobody anticipated his extreme reaction. At the time, it seemed like the right way to go…the only way. *Nobody* is to blame. Abe was right: 'When you deal with the Philistines….'"

His gaze remained fixed and probing. I nodded.

"Okay. Let's go to bed. Your aunt is gonna wonder what we're doing down here. Tomorrow…we'll find out more about DiNardi. Let's keep our fingers crossed that he's on his way out."

I slept late, dead to the world until a series of dreams began to intrude. Some old, some new, merging crazily, beginning with Remson in the alley. Then I had returned to Burt Street to live with my mother, which had been her cherished wish. But now there was nothing I could do to please her, nothing I could do to reduce a profound unhappiness caused by Davey's abrupt and inexplicable estrangement. She kept begging me to find him. So I searched everywhere I knew. I was about to give up when I entered a forest and there he stood in a shaded glen, on the deck of a cabin. Wary.

When I approached, instead of acknowledging me, he went inside. Avoiding me, keeping his distance and keeping silent, he cast distrustful glances. I couldn't believe it. I followed him. It was dark inside. He was packing his meager possessions into a duffel bag. Now that I'd found him, he didn't want to have anything to do with me or even ask the purpose of my visit. This killed me.

I went back to my old school to try to find someone who could help, but masked demons leapt from the wall murals and forced me to run a gauntlet, and at the end was Donny Reed. I fought past him and ran, turning to fight him again when he ran me down, until I reached a door. It wouldn't open and I pounded on it. Phaedra opened it. I tried to speak but words wouldn't come.

"Why, Daniel," she exclaimed, rubbing up against my leg, clinging to my hips, smiling her superiority: "You stutter!"

Just when I became aroused, she peeled away from me, laughing, sauntering toward another man, climbing onto his leg and pelvis. I tried to intervene, but the man kept pushing me away. Then Grandfather appeared, tugging on my arm, hammering a ringside bell, repeating a refrain: "Sometimes you have to be hit.... Sometimes you have to be hit.... Sometimes you ...."

I felt like I wanted to kill this man with Phaedra, but I couldn't take Grandfather's repetition anymore; I couldn't breathe; and gasping for air, I found myself kicking and flailing upward through water to the surface, like breaching from a turbulent sea, and there I lay, clutching the back of a turtle, the wet turf of his back which became my bed and, in the real familiarity of my surroundings, fragments of my dream subsided, and I remembered last night. The longest night of my life.

I wanted to go back to sleep. To never wake up. To never have to get out of bed or face anyone.

With my eyes closed, I tried to recollect laying in a hospital bed. Tried to imagine that I had the ability to unplug. To will myself to do this now. Will myself to fade to darkness. Bit by bit, I slowed my breath to palpable limits. Until heavy footsteps pounded down the hallway and the bedroom door flew open and Victor took hold of my shoulder. Shaking me.

"Daniel. Get up and get dressed. My father wants to see you in the kitchen."

I rolled onto my side and looked at him. He didn't even try to hide his resentment of me now. Reporting to Aunt Charlotte whenever he thought I was behaving badly, like drinking too much or coming home too late. Even making up stories about me misbehaving at school, or taking things of his—like money or jewelry—or ignoring him or not treating him properly when he suffered his seizures. Anything to get me reprimanded or punished in some way.

"You better hurry up!" Victor fumed. "He said it was important!"

I slid from beneath the covers, dug my feet into my slippers, pulled an old sweatshirt over my pajama top, and strolled down the hallway to the bathroom. The swelling on my cheekbone had subsided. A bluish shadow remained, but it was partly camouflaged by a patina of dark stubble. I was beginning to look like a derelict. I pushed open the shower curtain.

"You don't have time for that! He wants you downstairs! Now!" Victor yelled. He'd followed me down the hallway. I shut the door in his face. I was so tired I sat down on the toilet seat to piss, and when I finished I forced myself to think of reasons to get up, to stand. I wet my eyes and hair in the sink and took three aspirin with water cupped in my open hand.

When I came downstairs, Uncle Jack and a police officer—a tall, beefy man with a silver bar on each epaulet of his jacket—were sitting in the sun parlor drinking coffee. Uncle Jack waved me over. An empty cup and saucer were set for me. Bursting to speak, he yelled:

"Charlotte! Danny's here!" My aunt brought a pot of coffee on a tray. The alarm I felt was dissipated by her sunny greeting.

"Good morning, dear. Did you have a good sleep?"

Victor sat across from us in a high-backed easy chair, dour, oblivious to his mother's good cheer. The police officer looked familiar to me.

"You remember Sgt. Maguire from a few years ago," Uncle Jack said. "At Burt Street when we had all the trouble?"

The police officer leaned across the table to shake my hand. He seemed very much at ease.

"He's now Lt. Maguire, with the Violent Crime Squad."

He appeared even larger and more imposing than the last time I saw him. What I wondered about was his competency.

"Well, Danny," Uncle Jack began, "it looks like Uncle Abe was right. We didn't have to do anything to 'Rotten Raymond' to get our revenge; he did it to himself."

Aunt Charlotte's knowing look deepened to one of sublime satisfaction as she poured the coffee. I realized how tired and hungover I was when the aroma of it hit me. I quickly added cream and sugar and downed the first cup, then watched her pour me another.

"Why? What's happened?" Did Uncle Jack say that to echo Uncle Abe's admonition that God would "bring DiNardi down?" And I remembered my impatience with the lack of immediacy in that promise, its lack of clarity, like having to wait until some end-game.

Uncle Jack took a sip of coffee, leaving Lt. Maguire to tell me.

"One of my officers found DiNardi's car about 4 a.m.," Lt. Maguire said, "burned up, behind his tavern. A charred body was slumped in the front seat. It's been taken to the Medical Examiner. But shoes from the victim—intact enough to be identified—belonged to DiNardi."

"Investigators think it was an assassination," Uncle Jack added, barely containing his glee. "They found a .22 revolver in the back seat, one chamber empty."

Lt. Maguire appraised my reaction, wrongly, as it turned out.

"You can finally relax, son. He's out of your hair for good."

Maybe *he* is, I thought, but I wanted a more satisfying ending. Once DiNardi's death was broadcast over the radio, the phone at Uncle Jack's house never stopped ringing. One of the calls came to the telephone in my room. It was Uncle Abe.

"Oh, good! I'm glad you answered, Danny. I heard on the radio just now. What do you know about it? Don't leave out any details." He wanted to know exactly what Lt. Maguire had said and everything about how Uncle Jack responded. I spoke as quietly as I could into the receiver and still make myself understood.

"Jack is right," Uncle Abe said. "God did deliver the verdict, but DiNardi destroyed himself. He made reckless decisions and lots of enemies. Evil people worse than him hounded him to this end. Sometimes it's a surprising irony the way God works. None of us had to lift a finger to make it happen."

Well, somebody did, I thought. I told him about meeting Joey last night but that we'd been interrupted—that just when he seemed to be forthcoming he wasn't able to finish what he seemed ready to tell me. Uncle Abe shushed me.

"Not over the phone," he blurted. "Take a bus to my house. I want to know all about it."

"I don't know," I said, annoyed at the interference. "I was supposed to call Joey today and meet him for coffee."

"This is important, Danny; let me come with you. Don't go alone."

I told Uncle Abe that Prado and Lonnie Starr had planned to accompany me to any meeting.

"That's no good, Danny. No disrespect, but things have changed. This is no time to let your guard down. It still pays to be cautious. You need *me* to be there with you. Somebody experienced, not two of your friends. Tell him you're bringing me…if it's even possible to meet, which I kind of doubt. After all, with DiNardi's death, that whole gang will be in a turmoil. Helping the family will be his priority, too."

I hung up, but almost immediately my phone rang again. It was Prado.

"Hey, man; how's your *toches?*"

I told him my plan. "Your Uncle Abe probably knows best," he said. "But if you need a ride, or help, let me know. I'll either be here or at Lonnie's. We'll wait around. Call me when you know where you're going to meet."

I opened the matchbook to a scrawled telephone number Joey had written. I dialed it, but there was no answer. I tried DiNardi's tavern. A police officer answered. No one there, he said. Roped off for investigation. No answer either at the Chez Ami.

Heeding Uncle Abe's advice, I dialed information and asked for

Pirrone's Funeral Home. I was connected. But when a gruff voice answered, I disguised my voice. Made it deeper. I was asked who was calling. "A friend." It worked.

Joey took the phone. The first thing he asked after I identified myself was, "Did you tell your uncle what happened last night?"

"Yes, last night, when I got home."

"What did he say?" After he took in what I told him there was a silence. I wondered whether I should be more cautious and wondered whether he felt the same way. But I also felt compelled to carry out my scheme.

"Can we talk today?" I told him that Uncle Abe wanted to come with me.

"Just him?"

"Yes."

"So you and him really think there's more to the story than what your Uncle Jack told you? And Uncle Abe trusts me to tell you the truth about what I know?"

For the first time, it sounded like he did have something to tell me.

"Yes," I said, trying to generate conviction. Until taking a risk and standing apart from Uncle Jack, it didn't seem reasonable to me that Joey would meet with us. But why was I pushing this proposition? What was I really looking for?

"Do you know where All Souls church is?"

I told him I did.

"I'll be finished here in about an hour. Meet me at the side door entrance of the church, 4 p.m."

"Is Ray Jr. with you now?"

"Yeah. He and his mother."

"Tell him I'm sorry about his father."

Another silence.

"He probably shouldn't know we had a conversation."

"Oh.... Well...later, when we're through? You'll tell him then?"

"Yeah...tomorrow. Tomorrow is better."

After showering, shaving, and dressing, I called Prado to let him know of my plan to meet Joey, but that I was taking Uncle Abe with me. Then I went downstairs. Uncle Jack was gone. To the office, Aunt Charlotte said, placing two briskets into the oven to bake.

"He's going to be busy the next few days," she said. Victor had fallen asleep watching television. I grabbed a jacket out of the closet, Davey's old leather one, and a knit cap and gloves and quietly eased my way out the front door and down to the bus stop.

Uncle Abe was sweeping a downy layer of fresh-fallen snow off his porch and steps when I arrived. Inside, his water kettle was gently boiling. He made us a pot of tea.

"Have you had anything to eat today?"

"I don't know if we have time for tea, Uncle Abe; not if we're going to catch a bus and transfer to All Souls."

"Your uncle lets you stay out all night and sleep all day?"

"Football season is over, Uncle Abe."

"Season, shmeason. I don't know from seasons. I know years, months, weeks, days. Days, Daniel. Every day is a struggle. You need some nour-ishment. We'll make a little time here; I've called a taxi. Sid, my trusty Iroquois driver," he said, arranging a bowl of sugar cubes and a creamer on a tray next to a box of macaroons that he carried from his cramped kitchen into the living room.

"Sarah called me a little while ago. She said she was worried about you, wanted to know whether you got home okay last night."

Uncle Abe held his head off-kilter, peering at me through his glasses.

"I told her I didn't quite know," he said, "but that I would find out. From the looks of you, I'm not so sure."

Typically, he wanted to know the complete story of the evening, chronologically, saving Joey and the Chez Ami for last.

"This drinking of yours has been going on for a few years now," he said, diplomatically. "Your father never caroused the way you and your friends do. Is it because going to bars is the way young men get together these days? Or are you trying to drown your sorrows?"

I shrugged and sipped my tea. I felt too unsettled to eat a macaroon. But I took a bite anyway. It tasted so good, so sweet, I wolfed down two more, then another.

"This girlfriend of yours, Phaedra? What is your problem with her? From what Sarah said…."

I really didn't want to get into this burden. "It's complicated."

"Uncomplicate it for me," he insisted. "You can tell me. Let's get this out of the way first."

"We have a strange relationship," I began.

"Maybe not so strange, Danny. Maybe just not good for you. Look, I don't want to pry into the specifics. They're none of my business. Let's just boil it down to the basics: Is she an angel or a devil?"

When I couldn't answer, Uncle Abe shrugged and sipped his tea.

"All right, so she's both?" he asked. "At first she was an angel, and now she's a devil? Or she's an angel with a devilish sensibility?" He was chipping away at the heart of my dilemma with her, but in no way was I certain myself of what it was. So I shrugged.

"Both."

"Did you meet her during the day or night?"

"Late at night, at a party. She asked me to dance. It went on from there. Pretty well, I'd say."

"Does she have a brother?"

I shook my head.

"Does her mother like you? Does the mother treat you well, like the brother her daughter doesn't have, like the son you could be?"

I shook my head again.

"Has Phaedra committed any wrongdoing that you're aware of?"

I looked away, toward the mandala on his window. "She had an abortion when she was 15."

"Sarah said you actually fought with her last night. Is that an exaggeration?"

"An exaggeration. Last night was...an accident. We were in a crowded nightclub. There was a misunderstanding. The fight, if you could call it that, was really with her...friend."

"Have you two ever fought before? I mean physically?" He was honing in on this part.

"Once.... A couple of times. She...likes that."

"And you accommodated her And she liked it?"

I nodded.

"And did this become a pattern?"

"Sort of."

"And at any of these times, did she transform?"

"What do you mean?"

"Did she seem to change at all, to you, in her appearance?"

I explained how last night she seemed to age right before my eyes, how it was like seeing her over the span of her life. He frowned and shook his head.

"That night you met, did she seduce you? And is she so very enticing that you feel you can't stay away from her? Even though her parents don't approved of this relationship? And this violence is something you might be unhappy with? Is all of this weighing on you?"

"Yes."

"We don't have time to go into this in depth right now, but let me tell you something, and I'll show you passages to read when we come back."

He stood, prodded a book from his little library, looked in the index, skimmed to a page, and handed it to me.

"She is a Lillith. A historical figure. When you read this and some other passages I'll show you, you'll understand. And when you get rid of her, you'll have one less problem. You want a girlfriend, go back to Yvonne. She's is an angel just waiting for you."

I shook my head at how crisply he'd summarized my situation, with such certainty.

"But Yvonne says we're both Wolf clan. Her parents would object to me, too."

"Danny, Yvonne has loved you from…from the time she first set eyes on you. And if there's anything I know about the Iroquois, it's their flexibility. I know her family. This can be worked out. Trust me. Have you forgotten your own family history? Hasn't a similar thing happened between Mary and Davey? Look at what happened with them."

I nodded, half-heartedly.

"Okay, tell me what happened last night with Joey. Then tell me what Jack said when you came home."

CHAPTER 33

It was already turning dark by the time Sid parked his taxi in front of All Souls Church. A dry, light snow had begun to fall, dusting the sooted snow banks at curbside. As I helped Uncle Abe out of the back seat, he grunted and leaned heavily into me before I closed the door.

"So, Sid, you'll come back for us in about one hour?" he said to the Indian driver, more a command than a question. The driver hadn't said a word throughout our trip. As a matter of fact, I'd never heard Sid speak during any of the times I'd been a passenger in his taxi. Instead, he nodded through his side window and gunned the engine. Too forcefully, as it happened. His taxi's rear wheels whirled and whined for several seconds until they finally broke through snow and hit pavement.

"Maybe you'll put on some chains, too!" Uncle Abe yelled as the taxi pulled away.

A light at the end of the alley heralded the familiar rear entrance to the church, and once we stepped onto the shoveled walkway, Uncle Abe eased his grip on my arm. I felt again like I was walking from one uncertain world into another. I had zig-zagged from Burt Street to the reservation, from Jessie's attempt to heal me through communal ritual to not trusting anyone, from my insistence on skepticism and self-reliance to deciding to trust and depend on the one person who promised he could make things right for me, my Uncle Jack.

But what did I *really* know about trusting Uncle Jack with my future, with my life? How could I know enough to trust anyone, let alone Joey, who had betrayed my father? How could I trust him to shed any light on what Uncle Jack had seen only as a moral crisis created by a deluded Uncle Abe, the seer of black and white? And why should I believe in Uncle Abe's certainty about discovering the truth when he'd been so ineffectual at preventing transgression even as he'd witnessed it unfolding? How could I allow myself to undertake such a dangerous and, perhaps, foolhardy inquiry as this when I had no faith that anyone knew the truth about anything at all? Or if they did know something, it might not—in the long run—even matter now that DiNardi was dead. Worse, what I was about to embark on might cause me even greater harm than what had happened to me in the past. What was really the point of trying to set the record straight?

The church door was unlocked, and Joey was waiting in the vestibule, standing next to the same priest who'd called off the LaSalle boys two years ago.

Tentatively, Joey extended his hand, but Uncle Abe waved it off and opened his arms. Joey stepped into them and clung for a few seconds like a large, clumsy child, breaking away finally, slightly embarrassed, blinking his eyes and gripping the dented bridge of his nose as if to stem some tide. It struck me how Uncle Abe remained calm, even enthusiastic in a circumstance when other people's emotions got the better of them. He reminded me of Jesse and Jacques the quarterback, always knowing the correct response when things seemed uncertain or complicated or even unraveling. His presence was remarkably dogged and charismatic, an ability I marveled at, and which led me so easily to follow in its wake, despite lacking faith that it could elicit a substantial outcome.

At the very least, however, perhaps he was right in saying I needed to bring him to this meeting. After all, I didn't really know what I was doing other than plodding forward in an amateurish way to discover some apparent truth. I didn't even know what questions to ask.

"Hello, Father. I'm Abraham Mendoza."

The priest, wearing an ankle-length cassock and a bright gold crucifix around his neck, bowed and extended his hand.

"Father John O'Brian. My friends call me 'Bounce'."

Uncle Abe took his hand in both of his.

"Bounce O'Brian? Not the welterweight Golden Gloves champion of a decade ago? The knockout artist whose victims hit the canvas so hard…?"

"They bounced…. The very same, Mr. Mendoza."

"This is my grandnephew, Daniel."

"We already met, Mr. Mendoza, two years ago. He used to come to our Friday night open house, with a friend of his."

Uncle Abe turned his gaze on me and arched his eyebrows in surprise. "Open house?"

"Dances, Uncle Abe. I used to come with Chad Call. We dated two girls who went to school here."

"This boy gets around," Uncle Abe said, in a hard-to-define tone.

Father O' Brian led us down a shadowy nave to his office, a small room lined with bookshelves from floor to ceiling, illuminated by several small, strategically-placed brass lamps that enhanced a large stained-glass window behind his desk.

"You gentlemen make yourselves at home here. I have a few chores to tend to on the other side of the building."

Uncle Abe and Joey took chairs in front of Father O'Brian's massive and cluttered desk, while I sat in the priest's swivel chair behind the desk, tense and trying to adjust to the chair's unstable ballast that perfectly matched my condition. I decided to surrender the imperative, but Uncle Abe wouldn't let me. He rubbed his hands together as if at the outset of some great physical task, then gestured for me to begin. I nodded and cleared my throat.

"I talked with Uncle Jack last night.... His story about the Maxim fight is the same as what I told you, that he paid the Combination to make the fight with Davey."

"Did he tell you how much?"

"Yes, $25,000, which he said was pretty much the family's savings."

Joey shook his head. "That wasn't your family's savings; it was Ray DiNardi's money."

"What?" Uncle Abe sat forward and leaned against the desk.

"R.D. gave that money to Jack. It was the negotiated payment Jack wanted in exchange for a percentage of the fighter."

"You mean for Davey?" Uncle Abe asked. "You mean Jack agreed to let DiNardi have a piece of Davey, a piece of the family enterprise?"

"Right. And in exchange, R.D. was going to fix the ratings and set up the Maxim fight. Except Jack beat him to it. Jack took the money from R.D. and wired it to New York. Direct to Christenberry. Then Christenberry shared the $25,000 with Frankie Carbo. He and Carbo fixed the ratings and made the fight."

"But if DiNardi still worked for Carbo," I asked, "why would DiNardi sabotage the fight? I don't understand."

Joey's thumb raised out of his clenched fist.

"Number one, when R.D. found out what happened, he complained to Carbo. But Carbo told him to forget about it. Carbo said that for years R.D. hadn't been able to deliver Davey to the Combination. He told R.D. that he had been outsmarted and that he had to live with this failure.

"Number two, before the fight deal there was this year-long dispute over money between Carbo and R.D. It had to do with percentages from a local Negro bookmaking operation R.D. had taken over and never told Carbo about or shared the proceeds from. And so Carbo said that now they were even."

Joey was revealing pieces of a puzzle, pieces of a large puzzle that were beginning to fit together. Its magnitude and the dimensions of it astonished me.

"Was the bookmaking operation run by Lonnie and Brenda Starr's father?"

"Octavius Starr? Yeah. He ran a book for the entire ghetto, The Ward. R.D. wanted a piece of it, but Octavius wasn't going to give him a nickel, so R.D. had him killed. Took the whole thing," Joey said. "Your uncle knew all about it and he told Carbo; he told him because he figured Carbo would take R.D.'s money as a way of putting him in his place. And Jack figured R.D. wouldn't be able to do a damned thing about it."

Uncle Abe interrupted. "So, as far as Jake and Davey were concerned, R.D. had nothing to do with making the Maxim fight? They were still on the outside trying to get in? They thought, 'Ah, the Combination has finally relented under pressure from the sportswriters.' You know how Davey reveled in R.D.'s never getting a piece of him."

"Right," Joey said. "The only thing Jack didn't realize...the one big mistake he made is he didn't realize just how angry and how upset over these two things R.D. was."

Joey's revelation caused me to rock backward in the swivel chair but so incautiously that I lost my balance and fell to the floor. Uncle Abe tried, but he was too frail to help me up. Joey came around. He knelt beside Uncle Abe. I was too disoriented to take his extended hand.

"Danny, get up," Uncle Abe ordered. "We're not through."

Joey nodded and stood.

My arms and legs felt lifeless. I rolled backward out of the downed chair just to right myself. It got me to one knee. How much more could there be?

I stood up and righted the chair. Joey helped me settle into it. Uncle Abe poured me a glass of water before he resumed the thread of the inquiry.

"So, when the fight was postponed because of the fire," Uncle Abe said, "when Davey was unable to fight, what happened to the $25,000?"

"It was returned to Jack," Joey said, "eventually."

"*Before* or *after* he went to Brooklyn with Davey?"

"After. Christenberry felt sorry for the family, said it was highly unusual to return a fee of this nature, but that under the circumstances...."

"What did Uncle Jack do with the money?" I asked.

"He probably used it to go to law school," Uncle Abe mused acidly. "We'll have to ask him."

"What's interesting," Joey said, "is he goes to law school, then comes back here, gets himself a job in the D.A.'s office, finds out about R.D. setting up the big meet in Apalachia because he's trying to get back in the good graces of Carbo and the boys. And then Jack tips off the State Police. That was the beginning of the end for R.D. That was seen by the big people—let alone the cops—as a huge fiasco. From then on, R.D. is feeling pressure from both the law and his own people."

"And it finally became unbearable?" Uncle Abe asked.

"He was losing everything. He was being investigated by the state, by the feds, locally. That's when he started acting crazy, burying slot machines, burning his records. Nobody downstate would help him—he was so *persona non grata* they wouldn't let him do his own business. And then they didn't want him to testify in case he was indicted."

"So you think they had him killed?" I asked, looking first at Joey then at Uncle Abe who sat stiff, unmoving, as if paralyzed by Joey's testimony.

Joey sighed and sat back in his chair. "I think that remains to be seen."

"What do you mean?" I asked.

"The Medical Examiner hasn't released the body to the family yet. The reason why I was able to leave Pirrone's is because there's not a heck of a lot for me to do for the family yet. They can't plan a funeral until they have the body."

This brought Uncle Abe forward in his chair.

"And the Medical Examiner is keeping the body...?"

"...just to make sure...."

"Make sure of what?" I asked.

"Cause of death?" Uncle Abe said. "Murder, or...."

"Murder or suicide."

"But how could he shoot himself and there be a fire, too?" I asked.

"Anything's possible, Danny," Uncle Abe said, measuring Joey. "Some people take elaborate steps...." Then, as an afterthought: "You think it could've been suicide?"

Joey stared at Uncle Abe. He thought carefully before he spoke.

"It's hard to say, but I think it's possible. He was about as…upset about the way things were happening to him…about losing…as I've ever seen him."

"You said earlier he was burying slot machines, burning records. Do you think he also made provision for his family?" Uncle Abe asked. "In case anything should happen to him?"

Joey sat back in his chair. He thought this question over carefully, too. "I don't know. He'd lost a lot. The big people were taking business away from him. He paid out a lot to lawyers. That's what was making him the most…upset."

Uncle Abe struggled to his feet. "Well, you've got troubles of your own, Joey. We don't want to keep you. I think we've got the information we came here to get." He looked over at me. "Unless there's something you want to ask, Danny?"

What was left for me to ask? I was stunned by the revelation that my uncle—my father's brother—was the one ultimately responsible for the death of my mother, my father and my grandfather.

Betrayal occurred in politics, among business associates and criminals; it was exhibited perhaps by one-time friends like Joey. But, family? My family? The Mendoza family? This was beyond the pale.

And, yet, hadn't I betrayed my family? Hadn't I deceived everyone into thinking that I was cut from the same cloth? And wasn't I the one…? If I hadn't left my magazines in Grandfather's store that day…? The fire…?

What was most disorienting to me was the strange combination of numbed disappointment and elation that I felt. My throat felt suddenly constricted. Tears welled in my eyes. I tried to fight this emerging feeling. I'd been so successful so many times before, but now the tears just spilled. I was crying just like Yvonne had cried that night we were together, the kind of tears I'd never seen anyone cry before.

Uncle Abe gripped my shoulder. Joey stood and put his arm around me.

"This has been a tough few days…for all of us," Uncle Abe said. But there was no emotion in his voice, not even a tremor. It was almost as if he'd known all along, known everything, just wanted me to find out.

Joey cleared his throat. "I don't know what's keeping Father O'Brian. I'd like to say goodbye to him and thank him for letting us have this place to talk."

"You're right," Uncle Abe said, "but it's late and we've probably got a taxi outside waiting for us. Do you need a ride, Joey? Can we take you anywhere?" I blew my nose into a handkerchief and wiped my eyes.

"Thanks, Abe. But I don't live too far from here, just a few blocks, actually. I could use the walk. Maybe we'll catch Father O'Brian on the way out." They shook hands. Joey stared again at Uncle Abe, a mixture of sad sincerity and indecision. Uncle Abe's smile imparted gratitude. I stood, too, moved my feet in place to get the blood moving again, and shook Joey's hand.

"You'll be okay, kid," he said, smiling. "From what I hear, you got a great future ahead of you. Get yourself a scholarship next year, a college education, make a good life for yourself. Just like your dad would've wanted."

I appreciated his sentiment and the hopeful tone of his voice, but with his revelation, the bottom had fallen out from under me. I could never go back to Jack's house now or even face him or Aunt Charlotte, let alone accept his sponsorship of my life at East Brant High. I was turning a corner onto different terrain. Maybe it'd even been foretold. I could sense it now; everything had been leading up to this.

We put on our hats and gloves and walked back through the nave to the back door. It was already so late that only a lamp from the alley illuminating a panel of stained-glass windows marked our way. Disoriented, Uncle Abe had trouble finding the exit door.

"Father O'Brian!" Joey called out. The priest didn't answer. He took a deep breath and tried again. "Father O'...."

Joey was interrupted by a swift scuffling of feet. Several bodies rushed into the vestibule, thudding into us from the dark margins of the nave near the doorway. An arm hooked around my neck from behind. Someone pushed Uncle Abe into the door and held him fast. Several men—I couldn't tell how many—grappled with Joey. They must've tripped him because within seconds he was on his stomach, his face shoved hard against the floor.

"Bring them out to the alley!" one voice shouted.

Outside, two other men had Father O'Brian's arms pinioned behind him.

"Put him back inside! Rip out his phone and lock him in his office!"

Uncle Abe, Joey and I were hustled out of the alley to several cars idling by the curb. A light snow was still falling. The rear passenger window of one car was rolled down.

"Bring them all over here for a minute," a voice from the back seat ordered. Three men in overcoats and fedoras pushed Joey forward, his hands tied behind him. Another man had Uncle Abe by the arm, holding him up and constraining him at the same time. I was thrust forward by the man holding me from behind.

"Well, look what a nice little party this is," the voice said. "Planning some kind of occasion were you? A confirmation? A wedding? Somebody's funeral, perhaps?"

Uncle Abe was the only one of us to respond. "Just reminiscing about the old days, Raymond," he said evenly. "And making plans to attend your funeral."

The man in the back seat laughed. "To quote from a great writer, rumors of my demise have been greatly exaggerated; but I can't say the same thing about you."

Uncle Abe struggled with the man who held him captive, but it was a futile gesture. The man held him securely and kicked his cane away. Joey and I remained passive.

"What should we do with Joey?" one of the men holding him asked.

"Put him in the lead car," DiNardi ordered. "I'll take the other two and meet you."

"Wh...wh...where are we g...g...going?" I asked, feeling the fear rise from my stomach to cut off my breath.

"Tell me what our friend Joey told you."

"N...n...nothing," I stammered, "h...he just....."

"Don't tell him anything, Danny!" Uncle Abe shouted. "He's just trying to scare us."

"See? No matter what you tell me, it don't really make any difference," DiNardi said confidently. "I can't let you two go and run back to your uncle and let him know I'm still alive, and that some poor bum dressed in my clothes and wearing my jewelry got burned to a crisp. It would spoil everything."

He reached out and grabbed Uncle Abe by the throat. "You're all going back to Joey's apartment; Joey's gonna get it because he betrayed me, and you're going to get it because I'm gonna finish off the rest of this fuckin' family like I shoulda done years ago. And I'm gonna bury you all so deep nobody's ever going to find you."

The man holding Uncle Abe left him and ran to one of the waiting cars.

"How did you know we were here?" Uncle Abe asked, choking in

DiNardi's grasp. The question struck me as so logical, so typical of Uncle Abe, even amidst our dire situation. Not that I understood the point. In fact, it seemed ludicrous since it wasn't going to help us out of our jam. My mind was spinning between fear and this preposterous curiousity, wanting to know who set us up. And were we going to die? I stood trembling. Impotent.

DiNardi laughed. "A little bird told me."

He leaned closer to the window so that what little street light that was available revealed his face and a smirk that was cunning and cruel. He looked directly at me.

"Your cousin, Victor. Jack's boy. He phoned Ray Jr. after you left. You should be more careful when you talk on the phone at his house. The apple doesn't fall too far from the tree."

He laughed again and tried to pull Uncle Abe closer to the door, but the old man stubbornly dug his heels into the pavement and stretched DiNardi's arm all the way out of the car window. At the same time, he turned his head just enough to give me a look that sent chills up my spine. It was a look that Jacques and Coach Acquilino and Jesse had given me when I had taken the field before important games, when I was ready but hesitant, when I was there but not in a willing way: a look freighted with purpose, imploring me to do my best. And Uncle Abe's eyes said it all. *Come on! What are you waiting for!*

I stomped on the instep of the man behind me, wheeled, and—as he bent over in in pain—I grabbed both sides of his hat brim and kneed him in the face. Uncle Abe had slumped away from the car, as if he were trying to sit on the pavement, pulling DiNardi's arm further out of the window. Bellowing incoherently, I lunged toward DiNardi, grabbing his wrist and pumping his arm over the edge of the car door with such force it gave way like a rotted tree branch.

He screamed and clawed his way head-first out of the window, following the pain.

"Help me! Over here! Get this fucker!"

As I pulled Uncle Abe to his feet, the driver of DiNardi's car opened the door and began to get out. I left my uncle, grabbed the door and slammed it repeatedly, catching the driver's neck between the door and the doorpost, slamming it over and over until his face was bloody and broken.

Somebody spun me around. A tire iron arced overhead and I turned my head just enough so that it glanced off my shoulder. I spun away and chased after one man trying to hustle Uncle Abe toward the lead car where

Joey had been taken. I dove into the back of his knees and heard a crisp pop as we collapsed to the pavement.

Two pairs of hands lifted me by the shoulders and hurled me head-first into the rear fender. Stunned, I tried to push myself up but a blow across my shoulders knocked me to the pavement again. It was the man with the tire iron.

I rolled away from a second swing and it clanged against the sidewalk. Another man kicked me hard in the stomach. I could barely free one arm in time to ward off a second kick to my face and before he could kick again I grabbed onto his ankle and turned it sharply with both hands, as if I were steering a car away from a cliff. This put him down, but the man with the tire iron leaned in and swung again. Even though I rolled, he caught me in the back. My legs went numb and I felt paralyzed with pain.

I couldn't escape another swing, couldn't roll any further. I was trapped between the curb and a car tire. An unreal feeling of helplessness overrode whatever sense of desperate action I'd managed to muster when a sudden convergence of lights blinded me, accompanied by a screeching of tires.

The man with the tire iron must've swung again, but he missed my head and sparks danced as it ricocheted off the bumper and skittered into the gutter. I still couldn't move. The man knelt down, retrieved the tire iron, made ready to swing again. But somebody pushed him from behind and he sprawled over the car trunk. Two others leaped on top of him, rolled him to the ground and slammed his head into the pavement. Then more running footsteps scuffed close by, and I could hear blows and kicks and grunts and yelling.

Someone leaned over me. I couldn't see now because of the light blinding me, but I shielded my face with my hands. Whoever was leaning over me grabbed my wrists and hauled me out of the gutter.

"Danny, you all right?" a voice shouted.

Through my arms I could make out a face. It was Jesse and behind him Sid, the Iroquois taxi driver, peering at me with alarm. A raucous fight was still going on. Who else was there? I couldn't talk, couldn't move my head, only blink.

"Just lay still," Jesse said in a steady voice. "Lay still. The police and an ambulance will be here any second. We've got everything under control. You did a good job."

He and Sid threw blankets over me, and Jesse took off his coat and wedged it under my head. I was shaking uncontrollably and trying to catch my breath. In the distance a siren, then another, and another began to edge closer to the church.

"Uncle Abe...."

"Don't worry; he's okay," Jesse said. "Your friends are with him. He's not injured in any way."

"Friends?"

"About half the East Brant football team is here, plus Lonnie Starr. Sonny and Welcome came with us. A whole bunch of guys are sitting on 'Rotten Raymond' and his crew. Just waiting for the cops to come." Jesse grinned. "The Indians to the rescue."

As much as I hurt, I still managed a laugh. A smothered whelp of a laugh.

Feeling came back to my legs and arms the next day in the hospital along with steadily-throbbing back pain. But I didn't care; I felt like Sonny must've felt after he got hit with the "heavy shot." Purposeful. Especially when the guys who came to the rescue and Uncle Abe all stood around my bed grinning and cracking jokes, giving me the kind of treatment Sonny received when he recuperated from broken ribs.

"Was you the winner of this fight or the loser?" Lonnie asked. "From the looks of you, I can't hardly tell."

"Look at him all scrunched-up when he laughs," Prado said, sporting a red and swollen eye and a split lower lip. "Are you sure you're having fun?"

"Hey, Danny," Billy Pearl cracked, "forget about the sports page; you're the front-page headline in today's paper."

"Yeah," Jacques piped in, peering at me over Prado's shoulder, his lips flecked with spit like when we used to huddle up close to the goal line. "Don't forget, when they interview you, make sure they spell my name right."

Sonny and Welcome pushed through. "Go ahead, man," Sonny urged him and Welcome spread a khaki blanket across the foot of my bed, with three strands of Indian ribbon stitched across the top.

"Sonny had another dream last week," Welcome announced. "All three of us are joining up; we go to boot camp together. It's all arranged."

"Maybe you can, but Sonny and me aren't old enough yet," I protested. "We won't even be 17 until early summer."

"That won't hold us up. The recruiting sergeant told us that 16 and three-quarters is close enough," Sonny said, to a chorus of laughter. "He told us, 'It's a Marine Corps tradition to go in a little early.'" Sonny mimicked the sergeant's command voice. "He said, 'Go in early and you'll probably still be teenagers when you make corporal.'"

Uncle Abe pushed closer; the boys parted for him. Up close, he looked none the worse for wear. He raised his hands overhead, clenched together, although slightly trembling, in the sign of victory. Why wasn't I surprised that he was willing to entrust the Marines to supervise my development?

CHAPTER 34

I spent the remainder of the winter living at Jesse's cabin. His meager, spartan quarters and the pungent aroma of tobacco and firewood filled me with satisfaction. Even pumping water at the well and having to use the outhouse seemed remarkably gratifying. I couldn't believe how nostalgic I'd become for a place and experience I'd previously judged as lacking in merit for one such as me, a boy whose dynastic deliverance and ensuing rewards had once seemed so imminent, so pre-ordained.

One Saturday before *Purim*, Uncle Abe was driven over to spend the day. He, Sid, Jesse, Sonny, and I sat around the hatchcover table eating stew and fry bread, and savoring cowboy coffee. Uncle Abe brought a newspaper with him and, towards sundown as Jesse added logs to the fireplace and I cleared a place on the table, he unfolded it and spread it before us.

"DiNardi's latest indictment is for murder," Uncle Abe announced. "You and me and Joey DeYoung are going to be witnesses based on what DiNardi told us. There's plenty of evidence, too, so the wheels of justice will take care of that character."

"Who's prosecuting?" Jesse asked.

"District Attorney Halloran, the top man."

"So, Uncle Jack won't get the case?" I asked.

"He can't; too much conflict of interest. DiNardi's connection to our family will come out at the trial," Uncle Abe explained. "It's all part of explaining his motive for killing that derelict and placing him in the car to make it look like his own demise. Halloran says he has to build a case that takes in a certain amount of background history, how his disfavor with the Combination began, in part, with his pursuit of Davey's contract."

Jessie piped in. "Indirectly, then, he'll pay for those crimes, too."

"Yes," Uncle Abe said. "Halloran thinks that's how it will work out in the end."

"Did you see Uncle Jack at the Courthouse?" I asked.

"Of course, but we didn't talk. He knows there's nothing to say."

The first week in June, the day after our big farewell party at the Council House, Sonny, Welcome, and I took a bus downtown to the Federal Building to be sworn in. A staff sergeant who told us he'd served with the Navajo Codetalkers on Okinawa in 1945 made a big fuss over us. Indians were held in special regard by the Marines, and he especially liked it that we were athletes. He told me to be sure to have it put into my record at boot camp that I was an all-star who played on a championship high school football team. I'd be finishing Advanced Infantry Training just before football season and base teams were always looking for good players. He figured I was Iroquois, too, since Jesse, my guardian, had signed a document giving me permission to enlist. Sonny and I needed parental or guardian permission because of our ages.

But the sergeant was puzzled by my religious designation on the application: *Jewish.*

"My real father was Daniel Mendoza. When he died, I became an orphan, but I was adopted by my mother's brother."

"But your last name is still Mendoza, not Isaacs; Isaacs sounds like the Jewish name. Mendoza sounds…Puerto Rican."

"It's a different kind of adoption," was all I could think to say. The sergeant said he thought I didn't look full-blooded, like Sonny and Welcome, but he let it go at that. He still had that dumbfounded look on his face when we left the recruiting office.

To celebrate, the boys and I had a few beers at the Open Door then went across the street to tell Nate. He let us play a few games of rotation free of charge. Just after sunset, we left. I was planning on walking to Uncle Abe's house for a farewell dinner and to sleep over one last time, and Sonny and Welcome were planning on taking a bus back to the reservation. Then we'd reconnect in the morning at the train station for our trip south to the Parris Island Recruit Depot. But as we came down the stairs from Nate's and out onto the street, we ran into an unexpected obstruction: Donny Reed.

Summer weather had not yet arrived in Brant, and it was cool enough that evening for us to put on jackets. But Reed had only an unlined, dirty raincoat flung over one arm. I didn't recognize him at first. He was disheveled and beat-up looking—somewhat pinched at the shoulders, puffy around the ears and brows and with cross-hatched brush-burn scabs along one side of his face and cob-webbed blotches of broken veins across his cheeks and nose.

At first, he didn't recognize me; he was merely intent on the task at hand: pan-handling, ingratiating us with a smile, a sad-clown smile similar to Joey DeYoung's. We all chipped in spare change, adding up to a little over two dollars. Then he got an idea.

"Say," he said, in a peculiar stammer, "h…how about d…double or nothing?"

"For what?" Welcome asked.

"Hit me in the stomach as h…hard as you can, a…all of y…you, one at a time. If I don't f…flinch, I win."

"Nah," I said. "I don't know about these guys, but I gotta go; I'm late enough as it is."

Ever since, I've never had trouble describing this bizarre experience with Reed, but I've never been able to explain to anyone my aversion to what seemed like a God-given moment of retribution. I just wanted to be rid of my former nemesis, dismiss his absurd challenge, get to Uncle Abe's where my farewell dinner was waiting.

But he persisted, especially after he recognized me.

"C'mon, man," he pleaded. "What're you, a big shot? Too good for me now?"

Sonny and Welcome, on the other hand, seeing the humor in the absurdity and ever-willing to consider a sporting proposition, didn't hesitate to accommodate him.

So Reed placed his raincoat on the bus stop bench and assumed a stance with feet shoulder-width apart and knees slightly bent. He took a deep breath and set himself. Exposed in a wrinkled, stained tee-shirt, he seemed to have lost much of his hard-edged bulk.

Sonny went first, poking a faint-hearted straight right to Reed's solar plexus. Reed snorted and lurched a half-step back.

"Okay, you," he said, pointing to Welcome and re-setting his feet. "Y…you're next."

I shook my head in disgust and whispered to Sonny, "*We should just give him the money…. He doesn't even know the meaning of 'flinch.'*"

But Welcome decided to take the challenge at face value. He moved closer to Reed and put his weight behind a more forceful short punch. Gasping convulsively, Reed nearly caved in. He staggered back two steps, listing precariously until Sonny reached out and righted him.

"Now, Mendoza, y…you're n…next. You assholes b…better get your money ready."

His face was red from exertion, but he was determined; he sensed victory within his grasp. I stood behind the other two, still unwilling.

"C'mon, goddammit. I d…don't have all n…night."

"Nah," I said, more to Sonny and Welcome than to Reed. I felt too much pity to even address him.

"Sure! You kn…know I'll win the bet! You're just a tight Jew who doesn't w…want to part with his precious *sh…shekels.*"

Sonny and Welcome smiled.

"Go ahead," Welcome said, "don't back out now; give the guy what he wants."

"As hard as you can!" Reed insisted. "The bet is, hit me as hard as you c…can!"

I looked up at the night sky. Wind pushed a sheaf of clouds just enough to reveal a distinct scattering of stars.

Reed set himself more severely this time, edging one foot slightly ahead of the other and in a wider stance that would give him more stability.

Sonny and Welcome, grinning expectantly, waved me into position. It was my turn, and they were brimming with anticipation at what I would give him. I stepped up to Reed, much closer than the others. Reed grimaced once again, squeezing his eyes shut and thrusting his jaw forward, oblivious now to our history and to the momentum of impending retribution. Instead, I reached into my pocket and withdrew all the money I had left, a few crumpled singles, hugged him tightly and stuffed them into his back pocket.

Reed's eyes fluttered open. "Heeeeeyyyyy…."

Sonny, then Welcome, peeled off a few of their remaining dollars, slapped them into Reed's hand and steered him back across the street to a round of winner's drinks at the Open Door.

On the way to Uncle Abe's house, I pondered what had just transpired. How, at the first sight of Reed, no matter how evident the erosion of his once-mighty persona, a pulse-quickening fear had once again surged through me, reverberating to my very core.

What a fool I was to believe that the battle at All Souls Church had been a turning point in my development, a revival of some long-buried, inherited militancy that would forever vanquish fear. Or if not fear, at least the complacency that had nearly consumed me after DiNardi murdered my immediate family and destroyed my legacy, to bask in the glory, fame and fortune that would've accrued to Davey Mendoza, light heavyweight champion of the world. How deluded I had become that my reaction that night at All Souls, my simple and innate reflex to survive, had somehow been a heroic act that connected me, finally, to Davey, the patriarch, and to a long line of warriors and champions. What had happened, I wondered, to "The Fighting Marine?" Why had I recoiled in Reed's presence?

And why, when he had given me the perfect opportunity to exact revenge, when he'd all but pointed his chin at me, why hadn't I taken advantage of the situation? Why didn't I punish him, humiliate him like he'd humiliated me in front of my classmates, like he'd humiliated so many others? If I had transformed so much that night at the church, where was the reflexive, opportunistic instinct that gushes from anger? Where was the kind of destructive power I had so successfully unleashed only a few months ago? Why did I let slip away the satisfaction I could've so easily gained, a just reward handed to me on a platter at no cost? How far had I actually progressed since that night at All Souls? How much farther did I need to go?

As I walked, head down, oblivious to landmarks, just honing in on the direction I thought I needed to go but, really, detached from the process, I reconsidered how my mind worked in relation to the world. Terror seemed to haunt me whether I was in the world or in exile from it, whether I was in solidarity with my brethren or apart from them and going it alone. My predicament persisted, no matter what my personal circumstance.

Neither Jesse nor Uncle Abe seemed bothered by this reality. Even though they came from different worlds, they weren't pained by what God seemed to want, by the seeming inconsistencies. On the contrary, they were comforted by it. And they knew me better than I knew myself. Despite my resistance, they'd pushed me into situations by making certain that I would not grow attached to fear and become morally stagnant. They seemed to understand that I needed to be prepared when it came time to choose, that I needed to be pushed without letup, under constant scrutiny, so that I could perform at some majestic level of nonpareil. But I'd never reached that point, not against LaSalle, not against DiNardi. I hadn't gained anything the way they'd planned. Even my best games I'd played outside of myself.

I didn't realize how lost in my thoughts I'd become until my ears began ringing in a way I hadn't experienced in a long time, accompanied by the sensation of re-playing a long-buried scene from what seemed as distant as a previous life. And I didn't figure out that my mind had sought out and locked into one of the most compelling dreams from my childhood until I looked up and discovered that I had walked at least a mile out of my way and, instead, stood directly in front of my old house on Burt Street.

I was stunned. Not only because I'd become so distracted that I had sleep-walked blocks beyond the avenue that would've taken me to Uncle Abe's, but because I'd come out of my torpor just at the moment that I had reached my childhood home, now so weathered and neglected that not only its front porch, but also its entire framework seemed to sag with distress.

Not one light burned from within; its torn window shades and sun-faded curtains hung lopsided, as if abandoned. I walked around to the back of the house. The dirt boxing ring was no longer defined, just a bare patch of ground in the middle of scratch lawn and weeds and pocked with decaying sacks of garbage and busted crates.

A chill of bad memories settled along my spine, and I backed out of the alleyway and walked away, down the dank and musty street to the Adams Street hill. I leaned into the hill with a weariness that matched the tenebrous row of aged two-family houses with their caved-in steps and broken porch railings and apartment house vestibules rank with urine, and battered store fronts with their once-promising but now grimy picture windows that lined the street. I climbed the hill with shortened steps that made me feel like an old cripple making a final but futile pilgrimage.

By the time I climbed Uncle Abe's rickety porch steps and rang his doorbell, I kept wishing I wouldn't have to spend my last night in Brant resisting somebody's plan for how I ought to live my life, being an ungrate-ful guest taking sustenance with one hand while holding at arm's length Uncle Abe's parting advice.

I turned, catching one last glimpse of the synagogue across the street. Globes of soft light hung above the building's brass lettering and illumi-nated its Greek-styled pillars and platform stairs. I probably wouldn't see a synagogue of such stately proportions for a long, long time. Not that it mattered; I was going into exile once again.

I faced his front door, a little annoyed that I had to ring the bell for yet a second time, but when it opened, Yvonne stood on the threshold, eyes shining.

"Surprise! Your uncle invited me. I couldn't make your party last night, so I'm helping him cook your farewell dinner!"

She took me by the hand and led me into the parlor. Uncle Abe was filling three glasses with wine from Grandfather's antique glass decanter. He replaced the stopper into the bottle and limped across the room to embrace me. Tenderly, I patted his humped back.

"Where have you been? We thought you'd get here earlier than this; we're starving."

"Sorry. I lost track of time...."

In a forgiving gesture, Yvonne pointed to a space next to her on the davenport. I sat and told them about how Sonny, Welcome and I had signed the final papers and about being sworn in, about shooting our last game of pool, and about the strange encounter with Donny Reed, and my confusion over how I had reacted.

Uncle Abe responded as he so often did when he began to construct one of his abstract moral lectures.

"You gained and lost something of equal importance that night at the church. What you gained is not something innate, we all have to learn it. But most of us believed you didn't need to. You were to be a part of the new generation. Entitled. We were mistaken."

I waited for him to elaborate. Yvonne seemed to know what he was talking about and thinking. She and Uncle Abe not only harbored the same regard for me, but they also telegraphed it with the exact same and unmistakable look of adoring approval. I, of course, interpreted this as misplaced sentiment guided more by wishful thinking rather than logic.

"I'll set the table," she said, "and get everything ready."

I took a sip of Uncle Abe's sweet port wine. As this was my last night in Brant, I had to play guest to his host and seem willing, at least, to participate in his dialogue of religious commentary.

"Okay, so, at first, what did I lose?"

"Your philosophy of life," he said.

"What do you mean?"

"Remember the night you got drunk with those boys down by the creek?" Uncle Abe asked. "And you told Jesse the next day that you had discovered the secret of life, but you couldn't remember it, and it wasn't until later that you could? What was that secret again?"

It was embarrassing to recount. I drained my glass and took a refill. "That night, we decided that man was an island, that he shouldn't take unnecessary risks that might jeopardize his own well-being, that he shouldn't need anyone else...."

"Or trust anyone," Uncle Abe said. "Or sacrifice his own well-being for the sake of another." My ears burned with indictment. "You thought that was what being free was all about," Uncle Abe added, "that that was a wise man's goal to achieve. I wrote it down, what you said you'd learned. *'Bravery in the face of death is only for suckers. You have to look out for yourself; yourself only.'*

"Your sense of entitlement led you into that weakness—your unique destiny," Uncle Abe said, poised in his easy chair like a sage. "The loss of your loved ones threatened to drown you in it.

"That's when Jesse and Mrs. Hill and I thought that harboring you on the reservation after the death of your mother and Jake and then Davey would keep you in touch with spirit, would bring you out of your malaise. But you were too far gone, and the little challenges we devised for you to experience and the ones that just happened, seemingly without cause, weren't enough to lift you up.

"Then Uncle Jack came back and I figured it'd take something big," Uncle Abe said. "So big that I was sorry I pushed you into it, and I wondered at the time, the night we sought out Joey, whether I'd gone beyond what God had in store. There is a delicate balance, you know. It's a problem maintaining that…in our family."

"I'm sorry, I don't quite understand what you're getting at," I blurted, impatient with his rabbinical lecturing, yet, at the same time, wondering how I could resist him. Why shouldn't I embrace his ecumenical spirit, despite my misgivings? And what, exactly, are my misgivings? What's wrong with me?

"You don't hold to that old philosophy now, do you?" Uncle Abe asked.

I lied, not wanting to be a complete ingrate. "I'm not sure what to believe anymore. All I know is I acted that night at All Souls…I fought the way I did out of desperation. I didn't confront my fear, I went all-out…. It was a desperate act."

"No," Uncle Abe said. "Something came into you that night. You're just not certain what it is, or whether it is a benefit or a burden. You couldn't betray me. If you hadn't intervened, we both would've been killed. DiNardi said so. Your old philosophy didn't come to your rescue. You had to look beyond," Uncle Abe said, gesturing with his hand, a gesture that so mimicked one of Jesse's, so Indian and, at the same time, so Jewish in its reach and direction.

"Because of the deaths of your parents and grandfather, you despaired. And because of their deaths and your own survival, you were filled with remorse. And then you lost faith in God, you lost hope, you walked away from forgiveness. That's why Davey turns away from you in your dream. He's not blaming you, he wants to show you what you'd be like if left to your own devices—alone, distrustful, a miserable creature hiding from God.

"Jesse, Mrs. Hill and I tried to give you something to do—a good deed, good play—and companions, to help relieve you of your burden. In time, you rose somewhat to the occasion, you fought self-doubt, and God blessed you for your faith. He gave you the strength to take things into your own hands and, eventually, to take on your biggest monster."

Uncle Abe humbled me with these reminders of his and others' generosity and by giving me the benefit of the doubt, both his and mine, with his confident vision. If anything possible could reconcile me to at least consider faith's possibility, it was his and Jesse's selfless generosity, their vision and their persistent willingness to cleave me to it.

"I was afraid that if you remained with Uncle Jack, he would corrupt you to the ways of the world and to that philosophy you thought was so profound and which he has so greatly profited from. He has sinned so often it has become his commandment. I didn't want it to become yours. He has left God and lost God's love. He is diminished as a human being. I couldn't let that happen to you.

"To be truly free, Daniel, means rising to the occasion. Taking risks. Not just for a singular purpose, like being an accomplished athlete or a successful lawyer. Not to prove yourself to yourself. But for a greater purpose. Which is what you did that night at All Souls. And tonight is further proof that you're on the right track."

I couldn't take it anymore. "Uncle Abe, nothing came into me that night or the night against LaSalle. I was outside of myself. Or, rather, I acted in spite of myself, out of extreme fear."

"No other reason?"

I shook my head. "No other reason I can think of."

"You're wrong," he persisted. "Tonight proved it."

"You mean with Reed?"

He nodded. "Fighting injustice is one thing. But retribution often comes with a hard heart. Sometimes a better retribution is the kind served with empathy. Even love."

At this point, my head began to hurt. Sorting out my own contradictory feelings was one thing, but allowing Uncle Abe's elevated concepts into the mix was more than I could handle, and it put me into a mindset where I wanted to object, close off his tutelage, no matter how well-intentioned.

But, at the same time, out of an ingrained sense of being a gracious guest, I fought against giving up.

"A hard-hearted retribution is self-destructive. Donny Reed is living proof of that. I don't know what made him into a mean person but, you know, this was your father's Achilles heel, too, I'm sorry to say. He was tutored in an avenging spirit and it may have contributed...."

Uncle Abe paused. He was so transparently measuring how he wanted to conduct this lesson. Denigrating Davey wasn't going to be a part of it.

After a deep breath and a sip of wine, he continued. "You just need practice rising to the occasion. It's a long, hard process—taking risks, deciding which authority you want to commit to. But, don't you see? If you had acted the way you thought you should, you'd have acted just like those boys who tried to grind you into the ground that day at football practice. You'd have become like them, a bully. You'd have become like your enemy."

I found myself in the same old predicament, not really believing, yet wheedling advice just the same. "Is that why you want me to go into the Marines?"

"In part," he answered. "It's a next step. A good one now that there is no war, thank God. They'll teach you more of what you need to learn. Give you chances to test yourself. But then you have to come up with some results—results particular to your larger destiny. Jesse says after basic training an officer he knows from some camp...."

As a polite guest, I could've helped him come up with the name of the camp. Instead, my attention digressed. A thought flashed through my mind about being completely free, about the Café Jake and the All-Stars, and how they'd created a different and profound reality where they and their fans dwelled, within a steady, willful syncopation and melody that seemed like a kind of beckoning that everyone fervently wished could be followed: toward a free, cool life, aloof from the ordered choices which preoccupied us all.

"...Camp LeJeune?"

"Yes," I said, snapping out of my trance of ingratitude.

"Some officer he knows will arrange for your transfer there to play football for him, and you and Sonny will have an opportunity to join the boxing team."

"What about Welcome?"

"He has it in his mind to do some serious soldiering like Jesse."

That level of devotion surprised me. "You mean, be a scout?"

Uncle Abe nodded. "That's what he wants. But you'll have an unusual opportunity to be an athlete again, and you all will be able to earn your high school diplomas. And Jesse says...."

"...to come back home when you're finished and go to Brant University with me," Yvonne added, re-entering the parlor wearing one of Uncle Abe's aprons and carrying just a hint of stipulation in her voice.

Uncle Abe retrieved his empty wine glass from the coffee table and pushed himself to his feet, painfully and with great effort. "It's getting late. If we're ever going to have this farewell feast, we'd better get going."

He led us to the dining room table which was set up for a formal occasion with candles, good china, covered casserole dishes, and a brisket of beef.

Yvonne and I were last in the procession. She was humming a tune which at first I could not place. But when our shoulders touched, and we took the final steps together to the table, with her confidence and my uncertainty forming a strangely-compelling bond, I recognized its ancient Iroquois melody from long ago, from the first Midwinter ceremony we attended together as children.

The chant of thanksgiving.

ACKNOWLEDGMENTS

This novel was originally inspired by a newspaper article, "Joined Tribes: Jewish Indians Are Ultimate Outsiders," written in 1994 by Jonathon Tilove (Newhouse News Service), which featured Sharon Skolnick, an Apache who married a Jewish husband and whose daughter Debbie was a Chicago Indian Princess. The article also contained a quote by Suzan S. Harjo, a Cheyenne poet and former head of the National Congress of American Indians who compared Indians and Jews as "survivors who have lived life on the run…and who have been the victims of the most hideous kinds of politics and personal attacks." In the novel, these words are repeated.

I was also inspired by Joseph Campbell's concept of "the collective unconscious," and two books: *Human Universals* by Donald E. Brown (1991), anthropology professor emeritus at U. C. Santa Barbara, and *Consilience: The Unity of Knowledge* by Edward O. Wilson (1998). Brown challenged the assumption that human behavior is determined by individual cultures; instead, behavior, ideas and concepts are shared by virtually all human cultures. Wilson called for a synthesis of information and unity of the natural sciences with the social sciences and humanities. Or, as one reviewer put it: "The goal of consilience is to achieve progressive unification of all strands of knowledge in service to the indefinite betterment of the human condition."

As a community college English instructor, I used to teach multicultural literature. What that meant in the late 1980s and early 1990s was using a course reader containing articles by American writers of various races and ethnicities or, for example, teaching two coming-of-age novels (*Rumors of Peace* by Ella Leffland, and *Fools Crow* by James Welch). Unconsciously, I reinforced the idea that America is a salad bowl and not a melting pot; I unconsciously reinforced the concepts of *difference* and *other* and eventually I became uncomfortable with this approach.

With a recent change in the way the U.S. Census categorizes bi- or multi-racial and ethnic citizens, and with the election of Barack H. Obama as president, a new concept of American diversity has come to prominence. Perhaps this reality—that American identity is the result of commingling races and cultures—will do more to create a sense of national unity for the betterment of us all. It is in this spirit that I wrote my novel.

For Jewish spiritual aspects of the novel, books I relied on include: *Kabbalah: Tradition of Hidden Knowledge* by Z'ev ben Shimon Halevei

(1979) which contains images of the *sefiroth* or divine tree, *Kabbalah* by Gershom Scholem (1978), and *Jewish Mysticism and Jewish Ethics* by Joseph Dan (1977) which discusses divine will, law, communal responsibility, and "the cosmic struggle between good and evil that no Jew can refrain from taking part in." I also read *When Bad things Happen To Good People* by Rabbi Harold S. Kushner (1981).

For Iroquois aspects of the novel, I read: *Apologies to the Iroquois* by Edmund Wilson (1959), an edition that included a study, "The Mohawks in High Steel" by Joseph Mitchell (1949); *The White Roots of Peace* by Paul A. W. Wallace (1946) which discusses the legend of Handsome Lake and the founding of the Iroquois Confederacy; *Onondaga: Portrait of a Native People* featuring the photographs of Fred R. Wolcott (1986); *The Role of Games, Sport and Dance in Iroquois Life*, a master's of arts thesis by Karen Lynn Smith (1972) including description and images of snow snake *(ga'-wa-sa)* and lacrosse; *Iroquois Ceremony of Midwinter* by Elisabeth Tooker (1970); *Costumes of the Iroquois* by Robert Gabor; *The Iroquois Book of Rites* ed. by Horatio Hale (1883) including description of the condolence ceremony which I adopted in a modified form to include in a scene in the novel; *The False Faces of the Iroquois* by William N. Fenton (1987); *Indian Givers: How the Indians of the Americas Transformed the World* by Jack Weatherford (1988), especially Chapter 8, "The Founding Indian Fathers." I also read a number of *New York Times* religion columns written by Gustave Niebuhr pertaining to Iroquois spirituality, and a number of *Syracuse Herald-Journal* columns on Iroquois life written by Doug George-Kanentiio.

Special thanks go to Lorraine Shenandoah for giving me an intimate tour of the Onondaga Nation, including stories growing up there, and to Judy Lewis, who was a tribal judge for the Oneida Nation of Oklahoma during the mid-1990s when I was researching the novel. Judy told me many stories about growing up on the Onondaga Nation, participating in ceremonies, and going to school there and at Valley Academy.

In the novel I pay homage to Oren Lyons, Onondaga Nation Faith-keeper, by creating two characters (one an adult, one a boy) based on aspects of Lyons' life and, while I was unable to interview him, I did read several fascinating articles: "Keeping the Faith for the Iroquois" by Robert Lipsyte (*New York Times*, Jan. 29, 1993) which contains the anecdote about Lyons, a teenage goalie playing in a Red League game and being hit by a "heavy shot" from Angus Thomas. From that article, I borrowed a Lyons quote to give to a character in my novel, Jesse, who tells his nephew about how that incident proved a boy's manhood. In another Lipsyte profile of Lyons that appeared in *Esquire* magazine (February 1994), "R.I.P., Tonto," I borrowed an anecdote spoken by another character, Sonny, when his dog is shot by a curmudgeonly farmer. I was also inspired by Lyons' painting, *Tree of Peace*, which has been exhibited at the Smithsonian Institution's National Museum of American History in Washington, D.C.

Another painting which inspired me was *Haudenosaunee Creation* by Arnold Jacobs (no relation), Onondaga Nation, Turtle Clan, which represents his understanding of the Haudenosaunee creation story.

I also pay homage to Audry Shenandoah, Onondaga Eel Clan, who taught a daily course, "Onondaga Language and Culture," at the Onondaga Nation School, and who was very kind to give me a tour of the school in 1995. I also read her article, "Women: Sustainers of Life," which appeared in the Turtle Quarterly, Summer 1990.

For aspects of lacrosse, especially box lacrosse, Red League lacrosse, and intercollegiate lacrosse, I feel a deep sense of gratitude to Roy Simmons Jr., acclaimed lacrosse coach emeritus at Syracuse University. He told me many stories about his own days of playing, about playing with Oren Lyons, and about his father, Roy Sr., one of the greatest athletes and coaches in S.U. history (lacrosse, boxing, football), who coached me in 1963. It was through Roy Jr. that I came to read *American Indian Lacrosse: Little Brother of War* by Thomas Vennum Jr., a brilliant history of the game published by Smithsonian Institution Press. I also read *Tewaarathon (Lacrosse): Akwesasne's Story of Our National Game* published by the North American Indian Traveling College (1978) which included creation stories, an account of Colin Chisholm's lacrosse stick factory located at St. Regis, and a photo of the legendary Angus Thomas, who played Red League box lacrosse for the St. Regis Indians. In the novel, I create scenes and situations of historical significance based on Roy Sr., Chisholm, and Thomas.

For boxing, I read *The Jewish Boxers Hall of Fame* by Ken Blady (1988), and *A Pictoral History of Boxing* by Sam Andre and Nat Fleisher (1981 edition). I also read several articles: "I Say The Boxing Business Smells" by Dan Parker (1953, *Ring* magazine); "My Story," Pt. 1 and 2 by Joe Louis (1952, *Life* magazine; "My Rugged Education in Boxing," by Robert K. Christenberry, chairman of the New York State Athletic Commission

(1952, *Life* magazine), and several news articles from the *New York Times* 1952-55 regarding federal civil antitrust lawsuits against the International Boxing Club.

I also pay homage to my father, David Jacobs, a renowned high school athlete (Vocational High School, Syracuse) and a New York State heavyweight boxing champion in the early 1920s, and to my mother, Mary King Jacobs, that red-haired Irish beauty who could cook a kugel with the best of 'em.

Other characters in the novel will be recognizable to many readers, like Dick Tobin, a former boxer and endearing ring announcer at the Syracuse War Memorial Auditorium during the 1950s; Jacques Shure, a quarterback at Nottingham High School who led one of the city championship teams (1956-58) I played on; Pat Testa, a coach who most inspired me to play my heart out which, occasionally, I did; and Si Simpson and the All Stars, who performed at the now-defunct Club 800 on East Fayette Street.

Some places will also be recognizable to many Syracuse readers, such as the late-night diner, Poodle's and Jim's; city taverns, the Open Door and Tippin' Inn; and the Tic-Toc Club, a burlesque club in downtown Syracuse which epitomized genteel strip-tease.

I am grateful to many people who read and/or helped edit portions of the manuscript before publication, including Clark and Barbara Sturges of *Devil Mountain Books*; my writing coach, Mike Sirota, from San Diego, CA; Rabbi Eric Wisnia of Congregation Beth Chaim, Princeton Junction, N.J.; Roy Simmons Jr.; and Kevin Lynch, who writes about the San Francisco Forty-Niners for *SFGate.com*, a website belonging to the *San Francisco Chronicle*. Special thanks go to my typesetter, Carol Yacorzynski of Encore Design and Type; and my graphic artist, David Johnson from Berkeley, CA. Final editing kudos go to my dear wife, Susan Springer, whose keen eye and sense of aesthetics greatly improved the final product. She wouldn't let me stop working until the novel met her highest standards, and my debt to her is immeasurable as is my love.

Finally, although I extensively researched elements of Iroquois and Jewish religion and rituals, and boxing history (including the career of Daniel Mendoza, English champion, 1791-1795), and included parts of some scenes from historical documents, this book is a work of fiction and should be construed as nothing but. I am solely responsible for everything portrayed.